... ...y decided tha... ...
she was right. That dream stayed with her until she was ... ... when she decided that people like her – ordinary people – didn't write books, and so she trained to be a teacher instead. But it was only after working in various other jobs that her family nagged and dared and finally persuaded her to take up her pen. And the rest, as they say, is history!

Margaret McDonagh can't remember a time when her nose wasn't buried in a book. She reads avidly, but always knew that she had to write. In 2005, after twenty years of writing novellas for *My Weekly* Story Collection and Linford large print, plus serials and magazine short stories for *The People's Friend*, her manuscript was accepted by Mills & Boon. She has been writing novels ever since! You can contact Margaret via her website: www.margaretmcdonagh.com

Caroline Anderson's been a nurse, a secretary, a teacher, and has run her own business. Now she's settled on writing. 'I was looking for that elusive something and finally realised it was variety – now I have it in abundance. Every book brings new horizons, new friends, and in between books I juggle! My husband John and I have two beautiful daughters, Sarah and Hannah, umpteen pets, and several acres of Suffolk that nature tries to reclaim every time we turn our backs!'

Finding Forever

Finding Forever: A Passionate Proposal

MAGGIE KINGSLEY

MARGARET McDONAGH

CAROLINE ANDERSON

MILLS & BOON

First Published in Great Britain 2022
by Mills & Boon, an imprint of HarperCollins*Publishers* Ltd,
1 London Bridge Street, London, SE1 9GF

www.harpercollins.co.uk

HarperCollins*Publishers*
1st Floor, Watermarque Building,
Ringsend Road, Dublin 4, Ireland

FINDING FOREVER: A PASSIONATE PROPOSAL © 2022
Harlequin Enterprises ULC.

A Baby for Eve © 2008 Harlequin Enterprises ULC.
Dr Devereux's Proposal © 2008 Harlequin Enterprises ULC.
The Rebel of Penhally Bay © 2009 Harlequin Enterprises ULC.

Special thanks and acknowledgement are given to Maggie Kingsley for her contribution to the *Brides of Penhally Bay* series.
Special thanks and acknowledgement are given to Margaret McDonagh for her contribution to the *Brides of Penhally Bay* series.
Special thanks and acknowledgement to Caroline Anderson for her contribution to the *Brides of Penhally Bay* series

ISBN: 978-0-263-30453-4

MIX
Paper from
responsible sources
FSC® C007454

This book is produced from independently certified FSC™ paper to ensure responsible forest management.

For more information visit: www.harpercollins.co.uk/green

Printed and Bound in Spain using 100% Renewable electricity at CPI Black Print, Barcelona

A BABY FOR EVE

MAGGIE KINGSLEY

This book is dedicated to five extremely talented and generous writing friends. Kate Hardy, Jessica Matthews, Margaret McDonagh, Alison Roberts and Jennifer Taylor. Without their encouragement I can truthfully say this book would never have been finished.

CHAPTER ONE

A WRY smile curved Eve Dwyer's lips as the door of St Mark's Church creaked open then closed again. Somebody was cutting it fine. Very fine. Another five minutes and the wedding ceremony would have begun, and curiously she glanced over her shoulder to see who the latecomer might be only for the smile on her face to freeze.

It was him. His thick black hair might be lightly flecked with grey now, and there were deep lines on his forehead that hadn't been there twenty years ago, but Eve would have recognised the man walking rapidly towards an empty seat near the front of the church anywhere. Tom Cornish was back in Penhally Bay and, if she hadn't been sitting in the middle of a packed pew, surrounded by her colleagues from the village's medical practice, Eve would have taken to her heels and run.

'Good heavens,' Kate Althorp, the village's senior midwife, whispered from Eve's left. 'Is that who I think it is?'

Other people were muttering the same thing, Eve noticed, seeing the number of heads suddenly craning in Tom's direction, the nudges people were giving their neighbours. Not the younger members of the congregation. They wouldn't remember a Dr Tom Cornish but those aged over forty-five certainly did, and not very kindly if the frowns on some faces were anything to go by.

'Is that who?' Lauren Nightingale asked from Eve's right, but Kate didn't have time to answer the physiotherapist.

The organist had launched into the wedding march, which meant the bride had arrived. A bride Tom Cornish wouldn't have known from a cake of soap, Eve thought, gripping her order of service card so tightly that the embossed card bent beneath her fingers. Both Alison Myers and her bridegroom, Jack Tremayne, would have been children when Tom had last been in Penhally Bay so why was he here, and why had he come back when he'd always sworn he never would?

'Doesn't Alison look lovely?' Lauren sighed as the girl walked past them, radiant in a simple long gown of cream satin.

Alison did, but any enjoyment Eve might have felt in the occasion had gone. The flowers in the church, which had smelt so sweet just a few minutes ago, now seemed cloying. The crush of bodies, which had once felt so companionable, now simply felt oppressive, and even the sight of Jack and Alison's small sons, walking solemnly down the aisle behind Alison, failed to give her pleasure.

'Eve, are you OK?'

Kate was gazing curiously at her, and Eve faked a smile.

'I'm fine,' she murmured. 'It's just a bit…crowded.'

The midwife chuckled. 'Penhally loves a wedding. A christening's good, but a wedding is the only thing guaranteed to get the whole village out.'

But not Tom Cornish, Eve thought, stiffening slightly as she saw him half turn in his seat. Tom who had once said marriage was a prison he had no intention of ever inhabiting. Tom who'd said he wanted to be free, to travel, and was damned if he was going to rot away in the village in which he had been born.

'Oh, aren't they sweet?' Lauren exclaimed as Alison's three-year-old son, Sam, and Jack's equally young son, Freddie, held out the red velvet cushions they were carrying so everyone could see the wedding rings sitting on them.

'Yes,' was all Eve could manage as a collective sigh of approval ran round the congregation.

Why was Tom here—*why*? She'd read in a medical magazine a few years back that he'd been appointed head of operations at Deltaron, the world-famous international rescue team, so he should have been somewhere abroad, helping the victims of some disaster, not sitting in the front pew of St Mark's, resurrecting all her old heartache, and anger, and pain.

'Eve, are you *quite* sure you're OK?' Kate whispered, the worry in her eyes rekindling.

'I…I have a bit of a headache, that's all,' Eve lied. 'It's the flowers—the perfume—strong smells always give me a headache.'

Kate looked partially convinced. Not wholly convinced, but at least partially, and Eve gripped her order of service card even tighter.

Pull yourself together, she told herself as the service continued and she found her eyes continually straying away from the young couple standing in front of Reverend Kenner towards Tom. For God's sake, you're forty-two years old, not a girl any more. Tom probably won't even remember you, far less recognise you, so pull yourself together, but she couldn't. No matter how often she told herself she was being stupid, overreacting, all she wanted was to leave. Immediately.

'Eve, you look terrible,' Kate murmured when Jack and Alison had walked back down the aisle as man and wife, and everyone in the congregation began to get to their feet. 'I have some paracetamol in my bag—'

'Air,' Eve muttered. 'I just… I need some fresh air.'

And to get as far away from here as I can before Tom sees me, she added mentally as she hurried to the church door and out into the sunshine. She wasn't tall—just five feet five—so, if she was quick, she could lose herself amongst the congregation, then hurry down Harbour Road and go home. She'd tell everyone at the practice on Monday she'd had a migraine, and her colleagues would understand, she knew they would. All she had to do was keep walking, not look back, and—

'*Eve Dwyer*. By all that's wonderful, it's you, isn't it?'

His voice hadn't changed at all, Eve thought as she came to a halt, moistening lips that had suddenly gone dry. It was as deep and mellow as it had always been, still with that faint trace of Cornish burr, and she wanted to pretend she hadn't heard him, but she couldn't.

'Eve Dwyer,' Tom repeated, shaking his head in clear disbelief as she turned slowly to face him. 'I never expected to run into you within minutes of coming back to Penhally. It's Tom Cornish,' he added a little uncertainly when she stared up at him, completely unable to say a word. 'Don't tell me you've forgotten me?'

How could I? she wanted to reply, but she didn't.

'Of course I remember you, Tom,' she said instead. 'You're…you're looking well.'

He was. Up close, she could see he was heavier now than he had been at twenty-four but on him the extra weight looked good, and the grey in his hair, and the lines on his forehead, gave his face a strength it hadn't possessed before, but it was his eyes that took her breath away.

For years those startlingly green eyes had plagued her dreams, teasing her, laughing at her, and she'd told herself that time and absence had created an unreal image of him, but they were every bit as green as she had remembered, and every bit as potent, and she had to swallow, hard.

'So…'

'So…'

They'd spoken together, and she felt a tingle of heat darken her cheeks.

'I didn't realise you knew Alison and Jack,' she said to fill the silence.

'Who?' He frowned.

'The couple whose wedding you've just been at,' she declared, moving swiftly to one side so the people who were still leaving the church could get past her.

'Never met either of them in my life,' he said.

'Then why come to their wedding?' she asked in confusion.

'I arrived in Penhally just before twelve o'clock, found the place deserted, and when I asked at the shop I was told everybody was probably here.'

Which still didn't explain why he'd come.

'Tom—'

'Tom Cornish.' Kate beamed. 'What in the world brings you back to Penhally? I thought you were still in the States.'

For a second Tom stared blankly at the midwife, clearly trying to place her, then grinned. 'Kate Templar, right?'

'Kate Althorp now, Tom.' She laughed. 'Have been for years.'

And he hadn't answered Kate's question either, Eve thought.

'Are you coming to the reception?' Kate continued, waving to Reverend Kenner as he hurried towards his car. 'It's a buffet at The Smugglers' Inn so there'll be plenty of food, and I'm sure Alison and Jack would be delighted to meet you.'

'And I'm sure Tom has better things to do than go to a reception that will be packed with doctors and nurses who'll only end up talking shop,' Eve said quickly, and saw one of Tom's eyebrows lift.

'I can talk shop,' he said. 'I'm a doctor, too, remember, so I can talk shop with the best of them.'

'Yes, but—'

'Afraid I might embarrass you by smashing up the furniture, getting drunk and insulting all your friends?' he said dryly, and she crimsoned.

'Of course not,' she protested, though, in truth, she wasn't one hundred per cent sure about the insults. 'I just thought…'

She came to a halt. A small hand had slipped into hers. A hand that belonged to a little girl with long blonde hair who was staring up at her eagerly. 'Tassie, sweetheart. Where in the world did you spring from?'

'I've been out here since the wedding started,' the ten-year-old replied. 'Sitting on the wall, listening to the music.'

'Oh, Tassie, love, why didn't you come inside the church?' Eve exclaimed, her gaze taking in the girl's thin and worn T-shirt and her shabby cotton trousers, which weren't nearly warm enough to withstand the cool of the early October day. 'There's quite a breeze blowing in from the harbour—'

'Don't feel the cold,' Tassie interrupted, 'and I'm not really wearing the right sort of clothes for a wedding. Her dress is pretty, isn't it?' she added, gazing wistfully towards the lychgate where Alison and Jack were having their photographs taken.

'Yes, it's very pretty,' Eve murmured, her heart twisting slightly at the envy she could see in the little girl's brown eyes. Eyes which had always seemed too large for her thin face even when she'd been a toddler. 'Tassie, does your mother know you're here?'

'She said I was to get out from under her feet, so I did. She won't be worried.'

Amanda Lovelace probably wouldn't, Eve thought with a sigh, but that wasn't the point.

'Tassie—'

'I was wondering whether I could come to the reception?' the girl interrupted. 'I heard Mrs Althorp say there would be lots of food, so could I come? I won't be any trouble—I promise.'

Eve's heart sank. Normally she couldn't refuse Tassie anything. The child had so few treats in her life, but she didn't want to go to the reception. She didn't want to go anywhere but home.

'Tassie, the reception's not really for children,' she began. 'It's more a grown-up thing.'

'Nonsense!' Kate exclaimed. 'My son Jem will be there and he's only nine. And Alison's son Sam and Jack's son Freddie are both going, and they're only three, so I'm sure Tassie would enjoy it.'

'Perhaps,' Eve declared, 'but I really don't think—'

'Oh, I do, most definitely,' Tom interrupted. 'If Tom Cornish can be given an invitation then I think this half-pint should have one, too.'

'But her mother won't know where she is,' Eve protested, all too aware she was losing this argument, but determined to give it one last try. 'She'll be worried.'

Tom delved into his pocket and produced his mobile phone.

'Not if we use the wonders of modern technology,' he declared. 'Give her a quick call, and then I'll get to take two beautiful women out to lunch.'

Tassie giggled, and Eve sighed inwardly. There was nothing left to say—no argument she could come up with—and when she reluctantly took the phone Kate beamed.

'That's settled, then,' the midwife said as Eve made her call then handed back the phone to Tom. 'Tom, Eve can show you how to get to The Smugglers' Inn if you've forgotten where it is, and…' She stopped in mid-sentence as a dull, metallic thud suddenly split the air followed by the sound of breaking glass. 'What the…?'

'Sounds like someone's just backed into something,' Tom observed.

'And no prizes for guessing who the "someone" is.' Kate groaned as Lauren clambered out of her car, her hand pressed to her mouth.

'Oh, come on, be fair, Kate,' Eve protested. 'The cars are parked really close to one another. Whose car did she hit?'

Kate frowned. 'Don't know. It's a metallic blue Range Rover, not from around here by its number plate, so my guess is it belongs to some flash holidaymaker.'

Tom cleared his throat. 'I'm afraid I'm the flash holiday-maker, so who is the "she" who has just reversed into my car?'

Kate looked uncomfortably at Eve, and Eve bit her lip.

'Lauren. She's our practice physiotherapist, and a really lovely woman, but quite dreadfully accident prone.'

And currently absolutely mortified, Eve thought as Lauren hurried towards them, her cheeks scarlet, her eyes worried.

'I was certain I had enough space to reverse,' she exclaimed, 'absolutely certain, but… Does anyone know who owns the blue Range Rover?'

'Tom does,' Eve replied. 'Tom, this is Lauren Nightingale.'

'Not Florence?' he said, and Eve rolled her eyes.

'Tom, Lauren must have heard that joke about a million times.'

'A million and one now, actually,' Lauren said, 'but that's not the point. I'm so sorry about your car—'

'From the looks of it, your Renault's come off worse,' Tom interrupted, gazing critically at his car, then at Lauren's. 'You've scraped quite a bit of paintwork off your tail, whereas you've only broken my indicator light cover.'

'Which I will pay for,' Lauren insisted, digging into her bag. 'I have my insurance certificate in here—'

'Look, how about I simply send you the bill for the repair, and we don't involve our insurance companies at all?' Tom suggested. 'That way you won't lose your no-claims bonus.'

'Are you sure?' Lauren said uncertainly, and, when Tom nodded, she extracted a notebook and a pen from her bag. 'You'll need my address for the bill. It's Gatehouse Cottage. That's—'

'The cottage at the bottom of the drive that leads to the Manor House.' Tom smiled when the physiotherapist looked at him in surprise. 'I was born in Penhally, lived here for the first twenty-four years of my life, so I know where everything is.'

'Where are you staying so I can contact you?' Lauren asked.

'The Anchor Hotel,' Tom replied, taking the notebook and pen from Lauren, 'but I won't be there long so you'd better have my London address.'

His London address. So he didn't live in the States any more, Eve thought as she watched him scribble in Lauren's notebook, and he wasn't going to be staying in The Anchor for long, but did that mean he was moving back into his old home in Penhally, or what?

'You're staying at The Anchor Hotel?' Kate said before Eve could ask the questions she so desperately wanted the answers to. 'Very posh.'

'You mean, you're amazed they let anyone called Cornish through the door?' Tom said with an edge, and Kate coloured deeply.

'Of course I didn't mean that!' she exclaimed. 'I just meant...'

Her voice trailed away into awkward, embarrassed silence, and Eve came to her rescue.

'Kate, shouldn't you be making tracks for The Smugglers'?' she said. 'Alison and Jack headed off a few minutes ago, and they must be wondering where you are.'

'Oh. Right,' the midwife declared with a grateful smile and, as she and Lauren both headed for their cars, Eve turned to Tom, her expression sad.

'So, it still pushes all your buttons, does it, even after all these years?'

Tom's face tightened.

'Only in Penhally,' he said, then forced a smile as he noticed Tassie gazing up at him in obvious confusion. 'Well, half-pint, what are we waiting for? If we don't get to the reception fast all the best food will have gone.'

'Are we going in your car?' the little girl asked. 'The one that got hit?'

'We can walk,' Eve said hurriedly. 'The Smugglers' isn't far—just up the road.'

'We drive,' Tom insisted. 'If I'm taking two gorgeous women out to lunch then we go in style, even if my car is missing one indicator light cover.'

Walking would be better, Eve thought. Tassie would leap about as she always did, pointing things out to Tom, which would mean she wouldn't have to talk to him, but she could hardly insist on them walking. Tom would wonder why, and if Tom was the same man she had known—and she strongly suspected he was—he would badger and badger her until she told him.

'In style it is, then,' she declared, striding determinedly towards his car before she lost her nerve.

'Can I sit in the front?' Tassie asked, hopping excitedly from one foot to the other, her fine blonde hair flying about her shoulders, and Tom shook his head.

'Surely you know royalty always rides in the back behind the chauffeur?' he replied.

'But I'm not royalty,' the little girl pointed out, and Tom smiled the smile Eve knew could charm the birds off the trees.

'Today you are,' he said, helping Tassie up into the Range Rover. 'So, where to, ma'am?'

'Smugglers' Inn, as quick as you can, driver,' Tassie declared with an imperious air that was completely ruined when she dissolved into a fit of giggles.

'That was kind,' Eve murmured, as she got into the front seat, and Tom slipped into the driver's seat beside her.

'It's only manners to open a door for a lady,' he replied, and Eve shook her head.

'I meant it was kind of you to be so nice to Tassie.'

'She's a nice kid.'

'Not everyone sees that,' Eve observed, then managed a smile when Tom stared at her curiously. 'Do you honestly remember where everything in Penhally is, or do you want directions for The Smugglers'?'

'I haven't forgotten anything about Penhally,' he said abruptly, then grimaced as a slight frown creased Eve's forehead. 'Sorry. An hour back in the place, and already I'm defensive. No, I don't need directions,' he added as he drove out of the car park and turned left. 'The Smugglers' is at the top of Mevagissey Road.'

Odd, she thought as he drove north, that he should remember that. They'd never been to the inn when they'd been younger. It had been too expensive for them when he'd just qualified as a doctor and she'd just finished her nurse's training, and yet he'd remembered where it was. What else did he remember? she wondered, but she didn't want to go down that particular memory lane. It was fraught with too many dangers, too many complications.

'How long have you lived in London?' she said, deliberately changing the conversation. 'I mean, I thought you were still in the States,' she continued as he glanced across at her, 'but you gave Lauren a London address.'

'I haven't lived in the States for the past ten years,' he replied. 'I have a flat in London now, and an apartment in Lausanne overlooking Lake Geneva.'

'Sounds—'

'Posh?' he finished for her dryly, and she shook her head at him.

'Lovely—I was going to say lovely,' she said, and Tom shrugged.

'They're just places I stay in between trips, not proper homes. Homes have people you love in them. Wives, children.'

Don't ask, she thought as she stared out the windscreen at the trees flashing by. Trees that were beginning to lose their leaves under a sky that was as blue as only a Cornish sky could be. She didn't need to know, and it was better if she didn't, but she couldn't help herself.

'You're not married, then?' she said, glancing across at him.

'Nope,' he replied, braking slightly to avoid the rabbit that had dashed out in front of them. 'Never found anyone prepared to put up with the kind of erratic work patterns my job demands. At least, not for any length of time.' His green eyes met hers. 'What about you?'

She shifted her gaze back at the trees.

'No, I'm not married.' She took a deep breath. 'Tom, are you planning on coming back to Penhally to stay, or…?'

'I'm only here until Monday. I have things to do—sort out—then I'll be off again.'

A surge of relief engulfed her. Monday. This was Saturday. She could cope with that. If she should accidentally meet him again tomorrow, she'd be pleasant and friendly, talk about everything and nothing. She'd managed to keep silent for all these years so she could keep quiet for one more day because what good would it do to tell him? Telling him wouldn't change anything, alter anything, make it less painful.

'Eve?'

He was staring curiously at her, and she managed to smile.

'I read in a magazine a while back that you'd been made head of rescue operations at Deltaron,' she said. 'You must be very pleased.'

'Yeah, well, it's certainly a whole different ball game when your desk is the one the buck stops on. What about you?' he asked. 'Still nursing?'

She nodded.

'I actually just started work in Penhally last month,' she said. 'Before that I worked in Truro and Newquay, but Alison—the girl you don't know whose wedding you were just at,' she added, and saw Tom smile, 'is pregnant so I've temporarily taken over her position as practice nurse in the Penhally surgery.'

'Which means if she comes back after her maternity leave, you'll be out of a job,' Tom observed.

'Not for long,' she said briskly. 'There's a big shortage of nurses in the UK so I'll get something else pretty fast.'

'But you'd rather work here, in your home village.'

It was a statement, not a question, and her lips curved wryly.

'Well, you always did say I had no imagination.'

'Did I say that?' He shook his head. 'God, I had a big mouth when I was twenty-four, didn't I?'

'Uh-huh,' she replied, and he laughed. 'Actually, although you don't know Alison or Jack,' she continued, 'you do know Jack's father. It's Nick Tremayne.'

'Nick Tremayne, the doctor?' Tom declared.

'The very same,' Eve answered. 'He's the senior partner in the Penhally surgery now, and my boss.'

'Are you telling me I've just been to the wedding of the *son* of somebody I went to med school with?' Tom groaned. 'God, but now you've made me feel old.'

Eve chuckled. 'Do you remember when we thought anyone older than forty was decrepit?'

'And anyone over fifty might just as well be dead.' He nodded. 'Shows how little we knew, doesn't it?' His eyes met hers again. 'Eve—'

'Are we almost there yet?' Tassie chipped in from the back of the car. 'I'm *starving*.'

'In other words, quit with the talking,' Tom said ruefully, 'and drive faster.'

'Something like that.' The little girl giggled and, as Tom grinned across at Eve, and her own lips curved in response, her heart contracted.

No, she told herself. *No*. The past is past, nobody can ever go back, and if you allow yourself to be sucked back into his world he'll only hurt you again, and this time you might not survive.

'What's wrong?' Tom asked, his green eyes suddenly puzzled, and Eve shook her head.

'Just hungry, like Tassie.'

'Eve—'

'We're here!' Tassie interrupted with a shriek as the grey-stoned façade of The Smugglers' Inn suddenly came into view. 'And look at all the cars. I hope there's room inside for us.'

And I hope it's standing room only, Eve thought, so I can hide myself in the crush, but Tom must have read her mind because as she got out of the car he took her arm firmly in his.

'Now we eat, and socialise, right?' he declared.

'You go ahead,' Eve replied. 'I just need…'

She waved vaguely in the direction of the door leading to the ladies' cloakroom, but it didn't do her any good.

'We'll wait for you, won't we, Tassie?' Tom said, and Tassie beamed, leaving Eve with nothing to do but obediently disappear into the ladies' cloakroom.

At least it was empty, she thought with relief as she walked in. Company was the last thing she wanted right now, and quickly she washed her hands then pulled her hairbrush out of her handbag. Lord, but she looked awful. White face, panic-stricken brown eyes, her shoulder-length brown hair slightly windswept, and…

Forty-two, she thought bleakly as she gazed at her reflection in the mirror over the sink. I look forty-two. OK, so that wasn't old, but nothing could alter the fact that she was heavier than she'd been at twenty-two, that there were faint lines at the corner of her eyes, and her hair wouldn't be brown if Vicki at the hairdresser's didn't tint it every six weeks.

Impatiently, she dragged her hairbrush through her hair. What did it matter if she didn't look twenty-two any more?

Because I would like to have looked as I did when he last saw me, her heart sighed as her eyes met those in the mirror. Because it would have shown him what he lost when he walked away from me, and it was stupid to feel that way. Stupid.

'Feeling any better now?'

Eve whirled round to see Kate Althorp standing behind her, and forced a smile.

'Much,' she lied, and Kate shot her a shrewd glance as she ran some water into a sink and began washing her hands.

'It must have been quite a shock to see Tom again.'

'A surprise,' Eve said firmly. 'It was a surprise, that's all, seeing him back in Penhally.'

'Yes, but you and he were quite close before he went to the States, weren't you?'

Close. What an, oh, so very British, euphemistic way of saying 'lovers', Eve thought wryly, and of course Kate would remember she and Tom had spent that summer together. Kate was in her forties, too, and nothing stayed a secret for long in Penhally unless you really worked at it, and Tom hadn't given a damn about what people thought.

'Kate, I was twenty-two, he was twenty-four,' Eve declared, injecting as much careless indifference into her voice as she could. 'We shared a short summer romance, that's all.'

'Which wouldn't make it any the less painful when it ended,' Kate Althorp said gently.

The midwife saw too much—way too much—and Eve picked up her hairbrush again.

'Water under the bridge years ago,' she said. 'We've both gone our separate ways since then, led very different lives.'

Or at least Tom had, Eve thought as Kate looked for a moment as though she'd like to say something, then dried her hands on a paper towel and left the cloakroom. Tom had gone off to the States, full of determination to succeed, and he had, whereas she...

She squeezed her eyes shut. He was not going to do this to her. She had spent all these years rebuilding her life into something to be proud of, something that mattered, and she was not going to let his presence tear it all down, make it seem worthless.

'Enough, Eve,' she said as she opened her eyes and gazed at her reflection again. 'The past is past. Don't resurrect it.'

Except it wasn't that easy, she realised as she walked out of the cloakroom, and found Tom and Tassie waiting for her, grinning like a pair of conspirators.

'Tassie was convinced you'd slipped down the toilet,' Tom declared. 'I told her we'd give you another five minutes, then I'd go over the top in my capacity as head of rescue operations at Deltaron.'

'Promises, promises,' Eve said lightly, and Tom's grin widened.

'You think I wouldn't—or couldn't?' he replied.

'I think we should eat,' she said firmly, refusing to be drawn, but he knew what she was doing.

She could see it in the glint in his eyes. The familiar half daring, half challenging glint which had appeared in the past whenever he'd been about to do, or say, something completely outrageous, and a faint unease stirred in her. An unease which must have shown on her face because he smiled.

'I'm a mature man now, Eve,' he declared. 'No fights, no arguments, I promise.'

And he was as good as his word.

For the next hour Tom charmed his way round the crowded room as only he could when he wanted to. Of course it helped that most of the people at the reception were newcomers to the village, but even when some of the older villagers cut him dead he didn't rise to the bait. He simply moved away with a wry smile to gently reassure Lauren about his car, then make Chloe Mackinnon, the village's other midwife, laugh as her fiancé, Dr Fawkner, stood by, watching protectively.

'He's changed, hasn't he?' Kate observed, nodding towards Tom who was now engaged in an animated discussion about fund-holding practices with Dr Lovak.

'Tom always could string more than two words together, you know,' Eve said more caustically than she'd intended, and Kate's eyebrows rose.

'I never thought he couldn't,' the midwife replied. 'Just as you also know I never thought he got a fair deal in Penhally.'

'Still won't, judging by the reaction of some people,' Eve said, nodding across to a small group of villagers who were throwing deep frowns in Tom's direction.

'People have long memories and old prejudices. I'm not saying they're right,' Kate continued as Eve opened her mouth to interrupt. 'In fact, the longer I've lived, the less inclined I've become to judge anyone, but don't forget Tom has friends here, too, as well as detractors.'

Name one, apart from yourself, Eve was tempted to say, but she didn't.

'I must get Tassie home,' she said instead. 'She's beginning to look tired.'

Tom clearly wasn't because the minute Eve began to make her way through the throng he was instantly at her side.

'Trying to run out on me, are you?' he said, and she shook her head at him.

'It's time I took Tassie home,' she replied, sidestepping quickly as Freddie and Sam dashed past them, slipping and sliding on the polished wooden floor, whooping at the top of their lungs.

'Regular little bundles of fun, aren't they?' Tom said with amusement as the youngsters scampered off.

'You used to hate kids,' Eve reminded him. 'Said they should all be kept indoors by their parents until they were teenagers.'

'Yeah, well…' Tom glanced back at the two boys. 'Do you ever find yourself wishing you'd had children?'

Eve stared fixedly at the wedding cake sitting on the table by the window.

'No point in wishing, Tom,' she said. 'It's better to deal with the here and now.'

'I guess so,' he said, then smiled and waved to Tassie. 'But I still think I'd like to have kids.'

'And I think it's way past time Tassie went home,' Eve said through a throat so tight it hurt.

'Eve—'

'Well, well, well. If it isn't Tom Cornish. And what brings Penhally's local-boy-made-good back to Cornwall?'

Eve glanced over her shoulder to see Nick Tremayne standing behind them, and smiled.

'Tom,' she began, 'this is—'

'Nick Tremayne.' Tom grinned. 'No need for an introduction, Eve. I would have recognised this old reprobate anywhere. Good to see you again, Nick, and still doctoring, I hear.'

'And you're still globetrotting with Deltaron if all I've read about you is true,' Nick replied with no smile at all.

'You've been following my career?' Tom said lightly, but Eve could see a slightly puzzled look in his eyes. 'I'm flattered.'

'Oh, even in a sleepy little backwater like Penhally, we have the internet and satellite television now,' Nick replied, 'which means I'm all too aware of your exploits.'

'Tom is just back for a short visit,' Eve said, glancing from Tom to Nick, then back again uncertainly. Lord, but the animosity emanating from Nick was so patent it could have flash-frozen fish. 'He's leaving on Monday.'

'Back to singlehandedly, heroically saving the world, I presume?' Nick declared, and what little smile there had been left on Tom's face disappeared completely.

'If you want heroes, Nick, then it's the people who live in the countries my team and I go into to help who deserve that title,' he said tersely. 'They're the ones who have to tackle the long-term effects of any disaster.'

'I couldn't agree more,' Nick observed, 'but they don't get

the credit, do they? Because they get left with the boring, tedious stuff, like rebuilding their country, while you swan off on yet another photo opportunity.'

'Now, just a minute,' Tom began, his face darkening, and Eve caught hold of his sleeve quickly.

'Tom, we really *do* have to get Tassie home,' she said. 'She's very tired, and I told Amanda we'd make sure she wouldn't be too late back.'

For a moment she didn't think he was going to come with her. He certainly didn't look as though he wanted to as he glared at Nick, and Nick glared back, then he nodded reluctantly.

'Right,' he said, then added, 'See you around, Nick,' before he strode out of the room, leaving Eve and Tassie with nothing to do but hurry after him.

'I thought you said you and Nick Tremayne were friends?' Eve protested when she caught up with him in the car park.

'I thought we were, too,' Tom replied, 'but I've clearly done something to rattle his cage. Any idea what?'

'None at all,' Eve said. 'He can certainly be a bit brusque at times, but he's not normally so…so…'

'In your face?' Tom shook his head as he helped Tassie clamber into his Range Rover. 'Kate Althorp sure had a lucky escape.'

'From what?' Eve asked in confusion.

'From marrying him. Don't you remember how close Kate and Nick were at school?' he continued as Eve looked at him in surprise. 'Everyone was certain they'd get married.'

'Well, they didn't,' Eve replied. 'Kate married James Althorp.'

'So I gathered.' Tom frowned as he switched on his ignition. 'Which I have to say I find surprising. Don't get me wrong,' he added. 'James was a nice enough bloke, but I'd have thought he was a bit too laid back for Kate, which only goes to show you never can tell. Nick married that girl he met at med school, didn't he? Anne…Isabel…'

'Annabel.'

'Yeah, that was her name. Nice girl, she was, too, as I recall.'

'She died nearly three years ago now,' Eve replied. 'Her appendix ruptured and because she'd taken aspirin she bled out and there was nothing anyone could do.'

'I'm sorry about that,' Tom declared, 'but I still reckon Kate had a lucky escape.'

But Nick isn't normally like that, Eve thought with a frown, as Tom drove them down the winding road back into the village. The senior partner could certainly be sharp and cutting if he felt people weren't pulling their weight, but she'd never seen him verbally attack somebody for no reason, and yet that was exactly what he'd done this afternoon.

'Where does Tassie live?' Tom asked as they drove down Harbour Road.

'Just off Morwenna Road, but if you drop us at the post office we can walk from there,' Eve replied.

'But that will still leave you quite a distance to walk,' Tom protested.

'All to the good,' Eve said calmly. 'I need some exercise after what I've eaten.'

'But—'

'Drop us at the post office, Tom.'

He sighed but, after he'd crossed the Harbour Bridge, he obediently pulled up at the post office.

'Thanks for the ride, mister,' Tassie said when she and Eve got out of his car, and he smiled and ruffled her hair.

'Could you make yourself scarce for a couple of minutes, half-pint?' he said. 'I need to talk to Eve.'

'Tom, Tassie really does have to go home,' Eve began as the girl obediently skipped down the road for a few yards, then waited. 'The wind's getting up, and she's not dressed for the weather—'

'I was wondering whether you'd like to come out with me

tomorrow?' he interrupted. 'We could have lunch, and you could show me the sights of Penhally.'

'Tom, you were born here, you know what the sights are,' she protested.

'There's bound to have been some changes—new developments—since I was last here,' he argued back, 'and I thought—perhaps for old times' sake?'

She didn't want to do anything for old times' sake. Two postcards, that's all he'd sent her after he'd left for America. One from New York, saying he was homesick and lonely, and another one from California six months later, saying he'd applied for a job with Deltaron. After that, there'd been nothing. Not a card, or a letter, or a phone call, for the past twenty years during which she'd got on with her life, and if it hadn't been the life she'd planned, dreamed of, it had been a satisfying life, and now he was back, and she didn't want him to be back.

'I'm sorry,' she said firmly. 'I have things to do tomorrow.'

'Please.'

If he had been smiling at her with that old gotta-love-me smile she would never have wavered, but he wasn't smiling. In fact, he looked uncharacteristically unsure, uncertain, and Tom Cornish had never been unsure of anything in his life.

'I can't do lunch,' she said hesitantly. *Won't, more like.* 'As I said, I have things to do tomorrow.'

'Half a day is better than none,' he said. 'Do you still live in Polkerris Road with your parents? I'll pick you up at two o'clock—'

'Three o'clock,' she interrupted. 'And I'll meet you outside your hotel.'

He looked disappointed, then he nodded.

'OK, three o'clock it is,' he said, then to her surprise he added quickly, 'You will come, won't you?'

The uncertainty was back in his eyes, big time, and a slight frown creased her forehead.

'I said I'd come,' she pointed out, 'and I will.'

Though God knows why, she thought as she joined Tassie and the two of them began walking down the road together.

'He's nice,' Tassie observed, hopping from one paving stone to the next in some sort of elaborate game only she understood.

'Tom can be very nice when he wants to be,' Eve replied noncommittally.

'He told me you and he were best friends when you were younger,' Tassie continued with her usual directness, and Eve manufactured a smile.

'It was a long time ago, Tassie.'

'He still likes you. I can tell. In fact,' the girl added, 'I bet if we turn round right now he'll be watching you from outside the post office.'

'Tassie,' Eve began in consternation, but the girl had already stopped and was looking over her shoulder.

'Told you so,' Tassie said.

'He's watching us?' Eve said faintly.

'See for yourself if you don't believe me,' Tassie declared, and Eve shook her head, feeling her cheeks prickle with heat.

'I've got to get you home.'

'Chicken.' Tassie laughed.

Self-preservation, more like, Eve thought, walking on determinedly. I don't owe him anything, not after all these years.

But you've still agreed to meet him tomorrow afternoon, haven't you? a little voice mocked at the back of her mind, and she groaned inwardly.

She must have been out of her mind.

CHAPTER TWO

IT WAS strange, Tom thought as he leant back against the grey-stoned wall of the Anchor Hotel and breathed in deeply. He'd been all around the world in the course of his work, and yet no air had ever smelt quite the same as the air did in Penhally Bay.

And nobody had ever looked quite like Eve Dwyer, he decided when he heard the faint sound of footsteps in the distance, and turned to see her walking down Fisherman's Row towards him wearing a cherry-red sweater and a russet-coloured skirt, her brown hair gleaming in the early October sunshine.

Lord, but she'd scarcely changed at all. She still had the same cloud of brown hair, the same long, curly eyelashes, and even the same two dimples which peeked out when she smiled. Perhaps she was slightly curvier now than she had been when at twenty-two, but it suited her. It suited her a lot, he decided as his gaze swept over her appreciatively.

'Am I late?' she said, her brown eyes apologetic when she drew level with him.

He shook his head, and breathed in deeply again.

'You know, I think I would recognise Penhally air even if I was blindfolded.'

'You mean the pong of old seaweed and fish?' she said, her eyes dancing.

'I meant the tang of the sea, as you very well know,' he said severely, then his lips curved. 'And there was me thinking you'd still be a romantic.'

The light in her eyes disappeared, and a shadow replaced it.

'Gave up on romance a long time ago, Tom. So…' She spread her hands wide. 'Where do you want to start?'

'Start?' He echoed, still puzzling over what she'd said about giving up on romance.

'You said you wanted a tour of Penhally,' she reminded him. 'So, do you want to go north towards the lighthouse first, or down to the lifeboat station?'

'The lighthouse, I think,' he said. 'You always used to go there when you wanted to think, didn't you?'

She shot him a surprised glance.

'What an odd thing to remember,' she said.

'Oh, my mind's a regular ragbag of odd bits of information,' he replied lightly as she crossed the Harbour Bridge back into Fisherman's Row and he fell into step beside her.

'Of course, not many fishermen live in Fisherman's Row any more,' she declared. 'In fact, there aren't many fishermen left in Penhally full stop. Too few fish to catch nowadays, and too many quotas, to make it a viable way of life.' She waved to a dark-haired young woman who had come out of one of the cottages to scoop up a ginger cat. 'That's Chloe MacKinnon. You met her yesterday at Alison and Jack's reception.'

'Midwife like Kate, yes?' Tom frowned. 'Works in the village practice, and is currently engaged to, and living with, Oliver Fawkner?'

'That's the one,' Eve said as the woman waved back and disappeared into her house. 'You met Oliver at the reception, too.'

'I remember.' Tom nodded, then chuckled. 'You know, if one of the local midwives and a practice doctor had been living together when I was last in Penhally, they'd have been tarred and feathered then run out of town.'

'Times change even in Penhally, at least for some things,' she murmured, and before he could say anything she pointed across the harbour to where a pretty cottage sat high on the hill. 'That's where Kate lives. Her house must have one of the best views in Penhally.'

'Right,' he said, shooting her a puzzled glance.

'Dr Lovak used to live in Fisherman's Row,' Eve continued as they walked past the library and into Harbour Road, 'but he and his wife, Melinda, moved out into the country in the summer. I guess with a baby coming they wanted more space.'

Tom was sure they did, but talking about where the members of the village practice lived was not exactly what he'd had in mind when he'd asked Eve to meet him today, and if she was going to spend the whole afternoon pointing out the homes of her colleagues it was going to be a very long afternoon indeed.

'Eve—'

'I'm sorry,' she broke in, turning to face him, her expression contrite. 'I know I'm babbling a load of boring drivel, but the thing is…' She lifted her shoulders helplessly. 'We don't know each other any more, and I don't know what to say, or talk to you about. I know we were…close…in the past, but—'

'Us meeting again is fast turning into your worst date ever,' he finished for her, and she coloured.

'Maybe not quite that bad, but we're practically strangers now, Tom, so why did you ask to see me again—what was the point?'

Good question, he thought, but how could he tell her that part of him had hoped to find her happily married so he could finally squash the dream that had haunted him for years—that he could somehow go back, change things—while the other part had hoped she was still single so he might be given another chance at happiness.

She would say he wasn't making any sense, and maybe he wasn't. Maybe nobody could—or should—ever try to go back.

'Look, I won't take offence if you just want to give this up, and go back to your hotel,' Eve continued.

If her eyes hadn't met his when she'd spoken he might have been tempted to accept her suggestion, but, lord, she really was as lovely as he'd remembered, and how could he have forgotten her eyes weren't simply brown, but had tiny flecks of green in them? Because he'd forced himself to forget, he thought with a sigh, spent so many years trying not to remember, until a year ago, when…

Don't go there, his mind warned. It's better not to go there.

'Tom?'

She looked awkward and uncomfortable, and he forced a smile.

'Of course I don't want to go back to the hotel,' he said. 'Leastways, not until you've pointed out Nick's house and I've thrown a brick through his window.'

She gave a small choke of laughter. 'I thought you said you were a mature man now?'

'OK, I'll see if I can capture some greenfly and let them loose on his roses instead,' he said, and when she laughed out loud he linked his arm with hers, and began walking again. 'Eve, I know it's been a long time since we last met,' he continued, 'but it simply means we've a lot of catching up to do. And speaking of catching up,' he added when she said nothing, 'are you *quite* sure you don't know why Nick appears to consider me dog meat?'

'I thought you might know the answer to that,' she observed, and he shook his head.

'I knew him at school, and met him a couple of times when I went to med school, but he was a few years older than me, and his friends tended to be the more studious type, whereas mine…' He grinned down at her. 'Tended to be a little rowdier.'

'I bet they were,' Eve said dryly.

'How many kids does Nick have?' Tom asked, and Eve smiled as they reached the end of Harbour Road and turned towards the lighthouse.

'He and Annabel had three of a family. Lucy and Jack, who are twins, and Edward. They're all doctors.'

Tom pulled a face. 'All of them! I don't think I'd want any kids of mine becoming medics, would you?'

He'd said the wrong thing. He didn't know why, or how, but her face had suddenly closed up completely, and he longed to hug her, or say something totally outrageous to bring the smile back onto her face, but no words occurred to him, and as for hugging her... In the past he wouldn't have thought twice, but even thinking about doing it now made him feel ridiculously awkward, as though it would be too forward which was crazy when he remembered what they'd once meant to one another.

'Odd time of day for a church service,' he said, deliberately changing the subject as they passed the church and the sound of enthusiastic singing drifted out.

'It's not a service,' Eve replied. 'Reverend Kenner runs a club for the village youngsters on Sunday afternoons. Daniel's a nice man. A good one, too.'

'Single, is he?' Tom said, feeling a spurt of something that crazily felt almost like jealousy.

'Daniel's a widower like Nick, with a seventeen-year-old daughter.'

And she didn't look any happier, Tom thought as they walked on to the lighthouse. In fact, she looked even more strained and, in desperation, he pointed out to sea to where the wreck of the seventeenth century Spanish galleon, the *Corazón del Oro*, had lain for the past four hundred years.

'Remember when we wished we could dive down there, find loads of gold coins, and make our fortune?'

'Except neither of us could swim, so it was a bit of a nonstarter,' she replied. 'Still can't swim, which is a dreadful admission for somebody who lives by the sea. What about you?'

'I had to learn for my work so they sent me on a course and, believe me, being in a class of five-year-olds when you're twenty-four, and five feet ten inches tall, doesn't do a lot for your ego.'

Her lips twitched. 'You're making that up.'

'Scout's honour,' he protested, and she laughed.

'Tom, you were thrown out of the Scouts for disruptive behaviour when you were thirteen.'

'OK, so maybe I was,' he said, relieved to see her smile again, 'but I honestly was stuck in a kids' class. My boss reckoned it would concentrate my mind wonderfully, and it did. I always wondered why your dad didn't teach you to swim, what with him being a sailor.'

'He was too busy trying to make a living. My mum wanted me to learn, but you had to pay for lessons, and...' She shrugged. 'Money was always tight when I was a kid.'

'Are they still alive—your mum and dad?' he asked, as they turned and began walking back from the lighthouse.

She shook her head.

'My dad died of cancer fifteen years ago. Never would give up his cigarettes, though Mum nagged him like crazy about it. My mum died of a heart attack five years ago.'

'I'm sorry,' he said gently. 'I know they were apoplectic that summer when we started dating, but I liked them.'

'So did I,' she murmured, and Tom swore under his breath.

Hell, but she had that look on her face again. That bleak, almost haunted look as though he had conjured up memories that would have been better left buried.

'Look, why don't we go down to the beach?' he said quickly. 'Have a walk along the sand.'

'I'm not really dressed for it, Tom,' she replied, pointing down at her shoes. 'My heels will get stuck.'

'Then take your shoes off,' he said. 'Take off your stockings, too, and you can paddle if you want.'

'Tom, it's October,' she said. 'It's too cold to paddle.'

'Rubbish,' he said, steering her firmly towards the steps that led down to the beach. 'It's a gorgeous day.'

It was, too, Eve thought as she stared up at the sky. Seagulls were wheeling and diving overhead, their white feathers standing out in sharp contrast to the clear blue sky, and there was a deceptive warmth in the air despite the fact that it was October. Soon it would change. Soon it would be winter and the green-blue sea would become grey and stormy, sending breakers crashing onto the white sand, and only the very toughest would walk along the shore, but today there was enough heat in the day to make it pleasant.

'If you hurry up,' Tom continued as he sat down on the top step, and began pulling off his shoes and socks, and rolling up his trousers, 'we'll have the beach to ourselves—just the way you used to like it.'

How had he remembered that? she thought with surprise, and he'd also remembered she used to sit at the foot of the light-house when she wanted to think. They were such little things—such inconsequential things—and yet he'd remembered, and the water did look tempting, so very tempting, but she could just imagine what the gossipmongers would say if somebody saw her.

Eve Dwyer went paddling with that Tom Cornish yesterday. Paddling, *and with that Tom Cornish.*

'Tom, maybe we should just go back into the village,' she began, and his green eyes danced as he looked up at her.

'Eve, I'm not suggesting we go skinny-dipping. Though I'm game if you are.'

Her lips curved in spite of herself.

'In your dreams,' she said.

'Chicken.'

He was the second person to have called her that in twenty-four hours, and she discovered she didn't like it. She didn't like it one bit. OK, so skinny-dipping was completely out of the question but, hell's bells, even in Penhally she could surely paddle if she wanted to, and she discovered she wanted to.

'OK, move over,' she said, and he slid across the step so she could sit down beside him.

'So, are we paddling, or skinny-dipping?' he said, and, when she gave him a hard stare, his eyes glinted. 'Pity. I was kind of looking forward to shocking the good people of Penhally.'

'I bet you were,' she said dryly as she unbuckled the straps of her shoes and slipped them off. 'Right. Turn your back while I take off my stockings,' she added, and when his mouth fell open, she said, 'I'm not having you staring at my thighs, and making snarky comments about cellulite, so turn your back.'

'I don't even know what cellulite is,' he protested, but he did as she asked, and when she eventually stuffed her tights into her skirt pocket and stood up, he said, 'You're an idiot—you know that, don't you?'

'Probably,' she agreed, picking up her shoes by their straps, and walking down the steps. 'So, are we walking or not?'

He shook his head at her as he followed her down the steps.

'You didn't used to be so shy,' he observed, and a stain of colour spread across her cheeks.

He was laughing at her, she knew he was, remembering all the times he'd seen her completely naked, and she bit her lip, waiting for him to point that out, but he didn't.

'I don't think I'll ever forget you dancing and singing on this beach,' he said instead, completely surprising her. 'It was the height of summer—the place was packed with tourists, and families from the village—and suddenly you began singing that Whitney Houston song at the top of your lungs.'

'"I wanna to dance with somebody"!' she exclaimed with a choke of laughter. 'I'd forgotten all about that. I got into such a row with my mother after Audrey Baxter told her I'd made a public spectacle of myself.'

'Audrey Baxter would say that,' he replied with feeling as they began walking along the beach.

'And you told me I had no taste,' she reminded him. 'That if I wanted to sing, then I should have sung one of Bruce Springsteen's songs because he was the only singer worth listening to.'

'Still is,' he insisted, and when she rolled her eyes he laughed, and said, 'Do you still have that dress?'

'What dress?' she said in confusion.

'The red dress you wore that day. It had a big wide skirt, and puffy sleeves, and when I first went to the States I couldn't turn on the radio without hearing Chris de Burgh singing "The Lady in Red", and every time I heard it I thought of you, singing on this beach.'

'Did you?' she said faintly, and he nodded.

'You wouldn't believe how homesick I got whenever they played that song.'

But not homesick enough to write to me, or phone me, she thought, but she didn't say that.

'I'm afraid I threw the dress out years ago,' she said instead.

'Pity,' he murmured, picking up a pebble and sending it skimming across the water in front of them. 'I always liked that dress, and the little red boots you used to wear.'

'My *pixie boots*!' she exclaimed. 'I'd forgotten all about them, too. I *loved* those boots. Couldn't wear them now, of course.'

'Yes, you could. You've still got great legs. Great figure, too,' he added.

'Not that good,' she said, feeling the wash of colour on her cheeks return as his gaze swept over her. 'Years ago I could eat whatever I wanted and never put on a kilo. Now I just have to look at a cream cake, and, pouf, on goes the weight.'

He grinned. 'Well, you're looking good from where I'm standing.'

So was he, she thought. With the sun on his face, and the

wind ruffling his hair, he looked exactly like the town bad boy he'd been all those years ago, whereas she…

What had she been back then?

Naïve, yes. Trusting, most definitely, but mostly so full of dreams, and hopes, and plans. Tom had been the same, but her dreams hadn't been the same as his. He'd wanted to get as far away from Penhally as he could, to live a life of adventure and excitement, and she… She'd simply wanted him.

'Let's have some fun,' he'd said when he'd come back to Penhally as a fully qualified doctor that summer, and she'd been so happy because he'd finally asked her out that she'd chosen not to believe him when he'd told her he would be heading for the States at the end of September.

He'll change his mind, she'd told herself, and for four wonderful, glorious months they'd walked, and talked—lord, how they'd talked—and they'd made love. She'd been a virgin when they'd first started going out and he'd teased her about it, said a woman could have just as much fun as a man without fear of the consequences, and she'd gone on the Pill to be safe, and then after four far too short months he had left.

'What are you thinking about?'

She looked up to see him gazing at her quizzically, and managed a smile.

'I was just wondering where the last twenty years had gone,' she said. 'Sometimes it seems like a lifetime, doesn't it, and sometimes just a few months.'

'And I can't believe you're still single,' he observed. 'The men in Penhally must be either blind, or stupid, or both.'

'I almost got married once,' she replied, kicking the sand in front of her so it sprayed out as they walked, 'but…'

'It didn't feel right?'

'Something like that. What about you?' she asked. 'Were you never tempted to take the plunge?'

'I've had a couple of semi-serious relationships, but…' He

shrugged. 'My work makes it difficult because I never know where I'm going to be from one day to the next.'

'Maybe you're just not the marrying kind,' she said. 'Some people aren't.'

He stared out to sea, then back at her, and to her surprise he looked suddenly wistful, almost sad.

'And maybe I simply got my priorities all wrong.'

His eyes were fixed on hers, refusing to allow her to look away, and her heart gave an uncomfortable thump. This conversation was getting too personal, way too personal, and she had to change it. Now.

'Last one to reach the end of the beach is a wimp,' she said, and, before he could reply, she was off and running, her bare feet flying over the sand, her skirt billowing above her knees, her shoes swinging from her hand.

From behind her she heard him shout a spluttered protest, but she didn't stop. She just kept on running and when she heard his footsteps begin to thud behind her she suddenly, and inexplicably, began to laugh.

To laugh like the girl she'd once been. The carefree young girl who had once sung on a beach, feeling nothing but the joy of being alive, and she knew she probably looked like a demented lunatic, but she didn't care. For this moment—for just this one moment—with her hair streaming in the breeze, and the taste of the sun and the sea on her lips, she felt like that girl again, and it was wonderful.

'You *cheated*!' he exclaimed when he caught up with her, and grasped her by the waist, spinning her round so fast she had to catch hold of his shirt to prevent herself from toppling over.

'Sore loser,' she threw back at him, laughing breathlessly as she pushed her hair away from her face. 'You've been spending far too much time behind a desk.'

'Too much time…?' His eyes narrowed. 'I'll make you pay for that remark, Eve Dwyer.'

'Oh, no, you won't,' she said, turning to run again, and he made a grab for her, and she jumped back to escape him, only to let out a yell as she ended up ankle deep in the sea. 'Oh, my God, it's *freezing*.'

'Serves you right.' Tom laughed but, when she scooped up some water and threw it at him, he splashed into the water after her. 'Play rough, would you? OK, you deserve a complete ducking for that.'

'You wouldn't,' she cried, trying to evade him, but he caught her round the waist again and swept her up into his arms.

'You think?' he said, deliberately lowering her towards the water, and she shrieked and threw her arms round his neck.

'Tom, no!'

He grinned. 'OK, if you don't want to be ducked, you'll need to pay a forfeit, and I think you know what that forfeit is, don't you?'

A kiss. The forfeit had always been a kiss when they'd dated and, as Eve stared up into his, oh, so familiar face, she realised with a stab of pain that even after all that had happened, even after all the heartache and desolation, she wanted to kiss him, and the thought appalled her.

'Tom, let me go,' she said, but he didn't hear the strain in her voice.

'Nope, not a chance,' he said. 'The forfeit, or the sea. Your choice.'

'Tom, *please*.'

'Make a decision—make a decision,' he insisted as he whirled her round in his arms, but she didn't have to.

She had suddenly seen what he hadn't, and she tugged desperately on his sleeve.

'Tom, we have company.'

'Company?' he repeated, then swore under his breath as he followed her gaze. 'Oh, wonderful. Bloody wonderful. Is that who I think it is?'

'I'm afraid so,' Eve said, through gritted teeth, and when Tom quickly put her down she splashed out of the sea, feeling completely ridiculous and stupid, as Audrey Baxter walked towards them.

'Tom Cornish,' Audrey declared the minute she drew level with them, her faded brown eyes alive with curiosity and speculation. 'My heavens, but I never thought to see you in Penhally again.'

'Us bad pennies have a nasty habit of turning up again, don't we, Mrs Baxter?' he replied dryly.

'Oh, I wouldn't call you a bad penny, Tom,' Audrey declared. 'You were a little wild, to be sure—'

'I think the words you used to shout after me when I was a teenager were, "You're heading straight to hell in a handcart, Tom Cornish".'

Audrey patted her steel-grey curls and shook her head at him reprovingly.

'That was a long time ago, Tom.' She shifted her gaze to Eve, making her all too aware that her hair must be sticking out all over the place, and the hem of her skirt was wet. 'I see you and Nurse Dwyer are getting reacquainted.'

Tom moved up the beach a step. 'We are, but now I'm afraid we have to be going.'

'I thought you might have come back to Penhally two years ago, Tom, when your father died,' Audrey continued. 'I know you didn't always get on—'

'And I think your dog's looking for you,' Tom interrupted, pointing to the brindle and white greyhound which was splashing in the water further up the beach.

'Looking for crabs, more like,' Audrey replied. 'He loves them.'

'Indeed,' Tom declared, 'and now if you'll excuse us...'

But Audrey wasn't about to let him leave so easily.

'I hear your father left you his house in Trelissa Road?' she called after him, and Tom turned slowly to face her, his expression tight.

'What a very knowledgeable little community Penhally is,' he said, the sarcasm in his voice so plain that even Audrey couldn't miss it, and Eve grabbed his hand quickly, not caring that Audrey's eyes followed her action.

'Tom, we really do have to be going,' she insisted, and determinedly she urged him back up the beach, but it wasn't over as far as he was concerned.

'Nothing changes, does it?' he spat out when they reached the steps leading off the beach, and he glanced over his shoulder to see Audrey was watching them. 'Twenty damn years, and nothing changes. I could be the Prime Minister of Britain, and in Penhally I'd still be Tom Cornish, that drunkard, Frank Cornish's, son who no decent family ever wanted their daughter dating.'

'Tom—'

'If you're going to say Audrey meant no harm, you can save your breath,' he interrupted, sitting down on the step and beginning to drag on his socks, heedless of the fact that his feet were still covered in sand. 'And if you were going to ask me why I didn't come back for my father's funeral, you can save your breath on that one, too.'

'I know why you didn't come back, Tom,' she said gently, 'and Audrey… There's no question she can be an interfering busybody, but your father's dead and gone. Don't let him keep hurting you.'

'He left me his house, Eve,' he said furiously. 'After years of battering me from pillar to post until I was big enough to hit him back and make it count, he had the gall to leave me his house.'

'Maybe…' She shrugged helplessly. 'Maybe he was trying to make amends, at the end?'

'If I believed that for one second,' he retorted, 'I'd go round and torch the bloody place myself. No guilt gift can ever make up for the fact he hated me from the day I was born. Time and time again, he'd tell me of all the things he could have done—would have done—if my mother hadn't become pregnant, and her family hadn't forced him into marrying her, and when she died he hated me even more.'

'I know,' she said, sitting down beside him, aching at the pain she saw in his face, feeling a different kind of pain in herself, but he rounded on her furiously.

'No, you don't. You have *no* idea of what it's like to live with a man whose dreams you've shattered. No idea to feel, even as a seven-year-old child, that it would have been better if you'd never been born.'

She opened her mouth, then closed it again.

'I'm sorry,' she murmured. 'You're right. I don't know.'

Silently she brushed the sand from her feet, then pushed her feet into her shoes, but when she made to stand up he put out his hand to stop her.

'You've forgotten your stockings.'

'Doesn't matter,' she replied, and, for a second he said nothing, then he thrust his fingers through his hair, and she saw his hands were shaking.

'I'm sorry,' he said, his voice so strained it almost broke. 'So sorry for yelling at you.'

'It's all right,' she said.

'It's not,' he declared. 'I shouldn't have taken it out on you, and I'm sorry, too, that Audrey saw you in my arms. I know what this place is like—the gossip, the innuendo…'

'It's *all right*, Tom,' she insisted, and saw a small smile creep onto his lips.

'I've always created trouble for you, haven't I?' he said.

'Of course you haven't,' she lied. 'And now, come on,' she added, 'or we'll be completing this tour of Penhally by moonlight.'

'Which would really set the local tongues wagging, wouldn't it?' he declared as he fell into step beside her. 'Audrey—'

'Forget her,' Eve ordered as they began walking back down Harbour Road, and he shook his head.

'This is a professional observation, not a personal one,' he replied. 'Her colour's very high.'

'She has angina, and she's hopeless about remembering to use her glyceryl trinitrate spray. "I keep forgetting, Nurse Dwyer",' Eve continued in a perfect imitation of Audrey's voice. 'I don't think she realises, or will accept, how serious her condition is.'

'Denial can be a form of self-protection when people are scared,' Tom observed, kicking a pebble at his feet so that it ricocheted down the street in front of them. 'If they don't think about it, it hasn't happened.'

It was true, Eve thought, but denial had never worked for her. All the denying, and pretending in the world, had never made it go away for her, and when they reached Harbour Bridge she came to a halt.

'Tom, why did you come back?' she asked. 'You always said you wouldn't, so why are you here?'

For a moment she didn't think he was going to answer, then he shrugged.

'My dad's solicitor has been bending my ear about the house, wanting to know whether I want to sell it, or rent it out.'

'You didn't have to come back to Penhally for that,' she pointed out. 'You could just have told him over the phone.'

'I suppose,' he murmured as he stared down at the river Lanson flowing gently under the bridge beneath them, then he grinned. 'OK, you've rumbled me. I thought it might be interesting to see Penhally again.'

He wasn't telling her the truth. She didn't know how she knew that, but she did.

'Tom—'

'What happened to the cinema?' he interrupted. 'It used to be up there, in Gull Close, didn't it, on the right-hand side of the river?'

'It was on the left-hand side of the river, in Bridge Street, but it closed down years ago,' she replied, all too aware that he was changing the subject, but she had secrets so she supposed he was entitled to secrets, too. 'People gradually stopped wanting to go so much once they had television in their own homes.'

'I took you to see *RoboCop*.'

'No, you didn't.'

'I did, too,' he insisted as they began walking again. 'I remember us kissing in the back row.'

'Must have been someone else. Come to think of it,' she added wryly, 'it undoubtedly *was* someone else considering you were Penhally's answer to Casanova.'

'I was not,' he replied, the grin reappearing on his face.

'Yes, you were!' she exclaimed. 'Even when we were at school, every girl fancied you like mad despite you having the most dreadful reputation.'

'You didn't.'

Oh, but I did, I *did*, she thought, but you never noticed me. It was only when you came back from med school that summer that you realised I was alive.

'That's the Penhally Bay Surgery,' she continued, deliberately changing the conversation, and Tom let out a low whistle as his gaze took in the large building to the left of the Serpentine Steps.

'I remember when the doctor's surgery was that pokey little place in Morwenna Road,' he observed.

'Nick's made big changes since he took over the practice,' Eve replied. 'And he's making even more, as you can see,' she added, pointing to the scaffolding at the back of the surgery. 'In less than a week Lauren will have a state-of-the-art physiotherapy suite, and we'll have an X-ray room, and even more consulting rooms.'

'Well, he may have grown into a grumpy old so-and-so,' Tom said, 'but at least he wants the best for his patients.'

'He does,' Eve said, 'but you haven't told me anything about yourself, your work with Deltaron.'

'Not much to tell,' he said.

'There's bound to be,' she said, but he wasn't listening to her. He was already crossing the road, heading for the children's play park and playing field. 'Tom, where are you going?'

'I fancy a swing,' he shouted back, and though she shook her head she followed him.

'Big kid,' she said when she'd caught up with him.

'You'd better believe it,' he replied, then frowned slightly as he looked up at the new houses on the hill, then down at the older buildings clustered round the harbour. 'It's odd, but it seems so much smaller than I remembered it.'

'Hicksville. That's what you used to call Penhally,' she said. '"There's a whole world out there, Eve, and I want to see it, be a part of it."'

'Did I say that?' he said dryly. 'Yeah, well, I guess I always was a stupid kid.'

She stared at him for a second, then sat down on the swing next to his.

'Tom, what's wr—?'

'You wanted to know about my work with Deltaron,' he interrupted. 'There's almost fifty of us in the organisation, but normally we'll send in around fourteen people who are specialists in the sorts of conditions we're likely to encounter.'

'What sort of specialists?' she asked.

'Let's say we're going into an earthquake situation,' he declared. 'In that case, we'd want people who are familiar with the construction of buildings, plus experts in flammable and explosive materials, electricians, pilots, plumbers and medics.'

'And when you go into a disaster area, you're in charge.'

'Yup,' he said. 'I decide where we start looking for survivors, and I decide when we quit. When there's no point in looking any more.'

A harshness had crept into his voice, and his eyes… They had become bleak, empty, and desolate.

'It must be heart-breaking at times,' she suggested tentatively, and saw his jaw tighten.

'Bleeding hearts need not apply, that's for sure.'

'Tom…' She put her hand on his arm. 'Tom, are you OK?'

He stood up abruptly, letting the swing bang back against his calves, and faked a smile.

'Couldn't be better,' he said, 'and isn't that your little friend?'

For a second Eve continued to stare at him, then she glanced in the direction of his gaze, and saw Tassie running along the road, her blonde hair flying.

'She'll be going home,' she said. 'Tom, are you quite sure you're—?'

'What's the connection between you two?'

'None,' she said, getting to her feet, and leading the way out of the play park, 'apart from the fact I've taken an interest in her since she was about four years old. Her mother, Amanda… She's had to bring up five of a family virtually on her own so I help out by looking after Tassie one day a week.'

'Isn't there a Mr Lovelace?'

'He's in prison at the moment for petty theft. I'm afraid it always is petty theft with him, or selling on stolen goods.' Eve sighed. 'The whole family are completely out of control, including Tassie's twin brother, Terry, but Gary Lovelace is the worst. Seventeen years old, and already a complete and utter waste of space.'

Tom's eyebrows rose.

'It's not like you to write off someone when they're so young.'

Eve struggled with herself for a moment, then blurted out, 'Do you remember me telling you Reverend Kenner had a daughter? Well, she's pregnant, Tom. Rachel is just seventeen years old, and pregnant by Gary Lovelace.'

'Accidents happen, Eve,' Tom declared. 'You know that.'

'This was no accident,' she retorted. 'Rachel told Chloe MacKinnon it wasn't. Gary deliberately went after Rachel because he thought it would be fun to play around with the minister's daughter. What kind of boy does that, Tom? He's no job—no desire to get one—just hangs about with his friends… He—'

'Sounds exactly like I was at his age,' Tom interrupted, and Eve shook her head vehemently.

'You were nothing like Gary.'

'Hell, Eve, I was *exactly* like Gary,' Tom protested. 'God knows what would have become of me if it hadn't been for Gertie Stanbury.'

'Our old headmistress?' Eve exclaimed. 'What did she have to do with anything?'

'Do you remember the day when the bicycle sheds burned down at school, and I swore blind I didn't do it? Well, I did, and Gertie knew I did though she couldn't prove it. She called me into her office and said, "Cornish, you can either spend the rest of your life destroying things, or you can make something of yourself. Your father—and most of Penhally—have written you off, but you've got brains and ability, so are you going to prove your father and Penhally right, or show them they're wrong?" '

Eve shook her head in amazement. 'You never told me any of this.'

'Well, it was hardly my finest hour,' Tom said wryly. 'I was furious with Gertie—thought she was an interfering old bat, to be honest—but when I went home that night, and found my father lying dead drunk as usual on the sitting-room floor, I suddenly realised I was going to be him in a few years if I didn't knuckle down at school, and get some qualifications.'

'Which is what I want Tassie to do,' she declared, 'to get some qualifications. She's such a bright child, Tom, and Gertrude has been helping her by lending her books—'

'Gertie Stanbury is still alive?'

'Very much so.' Eve nodded. 'She thinks Tassie is clever enough to win a scholarship to the Lady Joan Mercer's Boarding School in Devon which would be wonderful because though Amanda wants what's best for Tassie she'll never be able to afford to let her stay on at school once she reaches leaving age.'

'And if she does go to this school?'

Eve smiled.

'At the moment Tassie wants to become a doctor. Of course, she'll probably change her mind, but if I can get her into Lady Joan's, and she studies hard, the world will be her oyster.'

A slight frown appeared on Tom's forehead.

'You do realise if you send Tassie off to this private boarding school, she'll lose her own family?'

'Of course she won't.'

'She will,' Tom insisted. 'She'll have nothing in common with them, could even end up looking down on them, while they'll simply think she's got above herself.'

'You're saying I'm wrong—I shouldn't encourage her,' Eve exclaimed, anger rising in her.

'I'm saying…' Tom stopped and rubbed the back of his neck awkwardly with his fingers. 'I'm saying Tassie's not your daughter, Eve.'

'I know that.' Eve flared. 'I know she isn't mine, but what's so wrong about me wanting her to have every opportunity?'

'Nothing,' Tom replied gently, 'just so long as she, and her mother, and you, understand it will come at a price.'

He was wrong, Eve thought furiously as she gazed at him. Tassie wouldn't lose her family, and when she thought of all the things the girl would gain…

'I have to go,' she said, her voice tight as she stepped back from him.

'Already?' he protested. 'But I thought we could have dinner together.'

'I can't.'

'Then what about tomorrow?' he declared. 'We could drive up to Newquay—'

'You're leaving tomorrow,' she reminded him, 'and I have to work.'

'Couldn't you ask for a few days off?' he demanded. 'Even just one day?'

It was clearly important to him that she said yes, but she had no intention of saying yes. She'd agreed to today but even during the few short hours they'd spent together he'd unsettled her so much, and she'd had enough unsettling.

'Tom, I can't,' she said. 'I've only just started work at the practice so it would hardly look professional if I took time off.'

'Then this is goodbye,' he said, making it a statement, not a question, and she stuck out her hand.

'It's been nice seeing you again, Tom.'

'Eve...'

He'd taken her hand in his, his eyes intent, earnest, and he was clearly hoping she would change her mind, but he was too late. Twenty years too late, and she pulled her hand free.

'Goodbye, Tom,' she said.

And she walked away from him, and she didn't look back.

CHAPTER THREE

'SOPHIE, tell me this isn't true?' Eve declared, gazing in horror at the sullen teenager.

'Look, I just miscalculated my insulin dose, OK?' Sophie Banks retorted belligerently. 'That's why my blood-sugar levels are all haywire today. I just made a *mistake*.'

'Mistake, my foot!' Sophie's mother exclaimed, her face tight, her eyes angry. 'I thought it was strange the way she kept rushing off to the bathroom, even wondered if she'd perhaps caught a chill, and then I heard her—bold as brass—on the phone to her friend last night, talking about this internet site she'd found—'

'You had no right to listen in to my private phone calls,' Sophie declared, outrage plain in her voice. 'I don't listen to yours—'

'Sophie, I know you weren't happy when you started putting on weight after your diabetes was diagnosed,' Eve interrupted quickly, seeing the mother and daughter round on one another, 'but skipping, or lessening your dosage in order to excrete more urine and stay thin is a recipe for disaster.'

'None of my clothes fit any more,' the teenager protested. 'I look *gross*.'

Or like a perfectly normal fifteen-year-old, Eve thought, but there was no point in saying that.

'Sophie, your weight gain is purely temporary,' she said instead. 'Once we get your blood-sugar levels under control, your weight will return to what it was before.'

'Yeah, right,' Sophie muttered under her breath, and Eve sat forward in her seat.

'This internet site you found,' she declared. 'Did it tell you that not only would you lose weight if you manipulated your insulin doses, you could also damage your eyes, and develop hypoglycaemia?'

'One mistake,' the girl said mutinously. 'All I did was make one lousy miscalculation, and now you all think I have a problem. I don't have a problem.'

Eve didn't believe her. Alison had warned her before she'd gone off on her maternity leave that Sophie seemed more interested in her weight loss than the fact she had diabetes, and when she'd tested the girl's blood-sugar levels this morning they'd been appalling. She didn't doubt for a second that Sophie had been deliberately skipping doses but warning the girl that she was, quite literally, dicing with death would achieve nothing. To a teenager, death was something that happened to other people, elderly people.

'I'm going to have a word with Dr Tremayne,' she declared. 'I'm sorry, Sophie,' she continued as the girl let out a hiss of irritation, 'but your temporary weight gain is clearly worrying you, so I think you should see an endocrinologist who will be able to advise you on your diet.'

And who will also be considerably more experienced than I am in dealing with eating disorders and diabetes, Eve added mentally.

Mrs Banks shot her daughter a that-will-sort-you-out-young-lady look, but, instead of getting to her feet and leaving as Eve had expected, the mother suddenly cleared her throat, her eyes sparkling with keen interest.

'I happened to meet Audrey Baxter on my way down to the surgery this morning, Nurse, and she said—'

Here it comes, Eve thought grimly. I thought I might have got away with it, but here it comes.

'She saw you and Tom Cornish on the beach yesterday.'

'That's right,' Eve said with the biggest smile she could muster. 'Now, as regards Sophie,' she continued determinedly. 'Hopefully, she won't have to wait long to see the endocrinologist, but until she gets an appointment I'd like to see her twice a week from now on to check on her blood-sugar levels.'

That Mrs Banks considered her a singularly disappointing source of information was plain. That she was itching to delve deeper into Tom Cornish's presence was even plainer but, unlike Audrey Baxter, Mrs Banks clearly possessed some scruples because she got to her feet, albeit reluctantly.

'We'll see you on Thursday, then, Nurse,' she said, then trooped out of Eve's consulting room, with Sophie trailing belligerently behind her, and Eve sighed wearily as she closed the teenager's folder.

Well, what did you expect? a little voice whispered in her mind. *When Audrey saw you in Tom's arms she was bound to spread the word, wasn't she?*

Yes, but couldn't she have kept quiet, just for once? she thought wistfully.

Fat chance in Penhally, Eve.

She could almost hear Tom saying that, and a smile curved her lips for a second then faded.

He'd be on his way to London now, back to the new life he'd made for himself, and their trip down memory lane was over. And that was all it had been, she reminded herself. One sunny October afternoon spent reminiscing about their youth although it had been strange how much Tom had wanted to look back. The Tom she had known had been forever planning, scheming, looking to the future, but this Tom… And he had no need to look back. He had it all right now, in the present.

'Eve, Mrs Baxter came in for a repeat prescription this morning,' Nick declared as he stuck his head round her examination-room door, 'and her BP's haywire again.'

'Like Sophie Banks's blood-sugar levels,' she replied, and when she told him what she suspected the teenager of doing Nick shook his head.

'Of all the stupid… What is it with women nowadays that so many of you want to look like stick insects?'

'I suppose it's the models we see in magazines and on television,' Eve observed. 'They're all extremely thin.'

'Idiots, the lot of them,' Nick declared. 'I'll send a letter to the endocrinology department right away, but you'd better keep an eye on her. The last thing we want is her going hypoglycaemic on us. Can you fit Mrs Baxter into your Thursday clinic, to check her BP for me again?'

'Unfortunately, yes,' Eve said dryly, and a rare smile appeared on Nick's lips.

'I know she can be a nosy old bat at times, but there's no malice in her.' The senior partner half withdrew, then paused. 'Tom gone, has he?'

The question sounded casual, indifferent, but Eve wasn't deceived.

'He left this morning,' she replied. 'Back to London, or it could have been Switzerland. I didn't ask.'

'Right.' Nick nodded, then seemed to come to a decision. 'It's better this way, Eve. It might not seem like it at the moment, but the past is simply that. Something over, done with, and attempting to recapture it can only be a mistake, especially—' his eyes met hers '—in the circumstances.'

He remembered, she thought, staring up at him, drymouthed. It had been one consultation all those years ago. Nick had been her GP even then while working in a practice in a town nearby. He must have seen hundreds of patients since, and yet he remembered, and not just remembered, had put two and two together and come up with the right answer. Not the whole answer, not the complete answer, but the right one.

'Nick…'

'Practice meeting in ten minutes, OK?'

She dredged up a smile, but when he'd gone she shut her eyes tightly. She should have gone to another doctor. She had, at the beginning. At the beginning she'd gone up to Bude because she hadn't wanted anyone to know, but then she'd caught an infection, and she'd had to go to Nick. A prescription for antibiotics, had been all she'd asked for, and when he'd examined her he hadn't said anything so she'd thought he hadn't realised, but he had. For all these years he'd known, and she couldn't bear the fact he'd known.

'Eve, do you have Stephanie Richards's file?'

Eve looked up with difficulty to see Kate standing in her doorway, and shook her head. 'Sorry, no, I don't.'

'Blast.' The midwife frowned. 'She's been on the phone—panicking again—and I thought I'd drop in on her after the practice meeting, but I wanted to check what her BP was the last time it was taken.'

'Can't help you—sorry. Maybe Dragan has the file,' Eve declared, and Kate tilted her head to one side.

'You OK?'

Eve didn't feel OK. She'd tossed and turned last night, her dreams plagued by memories she didn't want to have, and now to discover Nick knew…

'I'm fine,' she managed. 'And we,' she added, glancing down at her watch, and picking up her folders, 'had better get our skates on, or Nick will have our guts for garters for being late.'

He didn't. In fact, when Kate and Eve arrived in his consulting room, Nick was poring over plans laid out on his desk with Dragan Lovak, Oliver Fawkner, Chloe and Lauren.

'So, I should be able to move into my new physiotherapy unit by the end of the week?' Eve heard Lauren declare. 'Excellent.'

'Is Dr Devereux having one of the new consulting rooms when he arrives?' Oliver asked, and, when Nick nodded, the young doctor grinned. 'Which means Lauren will have the French charmer not only living next door to her, but also working beside her.'

'He's rented the Manor House, Oliver,' Lauren protested. 'That hardly makes him living "next door" to me.'

'Maybe you could drop in on him with a pot of soup when he arrives, make him feel welcome,' he replied slyly, and the physiotherapist shook her head at him.

'And maybe I won't.'

'And maybe we should remember this is a post-practice meeting, and not a dating agency,' Nick declared, rolling up the plans on his desk.

The consulting room became instantly silent, and Eve saw Oliver roll his eyes at Chloé, while Lauren exchanged a resigned look with Dragan. Only Kate was frowning quite openly at Nick, but he was completely ignoring her, and Eve sighed inwardly. Good doctor though Nick was, he really did need to lighten up. Tom would have handled the situation quite differently. He would have understood that sometimes they all needed to be a bit silly to relieve the stress of their jobs, but Nick either couldn't—or wouldn't—see it.

'OK, let's get down to business,' Nick continued. 'Eve, are your influenza inoculation clinics ready to roll next week?'

She nodded. 'I noticed from Alison's notes that the practice only had a 67 per cent take up rate last year.'

'Getting people to come in is proving difficult,' he conceded, 'but it *is* worthwhile particularly for those at high risk, like the elderly and those who suffer from asthma and bronchitis. We can't afford to ship them all off to drier climates for the winter.'

To places like Switzerland, Eve thought. It had a drier climate, despite the snow it got in winter. Tom had said he had a home overlooking Lake Geneva. She'd never been there—had never been abroad, full stop. She'd always meant to travel, but somehow—

'How's her BP?'

Eve felt a hot wash of colour creep over her cheeks. Dragan was gazing at her expectantly, and she didn't have a clue what he was talking about, and it was all Tom's fault. She had to get him out of her thoughts. He had gone, and he wasn't ever going to come back, so she had to stop this, and stop it now.

'I'm sorry,' she was forced to say, 'but whose BP are you talking about?'

She felt, rather than saw, Nick stiffen with disapproval, but Dragan merely smiled.

'My mind is always a bit of a sieve on Monday mornings, too,' he declared kindly. 'Lizzie Chamberlain. I saw her coming out of your room, and she looked decidedly stressed.'

'She is,' Eve replied, smiling gratefully at him. 'Her blood pressure is still way too high, but she's so worried about her mother. I know you all felt Lizzie needed a break, that nursing her mother was making her ill, but she's got it into her head that by agreeing to her mum temporarily going into the Harbour View Nursing Home she's abandoned her.'

'I have to say Mrs Chamberlain isn't doing nearly as well in there as I'd hoped,' Dragan admitted. 'I thought she might see it as a mini-holiday, but the last time I saw her she seemed very lethargic, and not really interested in anything.'

'It's a Catch-22 situation,' Eve observed. 'Nursing someone with Parkinson's is exhausting, but if Lizzie's feeling guilty, as she obviously is…'

'Would you like me to drop in on Mrs Chamberlain?' Lauren declared. 'I'm on home visits today, and I could see her before I call in on Harry Biscombe in Gow Court. It wouldn't be a bother.'

Both Eve and Dragan nodded their agreement and, to Eve's relief, Oliver then launched into an account of the patients he'd seen that morning, leaving her with nothing to do but simply appear interested.

And she *was* interested, she told herself as she constantly found her mind wandering. She loved her work—always had done—so why did she feel all unsettled, and shaken up, like leaves in an autumn gale, or the flakes of snow in a snow globe, tumbling everywhere?

Because Tom came back, her mind whispered, and unconsciously she shook her head. It was over. It had been over a long time ago.

'No prizes for guessing who he's phoning.' Chloe chuckled when they all trooped out of Nick's consulting room, and Dragan immediately extracted his mobile phone from his pocket.

'I think it's sweet the way he keeps checking on Melinda, to see if she's OK,' Kate protested.

'Melinda doesn't,' Chloe said as Dragan disappeared into his room. 'I think the words, "He's driving me crazy" were the ones she used last week when she came in for her prenatal check-up. In fact, she's actually started turning off her mobile so she can get some peace and quiet.'

'No—really?' Kate laughed. 'Well, I'm off. I'll be in Bridge Street, if anyone needs me, reassuring Stephanie Richards—yet again—that her symptoms are perfectly normal, and she'll have a lovely, healthy baby in a couple of weeks' time.'

'And I'll be home if I'm needed,' Chloe declared, then shook her head as Oliver's eyes lit up. 'Defrosting the fridge, so you can forget any ideas about slipping home for a cup of coffee.'

'Coffee wasn't what I had in mind, babe,' he murmured, and the midwife chuckled, and he laughed and, as they walked away together, Eve felt her heart twist slightly.

The young couple were so much in love. Tom hadn't been in love with her, she thought sadly as she tightened her grip on the pile of folders she was carrying and started walking towards Reception.

'Let's have fun' was all he'd said that summer, and for him their romance had simply been that, a bit of fun, whereas for her… She had loved him so much, and when he'd left, when he hadn't phoned, had sent her only those two postcards, she'd felt as though her heart had been ripped out and trampled on.

'Oh, damn, blast and bloody hell!' she exclaimed as she rounded the corner and cannoned straight into someone coming the other way, sending the folders she was holding clattering to the floor.

'Language, Nurse Dwyer, *language.*'

It couldn't be, she thought, feeling her heart give an almighty leap, but as she looked up and met a pair of sparkling green eyes she saw that it was.

'You're not supposed to be here,' she blurted out before she could stop herself, and Tom grinned.

'Decided to stay on for a few more days. Thought I'd let the local garage mend my broken indicator light, make it easier for your physio.'

Pathetic, she thought as she stared up at him, wondering how he could possibly manage to look quite so heart-tinglingly handsome in an old, threadbare blue sweater and a pair of jeans. That was the most pathetic reason for staying on in Penhally she'd ever heard, but she had no intention of calling him on it. Calling him on it might mean he'd give her the real reason, and something told her she was better off not knowing the real reason.

'I'm afraid Lauren isn't here,' she said, getting down on her hands and knees to begin retrieving the files. 'She's just gone out on her home visits.'

'I didn't want to see Lauren,' he replied, hunkering down beside her. 'I wanted to see you.'

'Me?' she said faintly.

'I wondered if you'd like to come out to lunch with me?'

'Lunch?' she repeated, and his green eyes twinkled.

'As in food. A substance which sustains every living thing,' he said.

'I know what lunch is,' she protested. 'I just…' Absently, she reached for the last file, just as Tom did, too, and when their hands touched she snatched hers away quickly, all too aware that a disconcerting crackle of heat had raced up her arm. 'I just…'

'Is there a problem here?'

Eve glanced over her shoulder to see Nick standing behind her, his expression colder and stonier than she'd ever seen it.

'No problem,' she mumbled. 'Tom…he's decided to stay on for a few more days.'

'So I see,' Nick replied.

'I was also hoping to entice Eve out to lunch,' Tom declared. 'You do allow your staff to have lunch, I presume?'

'Naturally,' Nick said, his voice every bit as tight as Tom's. 'But it's my staff's choice as to who they eat that lunch with.'

And frankly I'd be happier if Eve had lunch with Genghis Khan.

Nick didn't say those words, he didn't have to. His whole body language said it for him, and although Eve now knew why the senior partner was being so antagonistic towards Tom, she didn't need—or want—him protecting her.

'It's all right, Nick,' she said, and for a second she thought the senior partner might actually argue with her, then he nodded and walked abruptly away.

'What *is* it with that guy?' Tom demanded. 'We haven't seen one another in years, and yet every time we meet it's obvious he'd dearly like to stick a knife in me.'

'Personality clash, maybe?' Eve suggested evasively. 'Give me a couple of minutes to offload these with Hazel,' she continued quickly, indicating the folders in her arms, 'and to change out of my uniform, and I'll be right with you.'

And it would be only a few minutes, she thought as she

handed the folders to their practice manager. Any longer, and she dreaded to think what Nick might come back and say.

But it wasn't Nick who was uppermost in her mind when she went into the ladies' cloakroom to change out of her uniform and saw how flushed her cheeks were, how bright her eyes. She should have looked angry, horrified, because Tom hadn't left, but the truth was she looked more alive than she had in years, and she closed her eyes to shut out the image.

What was happening to her? Just two short days ago she'd had a life. OK, so maybe it hadn't been the world's most exciting life, but she'd had her patients, and Tassie, and she'd been in control and content, and yet now…

She couldn't still have feelings for Tom, not after all these years. He'd left her without a second's thought, and though she'd been heartbroken for a long time she'd eventually picked up the pieces of her life, had dated other men. Dammit, she'd even got engaged once.

But you broke off the engagement, her mind whispered.

Only because I realised it was a mistake, she argued back. That it would be wrong to marry someone, and keep secrets from him. It wasn't because I still had feelings for Tom.

Oh, really? Her mind laughed, and she gripped the edge of the sink tightly.

Somehow, some way, she had to pull herself together. Somehow, some way, she had to keep her emotions in check, because she couldn't go down that road again, Nick had been right about that. Recapturing the past would mean resurrecting it, and she couldn't do that, not ever.

'Eve, we were just talking about you,' Dragan said when Eve emerged from the ladies' cloakroom to find him and Tom laughing about something.

'Saying something nice, I hope?' Eve said lightly, and Dragan smiled.

'Tom was telling me about his home in Lausanne, and I was

saying he must take you there some time. It's a beautiful part of Switzerland.'

'You know it?' Eve asked, deliberately sidestepping the suggestion that she would want Tom to take her anywhere.

'I do, indeed,' Dragan observed. 'When I was young, my family and I went there a couple of times for holidays before… Before everything changed.'

A shadow had appeared in his eyes, and Eve knew the Croatian doctor was remembering happier times when his homeland hadn't been torn by war, when all of his family had been safe, and alive.

'Dragan,' she began hesitantly, and he shook his head and forced a smile.

'Sometimes it's good to remember the past, and sometimes it's not,' he said. 'But you must let Tom take you to Switzerland. It truly is a beautiful place.'

'I'm sure it is,' Eve said, then added quickly when she saw Tom open his mouth, clearly intending to interrupt, 'How's Melinda?'

'Tired,' Dragan admitted. 'Tired of waiting, tired of looking—she says—like a hot-air balloon that's about to go pop.'

Eve laughed.

'At least she hasn't got much longer to go,' she said. 'Just two more weeks, and then you'll be a proud papa.'

'Do you know whether it's a boy or a girl?' Tom asked, and Dragan shook his head.

'Melinda and I didn't want to know. We wanted it to be a surprise. And speaking of surprises,' he added, glancing at his watch, and letting out a muttered oath, 'if I don't get my home visits started the only surprise will be me managing to have them finished by midnight.'

'Brave man,' Tom observed as Dragan hurried away, 'coming to the UK, making himself a new life in a foreign land.'

'It wasn't easy for him—not at first,' Eve replied, 'but then he met Melinda, and…' She smiled. 'The rest, as they say, is history.'

'What I don't understand is why I keep feeling I know him from somewhere,' Tom said. 'I thought the same thing when I met him and his wife at the reception on Saturday, but I can't for the life of me figure out why.'

And I'm not about to jog your memory, Eve thought as she slipped on her jacket, and led the way out of the surgery. Melinda and Dragan had endured more than enough harassment back in April when their photographs had been plastered all over the newspapers, and they were entitled to some privacy.

'Where do you want to have lunch?' she said, deliberately changing the subject.

'I thought maybe The Grape Seed.'

'I'm afraid it closed down years ago,' she replied as they began walking up the road past the surfing and souvenir shops, skirting the puddles left from the thunderstorm that had deluged the village earlier that morning. 'When Mr Forrest retired, his son didn't want to take it over, so it became an estate agent's.'

'Damn!' Tom exclaimed. 'I loved The Grape Seed. Remember when you could choose all those different sorts of salad dishes, like grated carrot mixed with coconut, curried eggs, and pasta salad with tuna, and we thought we were the height of sophistication?'

Eve smiled and nodded, but she wished he'd stop this. She didn't want to keep dwelling on the past. It was over, gone.

'We could have lunch at the Anchor?' she suggested, and he shook his head.

'Too stuffy. I always feel as though they're itching to check my pockets for cutlery after I eat there.'

She let out a small snort of laughter.

'We could just buy some tortilla wraps, and eat them down by the harbour,' she said, then glanced up at the sky. 'And, then again, perhaps not. I think it's going to rain again.'

And it would be yet more heavy rain. The sea might currently be a sheet of near-Mediterranean blue, and the houses and steep roads that made up Penhally Bay might be standing out in sharp relief against the cliffs behind, but she could see another band of black clouds gathering over the cliffs.

'What's that café like?' Tom asked, inclining his head towards it.

'They do very nice soups, and puddings, and if you want something a bit more substantial—'

'*Lovak!*' Tom exclaimed, coming to a sudden halt in the middle of the pavement. 'Melinda and Dragan *Lovak*. She's that European princess. The one who gave up her throne to marry the Croatian refugee.'

Eve sighed. 'So it reached the London newspapers, did it?'

'It reached *every* newspaper, Eve.' Tom shook his head in disbelief. 'I should have recognised them immediately.'

Eve wished he hadn't recognised the couple at all.

'Tom, as far as Melinda is concerned, she's Mrs Lovak, the local vet, and a soon-to-be mum,' she said. 'And as far as Dragan is concerned, he's simply one of the Penhally doctors.'

'I can see why,' Tom observed. 'I wouldn't want my past splashed all over the papers. You'd be OK with your blameless history, but me…' He laughed. 'I doubt if my bosses would be overjoyed to learn I burned down bicycle sheds when I was at school.'

And he'd somehow put his foot in it again, Tom thought as he saw Eve's face set. He'd only been making a joke at his own expense, and yet the shutters had quite clearly come down and he could almost feel her physically withdrawing from him.

'Is Dragan taking paternity leave after his wife's given birth?' he continued quickly. 'I know I would be if I were in his shoes.'

'Yes, he's taking paternity leave.'

And that hadn't helped at all, he realised, seeing her face set into even more rigid lines. *OK, change the subject*, he told himself. *Talk about something else—somebody else.*

'I met your minister on the way down here—Reverend Kenner,' he declared. 'He had his daughter, Rachel, with him. Nice kid. When's her baby due?'

'December.'

Which didn't seem to please Eve any more than his comments about Dragan and Melinda had, he thought with a sigh.

'Look, I know you're not happy about the situation,' he said. 'Her being only being seventeen, and Gary Lovelace being the father, but I've always been a very firm advocate of a woman's right to choose. She didn't have to go ahead and have the baby, Eve. She could have opted for a termination, but she didn't. Her decision, her choice, and I admire her for it.'

Eve clearly didn't if her complete silence as she led the way into the café was anything to go by, and Tom groaned as he followed her.

Hell, was he always going to be fated to somehow inadvertently say the wrong thing? Maybe he should just have gone back to London this morning, but he hadn't wanted to leave, hadn't wanted the last words they'd exchanged to have been remote and distant ones.

And was that the only reason you didn't want to leave? his mind whispered, and he sighed.

He wished it was. It would have made things so much easier, but he'd spent the last twenty years of his life trying to convince himself he'd done the right thing only to have that illusion blown straight out of the water the minute he'd seen her again. All it had taken was one smile from her and the great weight that had been lying on his heart for so long had suddenly lifted and the world no longer seemed such a dark and empty place.

But how to tell her this? he wondered as they sat down at a table, and both picked up a menu. How to confess he'd made a mistake all those years ago?

'Eve—'

'I'll have the carrot and coriander soup, then lemon meringue pie, please,' she told the smiling waitress who had appeared at their table.

'The same for me,' Tom said, not bothering to look at the menu. He glanced around at the café as the waitress bustled away. 'Nice place,' he continued awkwardly. 'I'm surprised we're the only customers.'

'They'll be closing at the end of the week,' Eve replied. 'They haven't gone bankrupt, or anything,' she added. 'A lot of the restaurants, and most of the craft and gift shops, in Penhally close down at the end of the summer. It's not really viable for them to stay open over the winter.'

'Right,' he said, then cleared his throat. 'I want to apologise to you for what I said about Tassie yesterday. I don't know the family—don't even know the girl—so I spoke out of turn.'

'Yes, you did.'

Which pretty well finished that as a topic of conversation, he thought.

'It's raining again,' he ventured, as he stared out of the café window looking for inspiration. 'And the Lanson's running pretty high.'

'We had a lot of rain this morning,' Eve replied. 'We often do in October.'

And I'm dying a death here, Tom thought ruefully, if we're reduced to talking about the weather. Hell's teeth, it shouldn't be this hard to start a conversation, and keep it going. All he had to do was not mention Tassie Lovelace, Melinda and Dragan Lovak, Rachel Kenner or Eve's parents, and surely he'd be on safe ground.

'*Dirty Dancing*,' he said quickly. 'I've just remembered the film I took you to see at the old La Scala was *Dirty Dancing*, and you made me see it three times because you had a thing about Patrick Swayze.'

'It wasn't so much Patrick Swayze,' Eve said as the waitress appeared with their soup. 'It was more… I think I liked the film because it was about trying to fulfil your dreams.'

'Don't tell me you actually sit down and watch it when it comes on TV?' He laughed, and saw her jaw set as she picked up her spoon.

'No. I don't.'

OK, he thought. Let's try something else.

'Do you remember—?'

'Stop it, Tom.'

Her large brown eyes were unexpectedly hard, and he gazed at her in confusion. 'Stop what?'

'All these reminiscences, this trip down memory lane. We're not in our twenties any more. We've both moved on, we're different people now.'

'I don't think you've changed very much from the person I once knew,' he said with a smile, and she shook her head.

'You didn't even know me twenty years ago, Tom, not really.'

'Of course I did,' he protested, then glanced over his shoulder to see where their waitress was. 'Hell, Eve, we were lovers. If anybody knows you, it's me.'

'You might have known my body,' she said quietly. 'But you didn't know me.'

'You're talking in riddles,' he replied. 'Of course I knew you. Just as I also feel…' He lowered his voice still further. 'The old attraction between us… It's still there, isn't it?'

A peal of thunder had rung out, followed by a jagged fork of lightning, but Eve ignored them both and put down her spoon, cynicism and anger plain in her eyes.

'What you're feeling is a desire for the past, Tom,' she replied, 'for when your life was simpler. It's isn't me you want back. It's your youth.'

Was she right? he wondered as he stared back at her and unconsciously he shook his head. It was more than that, so much more than that.

'If you're saying I want to be young again, then the answer's no,' he replied. 'If I could go back, knowing what I know now, that would be different, but to go back to the thoughtless man I was then...' He reached out and clasped her hand. 'All I do know is I never forgot you.'

'Your never forgetting me didn't extend to you keeping in touch, did it?' she exclaimed, pulling her hand free, and he winced at the hardness in her voice. 'Two postcards, Tom. Two lousy, miserable postcards. One saying you were lonely, the other saying you had applied for a job with Deltaron, and then nothing.'

'I meant to write,' he began hesitantly, 'but the longer I was away, the more—'

'You forgot about me?' she finished for him, and he dragged his fingers through his hair.

'No,' he protested. 'I just thought—as the years passed— you'd be bound to be married—have a family.'

'And now you've discovered I'm not, you think it might be nice to try to pick up where you left off,' she said, her voice brittle. 'Well, you can forget it, Tom.'

'Eve—'

'Something wrong with the soup?' the waitress interrupted, appearing without warning at their table, and glancing from Eve's scarcely touched bowl to Tom's.

'It's lovely—perfect,' Tom said with an effort.

'Better than the weather.' The waitress laughed as another peal of thunder rang out and rain began bouncing onto the street outside, filling the drains and gullies so quickly they started to overflow.

'Eve, I didn't come back to resurrect the past,' Tom said the second the waitress had gone. 'I came back for two reasons. One I can tell you about, the other...' He shook his head. 'I can't tell you that, not just yet.'

'Then tell me the one reason you can,' she said, folding her arms across her chest with a look on her face that said all too plainly, you'd better make this good.

'I came back because...' He took an uneven breath. 'I wanted to see if I could still feel anything. Even if all I felt in Penhally was the old resentment, the old hatred, at least it would mean I could still feel *something*.'

Eve gazed at him, open-mouthed. Whatever she had been expecting him to say, it hadn't been that.

'I...I don't understand,' she faltered, and Tom pushed his soup away.

'Eve, during the years I've worked for Deltaron, I've witnessed the most wonderful—amazing—acts of courage and self-sacrifice. I've seen men and women tear at rubble with their bare hands in a desperate attempt to rescue people they've never met, but I've also seen men and women trample on children—babies—crushing them into the mud, in order to save themselves or to grab a crust of bread.'

'I suppose disasters always bring out both the best, and the worst, in people,' she said awkwardly, and his lips twisted into a bitter smile.

'It also breeds indifference, Eve. I was in New Orleans, and Colombia, and Phuket. Horrendous, all of them, but they got help because they made the headlines, whereas in so many places—too many places—I've had to watch people die because the food, and the shelter, and the medicine never came.'

'Tom—'

'Jean Paul Sartre, the French philosopher, said Hell was other people. He was wrong, Eve. Hell is people ceasing to care.'

'But you care,' she protested, seeing the desolation in his face. 'You wouldn't be doing the job you're doing if you didn't.'

'But the trouble is...' He picked up his spoon and put it down again. 'I'm ceasing to care. Ceasing to feel anything. So a hundred people were killed a month ago, a thousand the month before that. Maybe they're better off dead rather than being rescued by my men simply to survive for another month, or a year, only to be hit by yet another catastrophe, yet another disaster, and lose more loved ones.'

It was so dark outside the café now it could almost have been night, and vaguely Eve was aware of people scurrying past the café window, hurrying to get out of the rain, but what she was most aware of was the bleak, raw despair in Tom's face. Never had she seen such utter desolation on someone's face before and, as she stared at him, she suddenly realised she was feeling an emotion she would never have believed she would ever feel for him, and it wasn't attraction, or anger, or hatred. It was pity.

'Tom, you can't—you mustn't—think like that,' she said quickly, but he didn't seem to hear her.

'So many children orphaned, Eve,' he murmured. 'So many babies, sitting in cots all over the world, who are given enough food and water to live on, but no love, no affection, because there's simply too many of them, and every year their numbers increase.'

'Tom—'

'Maybe Nick was right,' he continued with a shuddering sigh. 'Maybe my whole working life has been nothing but a series of photo opportunities.'

She caught hold of his hand and held it tightly.

'Nick was wrong,' she protested. 'Your work is vitally important.'

'Yeah, right,' he said, with a smile that tore at her heart. 'Dr Tom Cornish, head of operations for Deltaron, the big cheese, the head honcho, but, when it comes right down to it, you're the one who's made something of your life.'

'But you've made a wonderful success of your life,' she said, even more confused. 'I'm just a nurse, Tom, whereas you… There are people alive today who wouldn't be if you hadn't rescued them.'

'But at the end of the day, it's you people remember, isn't it?' he said, turning her hand over in his, and staring down at it. 'You're that nice, kind, sympathetic nurse at the surgery. The one who holds people's hands when they're scared, the one who gives them a cuddle when they need it.'

The misery in his face was palpable and she had to swallow hard before she could answer him.

'Tom, people remember you,' she declared, her voice uneven. 'You're the man who arrives whenever there's an emergency, the man who helps. What you do, it's what you always wanted to do—so how has it all gone wrong? I can see how constantly facing so much death and destruction must wear you down, but what's happened to make you feel your work—your whole life—has been pointless?'

He didn't get a chance to reply. Another peal of thunder rumbled overhead, the lights in the café flickered and went out, and the waitress bustled towards them.

'Thought as much,' she said with resignation. 'Sorry, folks, but I'm not going to be able to give you your puddings.'

'It doesn't matter,' Tom said, getting abruptly to his feet and extracting his wallet. 'We've discovered we're not very hungry.'

'I'd get home as quickly as you can if I were you,' the waitress declared as she took Tom's money. 'The Lanson's running higher than I've ever seen it.' She glanced at Eve's light jacket, and Tom's sweater and jeans. 'You'd better borrow these umbrellas or you'll both be soaked in seconds.'

The waitress was right, Eve realised when she and Tom left the café. Not only was the rain—if anything—even heavier, the Lanson was now lapping ominously close to the top of its banks.

'I don't like this,' Tom murmured as he stared at it. 'Look at the colour of the river, Eve. It's almost black, and can you smell it? That's earth—lots and lots of earth. We have to get back to the surgery, and phone the emergency services, because I think this means trouble. Big trouble.'

'The Lanson's breached its banks before,' Eve protested. 'See, people are already putting sandbags round their doors, and boarding up their shop windows. OK, so we'll probably get an inch or two of water on the pavements, but once this thunderstorm's over—'

'Eve, we have to get away from here *now*,' he interrupted.

He was overreacting, Eve told herself, shivering slightly as more thunder and lightning split the sky. Yes, the river was high—incredibly high—and it smelt and looked odd, but calling the emergency services was far too extreme.

'Tom—'

He didn't even acknowledge she had spoken. He was already hustling her down the road, but, just as they reached the bottom of Harbour Road, they both came to a halt as a sound shattered the air. A bomb or a gas explosion, was Eve's immediate thought, but the sound was immediately followed by a roar. A terrible, screaming roar that made her look over her shoulder and what she saw made her heart stop.

'Tom.' She whispered. 'Oh, my God, Tom, *look*!'

A torrent of water was cascading out of Bridge Street, completely engulfing Harbour Bridge. Engulfing it in a raging, nine-foot-high torrent of black water in which dustbins were being tossed like toys before being spat out into the harbour, and when Tom grabbed her hand she didn't hesitate for a second. She began to run.

CHAPTER FOUR

'Has a gas main exploded?' Hazel, the practice manager, exclaimed, her face white with shock, as Tom and Eve raced into the surgery. 'I heard this awful sound, then our landline went dead, and I've been trying to get the police on my mobile—'

'Where's Nick?' Tom demanded, cutting right across the practice manager without compunction.

'He's not here,' Hazel replied. 'Kate rang about fifteen minutes ago, saying she wasn't happy about Stephanie Richards, so he went to help her.'

'Who's Stephanie Richards?' Tom asked, looking from Eve to Hazel, but it was Eve who answered.

'Mum-to-be, due date the 20th of this month. Her boyfriend walked out on her when he discovered she was pregnant, and she's not had an easy pregnancy. She…' Eve swallowed convulsively. 'Tom… She lives in Bridge Street.'

'Not the best place to be at the moment,' Tom said evenly, and Eve let out a cry that was halfway between a sob and a laugh.

'*Not the best place?*' she repeated. 'Tom, you saw that water—'

'What the hell was that noise?' Oliver interrupted as he came running out of his consulting room. 'I was ploughing through my paperwork, listening to the rain bouncing off the roof, then it sounded as though a bomb had gone off.'

'The river Lanson's broken its banks,' Tom declared, 'and, at a rough guess, I'd say it's running nine feet higher than it should be.'

'Nine *feet*?'

'Oliver, it was awful—truly awful!' Eve exclaimed, as the young doctor stared at her, open-mouthed. 'One minute the Harbour Bridge was there, and the next…'

'You mean, the bridge has collapsed?' Oliver gasped, and Eve shook her head helplessly.

'I don't know. It might still be there, under the water, but…' She clasped her hands together to try to stop them shaking. 'Tom—Kate and Nick, and the people who live in Gull Close and Bridge Street like Gertrude Stanbury, Audrey Baxter—we have to help them. That water…'

'I know,' Tom said, his gaze steady, his voice calm, 'but we both also know we haven't a hope in hell of getting up either of those streets. Hazel, phone Nick on his mobile—'

'I can't, Tom,' the practice manager interrupted. 'Bridge Street, Gull Close and Penhally Heights—they're all blind spots as far as mobiles are concerned. I could try reaching them by radio, but if they've left their handsets in their cars…'

'We'd be better off using smoke signals,' Tom finished for her grimly. 'OK, Oliver, as Nick isn't here, you're in charge.'

'No,' the young doctor declared immediately. 'Absolutely not. Hell, Tom, you're head of operations at Deltaron. If anyone has the expertise for a situation like this, it's you.'

That Tom didn't want to be in charge was plain. A shadow had crossed his face, making him look, Eve thought, suddenly every one of his forty-four years, but Oliver was right. Only Tom had experience of dealing with this sort of situation, and whatever had happened to him, whatever he had witnessed that had made him feel he had wasted his life, it didn't alter the fact that they needed him.

'Tom?' Eve said hesitantly, and saw a small muscle clench in his cheek, then he nodded.

'All right, but one thing has to be understood,' he said. 'If I'm in charge then whatever I decide we go with, no argument, no discussion. Even if you don't like my decision—feel it's the wrong one—my decision stands.'

'I hardly think any of us are going to query your judgment,' Oliver said, and when Eve and Hazel nodded their agreement, Tom's lips curved slightly.

'I'll remind you of that later,' he said, then turned to Hazel. 'Phone the coastguard, the fire brigade, and keep phoning the police. Tell them the Lanson's broken its banks, and we need help now.' He glanced at his watch. 'It's just after two o'clock, which means the kids will still be in school. Oliver, phone both the primary and secondary schools, tell them not to let any of the children go home. Eve, I need a map of the village—the more detailed the better.'

Eve scarcely heard him. Try as she may, she couldn't forget the wall of surging, churning water, and when she thought of Audrey, and Gertrude, the people who might have been walking down those two streets... And Tassie. Her heart clutched and twisted inside her. Tassie was always calling in on Gertrude to borrow books. What if she was there, in Gull Close, trapped?

She won't be, her mind insisted. It's a school day, so Tassie will be in school, safe, and, as she felt a surge of relief course through her, she dug her fingernails deep into the palms of her hands, hating herself for feeling such relief when so many others were in danger.

'Eve, we can stand here worrying, or we can do something, and right now I need that map.'

She looked up to find Tom's gaze on her, and though there was understanding in his green eyes, there was impatience in them, too, and with an effort she straightened her shoulders.

'There's an aerial photograph of Penhally in the waiting room,' she said. 'Would that be any use?'

'Perfect,' Tom replied. 'Absolutely perfect.'

'Tom, how can this have happened?' she said as she followed him into the waiting room. 'We've had violent thunderstorms before, but never anything like this.'

'My guess is the thunderstorm earlier this morning caused something to collapse further up the hill, forming a dam,' Tom replied as he took the photograph off the wall. 'Then, when we had the second thunderstorm, the sound we heard was the dam breaking. I can't think of anything else which would cause such a volume of water to travel down at such speed.'

'Schools alerted,' Oliver announced when Tom and Eve returned to Reception, 'and I've phoned St Piran Hospital, warned them to be on standby for possible casualties.'

'The firemen are on their way,' Hazel chipped in, 'but whether they'll be able to get here is another matter. Roads seem to be flooded everywhere. The coastguard have scrambled their helicopter, and the Royal Navy are sending three more.'

'What about the police?' Tom demanded, and Hazel shook her head.

'All of their mobile phone numbers seemed to be permanently engaged. Not surprising, really, under the circumstances.'

'Keep phoning them,' Tom said. 'They need to start evacuating people in case that water spreads, and we have to find somewhere safer, too.'

'But surely we're safe here?' Eve protested. 'The water was racing straight out of Bridge Street into the harbour.'

'We need to be higher, much higher,' Tom insisted. 'Do either of the schools have a generator?'

'The high school does,' Hazel replied.

'Then the high school would be the best place for us to relocate to, and it would also be perfect for the villagers living on the west side of the Lanson to assemble,' Tom observed. 'For the people who live east of the river…' He squinted at the aerial photograph. 'The Smugglers' is the highest, and there's also fields behind it where a helicopter could land. Would there be anybody at the inn at this time of day?'

'Tony—the owner,' Eve replied. 'He's always there, and I know he'd be more than willing to help, but won't we need a medic on site in case someone comes in injured?'

'Dragan,' Tom said. 'He was going out on home visits today, wasn't he, so where's he likely to be?'

Eve picked up the home-visits notebook, and scanned it quickly.

'At a guess, I'd say he should have reached Mrs Young at Penhally Heights by now.'

'Excellent.' Tom nodded. 'Oliver…' The young doctor wasn't listening. He was punching numbers into his mobile phone, and with a flash of irritation Tom turned to Hazel. 'Phone Tony at The Smugglers', explain the situation, and then see if you get Dragan. If you do, tell him not to attempt to come back into the town, but to head for The Smugglers'. Where's your physio? Laurie—'

'Lauren,' Eve corrected him. 'She said she was dropping in on Mrs Chamberlain at Harbour View, then going on to Gow Court.'

'Where's Gow Court on this photograph?' Tom asked, and Eve pointed to it.

'It's a newly built sheltered housing complex, in this small cul-de-sac running off from Trelawney Rise.'

'Which means, if Lauren's already left the nursing home, and is on her way to Gow Court,' Tom murmured, 'she'll either be driving down Penhally View, then into Polkerris Road, and on to Gow Court, or…'

'She could have taken the quicker route down Bridge Street,' Eve said.

Tom's eyes met hers, blank, unreadable.

'Then let's hope she's taken the scenic route,' he said evenly. 'Hazel—'

'Chloe's not answering, Eve,' Oliver exclaimed in frustration. 'I've rung her over and over, and she's not picking up the phone.'

'Maybe she's asleep,' Eve declared, seeing the worry on the young doctor's face. 'Maybe she had to go out,' she continued, only to realise too late that this hadn't been the wisest wise thing to say. 'I mean—'

'I've left a message on Dragan's mobile, telling him to make for The Smugglers',' Hazel interrupted. 'I've also got Chief Constable D'Ancey on my mobile. Do you want me to tell him we've agreed on two places of safety—the high school and The Smugglers'?'

Tom nodded, and turned back to Eve. 'Does Gow Court have wardens as it's a sheltered housing complex?'

'Carol and Florry Ford,' Eve replied.

'Phone them. If Lauren's there, tell her to make straight for the school hall.'

Eve didn't say, *But what if she isn't there?* But Tom must have realised she was thinking it, because as she picked up her mobile he smiled encouragingly at her.

'One step at a time, Eve,' he said, and she managed to smile back, but she felt less like smiling when she couldn't get a reply from Gow Court, and her smile disappeared completely when the lights in the surgery began to flicker.

'I'm surprised that hasn't happened before,' Hazel observed. 'Our emergency generator will kick in but…'

'It's time for us to move,' Tom finished for her. 'Where's your radio equipment?' he continued, and when Eve led him through to the back of Hazel's office to show him, he let out a low whistle. 'I'll say one thing for Nick, he hasn't stinted on anything. OK, we need to take this, and every piece of movable medical equipment we think we might need up to the school hall. Where's Oliver?'

As though on cue, the young doctor appeared behind them, his face white with worry.

'Chloe's still not answering,' he said. 'Where is she—*where the hell is she*?'

'Oliver, you have my permission to keep phoning your fiancée,' Tom exclaimed, not bothering to hide his irritation, 'but can you do it while you're also carrying some medical equipment out to your car?'

Oliver opened his mouth, then closed it again, and grimly picked up two of their portable defibrillators and disappeared with them.

'Tom, he's worried about Chloe,' Eve said awkwardly. 'He loves her.'

'And as far as we know she's safe, whereas a lot of people in Penhally aren't,' Tom retorted, 'so can we start moving things to the hall, or are we going to wait until the Lanson is lapping round our ankles?'

He was right, Eve knew he was. Speed was of the essence, but she wished he'd been a little kinder, a little gentler, with Oliver. She would have been frantic, too, if she'd been in the young doctor's shoes, and it didn't surprise her when she saw Oliver constantly checking his phone as they moved their portable medical equipment out to their cars, and he was still attempting to contact Chloe when they were carrying it through the rain and into the school.

'She said she was going to spend the whole afternoon at home, Eve,' Oliver muttered when they began setting up the radio equipment in the small office leading off from the school hall. 'You heard her. That's where she said she would be, so *why* isn't she answering the phone?'

Eve wished she knew. She wished, even more, that she could find some words of comfort to give to the young man, but she couldn't think of anything to say apart from, *She'll be all right*, and there was no point in saying that. Oliver would quite rightly turn round and demand to know how the hell she knew, so she simply squeezed his arm, and tried to look as reassuring as she could as they finished connecting all the radio equipment.

'OK, this radio must never be left unattended,' Tom declared when he joined them. 'When our mobile batteries run out—as they assuredly will—it's going to be our only means of contacting the outside world. We'll take it in rotas, but somebody needs to be by the radio at all times.'

'I'll take the first shift,' Eve said quickly. 'I mean, I haven't exactly been of much use up until now,' she added as Hazel hurried off in answer to Oliver's beckoning wave, 'so can I take the first shift on the radio?'

'Of course you can,' Tom said, 'but what do you mean, you haven't been much use?'

Eve shrugged helplessly.

'Hazel… She's been so efficient, on the ball, and I…I just keep seeing that wall of water, thinking if anyone was walking down Bridge Street, or Gull Close, when the dam broke…'

'Considering how heavy the rain was beforehand, I should imagine most people would have hurried indoors, don't you?' he said, and she forced a smile.

'I suppose so,' she said, then bit her lip. 'How do you do it—manage to stay so calm?'

'Because it's my job,' he answered simply. 'Running around like a headless chicken isn't going to get me anywhere.'

'No,' she muttered. 'Sorry. Memo to self. Stop behaving like a headless chicken. It's just…' She shivered involuntarily as the sky outside the office window lit up with lightning. 'I'm so cold, Tom. I don't know why, but I'm so cold, and I can't seem to get warm.'

He walked towards her, and before she knew what was happening he had wrapped his arms around her.

'Shock,' he said. 'What you're suffering from is shock.'

'Is that a professional diagnosis, Dr Cornish?' she said, resting her forehead on his chest, and holding onto him because he felt warm and solid, and so very good.

'Absolutely,' he murmured into her hair. 'Are your feet dry?'

She jerked her head up to look at him. 'What?'

'Wet feet make you feel cold, and cold hands made you feel downright miserable.'

'What medical textbook did that come out off?' she said, chuckling a little unevenly.

'The Dr Tom Cornish book of medical symptoms,' he said. 'It's never ever wrong.'

She put her head back on his chest, needing his warmth, his closeness.

'Tom…I'm scared—so very scared.'

'Glad to hear it,' he said to her surprise. 'A healthy dose of fear means you're not going to be tempted to do anything stupid.'

'I've got more than a healthy dose of fear at the moment, believe me,' Eve said with feeling, 'and yet you… Doesn't anything scare you?'

'Lots of things. Spiders the size of dinner plates, crocs, boa constrictors.'

She shuddered.

'You must think I'm such a wimp,' she mumbled, and to her surprise he tilted her chin so she had to face him.

'I think you're wonderful. I always have done.'

There was tenderness in his face. An unutterable tenderness that made her heart clutch, and desperately she tried to remember all the years they'd been apart, the times when she'd been so unhappy, the reasons why she'd hated him, but all she was aware of was that—stupidly—crazily—she wanted to stay in his arms for ever.

'Do you ever wonder what would have happened if I hadn't

gone to the States?' he said as though he'd read her mind, and she tried to avoid his gaze but couldn't.

'I think it's too late for regrets, Tom,' she said, feeling her throat tighten.

'Is it?' he said. 'Eve—this flood—if anything should happen to me—'

'Don't say that,' she ordered, quickly putting her fingers to his lips to silence him, feeling a chill wrap itself round her heart at his words. 'We're safe here. Nothing is going to happen to either of us.'

'But suppose it did,' he declared. 'I just want you to know—'

Whatever he had been about to say was lost as their radio crackled into life, and a deep, male, Irish voice suddenly rang out.

'Is that idle bastard, Tom Cornish, sitting on his backside somewhere nearby?' the disembodied voice said, and Tom turned quickly towards the radio with a broad smile.

'Hey, Mad Mitch,' he said, releasing Eve to pick up the handset and press the respond button. 'What the hell are you doing there?'

A booming laugh echoed down the radio.

'Well, the Navy contacted Deltaron, said Penhally was in a bit of bother, and asked if we could help. The boys and I hummed and hawed because there was a football match on the television, but when they said our contact was someone called Tom Cornish, we knew there couldn't be two lazy buggers by that name so here we are.'

'Who in the world is that?' Eve whispered, and Tom grinned.

'Michael Finnegan, known to everyone at Deltaron as Mad Mitch because he'll fly when no sane man would.'

Another guffaw came over the radio.

'Nice to know I'm appreciated, Tom, but maybe you ought to get your lady friend to show you how to use the mute button in case I hear something I shouldn't. I tell you, mate, they could put you in a men-only changing room, and you'd still manage to find a woman.'

'He's just kidding,' Tom said, colouring slightly as Eve's eyebrows rose. 'Where are you, Mitch?'

'Coming into Penhally over the sea, and let me tell you it's horrendous out here. Rain's just running off my blades, and visibility's virtually nil. All I'm picking up is what my strobes are hitting. I've been told to head for two streets called Bridge Street and Gull Close, but, if the floodwater's as bad as we've been led to believe, you know what that could mean. OAO until we're closer to you.'

'What did he mean by, "you know what that could mean"?' Eve asked as the radio went dead.

'At the moment, the water's flowing down Bridge Street and Gull Close, and out to sea,' Tom replied. 'What Mitch is worried about is if it encounters a blockage.'

'Is that likely?' Oliver asked as he joined them.

'If buildings start to come down, then, yes, it is,' Tom declared. 'All we need is a large enough fall of masonry and the water will have to find some other way out.'

'So, what you're saying is, nowhere in Penhally is safe?' Oliver exclaimed.

'Harbour View should be OK as it's high above the village, as should the two schools, and The Smugglers',' Tom replied, 'but other than that… Yes, I guess that's pretty much what I'm saying.'

'But isn't there something you can do if a building collapses?' Oliver faltered. 'Some way you can divert the water, make it flow elsewhere?'

'In an open environment there are things I could try, but in the middle of a village…' Tom shook his head. 'All we can do is hope and pray.'

'Is anyone there?'

The voice on the radio was faint, but unmistakably that of Kate Althorp, and quickly Eve lifted the handset.

'Kate, I'm here,' she said. 'Where are you?'

'Nick, are you sure this damn thing works?' she heard the midwife demand. 'All I'm getting is a lot of crackles.'

'Kate, you need to press the red button,' Eve said. 'Once you press that, you'll be able to hear me.'

'Oh. Right. Eve, is that you?' Kate said. 'Thank God. I thought… Never mind what I thought. OK, I know this is probably a non-starter,' the midwife continued, 'but we really could do with some help here. Stephanie's in labour, and it's a breech. We've no electricity, scarcely any equipment except what's in our medical bags, and we can't leave because there's about three feet of water downstairs.'

Eve glanced across at Tom, and he took the receiver from her, and sat down.

'Kate, it's Tom Cornish here. Where are you in Bridge Street?'

'Number sixteen. Luckily, it's a two-storey building, so we're upstairs, but…' They heard the midwife take a quick, and unsteady intake of breath. 'The building is shaking rather ominously, and Stephanie really does need to get to hospital, and the faster the better.'

'Can you hang a white pillowcase—something visible like that—out of the window of the room you're in so the choppers know where you are?' Tom asked.

'We can do that,' Kate replied. 'But, Tom…' The midwife took another uneven breath. 'We really do need help.'

'I know,' he said softly, then flipped the off button on the handset.

'Kate must be terrified,' Eve said as she saw him change the frequency on the radio, and knew he was trying to contact his colleague, Mad Mitch. 'Her husband—James—he drowned ten years ago, trying to rescue children who were cut off by the tide. Kate's always been scared of water, and if anything should happen to her… Her son's only nine, Tom.'

'I *know*,' Tom flared, then shook his head when Eve flinched. 'Sorry—sorry. Mitch, are you there, and if you are, where are you?'

'I'm over the harbour, Tom, and this is a bad one,' the Irish pilot declared. 'I've been talking to the coastguard pilot, and the Navy blokes, and we're all agreed. We're going to have to fly in singly, and do a snatch and grab. The access into Penhally over the harbour is too narrow, and if our blades collide…'

'Mitch, we have a woman in labour in Bridge Street,' Tom declared. 'She has two medics with her, but they've no electricity, and she needs to be in hospital pronto.'

'I hear you, Tom, but I can see people on roofs, people hanging out of windows. Men, women, children, and… Holy mackerel, part of a building's just gone. It looks like a hotel, but…' There was silence, then Mitch spoke again. 'Bob says that according to his map it's the Anchor Hotel, and the water's now spreading into…' There was another silence. 'Fisherman's Row. Bob says the water's now in Fisherman's Row.'

Eve heard Oliver's sharp intake of breath, but Tom ignored him.

'Mitch, can you see any people in danger of drowning?' he asked with a calmness that Eve could only wonder at.

'Hell, mate, I can see people everywhere in danger of drowning,' the pilot replied, and Tom's eyes met Eve's, then Oliver's.

'OK, save any children you see first,' he said.

'But, Tom,' Oliver protested. 'Chloe—'

'I repeat, Mitch,' Tom declared. 'Save any children you see first.'

Deliberately he cut the radio connection, and Oliver stared wordlessly at him for a second, then straightened up.

'I…I have to go,' he said with difficulty. 'Chloe…she's in Fisherman's Row.'

'You're going nowhere,' Tom declared, swinging round in his seat, as Oliver made for the office door. 'Number one, you'll never get across the Lanson, and, number two, we need you here.'

'Chloe needs me more,' Oliver said tightly, and Tom shook his head, his face impassive.

'No, she doesn't,' he said. 'If she's not in the house, she's safe. If she *is* in the house, the only people who will be able to rescue her are the helicopter winch men.'

'But you said they were to rescue children first. Chloe—'

'You put me in charge,' Tom declared, his voice level, flat, 'and you said you would accept whatever decision I made. My decision is they lift any children they see first, and you are to stay here. It's a question of priorities, Oliver.'

'A lifeboat, then,' Oliver said, dragging his fingers through his hair in desperation as, overhead, they all heard the drum of helicopter blades. 'Can't you at least ask them to launch the lifeboat?'

'Oliver, the water's running too fast for a lifeboat to make any kind of headway,' Tom protested, 'and I can't—I won't—order men to put their lives at risk for one woman.'

'I notice you're not out there endangering yourself with the men you profess to care so much about.' Oliver flared. 'You're sitting in here, all nice and warm and comfortable.'

A flash of anger appeared on Tom's face and when he got to his feet Eve instantly moved between the two men.

'Oliver—Tom—please,' she protested, but neither were listening to her.

'If I were a pilot, I'd be up there, doing my damnedest to save people,' Tom said with difficulty, 'but I'm not a pilot. When the water ebbs I'll be out there with my men, but until then I'm doing what you asked me to do—co-ordinating, and organising this operation.'

'And that's all this is to you, isn't it, just another operation?' Oliver said, fury and fear mixed on his face. 'You don't give a damn about Chloe. To you, she isn't even a person, she's just a statistic, a nameless, faceless nobody.'

'Oliver…' Tom's mouth compressed for a second, and when he eventually spoke his voice was strained. 'Believe me, this is as hard for me as it is for you, but I have to prioritise.'

'And if Chloe dies?' Oliver exclaimed, and Eve saw Tom's eyes darken.

'I'm sorry, Oliver.'

'Sorry?' Oliver echoed in anguish. 'You're *sorry*? How do you live with yourself, Cornish—how do you sleep nights?'

'I live with myself because making hard decisions is what I'm paid for, and as for sleeping…' Tom's lips curved into a bitter parody of a smile. 'I actually sleep very badly, if you want the God's honest truth, but I'm still not ordering the lifeboat to put to sea, and I want you to go back into the hall and see if there are any people needing your medical services.'

For a moment Oliver looked as though he intended to argue, then his jaw set and he strode out of the small office, banging the door behind him, and Eve turned awkwardly to Tom.

'Tom, what Oliver said… He didn't mean it, not really.'

'I know,' he murmured, sitting down again, and turning his attention back to the radio. 'But there honestly isn't anything I can do but hope Chloe either isn't in the house, or when the water started to come in she had the sense to head for the attic.'

He sounded drained. Completely, and utterly drained, and for a moment she hesitated then walked up behind him and put her arms round him.

'It's hard to believe, isn't it,' she said, 'that a little over an hour ago we were walking up the street, discussing where we would have lunch, and you said not the Anchor Hotel because you felt they always suspected you of stealing their cutlery?'

He gave a husky chuckle.

'Yeah, well, this afternoon's the day they stopped needing to worry about their cutlery.'

She gazed out of the office window, seeing nothing but darkness illuminated by the strobe lights of a hovering helicopter.

'Is it always like this, Tom? The rescue missions you and your men go out on. Are they always like this?'

'Pretty much,' he replied and, as she held him tighter, she felt his head fall back against her chest.

'How do you stand it?' she said. 'How can you bear it?'

'Because I have to,' he said quietly. 'It's my job, what I signed up for, what I agreed to do. I know Oliver thinks I'm a completely unfeeling bastard, but children always come first in a disaster, and to launch the lifeboat, risk the lives of eight—ten—men in conditions I know would be suicide…'

'Tom…'

She didn't get a chance to say any more. The office door opened and, when Chief Constable Lachlan D'Ancey appeared, she stepped away from Tom quickly.

'I picked up the emergency message on my car radio,' the policeman gasped, pulling off his cap and sending rain drops scattering everywhere, 'so I knew it was going to be bad, but I never thought it would be as bad as this. I've got men out sandbagging Harbour Road, the council have brought in diggers, but nothing is stopping it from spreading.'

'Have you closed the roads into Penhally?' Tom asked. 'The last thing we want is people returning from work, adding to the chaos.'

'We've blockaded all the roads, and I can tell you it's holy murder out there. The word's already gone out that Penhally's in a bad way, and husbands—wives—are trying to get back into the village to find their loved ones. Luckily, a lot of the stay-at-home mums, and the elderly, seem to have taken police advice and made their way towards either Smugglers' or here, but we've no way of knowing just how many people are out there, trapped.'

'Lauren's just rung in,' Hazel declared as she appeared behind Chief Constable D'Ancey. 'She made it to Gow Court, and she's now going to try to make her way to the school hall.'

'Any word from Dragan?' Eve asked, and the practice manager shook her head.

'I'm guessing he's still out of range, and it's taking him a little while to get to The Smugglers'.'

But surely not this long, Eve thought, but she didn't say it and neither, she noticed, did Tom.

'I'd better get back outside,' Chief Constable D'Ancey declared, 'see what's happening.' His eyes met Tom's. 'Any orders—instructions—advice?'

'How about praying it stops raining?' Tom replied as another deluge began to bounce off the school roof, and the policeman smiled wryly.

'I doubt if I have a direct line to the Big Man upstairs, but I'll do my best.'

He didn't linger, and when he had gone, Hazel turned to Eve apologetically.

'Could you have a word with Lizzie Chamberlain? I've told her time and time again that Harbour View is probably the safest place in Penhally for her mother to be at the moment, but she's stressing like crazy.'

Eve glanced across at Tom enquiringly, and he nodded.

'Take a break—you deserve one,' he said, and Hazel rolled her eyes as she led the way out of the office.

'I don't think anyone could call this a break,' she muttered. 'Lizzie is a wonderful woman, and I admire her no end for all the work she does with abandoned animals but if her BP isn't through the roof mine certainly is after listening to her for the last half-hour.'

Eve chuckled, but it didn't take her long to discover that the practice manager wasn't exaggerating. Lizzie had worked herself into a complete panic attack, and eventually Eve had to concede defeat and call Oliver over to give her a sedative.

'I very much doubt she'll be the only one who cracks tonight,' Oliver declared, his face tight, strained. 'Look around you, Eve, see how crowded the place is, and yet there's scarcely a sound.'

The young doctor was right. Everywhere Eve looked she could see people sitting either in silent huddles, white-faced with shock, holding onto their families, or sitting alone, and those who were sitting alone watched the school-hall door constantly, clearly desperately hoping the next person who came in would be one of their loved ones.

'Eve…'

She knew what Oliver was going to say, just as she also knew she had no words of comfort to give him, but she was saved from saying anything when a familiar figure appeared beside her.

'Amanda, I'm so pleased to see you,' she said, turning towards Tassie's mother with relief. 'I was hoping you and your family would come here. Is there anything you need—anything I can get you?'

'We're fine, Eve,' Mrs Lovelace replied. 'A nice policeman told us to bring some food with us so we're not going to starve, but…' She glanced in the direction of her family. 'Do you think we'll have to stay long? My boys are getting a bit restless.'

They would, Eve thought as she stared at Amanda's children. The woman's three sons were looking as truculent and surly as ever, while Kelly, Amanda's eldest daughter, appeared to be painting her fingernails with an air of unutterable boredom.

'Where's Tassie?' she asked.

'Tassie?' Amanda repeated. 'But, I thought… I mean, isn't she with you?'

'No, she's not with me,' Eve said, seeing a flash of fear cross the woman's face, and knowing her own face had just mirrored it. 'Wasn't she at school today?'

'She said she didn't feel well—'

'Skiving, more like,' Tassie's twin brother Terry muttered sullenly, but his mother ignored him.

'She said she felt a bit better after lunch, and when she asked if she could go for a walk I thought she meant she was coming down to see you.'

'No, she didn't come to see me,' Eve said, fighting to stay calm, but knowing she was losing the battle. 'Have you talked to any of her friends—asked if they've seen her?'

'Nobody's seen her, Eve,' Amanda protested, panic plain now in her voice. 'You don't think—? You know how she liked to borrow books from Miss Stanbury—you don't think she could have gone to…to Gull Close?'

Please, God, no, Eve thought, as she stared wordlessly at Tassie's mother. Please, God, don't let Tassie be there, not there, and blindly she turned and hurried towards the office, her heart hammering.

'Tom—'

He held up his hand to silence her as she rushed in.

'OK, Mitch,' he said. 'Can you give me an update when you're closer to Stephanie Richards's house?'

'Will do,' the pilot replied. 'OAO.'

'Tom, Amanda doesn't know where Tassie is,' Eve said before he'd even hit the cut button on his handset. 'She wasn't at school today—she didn't feel well—but she went for a walk after lunch, and no one's seen her since.'

'And?' he said, getting stiffly to his feet.

'You have to find her,' she declared, wondering why he was suddenly being so unnecessarily dense. 'She must be out there somewhere so you have to find her.'

'The chopper pilots are picking up everyone who looks as though they're in trouble so hopefully they'll see her.'

'And that's *it*?' she protested, her voice rising despite her best efforts to prevent it. 'That's all you're going to do—*hope* Tassie is seen by somebody? Tom, she's just a little girl, just ten years old, and if she's trapped somewhere she's going to be terrified out of her mind.'

'As will be a lot of people at the moment,' he murmured, and she grabbed hold of the front of his sweater, knowing she un-doubtedly looked wild-eyed and deranged but she didn't care.

'Please, Tom, you have to do something. Get your friend—Mad Mitch—back on the radio, tell him what Tassie looks like—'

'For God's sake, Eve, the only lights out there are the heli-copter search lights,' Tom flared. 'The pilots will scour all the rooftops, but I can't—and won't—order them to look for one specific child. While they're doing that, other men, women and children could drown.'

'*I don't care!*' Eve cried, then took an unsteady breath when Tom stared at her in shocked astonishment. 'I'm sorry—I don't mean that—not really, but this is Tassie, Tom. *Tassie*.'

'Eve—'

'Tom—if you're there, mate, we have a problem.'

Tom eased Eve's fingers from his sweater and picked up the handset.

'What's wrong, Mitch?'

'I'm over Bridge Street, and can see the white pillowcase you mentioned for the woman who's giving birth, but, Tom, I can't take a woman in labour out of that small window. When the baby's arrived, we can do a scoop and run, but a woman in labour, over that water, I'm sorry, but I can't.'

'I understand,' Tom said. 'Mitch—'

'I have to go, mate. I can see a couple of kids—one about two, the other about three—sitting with a woman astride one of the roofs in Bridge Street, and there's a blonde-haired girl of about nine hanging out of an attic window in Gull Close.'

'*Tassie*,' Eve breathed. 'Tom, that'll be Tassie. Tell him to pick her up first—please tell him to pick her up first.'

Tom gazed at her for a long moment, then hit the 'talk' button on his handset.

'Pick up the youngsters on the roof and their mother first, Mitch.'

'*No!*' Eve exclaimed. 'Tom—'

'The child hanging out of a window in Gull Close is safe for the moment, Eve,' he replied, 'but those kids on the roof have no shelter, no protection. If one of them slips—'

'But—'

'It's a question of priorities, Eve.'

'You keep saying that,' she said, feeling tears begin to trickle down her cheeks, and she rubbed them away roughly with the back of her hand. 'Like…like it's some sort of justification.'

He caught her by the shoulders, his face dark, and forced her to look up at him.

'It's the only justification I have, Eve. Can't you see that?'

'Then I'll go and help her,' she said blindly. 'If you can't—won't—I have to. I'm not going to let her down. I'm not going to abandon her the way I—' She bit off the rest of what she'd been about to say. 'She's a little girl, Tom, just a little girl, out there in the dark, and she must be terrified.'

'Eve, you are not leaving this hall.'

'I have to—don't you see that?' she cried. 'I can't live with another twenty years of regret, spend another twenty years wishing I'd done things differently.'

'Eve, you're talking nonsense,' Tom declared, giving her shoulders a little shake. 'You have never let anybody down in your life.'

'But I have, I have,' she insisted, knowing she was crying in earnest now, that her words were coming out choked with sobs. 'And I won't do that again. I *can't,* Tom.'

'Eve, you're not making any sense. Who did you let down?'

She could see the complete bewilderment in his face, and she didn't want to tell him. She'd always sworn she never would, but if she told him maybe he'd understand, maybe he would send people to help Tassie, and she took a ragged breath.

'Our baby, Tom. I let our baby down.'

He stared at her blankly.

'Eve, we don't have a baby. Look, shock can play strange tricks, affect people differently. I'll get Oliver—'

'Listen to me, Tom,' she interrupted, clutching hold of him, 'you have to listen to me. I didn't realise I was pregnant until a month after you left for America. I hadn't been feeling well, and I thought it was simply something I'd eaten until I was talking to one of the midwives at the practice I was working at in Newquay, and the penny dropped.'

'But...' He shook his head. 'You can't have been pregnant. You were on the Pill. You told me so.'

'Maybe it took longer to begin working on me—maybe it just didn't work properly—I don't know,' she protested. 'But I took one of the pregnancy kits from the surgery I was working in, and when it came up positive I thought it was a mistake— was so sure it must be a mistake—that I went up to Truro and bought another one, and...'

'It came up positive, too?'

She nodded. 'I was pregnant, Tom.'

'And you had a miscarriage,' Tom said, grasping both of her hands tightly in his. 'Oh, hell, Eve, if I'd only known, had been there with you.'

'I didn't have a miscarriage, Tom.'

'You mean...' His eyes searched hers, and she saw amazement followed by dawning delight appear in them. 'You mean, I have a son or a daughter? Eve, that is—'

'You don't have a son or a daughter, Tom,' she interrupted, her voice uneven. 'I...I had an abortion.'

CHAPTER FIVE

HE DIDN'T believe her. She could see the disbelief and denial in his face, knew he was expecting her to suddenly smile and say, 'I didn't mean that,' but as she continued to stare silently back at him, she saw his incredulous expression gradually turn into one of shocked horror.

'You had an abortion?' he said hoarsely. 'You aborted our child?'

'I didn't want to do it, Tom,' she said, returning the pressure of his fingers, willing him to believe her. 'If there had been any other way—if I could somehow have kept the baby—but I couldn't, and believe me there hasn't been a day since then when I haven't regretted what I did.'

'You had an abortion,' he repeated as though by saying it he could somehow make it untrue.

'Yes,' she whispered, and he let go of her hands, and stepped back from her, revulsion flooding his face.

'How *could* you have done that?' he demanded. 'How *could* you have taken the life of an innocent child and just thrown it away?'

His words and his expression cut her to the bone but, as she stared back at him, saw the disgust in his eyes, it wasn't pain she felt, it was anger. A blind, furious anger that he could judge her so easily, and so instantly.

'You think,' she said, her voice shaking so much she could hardly get the words out, 'you think I just did the test, and thought, Oh, good heavens, I'm pregnant, now that's really inconvenient, but never mind, I'll *get rid of it*?'

'I don't know what you thought,' he threw back at her. 'How can I when I don't feel like I know you at all? All these years and you said nothing. All these years when I could have had a son or a daughter, but you chose to go ahead...to...without telling me... It was my child, too, Eve.'

'A child you wouldn't have wanted—not then,' she cried, her heart thumping so hard she was sure he must hear it. 'Time and time again, that summer, you told me you didn't want to be tied down, didn't want a wife, or a family, wanted to be free, to make something of your life.'

'You didn't give me the chance to say whether I wanted our baby or not,' he declared, his face twisted with fury and anguish. 'You just decided, without a word, a call...'

'*How* could I have contacted you, Tom?' she protested. '"I'm off to the States," you said, and then I got a postcard from New York, and another one from California saying you were applying for a job with Deltaron, but you never even bothered to tell me whether you'd got the job. All I knew—guessed—was you were somewhere in America. Well, America is a pretty big place, Tom.'

'You...you could have phoned the offices of Deltaron,' he said defensively. 'They would have told you where I was.'

'And if I'd done that—turned up on your doorstep—and said, "I'm pregnant, Tom," how would you have felt?' she demanded. 'What would you have done?'

'I would...I could have offered to help,' he said, beginning to pace backwards and forwards across the small office, his face a tight mask of anger, his green eyes blazing. 'OK, so maybe I wasn't making very much money then, but I could have sent you something every month to help you take care of the baby.'

'And resented me and the child for the rest of our lives for putting you in that position.'

He whirled round at her, his face so contorted that she involuntarily took a step back.

'How *dare* you say that?' he exclaimed. 'I would *never* have resented my child. You know how I feel about children.'

'I know how you feel now,' she countered, bunching her hands into tight fists at her sides, 'but that wasn't how you felt when we were young.'

'Eve—'

'You wanted freedom. "No emotional baggage", that's what you said you wanted, and if I'd told you about the baby… Do you think I wanted you to hate him or her as much as your father hated and resented you?'

'So, it's my fault, now, is it?' he flared.

'Tom—'

'Eve—Oliver—is anyone there?'

Dragan's voice crackled over the radio, insistent, concerned, and when Tom made no move to answer it Eve shakily lifted the handset, and hit the reply button.

'I…I hear you, Dragan,' she said with difficulty. 'Where are you?'

'The Smugglers' Inn, as per instructions. I gather things are pretty bad in Penhally?'

Eve glanced across at Tom's rigid back.

'You could say that,' she replied.

'Well, I'm sorry to add to your troubles, but I need a helicopter asap,' Dragan continued. 'Tony, at the Smugglers', has apparently been experiencing chest pains for the past month, but he's been ignoring them, thinking they were due to indigestion, but the pain's so bad even he can't ignore it. Chloe says—'

'Chloe's there?' Eve interrupted quickly.

'She was visiting Rachel Kenner at the manse when the word to evacuate went out, so she and Rachel came here. Why?'

'She hasn't had her mobile switched on, and Oliver's been a bit worried about her,' she said. *Which had to be the biggest understatement of the year.* 'You think Tony's having a heart attack?'

'His BP's 130 over 90, his skin's sweaty, and the pain's radiating from his chest down his left arm and up into his jaw, so I think we can safely say he's having a heart attack,' Dragan replied. 'I've given him nitro to relieve the pain, and Chloe's started an IV line of morphine, but he needs hospital, Eve, and fast.'

Out of the corner of her eye, Eve could see Tom holding out his hand for the handset, and she gave it to him.

'I'll get one of the Navy guys to Smugglers' Inn right away, Dragan,' he declared. 'Could somebody put out a light, or a flare, to show the chopper where you are?'

There was a distant murmur of conversation from Dragan's side of the connection, and then Dragan's voice rang out.

'We're on it, Tom, but can you be quick? Tony's not in good shape.'

Tom handed the handset back to Eve, then picked up their spare.

'Keep him on the radio,' he said abruptly. 'I can page the Navy with this, and then give him an ETA.'

Eve nodded.

'Is Melinda all right, Dragan?' she said, turning back to the radio.

'Would you believe she's actually watching what's happening in Penhally on television?' the Croatian doctor replied. 'She said she couldn't believe it when part of The Anchor collapsed.'

'Someone's been filming this?' Eve gasped, and heard the Croatian doctor give a wry chuckle.

'Eve, people would film a car crash if they thought they could make a quick buck out of it.'

'Tell him the ETA for the helicopter is five minutes,' Tom declared.

'No need to tell me,' Dragan said. 'I heard it myself. Thanks, Tom, and now I'd better go,' he added. 'There's quite a crowd gathering here, and some of them are panicking pretty badly.'

'Tell Melinda to stay where she is when you next talk to her,' Eve said. 'And tell her not to do anything stupid, like going out to check her animals.'

'I've already told her that,' Dragan replied. 'Got an earful back for my pains, of course, but when I first heard about what was happening in Penhally, all I could think was, Please, God, don't let her be there. Just the thought of losing her, and the baby…'

'I know,' Eve said softly, and heard Tom draw in a ragged breath behind her, but she didn't turn round, couldn't. 'Call us if there's anything else you need, OK?'

She heard Dragan's muttered assent but, after she'd switched off the reply button, she stared at the radio equipment for a long moment before she hesitantly turned towards Tom.

'That's good news,' she said. 'About Chloe, I mean.'

He nodded, but he didn't meet her gaze.

'Tom…' She moistened her lips. 'Tom…'

'I'll tell Mitch to pick Tassie up next.'

'Thank you,' she said, wishing he would look at her, wishing she could touch him, but not daring to. 'Tom—'

'You'd better tell Oliver about his fiancée.'

His face was cold and forbidding, but she couldn't leave it like this—simply couldn't—and hesitantly she took a step towards him.

'Tom, about our baby,' she said, her voice choked, and he made a convulsive movement with his arm, clearly warning her not to say anything else, but she couldn't remain silent. 'Tom, you cannot possibly regret what I did more than I do.'

'You *think*?' he exclaimed, his green eyes dark, pain-filled.

'Tom… *Please*.'

The raw pain in her face tore at his heart, and part of him wanted to go to her, to hold her and comfort her, but the other part—the part inside him that hurt so much—never wanted to see her ever again.

'Just go, Eve,' he said. 'Just…*go*.'

She did. She walked stiffly out of the office, but, when she'd closed the door quietly behind her, he let his breath out in a long, shuddering gasp of pain.

How could she have done that? he wondered. She'd said she'd had no choice, but other women were single mothers, other women had brought up—were bringing up—children on their own, and for her to have…

A son. He might have had a son he could have taught how to play football, taken to matches, joked with, laughed with, advised so he wouldn't make the same mistakes he had. Or a daughter. He squeezed his eyes shut, but that didn't stop him seeing her in his mind's eye, a smaller version of Eve with big brown eyes, and a cloud of dark hair.

How could she just have gone ahead and had an abortion? He'd thought he'd known her. He'd thought in the mêlée of death and destruction that his life had become, she was the one constant, the one calm haven, and to discover she'd…

'Eve… Oh, sorry,' Hazel declared as she stuck her head round the office door. 'Where's Eve?'

'She…' Tom stared at the radio equipment, deliberately avoiding the practice manager's eye. 'She's with Oliver.'

'Oh. Right,' Hazel said. 'It's just Amanda Lovelace—she's very worried about her daughter, and she seems to be under the impression Eve knows something, or can do something.'

'Tell Mrs Lovelace we think we know where Tassie is.'

'You mean she's safe—she's been picked up?' Hazel said.

'No, she hasn't been picked up, not yet,' he replied.

'But—'

'Hazel, I'm not God,' he snapped, then held up his hands

apologetically when the practice manager blinked. 'Sorry—
I…I'm sorry.'

'It's OK,' Hazel said, her face softening with understanding.
'I'll be as encouraging as I can to Amanda, without being too
specific.'

He nodded but, when the practice manager had disappeared,
he bit down hard on his lip to quell the sob he could feel welling
in his throat.

To think he'd told Eve just a few short hours ago that one of
the reasons he'd come back to Penhally had been to see if he
could still feel anything. Well, by God, he knew he could. He
was caring so much right now he felt as though he would die of
it, and, desperately, he glanced around the silent office, searching for some way to release the anger and despair he felt, but
there was no way, and he knew there wasn't. Nothing could ease
what he felt inside. Nothing could remove the knowledge that
he could have had a son, or a daughter, and that Eve had taken
that from him. Taken it without asking him, or even telling him
what she'd done.

How could she have told you? a small voice whispered at
the back of his mind, but he didn't listen to it, didn't want to.
All he wanted was the pain to go away, for him never to have
known, because the knowledge was tearing him apart.

'Eve, are you there?'

Tom swore as Nick's voice rang out on the radio. The senior
partner was the last person he wanted to talk to right now, but
he couldn't ignore the voice.

'It's me, Nick,' he said, flicking on the handset.

'Oh. Right.'

Nick's clipped tone said it all, and a horrible suspicion
suddenly crept into Tom's mind. Could Eve had gone to Nick,
all those years ago, asked him to authorise her request for a termination, and that was why Nick always looked at him as
though he was something unmentionable stuck to the bottom

of his shoe? It would have made more sense for her to have gone outside the area, to a doctor she didn't know, but, then, he didn't know anything with any certainty any more.

'St Piran's?'

Tom stared blankly at the radio equipment. Nick had clearly asked him something, but he hadn't been listening.

'Sorry, Nick, interference on the line,' Tom lied. 'Can you say that again?'

'I said,' Nick declared with clear impatience, 'that Stephanie's just given birth to a boy, and she really needs to be in hospital so we'd appreciate the appearance of a helicopter as quickly as possible.'

Despite everything, Tom could not prevent a wry smile from curving his lips at the senior partner's peremptory tone. When Nick said, 'Jump', he clearly expected people to obey irrespective of the circumstances.

'You're a priority two, Nick, if that's any consolation,' he said, then hit the talk button so he could speak to Mitch.

'Did you hear that?' Nick said, turning to Kate as he put down his handset. 'We're a priority two.'

'Good to know we're somewhere on the list,' Kate said with a wobbly smile, 'especially as our torches aren't going to last much longer.'

Nick nodded, then frowned.

'I feel so damned useless, stuck in here,' he protested. 'All my patients are out there, and I'm trapped in here and about as much use as a chocolate fireguard.'

'Stephanie Richards didn't think you were useless,' Kate pointed out. 'A breech birth isn't easy to pull off even with every surgical piece of equipment known to mankind, but you did it with just what was in your bag.'

Nick shook his head. 'Flattery will get you nowhere.'

'Not flattery,' she said. 'You're a good doctor, Nick, you

always were, and…' She came to a halt as the building swayed slightly. 'I wish it wouldn't do that.'

'Stop fretting,' Nick replied. 'This building's made of good Cornish stone. It can withstand worse than this.'

'Right,' Kate said without conviction, then flushed when Nick shook his head at her again. 'Sorry. I'm not doing positive and upbeat very well, am I? Trouble is, I'm a coward when it comes to water.' She took a shaky breath. 'Bad memories.'

'Nothing's going to happen to us, Kate,' Nick said gently, and she forced a smile.

''Course it won't.' She bent down to tuck a blanket round the young mother and her baby. 'Strange to think Stephanie was right all along. She kept saying she felt something was wrong, and I kept thinking, Here she goes again, panicking. And yet she was right.'

'I hardly think she can have known she was going to have a breech birth,' Nick observed, and Kate rolled her eyes.

'Must you be so pedantic, Nick? I didn't mean she knew she was going to have a breech birth. I just meant sometimes mums-to-be have a sixth sense about whether things are right, or not.' She gazed down at the sleeping young mother. 'Actually, although she doesn't know it yet, this is when the really hard bit starts, and it's going to be doubly difficult for her as she'll have to bring up the baby on her own.'

'She'll cope,' Nick said firmly. 'It never ceases to amaze me how strong women are, and she'll cope.'

Kate nodded, and cleared her throat.

'Do you think Jem's all right?'

Nick's eyes met hers, calm, unreadable.

'I should imagine they've kept all the kids in school,' he said, 'and, as both the high school and the primary school are up on a hill, he'll be fine.'

'Yes,' Kate said, more in an attempt to convince herself than in actual agreement. 'It's just he's like me—not keen on water.'

'Nothing's going to happen to him, Kate.'

'No, of course not,' she said with an effort. 'Do you think it will be Tom who will come with the helicopter?'

'God, I hope not.' Nick groaned. 'That would be all I'd need. The mighty Tom Cornish winching me out of a window.'

Kate tilted her head, and gazed at him speculatively. 'You seriously dislike him, don't you?'

'Yes.'

'Care to share the reason?'

'Can't,' Nick said tightly. 'Patient confidentiality.'

'It's got something to do with Eve Dwyer, hasn't it?' Kate pressed. 'She looked as though she'd seen a ghost when he turned up at Alison and Jack's wedding.'

'Kate—'

'Nick, given that we're both medical professionals, and we could well be dependent on Tom to rescue us,' Kate exclaimed, 'don't you think I have the right to know what he did that has made you dislike him so much?'

For a second she saw indecision warring with professionalism on Nick's face, then he sighed.

'Eve came to me twenty years ago, asking for a prescription for antibiotics. She told me she had a vaginal infection. Well, there was no way I was going to prescribe anything without examining her first, so I did. She'd had an abortion, Eve.'

'And you think Tom was the father?' Kate said calmly.

'Kate, it was common knowledge twenty years ago that they were lovers.'

'You mean it was Penhally gossip, twenty years ago,' Kate replied dryly, and Nick looked irritated.

'She wasn't going out with anyone else at the time, so I think we can safely say he fathered her baby. And what did he do? He skipped off to the US, leaving Eve to deal with it.'

'He might not have known she was pregnant when he left,' Kate protested. 'He might only have found out later.'

'He didn't come back, though, did he?' Nick countered. 'And what kind of man does that?'

'Nick—'

'Kate, I was just nineteen when Annabel and I got married, and I was a father to twins soon after. I don't know how Annabel and I survived those early years, never knowing where the next meal was coming from, always panic-stricken that we wouldn't be able to pay the rent, but I would never have suggested she have an abortion.'

'Nick…' Gently, Kate put her hand on his arm. 'Things are seldom black and white, right or wrong, and who are we to judge? Our haloes are hardly shiny bright. Ten years ago—'

'I don't want to talk about this,' Nick interrupted, throwing her hand off, and walking towards the window, but Kate followed him.

'Nick, we might die tonight,' she said, 'and I don't want to die with what I need to say to you—what I've wanted to say to you for the past ten years—left unsaid.'

His face contorted, and for a second she thought he was going to refuse to listen to her, then his shoulders slumped.

'Do you have any idea how much I deeply regret that night?' he said hoarsely as he stared out of the window into the blackness. 'It should never have happened, and I blame myself entirely.'

'Nick, it takes two to make love, and I didn't push you away,' Kate said softly. 'I could have done—should have done—and yet I didn't. I wanted you that night as much as you wanted me, and when I heard James had died…' She closed her eyes, then opened them again. 'I knew it was a punishment. That God had taken my husband from me to punish me.'

'Oh, Kate…'

'No, please, let me finish,' she insisted as he turned towards her, his face taut. 'We made love that night. You were unfaithful to your wife, and I was unfaithful to my husband, and it was wrong—so very wrong—and when I discovered I was pregnant…'

'Are you telling me you actually considered having an abortion?' Nick said, horror plain in his voice, and tears appeared in Kate's eyes.

'Maybe I should have done. It would certainly have made everything easier for us both, wouldn't it, with no living reminder of what we'd done, but despite all the guilt I've felt over the years, all the torment…' Kate's voice broke. 'As God is my witness, even though I know I will be damned for all eternity for saying this, I can't—and won't ever—regret having him.'

Nick reached out and jerkily clasped her hands in his.

'Kate, if there is a God, he would never condemn you, but what I can't forgive myself for—will never be able to forgive myself for—is cheating on Annabel that night, betraying my marriage vows.'

'And you think I can forgive myself for betraying James?' Kate demanded. 'You think I'm saying that because Jem has brought me so much happiness, his birth justified what we did? I'm not saying that, Nick, I would never say that, but…'

'But?' he prompted, and she could see the uncertainty in his eyes, and the pain.

'We can't undo it, Nick. We will both have to live with our guilt until the day we die, and if by some miracle we're spared tonight then what I want—what I hope—is for us both to perhaps be able to move on, move forward. Not forgetting what we did—we won't ever be able to—but living with it, accepting it, and for you—maybe in time—to let Jem become a part of your life.'

'Kate…'

His voice was deep, strained, but she didn't get a chance to find out what he'd been about to say. A light suddenly appeared at the window, followed by the sound of a gloved hand knocking against it.

'You have a woman and a newborn in here?' the winch man asked when Nick opened the window, and, when Nick nodded, the winch man grinned. 'Then your helicopter awaits, and Tom Cornish sends his compliments.'

'He would,' Nick said darkly.

'And Chloe really is safe?' Oliver declared for what felt, to Eve, like the hundredth time, and she nodded.

'Yes, she really is safe,' she said.

'No thanks to Tom,' the young doctor muttered as he gazed out over the crowded school hall, then flushed when he saw Eve's expression. 'I'm sorry, but he didn't exactly help, did he?'

'Oliver, it's not his fault only one helicopter can fly into Penhally at a time because the entrance to the harbour is so narrow,' she protested. 'It's not his fault the water's rushing so high and fast it would be suicide to launch a boat. What else could he have done—what would you have done if you'd been in his shoes?'

'Saved the woman I loved first,' he said simply, and Eve managed a smile.

'Which is why neither you nor I would make very good heads of operations at Deltaron,' she said. 'We can't see the bigger picture.'

'I'd rather keep my ability to feel, to care,' Oliver declared, and, as Eve caught sight of Tom coming out of the small office, her smile died.

'Tom has the ability to feel, Oliver,' she murmured, 'and to care, very deeply.'

And to hate, she thought, feeling her heart contract as Tom's gaze stopped momentarily on her without expression, then moved away.

'Eve?'

Oliver looked concerned, puzzled, and she forced her smile back into place.

'How's everyone doing?' she said.

'Those who have their families with them are obviously coping better than the others.'

'Are…?' Eve swallowed hard. 'Are there many missing?'

'We don't know,' Oliver admitted. 'What with half the village being here, the other half at The Smugglers', and some people away at work… Chief Constable D'Ancey has put the number missing at around eighteen, but that's purely guesswork.'

'*Eighteen?*' Eve echoed in horror, and Oliver squeezed her hand.

'It's guesswork only, Eve. We'll know better when it's daylight, when the water starts to go down. Hopefully, nobody is lost at all, and people are just sheltering where they can.'

'Lizzie Chamberlain's looking a little better,' she observed, and Oliver nodded.

'She should do, considering the size of sedative I gave her. Amanda Lovelace is understandably in a bit of a state, but she point blank refuses to let me give her anything.'

And Tom was talking to her, Eve noticed. He was bending down towards Tassie's mother, then suddenly she saw Amanda's face light up, and she was gripping his hand tightly, and he was shaking his head, his cheeks darkening slightly, at whatever she'd said.

Could this mean Tassie was on her way? She prayed the girl was. She prayed, too, that Gertrude Stanbury had survived. The elderly school teacher was a determined, spunky woman, but she was crippled with arthritis, and though Tassie was agile enough to have reached the attic she couldn't see how Gertrude could possibly have managed to clamber up there.

'Is…is Tassie safe?' Eve said hesitantly as Tom passed her, and he paused, but he didn't look at her.

'Mitch has picked both her and Gertie Stanbury up. He's going to drop them on the playing fields, and the police will bring them here.'

Eve closed her eyes tightly.

'Thank you,' she whispered. 'Thank you.'

'Nick knows, doesn't he?'

Eve's eyes flew open. 'What?'

Tom caught her by the arm, and steered her none too gently back into the school office.

'Nick—you went to Nick, didn't you, when you decided you weren't going to have the baby?'

'No— I— No,' she faltered. 'I went up to Bude when I discovered I was pregnant. I had…I had it done there.'

'But Nick knows.'

Tom's face was tight with barely suppressed anger, and she wished she could lie, but there was no point.

'He knows I had an abortion,' she said. 'I didn't realise until quite recently that he knew—had guessed—but I caught an infection afterwards, so I had to go to him for antibiotics and he must have guessed then.'

'Which is why he thinks I'm scum,' Tom said. 'He thinks I walked out on you when you were pregnant, forced you into having the abortion.'

'Why would he think that?' she protested. 'Why would he even suspect you were the father?'

'Oh, give me credit for some intelligence,' Tom said, his voice harsh, bitter. 'You and I were an item that summer so he had to suspect it was me, didn't he?'

'Tom—'

'What else haven't you told me?' he said, talking right over her. 'What else don't I know?'

'You know everything now,' she said wretchedly. 'You're the only one who does. No one else. I told no one else.'

'Couldn't your parents have helped?' he demanded. 'I know they didn't have much money, but—'

'They didn't know either.'

He stared at her blankly.

'They didn't know? But—'

'Tom, you know what my parents were like,' she cried. 'My dad—he was a kind man, a generous man, but he disapproved of me even going out with you. He would have said I'd made my bed, and I had to lie in it, and my mum... She would have wanted to help, but this was twenty years ago, and her first thought would have been, What will the neighbours say?'

'So, you kept this from them,' he said, 'just as you kept it from me.'

'And I paid for it, Tom,' she said, her voice thick with unshed tears. 'Because I couldn't tell them, because they never knew they could have been grandparents, it got harder and harder for me to face them so I visited them less and less, so I lost my parents, too. I didn't just lose my baby, I lost my parents, too.'

'But you didn't have to,' he protested. 'Even twenty years ago, women had babies without being married, without their parents' approval.'

'Tom, I'd only just qualified as a nurse, and you know what the wages were like back then,' she said, willing him to understand. 'I thought of adoption, but what was I going to live on while I was pregnant, unable to work? I was twenty-two, Tom, and I was scared witless. I couldn't see any other way out.'

'If you didn't want it—'

'Don't...don't you *dare* say that to me,' she said, her voice breaking on a sob. 'Don't you *dare* say I didn't want my baby. I would have given anything to have kept that baby.'

'Except given birth to it.'

'I *loved* you, Tom,' she replied, feeling her heart splinter with absolute loneliness at the coldness in his voice. 'I loved you back in school even when you and your friends used to shout "Starchy Dwyer" after me in the corridor. And when I discovered I was pregnant, knew there was a part of you growing inside me, I wanted to keep your baby so badly, but I couldn't—I *couldn't*.'

'So you just...you just...'

'Took the easy way out,' she finished for him. 'That's what you're accusing me of, isn't it, taking the easy way out?'

'Perhaps not the easy way out,' he muttered, hot colour darkening his cheeks. 'Maybe that was the wrong thing to say.'

'You want to know how easy it is to have an abortion, Tom?' she said, her voice every bit as hard as his now. 'Then maybe I should tell you. Maybe I should tell you *exactly* how easy it is to have an abortion.'

'I know what the procedure involves,' he said, turning his back on her, and she came after him, and grabbed his arm.

'Maybe you do—medically,' she said, forcing him round to face her. 'But you don't know what it's like emotionally. You don't know what it's like to sit in a waiting room full of women where nobody makes eye contact, and nobody talks, because you all know why you're there, and you're all locked inside your own private little hell.'

'Eve, I don't want to hear this,' he said, pulling his arm free and walking away from her, but she followed him.

'And the nurses,' she continued, 'maybe it was my imagination, but I felt—I thought—that all I could see in their eyes were the unspoken words, "You should have known better. You should have been sensible, should have used a condom, or been on the Pill," and I wanted to yell at them that I had been on the Pill, that this wasn't supposed to have happened, but I didn't say anything because I knew...' Her lips trembled. 'I knew if I started yelling I would never stop.'

He turned to face her, his face white, taut. 'Look, if I've implied—'

'And all the time you're sitting in the waiting room you're thinking, you're thinking...' She choked down a sob. 'That you can still change your mind, you don't have to go through with this, you can still change my mind, but you know you won't because you've been through all the options in your head a thousand times, and you know there isn't anything else you can do.'

'Eve—please—I don't want to hear any more,' he said, his voice cold.

He clearly didn't, she realised as she met his gaze and saw no sympathy or compassion at all in his green eyes, only complete condemnation, and, as tears began to trickle down her cheeks, she felt as empty and as utterly alone as she had felt all those years ago.

'Maybe you don't want to know, Tom, but there's one thing you should know,' she said, wiping her face with a shaking hand. 'Afterwards, when it's done, and the doctor says you can leave, they tell you it's over, but it isn't over because what you don't know—what no one tells you—is that abortion doesn't end anything. It simply starts something else.'

'I don't know what you mean,' Tom said harshly, and Eve shook her head.

'I know you don't,' she said, 'because, you see, nobody warns you that from then on you'll live a lifetime of regret. Nobody tells you you'll discover that the world is full of babies and pregnant women, and every pregnant woman you see, every…every baby you see, will remind you of what you did— what you gave up.'

'Eve—'

'And it never goes away, Tom,' she said. 'Oh, gradually, you pick up the pieces, learn somehow to go on, but it can't ever go away because there are all these dates, you see. The day when he or she would have had their first birthday, the day they would have started school, and all…' She took a ragged breath. 'All the Christmases you never share with them.'

'Eve, I—'

'You implied I took the easy way out, Tom,' she said, catching his gaze, refusing to allow him to look away. 'Well, you tell me whether you think it's been easy for me.'

He opened his mouth to reply, but, before he could say anything, Hazel had appeared, her eyes shining.

'Eve, someone's just arrived I know you'll be delighted to see,' the practice manager declared.

Quickly Eve hurried out into the school hall and when Tom followed her he saw her glance around, expectant, hopeful, and then the hall door opened, and Tassie raced in. For a second Eve's face lit up with a blinding smile but, as she held out her arms, and Tassie raced straight past her towards her mother, Tom saw her smile slide slowly sideways. Slide—just for an instant—into an expression of hurt, and then into an accepting, rueful, wistful yearning that tugged at his heart.

Tassie wasn't simply a child Eve was trying to help. Tassie was the child Eve had never had, the child she had lost.

Not lost, a small voice reminded him. Didn't want, but the small voice held no conviction. In truth, it never had. It had been his own guilt which had made him stand coldly by while Eve had poured out all her anguish and suffering. His own guilt which had kept him aloof from her, because she had been right.

He wouldn't have wanted a child when he'd been twenty-four. All the plans he'd had then, his aims, his dreams… He would have seen a child as an encumbrance, something he had been saddled with, and what kind of life would that child have had, with him rejecting her or him, giving money perhaps but even then grudgingly? He would have been his father all over again, not in the violence—never in the violence—but in the resentment, the feeling of having been cheated out of the life he had wanted, dreamt of.

Savagely, he bit his lip. How could he have accused her of taking the easy way out? She'd taken the hardest decision any woman could ever make, taken it alone, had had to live with it alone, carrying the knowledge, and the pain, for twenty years, and what had he done? He'd watched impassively as she'd broken her heart all over again in telling him. He'd been wrong—so wrong—and somehow he had to tell her that, but how could he get her to listen to him after what he had said, what he'd accused her of?

'I don't believe it,' Gertrude Stanbury declared, as she walked towards him, leaning heavily on the arm of a young policeman. 'I wondered when the pilot said he'd been sent by a Dr Cornish, but I didn't believe it really could be you, not after all these years. It's good to see you again, lad.'

'It's good to see you, too, Miss Stanbury,' he managed to reply. 'I understand you and young Tassie have had quite an afternoon.'

The old lady chuckled.

'You could say that,' she said. 'In fact, I wouldn't be here at all if it hadn't been for the girl. I told her I'd never get up into the attic—that she was to save herself—but she refused to take no for an answer, and somehow, between the two of us, she got me up there.'

'Would you like something hot to drink, Miss Stanbury?' Eve asked as she joined them. 'We've tea—coffee—cocoa…'

'Cocoa,' Miss Stanbury said firmly, 'and a seat if one's available. The young man who winched me out of my house was most kind, and reassuring, but dangling above Penhally, held only by a harness and a stranger's arms, is not my idea of a fun time out.'

Eve laughed. Gently, she and Tom helped the elderly lady across the hall, but once Eve had settled Gertrude into a seat, she straightened up and there was no laughter in her face, only an unreadable blankness.

'I expect you'll be wanting to get back to the radio, Tom,' she said.

The finality in her voice was plain and he knew, as he watched her walk away to get Gertrude cocoa, that he had been dismissed as effectively as if she'd actually closed a door on him, and he deserved it. Twice in her life he had let her down. Twice he hadn't been there for her when it had really mattered, and this last time…

'Whatever it is, lad, I'm sure you'll sort it.'

He glanced down to see Gertrude staring up at him, her small face oddly understanding, and shook his head.

'I don't think I can this time, Miss Stanbury,' he said. 'I think this time I've screwed up big time.'

CHAPTER SIX

THE sun was shining. It was unbelievable, Eve thought as she
stared up into the cloudless blue sky, but the sun was actually
shining and as long as she kept looking up she could almost
believe that the devastating flood which had hit Penhally yesterday had never happened. Almost, but not quite.

'I suspected it might look pretty bad this morning,' Kate
murmured, 'but I never for one minute…'

The midwife's voice trailed away into silence and Eve could
understand her difficulty. Yesterday Penhally had been a
picture-perfect village, full of people going about their daily
business, but this morning the area around the harbour looked
as though some malevolent giant had taken a hammer and
smashed his way through the buildings, heaping boulders, trees,
telephone poles and dustbins onto roofs, and tearing up roads
and pavements in his relentless march onwards.

'I'm amazed the surgery wasn't touched, or any of our
homes, apart from poor Chloe and Oliver's,' Eve observed.
'They're going to stay with Lauren, aren't they, until their house
can be dried out?'

'*If* it can be dried out,' Kate said dubiously. 'Tom says all the
houses can be made habitable again but when you look at
this…I know the Lanson's flowing within its banks again, and
somehow the Harbour Bridge is still intact, but one of Tom's

men told me all of the houses have at least three feet of water and mud in them.'

'I suppose Tom's the expert,' Eve said uncertainly, though she had to admit she couldn't see how anyone could ever live in Bridge Street or Gull Close again either.

'I'm just so glad Tom is here,' Kate continued. 'I wouldn't have a clue about how to begin searching for the people who are missing, would you?'

Eve shook her head as she glanced over to where Tom was deep in conversation with Nick, Chief Constable D'Ancey and a group of men dressed in coveralls emblazoned with the Deltaron insignia. It wasn't a task she would have liked and, judging by the expression on Nick's face, Tom's suggestions weren't meeting with his approval, whereas Tom…

She shifted her gaze quickly towards some of the shopkeepers who were standing in dazed huddles outside their ruined shops. She didn't know what Tom was thinking, didn't want to be anywhere near him for fear he would look at her with the same condemnation and disgust as he had done yesterday.

'How's Stephanie Richards?' she asked, deliberately changing the subject.

'She and her son are doing very well,' Kate replied, 'though goodness knows where they're going to stay when they're discharged from hospital.'

'Oliver said the owners of the Penhally Paradise Caravan Park have offered some of their caravans as temporary accommodation for people who can't go back to their homes,' Eve observed. 'And Tony has offered the use of some of the bedrooms at Smugglers' Inn.'

'Did you hear he was still giving out orders while they were carrying him out to the helicopter?' The midwife shook her head. 'The man was having a heart attack, for God's sake, and yet he was still giving out orders.'

Eve laughed. 'One of a kind, Tony.'

'So is Tom.'

Kate's gaze was fixed on her, and Eve couldn't meet the midwife's eyes.

'He's certainly a good organiser,' she said noncommittally, and Kate sighed.

'Eve, whatever happened in the past, let it go. You can't alter it—change it—so let it go.'

'What has Nick been say—?'

'This has nothing to do with Nick,' Kate interrupted as Eve's eyes shot to hers in alarm, 'this is just me talking to you, one woman to another. We've all made mistakes—me, more than most—but you have to forgive yourself your mistakes or they will simply corrode your present and your future.'

Which was easy for Kate to say, Eve thought as her gaze went back to Tom, but she couldn't forgive herself. She had learned to live with what she'd done, but she had never forgiven herself and she never would. Tom hadn't resurrected the old pain. He had simply ripped off the unhealed scab, exposing the old wound for the ugliness it was.

'Which of you two lovelies is Eve Dwyer?'

A tall man, with flaming red hair and a bushy beard, was gazing at them quizzically, and Eve managed a smile.

'I'm Eve Dwyer.'

The man's eyebrows rose.

'Do I know you?' he asked. 'Your voice sounds strangely familiar.'

She recognised his voice, too. It was Mad Mitch or, to be more accurate, Michael Flannery, the pilot from the radio last night.

'I'm the woman Tom found in the men-only changing room,' she said before she could stop herself, and the pilot threw back his head, and laughed.

'Pleased to meet you in the flesh, so to speak,' he said. 'Tom would like a word.'

'With me?' Eve said faintly.

'With you.' The pilot nodded. 'He has a suggestion to make, and your boss isn't very happy about it.'

Kate's eyes gleamed.

'Now, this I want to hear,' she said, and carefully the midwife followed Eve over the rubble-strewn pavement towards where Tom was standing.

'So, what you're basically saying is, according to your engineer, most of the shops and houses should be habitable once the water and silt have been pumped out, but the Anchor Hotel is a writeoff?' they heard Chief Constable D'Ancey declare.

'I'm afraid so,' Tom replied. 'For the moment I'd recommend you erect scaffolding to ensure no more of it comes down, but after that I'd say you're pretty well definitely looking at a demolition job.'

'When are people going to be allowed back into their homes to collect their personal possessions?' Nick demanded. 'The police can't watch every house, and people are becoming understandably twitchy about their valuables.'

'They'll become considerably twitchier if they're electrocuted,' Tom said dryly. 'The electricity company isn't sure all power has been disconnected to the village, and until they are nobody enters any house apart from me and my men.'

'Yes, but—'

'Nick, if you want to be useful, go and open up the surgery,' Tom interrupted. 'With all this polluted water lying about I should imagine you'll be inundated with people requiring tetanus injections.'

'I don't take orders—'

'I've the press at my heels wanting to come into Penhally to take photographs,' Chief Constable D'Ancey declared, cutting across Nick who shot him a fulsome look. 'They're also very keen to do an interview with you.'

'I've more important things to do than give interviews,' Tom said tightly, 'and neither do I want photographers scrambling over the rubble in search of a story. Keep them out.'

Eve saw Nick's lip curl as the chief constable hurried off to forestall the members of the press. So, too, she noticed, had Tom, and quickly she cleared her throat.

'Mitch said you had a suggestion to make to me?' she said, and Tom nodded.

'At the moment, I'm the only medic on the rescue team,' he declared. 'We have spare medi-bags but they're no use without someone who knows how to use the contents, and I wondered if you'd like to help.'

'And *I* have said,' Nick exclaimed, 'if another medic is required then Oliver or I will volunteer. Eve is not a qualified rescue worker, or a doctor.'

'But she's a fully qualified nurse, and she's small, and there may be areas that only someone small will be able to get into,' Tom said, his voice calm but with an unmistakable hint of steel beneath it. 'And I would like Eve to help, if she's willing.'

'Eve is a member of my staff, and I will not agree to this,' Nick retorted.

'I don't think it's a question of whether you agree or not,' Tom began. 'Eve—'

'Can make up her own mind, thank you very much,' she interrupted, 'so would the two of you both park your testosterone to one side for the moment, and concentrate on what's really important?'

Tom's jaw dropped, Mitch Flannery smothered a wry chuckle, and Nick looked absolutely furious, but Kate laughed.

'Well said, Eve,' she declared. 'Nick, it's Eve's decision,' she continued quickly as the senior partner opened his mouth, clearly intending to continue the argument. 'If she wants to volunteer then surely it's her choice, not yours.'

Eve didn't have the faintest idea of what she might be volunteering for but she didn't care. All that mattered to her was that Tom had specifically asked for her. She hadn't expected him to—was amazed that he had—and if he was holding out any kind of olive branch she had no intention of rejecting it.

'I want to help,' she said firmly, and saw Tom's lips curve into a hesitant smile, a smile she returned equally tentatively.

'I am Eve's boss,' Nick declared angrily, 'and I still don't think—'

'I know you don't, Nick,' Kate interrupted, 'but right now we have a surgery to open.'

And, with a backward wink at Eve, the midwife towed a clearly reluctant Nick away leaving Eve standing awkwardly beside Tom and Mitch Flannery.

'Do we know how many people we're looking for?' she asked.

'Thankfully only three people still haven't been accounted for,' Tom replied. 'Reverend Kenner, Audrey Baxter and Sophie Banks.'

'Sophie?' Eve gasped. 'But—'

'She should have been at school.' Tom nodded. 'Her mother thought she was, and so she didn't worry about her, thinking she was safe with the other kids, and the school weren't concerned because they thought Sophie had been told to take the day off after she'd been to the surgery to see you.'

'And Reverend Kenner and Audrey Baxter?' Eve said.

'A neighbour saw Mrs Baxter leaving her house just before the river broke its banks,' Mitch Flannery declared. 'Reverend Kenner appeared to be trying to persuade her to go back into her house but, since then, there's been no sign of either of them.'

'Mitch, do we have any protective coveralls and thermals that would fit Eve?' Tom said, his gaze taking in her jeans, sweater and sturdy boots.

'I doubt we've anything small enough,' the pilot said dubiously. 'Gregory's our shortest man, but even he's a good four inches taller than this lass.'

Gregory was.

'If you laugh at me, you're a dead man,' Eve warned a little later, when Mitch led her back to Tom and she saw his lips twitch as his gaze took in her rolled-up sleeves and trouser legs.

'Would I laugh?' he protested, and she nodded.

'Without a second's thought,' she said, and heard Mitch guffaw.

'Keeper, Tom,' the pilot observed. 'Trust me, this one's a keeper.'

'A keeper of what?' Eve said in confusion but, for an answer, Tom placed a string round her neck with a whistle at the end.

'Blow once on this if you spot somebody alive, and blow twice if you see a body. It's standard rescue procedure,' he continued as she stared down at the whistle.

'Right,' she said, swallowing hard, and praying she would only have to blow once on the whistle as Tom called for his men's attention.

'Does everyone have a thermal imaging camera?' he asked and, when his question was greeted with a series of nods, he added, 'OK, Mitch, I want you and your men to survey Bridge Street. Gregory, you and your team will do Gull Close, Frank, you take Harbour Road. I'll do Fisherman's Row, and if anyone spots any signs of life, it's the usual drill.'

Obediently, the men split themselves into four groups but, as Tom began to move off, Eve tentatively put her hand on his arm.

'Why, Tom?'

To her relief he didn't pretend to misunderstand her.

'Because—as I said—you're a qualified nurse, and small, and because…' He lifted his shoulders awkwardly. 'Yesterday, I said some totally unforgivable things to you, and apologising… You know I'm not good with words. If you want cutting and cruel, then I was taught by the best, but saying I'm sorry…'

'You don't have to say anything,' she said softly, and saw a muscle clench in his cheek.

'I do, but now's not the time to discuss it. I just wanted you to know…' He bit his lip. 'Asking for you, I hoped maybe you might see…'

'An olive branch?' she said. 'Seen, and accepted, Tom. Now, tell me how these thermal imaging cameras work.'

For a second he gazed at her silently, then he smiled.

'You're something else, Eve Dwyer.'

'Lippy, irritating, argumentative—yeah, I know,' she said lightly, unnerved by the intensity of his gaze, 'and you still haven't told me what a thermal imaging camera does.'

His smile widened.

'They detect and produce images of radiation, and since infrared radiation is emitted by all objects based on their temperatures, warm objects stand out well against cool backgrounds so humans and other warm-blooded animals become easily visible whether it's day or night.'

'Clever,' she said with admiration.

'Very.' He nodded, then his smile faded. 'Of course they can only pick up images of living things.'

'You think…' She swallowed. 'You think they might all be dead?'

'I think we have to be prepared for that given the silence.'

'The silence?' she repeated.

'Eve, if you were trapped, what would you be doing?'

'I'd be… Oh, I see,' she said with dawning comprehension. 'I'd be yelling my head off to attract attention, but nobody's yelling.'

'Exactly.'

She hoped he was wrong. She hoped it even more as the morning crept by with a painstaking slowness she found frustrating as Tom and his men scanned every square foot of rubble in Fisherman's Row with their cameras, and then checked and double-checked the results with a sound detector and fibreoptic probe.

'You thought a rescue operation would be a lot more exciting,' he observed with a slight smile, correctly reading her mind when he ordered his men to take a break. 'With people rushing from place to place.'

She coloured. 'I suppose so.'

'Sometimes it's like that,' he admitted. 'If a lot of people are trapped you can come upon them quite quickly, but when it's just three we have to take it slowly in case we miss something, plus there are a lot of potential hazards. Standing water can be electrically charged from underground or downed power lines, and we don't know how much untreated raw sewage there is in the water, not to mention the biohazards of dead animals, rotting food and liquid petroleum gases.'

She shivered as she stared up at the water line which showed how high the floodwater had reached in Fisherman's Row, and she knew it had been even higher in Bridge Street and Gull Close.

'I don't know how you can do this over and over again.'

'Somebody has to,' Tom observed.

'I know, but…'

She shivered again and, as though on cue, one of Tom's men appeared carrying a tray of steaming white polystyrene cups.

'What's this?' she asked, screwing up her nose after she'd taken a sip.

'Hot water, with three sugars,' the man replied, and she grimaced.

'I'd rather have a coffee,' she observed, and Tom grinned.

'Wouldn't we all, but both coffee and tea have caffeine in them, and that's a no-no because caffeine dehydrates you, and as we're all dehydrating rather a lot because we're sweating we don't want to add to it.'

'I'd still rather have a coffee,' she said with feeling as she sipped the hot water. 'Do you suppose…?' She came to a halt, seeing a dog appear at the top of Fisherman's Row. 'Tom, isn't that Foxy—Audrey's dog?'

He nodded as his eyes followed hers.

'Which would suggest Audrey is somewhere nearby. Dogs have a much more highly developed sense of smell than we do, and… Oh, hell.'

'What?' Eve said, in confusion, seeing Tom throw down his polystyrene cup, his face grim.

'He's pawing at the rubble by the Anchor Hotel. I think we may have found Audrey.'

They'd also found Reverend Kenner, too.

'My guess is the lady lost her footing when the river burst its banks,' Mitch declared. 'The reverend was holding her round the waist, so I'd say he was trying to keep her head above water, and then the outer wall of the hotel came down on them.'

Foxy was howling at the top of his lungs, desperately trying to get to his mistress, and Eve turned away quickly, not wanting anyone to see the tears that had filled her eyes at the sight of the two covered bodies lying on stretchers, but an arm came round her shoulders instantly.

'I shouldn't have asked you to do this,' Tom murmured. 'I'll get Mitch to take you back to the surgery.'

'No,' Eve insisted, wiping her sleeve across her eyes. 'Sophie is still missing so I'm not giving up. I just need…' Her voice became suspended, and she took a ragged breath. 'Why, Tom? Daniel Kenner… He was such a good man, such a kind man, and now Rachel has no father, her child will have no grandfather, and Audrey… Yes, she was a gossip, but to die like that… Why do some people live, and some people die, Tom?'

'An old Buddhist monk once told me that for some people it's simply their time,' Tom said, drawing her closer.

'It isn't for everyone—not always,' she said with difficulty, and she knew he understood what she meant because she felt his chin come to rest on the top of her head.

'Sufficient unto the day, Eve,' he said, his voice as uneven as hers. 'Sometimes that's all any of us can hold on to.'

'Tom, I…' She looked up at him, begging him to believe her, to understand. 'I didn't want to do it. Our baby. I truly didn't want to do it.'

'I know,' he said, his voice thick. Gently, he smoothed her hair back from her face with his fingers. 'Eve…' A loud blast from a whistle rent the air, and he turned towards it immediately. 'Someone's found a live one.'

He and Mitch were off and running before Eve could say anything, and by the time she'd caught up with them near the top of Bridge Street they were already deep in conversation with the man Tom had called Gregory.

'Is it Sophie?' she asked breathlessly as she stumbled to a halt beside them.

'Yes.'

Something about Tom's tone made her heart clutch.

'But I thought— One blast of the whistle—doesn't that mean she's alive?' she said.

'She is, but she's in big trouble,' Tom replied.

'I have glucagon in here,' Eve said, opening the medi-bag that Mitch had given her. 'If her blood-sugar levels are too low, and she's become hypoglycaemic—'

'She had the presence of mind to keep taking her glucagon, at least at the beginning,' Tom interrupted, 'but she was spending her day off school hiding out in one of the concrete sheds at the back of Bridge Street. That's why it's taken us so long to find her because Mitch and his men were concentrating on scanning the houses first.'

'And?' Eve demanded, wishing he would get to the point.

'When the shed flooded, part of it came down trapping Sophie by her leg.'

And not just trapping her by the leg, Eve realised when she followed the men down the narrow alley way to get to the back of the houses in Bridge Street. The piece of concrete had also come down at a right angle so all that was visible of the teenager was her head and upper body, and only somebody small would have any chance of being able to crawl close enough to her to assess her medical condition.

'It will have to be me, won't it?' Eve declared, cutting right across Mitch and Tom as they discussed how Tom might reach the girl. 'Look, you said one of the reasons you wanted me was because I'm a fully qualified nurse, and I'm small,' she continued, seeing Tom's eyebrows snap down, 'so it has to be me, doesn't it?'

'But if the rest of the shed comes down…' Tom said, indecision plain on his face.

'Tom, the longer we stand here debating this, the more likely it is that it *will* come down,' she said.

'She's right, Tom,' Mitch declared, and Eve saw Tom's eyebrows knit together still further.

'OK,' he said with clear reluctance, 'but if the shed begins to move I want your promise you'll get out of there.'

'I promise,' Eve said.

'Show me your hands.'

'What?'

'Eve, I know you've got your fingers crossed behind your back,' he declared, 'so let me see your hands when you promise.'

'OK—OK—I promise, no fingers crossed, and now can we get on with this?' she exclaimed, but she didn't feel anything like as confident when she began crawling under the concrete to get to the teenager.

Not only was the space a lot smaller than it looked, the water was filthy, and when she felt something brush against her leg and realised it was a dead rat, it took all of her self-control not to scuttle back out and run screaming from the building.

'Are you OK?' Tom called when she let out a gasp and Eve gritted her teeth until they hurt.

'Fine,' she said, but she felt even less fine after she'd examined the teenager.

Sophie was barely conscious and didn't even seem to be aware she was there and with a temperature of 91°F, and a GCS of 3-3-4, the girl was very ill indeed.

'I think she must be losing a lot of blood from her leg,' Eve said, and saw Tom shake his head.

'I think she's losing some, but not enough to cause those Glasgow coma scale results,' he replied. 'My guess is the main problem is she's been lying in freezing water for the past twenty-one hours.'

'A thermic lance,' Mitch declared. 'It's the only way, Tom.'

'What's a thermic lance?' Eve asked, glancing from Mitch to Tom, and it was Tom who answered.

'Basically, it's a long iron tube packed with a mixture of iron and aluminum rods. We feed oxygen through the tube, and when it's lit, it produces an intense flame that can cut through steel and concrete, but…'

'But?' Eve prompted.

'I don't know whether it will be able to cut through fast enough,' Tom said, 'and if it does whether the two halves will split away from her leg or impact down on her.'

'Tom, if we don't do something soon I think the question of what way the concrete might fall will be academic,' Eve replied. 'Her temperature's falling all the time.'

'OK, we use the thermic lance,' he said. 'Try to keep her awake, Eve. Sing to her—talk to her—but somehow keep her awake.'

It was easier said than done, Eve thought as Tom and Mitch began using the thermic lance to cut through the concrete that was pinning Sophie to the floor. Never had time seemed to pass so slowly as she crouched beneath the concrete, talking about everything and nothing while Sophie became increasingly unresponsive.

'Tom, her pulse ox is 80, her temperature's now 88, and she's not shivering any more,' Eve reported.

Because Sophie was developing hypothermia.

Neither she nor Tom said it, but they both knew it, and if Sophie's temperature continued to fall she'd start developing cardiac arrhythmias, then her heart would begin to fibrillate, and if her temperature slipped below 82°F there would be no way back for her.

'Fifteen minutes,' Tom replied in answer to Eve's unspoken question. 'We should be through the concrete in fifteen minutes.'

'Tom, I don't think she's going to hold on for fifteen minutes,' Eve said, and he let out a colourful oath.

'I know,' he exclaimed, 'but my only other alternative is to amputate her leg, and she's a kid, Eve, just a kid.'

But Sophie was going to die if she stayed in this water for much longer, Eve thought, and her feelings must have been all too apparent, because Tom thrust a dirt-grimed hand through his hair.

'Five minutes, Eve. Five minutes, and if we're no further forward, we amputate.'

She nodded and, as the seconds ticked by, she prayed as she had never prayed before. Prayed that the concrete would split in two soon. Prayed that Sophie would survive because there was no guarantee, no matter what they did, that she would. The girl was virtually comatose now, and her lips were beginning to turn blue which was a sure sign of cyanosis.

'It's moving, Tom,' Mitch shouted. 'The bloody thing's finally moving!'

Without a word Tom immediately crawled as far under the concrete as he could get, and Eve knew why. If the concrete fell on them he intended taking the full brunt of the fall, and her heart stopped for a second at the thought of him being crushed, of him dying in front of her eyes, and then—miraculously—

she saw a rush of bubbles in the water and Sophie sagged in her arms.

'She's free—I think she's free,' she declared, holding onto the girl for all she was worth, and Tom scrambled to his feet and splashed through the water towards her.

'Mitch, where's your chopper?' he demanded as he gripped Sophie under the armpits.

'The playing fields,' the pilot replied.

'Crank it up. This girl needs a hospital, and fast.'

Mitch couldn't have been faster. Within a short time he had Sophie and Tom airborne and in less than half an hour the girl was being admitted to St Piran's Hospital.

'Tom and his men—they're quite something, aren't they?' Lauren said when Eve told her about it later. 'It's not a job I'd like to do, but if I was ever in trouble I'd want the men from Deltaron coming over the horizon.'

And especially Tom, Eve thought as she helped the physiotherapist ensure that those who had sheltered in the school hall last night, and those who had taken refuge in The Smugglers', had all been allocated temporary accommodation in order to leave the hall free for Tom's men. He must have been exhausted when Mitch brought him back to Penhally but he'd stopped only long enough to tell them that the A and E consultant was hopeful Sophie would make a complete recovery and then he'd gone back out onto the streets with his men.

'I just wish I could find somewhere other than Harbour View for Miss Stanbury to stay in temporarily,' Lauren continued. 'There's no room left at The Smugglers', and I've put my foot down over a caravan, but she's such an independent woman, and staying in the nursing-home even for a short time… The last thing I want is her losing confidence in her ability to cope.'

'Who's losing confidence?'

Eve turned quickly at the familiar voice, and try as she may she couldn't prevent her heart lifting when she saw Tom smiling down at her.

'It's Miss Stanbury,' Lauren said, and after she'd explained the situation Tom shook his head.

'Not a nursing-home, not for Gertie. She can stay in my father's house in Trelissa Road. It's fully furnished, so she'll be quite snug and comfortable until her own home dries out.'

'Are you sure?' Lauren declared. 'I mean, lovely lady though Miss Stanbury is, I don't know what she would be like to share a house with and you'll be staying in your father's house yourself, won't you, now that the Anchor Hotel is uninhabitable?'

'Actually I won't,' he replied. 'I've made other arrangements.'

'Really?' Lauren exclaimed and, when Tom nodded, she beamed. 'Then you must come and tell her about your kind offer. She'll be so grateful.'

'Can't you tell her?' he said, already beginning to back awkwardly towards the school-hall door. 'I'm a bit tired—thought I might just head off, grab some sleep.'

He was out of the hall before Lauren could say anything else, and Eve laughed when she caught up with him.

'You fraud,' she declared. 'You just don't like people thanking you, do you?'

To her surprise, a faint wash of colour appeared on his cheeks.

'Not really, no.'

'And what are these other arrangements you've made?' she demanded, and saw Tom give a shamefaced grin.

'None, to be honest, but I can think of nothing I'd like less than staying in my father's old house, plus Gertie did me a good turn in the past and I figure it's time I repaid the debt. I can sleep in the hall with my men. It's no big deal, Eve,' he continued as she began to protest. 'I'll be perfectly fine.'

'I'm sure you will but not when there's an alternative,' she said firmly. 'My house has two bedrooms and you're more than welcome to use one of them. If…if you want to, that is,' she added, feeling her cheeks heat up when he stared at her in obvious surprise.

'I'd love to,' he said, 'but have you considered what people might say?'

'Tom, half of Penhally is covered in mud, silt and boulders. Half of the population are either sleeping with friends, or in a caravan, or at The Smugglers'. If anyone has the time or the energy to check up on where you're staying, then they need to get a life.'

He laughed.

'Well, if you're sure?'

'I'm sure,' she said. 'I can't offer you much to eat, but…' Her gaze took in his dirt-smeared face and hair, and bloodshot and weary eyes. 'I can offer you a bath.'

'You can heat water?' he said, his eyes lighting up, and she nodded.

'My dad installed a generator years back. He said he didn't much care if he couldn't watch TV when we had a power cut, but he was damned if he was going to sit in the dark, unable to have a bath.' She took a deep breath. 'I only have one condition to make.'

Tom grinned. 'Don't use all the hot water?'

She smiled. 'OK, two conditions. Don't use all the hot water, and…' Her smile faded. 'We don't talk about…about the baby. I know you want to,' she added quickly, seeing a flash of pain in his eyes, 'and I know we have to but, please, not tonight.'

He looked at her for a long moment, then smiled slightly crookedly.

'OK, not tonight,' he said.

'How do you feel now?' Eve asked when Tom joined her some time later in her small sitting room.

'A lot cleaner, that's for sure,' he said. 'I used some of your shampoo—I hope that was OK. Unfortunately you don't seem to have a razor so I couldn't get rid of this,' he added, rubbing his hand over the stubble on his chin, 'which means you'll have to put up with me looking scruffy.'

Or downright sexy, she thought, and stamped on the thought quickly as she put another log on the fire.

'Lauren and Chloe organised a clothes and general toiletries collection today for the people who can't get back into their homes,' she said. 'I should have thought to ask them to make up a bag for you, but I'm afraid I forgot you must have lost everything in the Anchor.'

'It doesn't matter,' he said dismissively. 'I've my wallet and my car keys. Everything else can be replaced.' He looked round awkwardly. 'Is there anything I can do—something to help?'

Aside from trying not to look quite so big, or so very immediate? she thought, but she didn't say that.

'Not really,' she said instead. 'I thought I would just heat up some soup, put it into a couple of mugs, and we could have it in here. It's warmer by the fire than in the kitchen.'

'Sounds good to me.' He nodded. 'Has Rachel Kenner been told about her father?'

'Nick went to see her this afternoon. As you can imagine…' Eve shook her head. 'It wasn't very pleasant, but Rachel's aunt and uncle have come over from Plymouth to stay with her. Audrey had no immediate family, but she had a sister who lives in Devon and we're trying to trace her.'

He sat down on the sofa and let his head fall back against it. 'God, but I'm tired.'

He looked tired. He also looked rumpled, and sloppy, and more attractive than any man had any right to be, and she put another log on the fire even though it didn't need it.

'When do you think they'll be able to restore the electricity to the village?' she asked.

'Perhaps tomorrow. Then we can send in the fire brigade to begin draining the houses, and my work will be done.'

And I'll leave.

He hadn't said the words, he didn't need to, and of course he would leave. He was only still here in Penhally because of the flood so it had been stupid of her heart to dip at his words but she couldn't deny it had dipped.

'Eve?'

He was gazing at her questioningly, and she forced herself to smile.

'I'll get the soup,' she said, but when she went into the kitchen she leant against the table and closed her eyes.

How had he managed to slip so easily back into her life? She'd always sworn she'd never let him get close to her again and yet, within the space of a few short days, it was almost as though he'd never been away, but he was going to leave again as he'd done before, and she was going to be alone again as she had been before.

Which was how it had to be, she told herself. Yes, she felt the old attraction—he had been right about that—but there was too much hurt and pain between them now and, even if he could eventually forgive her for what she had done, he had his life, and she had hers, and their time was past.

Except it wasn't that easy, she realised, when she went back into the sitting room with their soup and she found him fast asleep on the sofa.

Twenty years. It had been twenty years since they'd last met, and yet she only had to see him like this, his face so tired in the firelight, his hair still damp from his bath, his eyelashes dark against his skin, and she wanted him all over again. Wanted to go to him, to wrap her arms around him, to have him hold her as he used to.

You can't go back, Eve, her heart whispered, and yet before she could stop herself she had carefully put the soup down on the mantelpiece, and just as carefully stretched out her hand, meaning only to smooth his hair back from his forehead, but he was a light sleeper and his eyes flew open with a start.

'I'm sorry,' she said awkwardly, backing up a step. 'I didn't mean to wake you.'

'It's just as well you did,' he said ruefully. 'I never could fall asleep in a chair without waking up with an infernal crick in my neck.'

'Snap.' She laughed as she handed him a mug of soup, but to her surprise he didn't join in her laughter.

Instead, he stared down at his soup, then up at her.

'I'm thinking of resigning from Deltaron, Eve. Maybe going into general practice.'

Her mouth fell open, then she shook her head.

'Tom, you'd be bored witless in under a week,' she protested. 'You're used to immediacy, constant change. I know you said you were worried you were ceasing to care but, believe me, GP work is not for you.'

'Perhaps not,' he murmured, his face all dark planes and shadows in the firelight. 'But... I used to get such a buzz from the danger, Eve, from pitting myself against the elements—fire, flood, earthquake—and yet now... All the time I'm thinking, What if I get it wrong, make a mistake, miscalculate?'

'You haven't yet.'

His face darkened still further.

'I have.'

His voice was so low she barely heard him, and for a second she hesitated then she sat down on the sofa beside him.

'What happened, Tom?'

She didn't think he was going to answer, then he put his soup down on the floor beside him and gripped his knees.

'We were sent to India last year to help out after a very bad earthquake. The village we were assigned to had been pretty well flattened, but one house was still standing, and we could hear people calling for help from inside it. I knew…' Tom took in an uneven breath. 'I knew the house was unstable, that it could go at any minute, but I could hear kids crying so I took the gamble it would hold.'

She reached out and laced one of her hands with his, and held it tightly.

'Go on,' she said.

'Charlie Dobbs, the other medic on the team, and I went in,' he continued with an effort. 'We'd just reached the kids—I had actually caught hold of one of their hands—and the house collapsed. I was pulled out alive, but Charlie, the people, the kids, they were all killed.'

'It wasn't your fault, Tom,' she said softly. 'You were trying to give them a chance, and Charlie… He would have known the risks, just as you did.'

'That's what the head of Deltaron said,' he declared, his eyes desolate, 'but I keep thinking if I'd done it differently, maybe tried to shore up the house, maybe waited…'

'You did what you thought was right at the time, Tom,' she said, hating to see the torment in his eyes. 'That's all anybody can do.'

'I went to Charlie's funeral,' he continued as though she hadn't spoken. 'Deltaron flew his body back to the States, so I went to his funeral and there was nobody there but me and the minister. He had no brothers or sisters, and his parents were both dead, so it was just me and the minister standing at the graveside, and I thought…' He swallowed. 'I thought, One day that's going to be me.'

'No, it won't,' she insisted, but he shook his head.

'It will, Eve. I've given my whole life to the company, just as Charlie did, so one day I'll be buried with no one there to mourn me, nobody who cares enough about me to come and say goodbye.'

'I'll come, Tom,' she said, her lip trembling. 'You wouldn't be alone. I'd come.'

'But you wouldn't know, Eve,' he said, his eyes meeting hers, dark and empty. 'You'd be here in Penhally, and I could be anywhere in the world.'

'Tom—'

'Eve, there's something I have to tell you,' he interrupted. 'Something I want you to know. Do you remember when I said I had two reasons for coming back to Penhally? Well, the other reason…' He came to a halt with a muttered oath as his mobile phone began to ring, and impatiently he pulled it from his pocket, checked the caller ID, then punched the answer button. 'Mitch, this had better be important,' he said.

It clearly was, Eve thought as she watched the frown lines on Tom's forehead deepen at whatever the pilot was saying, and when the call was over Tom immediately got to his feet.

'Bad news?' she said uncertainly.

'They've found a fractured gas main in Gull Close,' he replied. 'I have to go.'

'But you're exhausted,' she protested, 'and you're not an engineer. Can't somebody else deal with it?'

'I'm the boss, Eve, so I have to be there. Don't wait up for me. I don't know how long I'm going to be.'

'Right,' she said, then added quickly before she could stop herself, 'Be careful.'

'I fully intend to,' he said with a small smile, 'because we have a conversation to finish, and I intend finishing it.'

And, to her surprise, he bent down and kissed her lightly on the forehead, then strode out of her sitting room, leaving her gazing open-mouthed after him.

CHAPTER SEVEN

THE WAITING room was crammed to overflowing with press people, and each and every one of them seemed to be armed with a camera, a notebook and an apparently unending supply of stupid questions.

'I wonder how long it's going to be before Nick hits someone,' Dragan murmured as he and Eve stood outside in the surgery corridor watching Tom, Nick, and Chief Constable D'Ancey field questions.

'I should imagine just until one of those reporters asks him—yet again—whether he's sure there's only been two fatalities,' Eve said dryly.

'Or maybe until someone asks him for yet another photograph of him and Tom shaking hands,' Dragan declared, and Eve let out a small choke of laughter.

'Yup, I reckon that would probably do it.'

'Ghouls,' Dragan said with distaste. 'The whole pack of them are nothing but ghouls. The paparazzi came out in droves when they found out about Melinda and me, but this...' He shook his head. 'I don't know how Tom keeps his temper when you consider how many of these press conferences he must have taken part in.'

'I suppose because he has to,' Eve murmured, glancing back into the waiting room and seeing Tom wearily rotate his shoulders, his face a carefully arranged expressionless mask. 'I think Tom has learned to do a lot of things because he has to.'

Including having to accept he wasn't God, she thought sadly, with all the attendant heartbreak that knowledge could bring.

'Looks like Nick's just reached breaking point,' Dragan said when the senior partner suddenly stood up, his face dark and stormy. 'Yup, he's reached it, and I think he's actually passed it.'

The senior partner had. With an angry nod at Chief Constable D'Ancey, Nick strode out of the waiting room without a backward glance and, when he went into his consulting room, he slammed the door so hard it shuddered.

'It doesn't look as though Nick has enjoyed his encounter with the members of the press, does it?' Kate said, her eyes dancing as she joined them.

'Perhaps it will teach him to have a little more sympathy for Tom in future,' Eve replied before she could stop herself, and the midwife laughed.

'We can but hope,' she said. 'Do you think we might be able to get on with afternoon surgery soon?' she continued as the press began to file out of the waiting room. 'I know the press is entitled to a story, but we've told them all we know, and what we need now is to try to get back to some sort of normality, and that means seeing patients.'

'I couldn't agree more,' Dragan replied, 'and in that spirit I'll be in my consulting room if anyone wants me.'

'And I'll be in my examination room,' Kate declared as Dragan disappeared, 'hoping at least some of my mums-to-be manage to make it down for their prenatal check-ups.'

'Is the embargo on evening home visits still in place?' Eve asked, and Kate sighed.

'Nick is adamant that unless it's an emergency none of us are to be out after dark, and he's even more against it since Lauren took a tumble yesterday. I know it makes sense,' Kate continued. 'Some of the pavements and roads in Penhally are lethal, but I have quite a few my mums-to-be who can't come in during the day because they're at work.'

'Do you think…?' Eve began, then stopped. Chloe and Oliver were walking down the corridor towards them and it was obvious from the woman's stricken countenance that something was badly wrong. 'Chloe, are you all right?'

'She insisted I take her down to Fisherman's Row this morning,' Oliver replied, 'and she's a bit upset by what she saw.'

'Chloe, your home can be repaired,' Eve said quickly. 'Tom said once all the mud and silt have been pumped out—'

'It's not the house,' Chloe interrupted. 'That's just bricks and mortar, but Cyclops and Pirate… Eve, there's no sign of them, anywhere.'

'Cats have nine lives, babe, you know that,' her fiancé said, putting his arm around her and giving her a hug. 'They're probably just hiding out some place, too scared to come home.'

'Truly?' Chloe said, and, when Oliver nodded, she gave a wobbly smile. 'You think I'm being stupid, don't you?'

'Babe, you could never be stupid,' he said gently. 'They'll be fine. I know they will.'

But he wasn't, Eve knew, as Chloe and Kate hurried away to start their afternoon clinic, and she knew why. The water level in Oliver and Chloe's home must have reached nine feet at the flood's height, and neither Cyclops nor Pirate were robust cats.

'What's the matter with Chloe?' Tom asked as he joined them. 'She looks as though she's lost a pound and found a penny.'

'It's her cats,' Eve replied and, after she'd explained, Tom frowned.

'So, Cyclops is a ginger cat and only has one eye, and Pirate is white with a black patch over one eye. OK, I'll ask my men to keep a special watch out for them.'

'Yeah, right,' Oliver muttered, but Tom heard him.

'Oliver, I know your opinion of me is about as low as it can be,' he said without heat, 'but when I make a promise I keep it.'

'Right,' Oliver said, his cheeks darkening slightly. 'Sorry,' he added, but as Tom turned to go, the junior doctor held out his hand to stay him. 'Look, I truly am sorry, Tom, and not just for the cats. On the night of the flood, I said some pretty appalling things to you—'

'Forget it,' Tom interrupted.

'Yes, but—'

'Forget it,' Tom repeated. 'We were all a bit fraught that night, and if someone I loved had been missing I would have behaved exactly as you did.'

'Yes, well…' Oliver thrust his fingers through his hair awkwardly. 'It's good of you to say so, and considerably more than I deserve. If your men do find the cats, and they're dead, could you tell me first? I don't want Chloe to see them looking… messed up. She…' His shoulders lifted helplessly. 'They mean so much to her, you see.'

'Not a problem,' Tom replied but, after Oliver had gone, Eve folded her arms across her chest and shook her head at him.

'He owes you a much bigger apology than that,' she said, and saw one corner of Tom's mouth lift.

'Eve, people say things in the heat of the moment, and I have broad enough shoulders and a thick enough skin to cope with it. Oliver was worried sick about Chloe that night, and if I'd been in his shoes I would probably have said a hell of a lot more.'

'Even so,' she protested, 'I still feel—'

'Plus, I hardly think I'm in a position to criticise somebody else's thoughtless words, do you?' he interrupted.

His eyes were fixed on her, and she felt a faint wash of colour creep across her cheeks.

'Tom…'

'I know.' He nodded. 'Not here, not now, but we're going to have to talk about it some time, Eve.'

She knew they would, but she didn't want to talk about it because talking changed nothing, altered nothing. Talking simply meant she had to relive it again, and she'd relived it so often in her mind—regretted it so often.

'Do you know what's going to happen to Audrey's dog, Foxy?' she said, deliberately changing the subject, and knew from the way Tom shook his head that he wasn't deceived for a second.

'The RSPCA is looking after him at the moment,' he replied, 'but to be honest they're a bit worried about him. He's not eaten anything since they picked him up, and there's no doubt he's going to be difficult to rehome because people generally want puppies, not older dogs. I'd take him myself, but the RSPCA say he's wary of men, plus a dog really shouldn't have a globe-trotting owner. Maybe if I had a wife, a family…'

His words hung in the air between them, and Eve plucked at a loose thread on her sleeve.

'I hope you find someone one day, Tom,' she murmured. 'You deserve to be happy.'

'But you don't think you do.'

The unexpectedness of his comment completely threw her.

'Of—of course I deserve to be happy,' she stammered, 'and I *am* happy. I have my work, and Tassie, and…' Desperately she tried to think of something else that made her happy but to her dismay her mind seemed suddenly blank. 'I'm *happy*, Tom.'

'Eve, you need more in your life than your work, and looking after someone else's child once a week,' he said gently, 'but until you let go of the past, move on, you're not going to believe that. You're going to continue to keep people at arm's length because you don't think you're entitled to happiness.'

'I— You—you're talking nonsense,' she said vehemently. 'You're making it sound as though—'

She didn't get an opportunity to finish what she'd been about to say. Dragan had appeared, looking white-faced and tense.

'I've just had a phone call from Melinda,' he said unevenly. 'Her waters have broken. She's having the baby, Eve, and it's two weeks early.'

'Which is no time at all,' she said soothingly. 'In fact, she probably got her dates wrong—it's not uncommon.'

'Right,' he said, though Eve doubted whether he'd actually heard her. 'I need to go to her, but I have surgery this after-noon— My patients—'

'I'll take your place,' Tom interrupted. 'I'm a fully qualified doctor, remember, and I'm sure Nick wouldn't object.'

To Eve's amazement the senior partner didn't. He simply gave Tom a long, appraising stare, then nodded.

'Just so long as you realise what you're letting yourself in for,' he said. 'General practice is not for everyone.'

'Then it's OK if I go?' Dragan said, clearly anxious to leave, and Nick gave him a gentle push with his finger.

'Of course you can go, you idiot. Give Melinda my best, and try not to faint. It reflects badly on the practice.'

Quickly, Dragan strode to the door, then came back and gripped Tom's hands.

'*Bog te blagoslovio!*' the Croatian doctor exclaimed. '*Hvala*, Tom. I just want to say—*hvala*.'

'Do you have any idea what he said?' Tom asked, bemused, when Dragan had rushed away.

'I imagine he was thanking you,' Eve declared, 'but I'm afraid I can't give you an exact translation as I don't speak Croatian.'

Tom grinned. 'In which case he could have been telling me in no uncertain terms to…um…remove myself.'

'Maybe somebody should,' she muttered, and walked off to her examination room, but Tom came after her.

'Eve, what I said earlier—about you needing to move on— I'm sorry if you feel I spoke out of turn.'

If, she thought angrily. How dared he imply—suggest—she was some lonely, unhappy woman, stuck in the past, who had spent the last twenty years punishing herself for what she'd done? She may not be able to forgive herself, but she'd created a full life, a satisfying life, and she was on her own through choice. Not everyone met someone they wanted to spend the rest of their life with. A lot of luck was involved, like being in the right place at the right time.

Like you and Tom, her heart whispered, and she crushed down the thought immediately.

'As you appear to make a habit of speaking out of turn, I don't suppose I should be surprised,' she said tightly.

'Eve, I was only speaking as I see it,' he protested, and she shook her head.

'Isn't that what people with big mouths, and even bigger egos, usually say to justify sticking their noses into other people's business?'

He opened his mouth, then closed it again.

'Fair point,' he declared. 'In future I will button my lip whenever I feel the urge to make any kind of observation.'

'You couldn't button your lip if your life depended on it!' she exclaimed, and saw his eyes twinkle.

'No, but I'm prepared to swear anything to get back into your good graces.'

He was gazing at her with a quite ludicrously hangdog expression, and anger warred with amusement inside her for a moment and amusement won.

'You're impossible, Tom Cornish. You know that, don't you?' she said.

'Yup.' He grinned. 'But I got you to laugh.'

'I don't think you're going to be laughing by the end of this afternoon,' she observed. 'In fact… Look, are you sure you know what you're doing—volunteering to take Dragan's clinic?'

He groaned. 'Not you, too. It's bad enough having Nick doubt my professional capabilities—'

'It's not your professional capabilities I'm worried about,' she interrupted, 'and I don't think it's what Nick is concerned about either. It's been a long time since you've met "ordinary" members of the public, Tom, and I think you're in for quite an eye-opener.'

Tom rolled his eyes with exasperation, but it didn't take him long to discover both she and Nick were right. He could tolerate the stream of people he saw that afternoon who had met with unfortunate accidents due to the uneven roads and pavements, but what he found impossible to cope with were the people who appeared to have blithely ignored every health leaflet Nick had sent out, and now felt distinctly aggrieved because they weren't feeling well.

'Is it my imagination or is the entire world populated by complete idiots?' he demanded, by the end of the afternoon. 'There's been a flood, the water supply has been contaminated, Nick has issued leaflets advising people to drink bottled water, and yet what do some people do?'

'You tell me,' Eve said, her lips twitching as her gaze took in his distinctly frazzled expression.

'They drink water out of the tap,' Tom retorted. 'They come in here, saying, "I thought it looked all right, Doctor, and now I've got a fever, and a really bad headache." Well, of course they have. The prats have contracted Weil's disease.'

'And did you tell them they were prats?' Eve asked, controlling the laughter she could feel bubbling up inside her with difficulty.

'No, but it was a close-run thing,' he admitted. 'And do you know how many people I saw this afternoon who decided it would be a whiz bang idea to light a camp stove to speed up the drying out of their houses?' he continued. '*Three*, Eve. That's three idiots who now have carbon-monoxide poisoning because they were too lazy, or too dim, to read the warning leaflets which specifically said the fumes from charcoal were deadly.'

'Oh, dear,' she said unevenly, and he gave her a hard stare.

'It is *not* funny, Eve.'

'The illnesses certainly aren't, but your face sure is,' she said with a peal of laughter. 'I'm sorry, Tom. It's not fair of me to mock,' she continued as his eyebrows snapped together, 'but Nick and I did try to warn you that general practice wasn't for you.'

He thrust his fingers through his hair, making it stand out all over the place, then smiled reluctantly.

'OK—all right—so you were both right, and I was wrong. Maybe becoming a GP would be a bad career move for me.'

'If you were on the verge of strangling the patients you saw after just one afternoon, then it sure would be,' she replied. 'Deltaron is where you belong, Tom. I think you need a break— a long holiday—but I think Deltaron is where you're meant to be.'

'But only if I get myself a life outside my work, just as you should.'

The smile on her face disappeared.

'I thought we agreed this subject was a no-go area?'

'Can't blame a bloke from trying.' He grinned, and she shook her head at him.

'You're completely incorrigible.'

'I think that was one of the nicer things Gertie Stanbury used to say about me when I was at school,' he replied. 'In fact—'

'The very person I wanted to see,' Lauren interrupted as she came out of her physiotherapy room and saw them. 'Tom, I have Miss Stanbury with me, and she'd very much like to thank you personally for the loan of your house.'

That he didn't want to be thanked was plain. In fact, he had the look of a man who would have preferred to have his toenails pulled out, but Eve wasn't going to let him get away with it, at least not this time.

'Tom, if she wants to thank you, you have to let her,' she

declared, and she saw reluctance and unwillingness war with each other on his face for a second, then he sighed.

'OK—all right,' he said.

'And I dare you to call her Gertie to her face,' Eve added in an undertone as she followed him down the corridor.

'Are you kidding?' he protested. 'I want to live to be fifty.'

Eve didn't think the elderly lady would have cared what Tom called her. She was far too overwhelmed by his generosity.

'It's almost like being at home,' she said, her small face wreathed in smiles, 'and I can't thank you enough for allowing me to stay there. I just hope I'm not inconveniencing you.'

'Not in the slightest,' Tom insisted. 'Stay for as long as you like, and most definitely until your own home is habitable again.'

'Amanda Lovelace drove me round to Gull Close this morning,' Gertrude continued. 'Seeing it… I can't believe Tassie and I got out of there alive.'

'It's not going to always look like that, Miss Stanbury,' Tom said softly, seeing the stricken look that had suddenly appeared in her eyes. 'Once the fire brigade has pumped out the water, and it's been dried out, you'll soon have it looking as it did before.'

'I just wish I'd thought to take my papers and photographs with me when I went up into the attic,' she said. 'When I looked in the window, they were all there—floating about in the water.'

'Miss Stanbury—'

'I know—I know,' she interrupted as Tom looked at her with concern. 'The most important thing is Tassie and I are here to tell the tale. As for my photographs, papers…' Her lip trembled slightly, and she firmed it. 'Not important.'

Tom hunkered down on his heels in front of her, his green eyes soft with understanding.

'You haven't lost them,' he said. 'If this was the summer we could air-dry them for you in a trice but at the moment what we need is a freezer. If we can find someone with a big freezer, all we need to do is to pop your photographs and papers in, freeze them, and they can be air-dried when the weather is better.'

'And that will work?' Gertrude declared, and Eve could see hope stirring in the elderly lady's eyes.

'Yup,' Tom said, and Gertrude shook her head in amazement.

'The wonders of modern technology.'

'Nah.' Tom grinned. 'Knowledge gained from a misspent youth.'

Gertrude chuckled wryly.

'You haven't changed a bit, Tom Cornish,' she declared. 'You're just the same lippy, opinionated, and—' she stretched out and caught hold of one of his hands, and gripped it firmly in her own frail one '—downright kind and decent human being you always were.'

'And there was me thinking I had you fooled,' Tom said, his cheeks darkening, and Gertrude shook her head.

'Not for a minute, lad. Not for one single minute.'

'That was kind of you,' Eve said when she and Tom left the surgery some time later.

'I wasn't lying to Gertie,' Tom replied, taking hold of her elbow to steer her round the rubble in Harbour Road. 'She might not be able to save all of her photographs and private papers, but she should be able to salvage most.'

'I didn't mean that,' Eve said. 'I meant the way you talked to her. You've a good heart, Tom.'

'Anyone else would have done the same,' he said dismissively, but she could see the embarrassment back on his face again, and stared at him curiously.

'Why does gratitude make you so uncomfortable?' she said, and to her surprise he didn't meet her gaze.

'I guess…' Tom took an awkward breath. 'Maybe it's because my father always battered it into me when I was a kid that nobody does anything for nothing. "There's no such thing as a free lunch, Tom." That was one of his favourite sayings, so I suppose I find it hard to believe people are on the level.'

'Gertrude is, and she knows you are,' she said softly.

'I'd rather you did,' he said, turning to face her, and it was her turn to look away.

'Your promise didn't last very long,' she said.

'Yeah, well, never trust a Cornish.'

She could hear the laughter in his voice, and shook her head.

'Ain't that the truth,' she replied. 'Tony at The Smugglers' has huge freezers. I bet he'd offer to help Gertrude in an instant.'

'I understand he's doing very well in hospital,' Tom said, and Eve couldn't help but laugh.

'You mean, you've heard he's giving the staff merry hell, demanding to be discharged.'

'I heard that, too.' Tom grinned. 'I'm afraid he's going to have to take things a lot easier from now on whether he wants to or not.'

'I think this flood is going to change quite a few people's lives.' Eve sighed.

'I'm hoping so.'

His words were innocuous enough, but she wasn't deceived for a second.

'I thought we agreed—'

His green eyes met hers.

'You can run, Eve, but you can't hide.'

He was right, she thought, and his words became even more prophetic after they'd reached her cottage and she made them both a simple meal of pasta Bolognese. Every time she looked up his gaze was on her, thoughtful, pensive. Every time she tried to start a conversation, he answered her in monosyllables and she knew why. He was waiting. Waiting for her to talk about the baby, and though she knew they had to talk about it, she didn't want to see his eyes darken again with pain or to relive the decision she'd made all those years ago.

'Would you like anything else to eat?' she said hopefully after she'd gathered up their empty plates. 'I have cheese and biscuits, and I managed to get some fruit from the corner shop. Goodness knows how it survived the flood, but it did.'

'No, thank you,' he replied.

'A coffee, then?' she suggested, knowing her voice was beginning to sound slightly panic-stricken but quite unable to control it. 'It's only instant but—'

'I don't want a coffee, thank you,' he interrupted. 'What I want is to talk to you.'

'Tom, I'm really tired,' she said quickly. 'In fact, I thought I might actually have an early night.'

He got to his feet, took the plates from her hands and put them back on the table.

'Eve, I could get a call at any time from Deltaron,' he declared, 'and I don't want to leave Penhally without us having spoken about…about our child.'

He was right about the call, and she knew from his set expression he wasn't going to take no for an answer, but when she walked over to the sofa she sat down wearily.

'Tom, what is there left for us to say?' she murmured. 'I was pregnant, I decided I couldn't have the baby, I had an abortion. I know you must hate me for what I did—'

'I don't hate you,' he interrupted, sitting down beside her. 'Maybe I thought I did, when you first told me—when I thought of the son or daughter I could have had—but those thoughts were the thoughts of the man I am now. The man I was all those years ago would have felt only relief that you didn't have the baby.'

'Relief?' she echoed, and he took a deep breath.

She had opened her heart to him, told him everything, and she deserved the same truth from him no matter how badly it reflected upon him.

'Eve, I'm ashamed to admit it, but if I'm honest—and I want

to be completely honest with you—I wouldn't have wanted a baby, not then. I had this wonderful career, you see,' he continued, his mouth twisting into an ironic and bitter smile. 'I was Dr Tom Cornish, all set to conquer the world, and a baby… I would have seen a baby as an encumbrance, that I was being trapped into a responsibility I didn't want to have, just as my father was.'

'And now you wish I hadn't done it,' she murmured, pleating and unpleating her fingers, 'but I can't undo it, Tom, no matter how much I might want to. I was weak all those years ago, took the easy way out, just as you said I did.'

'Weak?' he exclaimed. 'Eve, you took the hardest decision anyone can ever make, and you took it alone. When I think of you going to the clinic by yourself…' He shook his head. 'No one should have to go through that alone, and yet you did. You were the one who possessed the strength all those years ago, not me.'

'It wasn't strength, Tom, it was cowardice,' she said, her voice raw, harsh. 'I was so desperate. Desperate and scared that I wouldn't be able to cope, and I wish—I so wish—I could go back, and do things differently, but all the wishing in the world isn't going to make that happen.'

Awkwardly, he half reached for her, but he didn't know whether she would reject his touch—not want it—so he clasped her hand in his instead.

'If anyone's to blame for what happened, it's me,' he insisted. 'You should have felt you could come to me, and the fact you didn't… I let you down, Eve. Me.'

'I don't even know whether we had a son or a daughter, Tom,' she said, her lips trembling. 'I felt—I don't know why—it was a little girl, but one of the nurses… She said it wasn't a baby, not a real baby, just a collection of cells. But it was a baby, Tom. Our baby—and I killed it.'

He felt his heart twist with pain, but what deepened the pain, intensified it, were the tears he could see shimmering in her eyes, tears he knew were going to fall at any moment, and holding her hand was not enough—not nearly enough—and he put his arm around her, drawing her close.

'Don't, Eve, *don't*,' he begged, hating to see her suffering, but she misunderstood him.

'It's the truth, Tom,' she said. 'I did it. It was my decision, not yours. Mine, and I want so much to say I'm sorry to our daughter, but I can't. There's not even a grave I can stand beside so I won't ever be able to tell our baby that I'm sorry, and some-times…'

The tears in her eyes overflowed, and Tom put his other arm round her, and held her tightly, his own throat constricted.

'Eve, listen to me,' he said into her hair. 'If we had made love ten years ago, and you'd discovered you were pregnant, would you have had an abortion?'

'Of course I wouldn't,' she said into his chest.

'Why not?' he said, knowing full well what her answer would be, but knowing, too, that he had to make her say it, see it.

'Because I had a good job ten years ago,' she exclaimed, 'and a flat of my own in Newquay!'

'None of which you had when you were twenty-two. Eve…' He clasped her face between his hands and forced her to look at him. 'You did what you thought was right twenty years ago, and now you have to forgive yourself, to move on, and believe you're entitled to a future, to happiness.'

'I don't know if I can,' she said brokenly.

He smoothed her hair back from her damp cheeks.

'You asked me—oh, it seems a lifetime ago now—why I came back to Penhally. I said I could give you one reason, but not the other—not then. Well, I can give you that other reason now. I came back because I've never stopped loving you.'

She stared at him in open-mouthed amazement for a full minute, then drew back from him.

'You're asking me to believe you've been in love with me for the past twenty years?' she exclaimed.

'Is that so very surprising?' he said.

It clearly was to her, he thought, seeing her shake her head, and her words confirmed it.

'Tom, if you'd truly felt like that you would have kept in touch,' she protested, 'but you never phoned, or wrote, or made any attempt to see me.'

'Because I was the one who walked away,' he said, willing her to believe him. 'I was the one who'd said I didn't want to be tied down, didn't want a wife or a family. You would have been quite within your rights to say, *On your bike, Tom Cornish*, and, as the years passed, I told myself you must be married, so I thought—I felt—I couldn't come back.'

'And you've been pining for me for the last twenty years?' she said, not bothering to hide her cynicism. 'I don't think so, Tom.'

'No, I haven't been pining for you for the last twenty years,' he admitted, 'but, because I made the biggest mistake of my life, I have spent those years trying to convince myself that the image I had of you couldn't be a real one, that no one could be so special, or different.'

'I'm not different, or special, Tom,' she said.

'You are, and because you are I kept on dating, and dating, and…' He broke off awkwardly, with a crooked smile and a gesture of dismissal. 'When none of my relationships worked out, I finally had to admit what I'd known all along. That I was looking for someone like you, and there wasn't anyone like you, there never could be.'

'So you came back to Penhally hoping to find me unhappily married, or divorced, so you could become involved with me again?' she said, outrage plain in her voice, and he swore under his breath.

Hell, was he never going to be able to find the right words to say to her? Was he doomed always to screw things up, and he was screwing things up, big time, because he see her barriers going up, and he couldn't lose her a second time, simply couldn't.

'It wasn't like that,' he said vehemently. 'I thought...' He grasped her hands before she could draw back, and held onto them. 'Part of me hoped to find you happily married because I thought—if you were—I might finally be able to move on, to bury the dream I had of somehow undoing the mistake I'd made, and the other part...I thought if you were still single that maybe...you and I...maybe we could try again.'

Her eyes met his, and he could read nothing of what she was thinking in them, and then she cleared her throat.

'Tom, have you thought that what you've been wanting back for all these years isn't me, but your youth and your dreams, and I can't give you that. No one can.'

'You said that to me before,' he said, willing her to see the truth in his eyes, 'but it isn't that, I know it isn't. Since we parted there's never been anybody in my life like you. There have been other women—I won't deny that—but it was always you. Nobody ever came anywhere close to you.'

Gently, she slipped her hands free from his.

'Even if I believed that, Tom,' she murmured. 'Even if what you say is true, we can't go back. You know we can't.'

'Why not?' he said.

It was a good question and one Eve wasn't entirely sure she could answer. She knew nobody had ever touched her heart the way he had, but she also knew no one had ever hurt her quite so much either, and to go down that road again, risk everything again...

'Tom, we're not the same people any more, and our worlds—they're too different, too far apart.'

'Then I'll give up working for Deltaron, and come back to Penhally,' he said. 'I'm getting too old to be traipsing around the world anyway, and after what happened last year in India—'

'And what would you do in Penhally?' she interrupted. 'This afternoon must have proved to you beyond a shadow of a doubt you'll never make a country GP, and Penhally… There are too many bad memories for you here. You'd never feel you belonged.'

'Then you could come to London with me,' he declared. 'Or there's my flat in Lausanne. You'd love Switzerland, Eve. It's a beautiful country, and if you wanted to continue nursing you'd easily find work there.'

He looked so desperate, so anxious, and she didn't want to hurt him, but she knew she must.

'Tom, my home is here,' she said. 'And to uproot myself from everything I know, from everyone I know on the strength of…'

'A whim?' he finished for her. 'It's not a whim, Eve, it's a question of trust. A question of whether you believe me when I say I love you and I always will.'

He made it sound so easy, so simple, but he'd made it sound easy and simple all those years ago, too.

'Let's have fun,' he'd said, and she'd thought they'd get married, raise a family in Penhally, and within a few short months her dreams and hopes had all been left lying shattered in the dust.

'I can't, Tom. And you're assuming too much,' she continued as he tried to interrupt. 'Assuming I still feel the same way about you.'

He reached out and gently cupped her cheek with his hand. 'Don't you?'

His eyes were deep and green and dark, and she shivered at the intensity she could see in them and, when he traced her neck with the fingers of his other hand, she shivered even more.

'It's still there, isn't it?' he continued, his voice suddenly deep, husky. 'What you used to feel for me, it's still there?'

'No,' she said, trying to sound firm but unfortunately her voice wobbled.

'Then, if I kiss you, you'll feel nothing?'

He didn't even need to kiss her, she thought. She could already feel herself melting, responding to him, wanting to touch him, to hold him, but she also knew nothing had been resolved between them, and it never could.

'Tom…I don't…I…'

'I'll take that as a yes,' he said, and bent his head towards her, and before she could say anything his lips met hers and she was lost.

Lost on a tide of need and longing. Lost in a sea of old memories, and sensations, and she slid her arms up his back to bring him closer, heard him groan against her mouth as he deepened the kiss, and he threaded his fingers through her hair so she couldn't escape, and she didn't want to escape.

'I have dreamt about doing this for so long,' he said, his breathing ragged. 'Wanted it, longed for it, and now you're here, in my arms, and it's right, so right.'

It felt right to her, too, as he smothered her face and neck with kisses, and when he slid his hands up under her sweater, and she felt the heat of his fingers through the lace of her bra, she arched against him, feeling her nipples harden instantly. It would be so easy to let go, she thought with a sigh as he drew her closer to him, and she felt his heart beating rapidly against hers, felt a heat begin to spread out deep and low in her stomach. It would be so easy simply to enjoy the moment, and it had been so long since she'd been in a man's arms, so long since she'd made love, but though her body and her heart spoke loudly, her head spoke louder still.

Nothing has changed, her mind warned, nothing *can* change. In a few days' time—probably less—he'll be gone, and then what? Then you'll be left with even more regret, even more memories to hurt you. With a sob, she pulled herself free from his arms and stood up.

'I can't,' she cried. 'I'm sorry, but I can't do this.'

'Eve—'

'I'm scared, Tom.'

'Of me?' he said in horror, and she shook her head as she wrapped her arms around herself.

'Of what will happen to me if I let you get close again. I can't go down that road and have you leave me again. I can't.'

'Why would you think I'd leave you?' he demanded.

'Because you always do,' she said, her voice trembling. 'You make me feel special, and different, and then you leave.'

'Eve, I *love* you,' he protested, reaching for her only to see her back away. 'I want us to be together for always. Can't you believe that?'

'I want to—I truly want to,' she said, 'but I can't risk it—I *can't*, Tom.'

'Eve, listen to me—'

'No,' she interrupted. 'No,' she repeated. 'You'll just talk me round like you always could. Go back to your world, Tom, and I'll stay in my own little one. I know it's not an exciting place like yours, and maybe…maybe it's not always completely fulfilling, but it's safe. It's never going to let me down, or walk away from me, and I have to have that kind of certainty, don't you see?'

'I can give you certainty,' he protested. 'Eve—'

'No, Tom,' she said, and before he could stop her she'd fled, and he swore long, and low, and fluently.

CHAPTER EIGHT

'DOES anybody else have anything to add, or can I call this practice meeting to a close?' Nick said, leaning back in his chair.

'Has anyone heard anything from the hospital about Melinda?' Eve asked.

Nick shook his head.

'Dragan phoned Chloe a couple of hours ago, said he was hoping it wouldn't be too much longer, but we haven't heard anything since.'

'That must be—what?—nineteen hours now?' Oliver said.

'It's not unusual for first babies to take a while to arrive,' Chloe said calmly. 'I'm sure there's no need to worry.'

'I wouldn't tell Dragan that.' Her fiancé grinned. 'I bet the poor bloke's got no fingernails left.'

'I'm surprised Tom had any hair left after he took over Dragan's surgery yesterday afternoon.' Kate laughed. 'I see you didn't take up his offer to help out this morning, Nick.'

'I thought he'd suffered enough,' the senior partner said with a rare smile, 'though I have to say, with Dragan shortly going on paternity leave, I wish Dr Devereux was arriving sooner.'

'We'll manage, boss,' Oliver declared, and Nick's smile widened.

'I'll hold you to that.'

'Where is Tom this morning?' Chloe asked, and to Eve's dismay all eyes in Nick's consulting room turned to her.

'I don't know,' she said uncomfortably. 'He got a call this morning at breakfast, and I haven't seen him since.'

A breakfast that had been eaten in a strained, awkward silence with neither of them saying anything. A breakfast she'd eaten at breakneck speed, all too aware he was watching her every move.

'Sorry to interrupt,' Hazel declared to Eve's relief as she appeared at Nick's consulting-room door, 'but Mrs Banks is here, Eve, and she'd like a word with you.'

'With me?' Eve said in surprise.

The practice manager nodded, and Eve glanced across at Nick.

'I don't think we have anything else to discuss, do we?' the senior partner said, and, when everyone shook their heads, he said, 'you'd better see what she wants, Eve.'

Eve thought she'd better, too, though she couldn't imagine what Mrs Banks might want to talk to her about unless it was how Sophie was getting on in hospital.

It wasn't.

'I simply had to come in and thank you personally, Nurse,' Mrs Banks declared the minute she sat down in Eve's examination room. 'Dr Tremayne told me what you did for my Sophie, how she probably wouldn't have survived if it hadn't been for you, and I'll never forget it.'

'It's not me you should be thanking, Mrs Banks,' Eve replied with a smile. 'Dr Cornish, and his pilot, Michael Flannery, were the real heroes of the hour.'

'Yes, but they get paid to rescue people, you don't,' Sophie's mother said dismissively.

Eve stared, open-mouthed, at the woman sitting opposite her, then straightened in her seat.

'Dr Cornish and Michael Flannery may—as you say—be paid for the job they do,' she said, fighting to control her mounting anger with difficulty, 'but there are precious few people in the world who would be willing to put their own lives on the line every time they go into work. It takes a very special man—or woman—to join a rescue service, Mrs Banks.'

'Granted,' Sophie's mother observed, 'but Dr Cornish… Well, he always was a bit wild, reckless, and as for his father—'

'I'm afraid you'll have to excuse me,' Eve interrupted, getting abruptly to her feet and pointedly walking over to her examination-room door and opening it. 'I'm on a tight schedule this morning.'

She wasn't. In truth, she was actually finished for the day, but she knew if she sat in the same room as Mrs Banks for even a minute longer she wouldn't be responsible for her actions.

'Oh—of course,' Mrs Banks declared uncertainly. 'I know how busy you professionals are, but I felt I couldn't let another day go past without thanking you.'

Eve wished Sophie's mother hadn't said anything at all as the woman left.

How could Mrs Banks be so blinkered, so stupid? she wondered. Tom and Mitch might be paid for their work, but how could that possibly make their actions less courageous, less admirable?

She shook her head as she began gathering up the folders on her desk. And to think this was the village Tom had said he would be prepared to come back and live in. A village where people would never let him forget his origins or his youthful behaviour. He must have been insane.

Or very deeply in love with you, her heart whispered, and she bit her lip.

Part of her desperately wanted to believe he'd meant what he'd said. Part of her wondered if perhaps, this time, they might both be able to get it right, but she knew the part that wondered was her heart. Her heart which had deceived her all those years ago, telling he would change his mind, and stay in Penhally instead of going to the US, so she mustn't listen to it, she told herself as she picked up the last folder and strode down to

Reception to find Amanda Lovelace deep in conversation with their practice manager. This time she had to listen to her head. This time she had to be sensible because if it all went wrong again she knew she would never recover.

'Hello, there, Amanda,' she said, forcing a smile to her lips. 'I hope this isn't a medical visit?'

'Not at all,' Tassie's mother replied. 'Hazel loaned me a little portable gas stove to cook on while the electricity was off, and now it's back on again I thought I'd better return it.'

'How's Tassie?' Eve asked. 'None the worse, I hope, for her adventure?'

'She's fine. And talking about Tassie,' Amanda continued, steering Eve away from the reception desk, 'I just want to say thank you. Thank you *so* much.'

'For what?' Eve said in confusion, and Tassie's mother tapped the side of her nose and winked.

'You don't have to pretend, Eve. I have to say I wasn't very happy when Dr Cornish first suggested it—felt I couldn't be beholden—and I know he doesn't want thanks, or for anyone to know—he was most insistent about that— but I had to thank you because I'm guessing you came up with the idea.'

'Amanda, I don't know what—'

'I have to go,' Tassie's mother interrupted. 'I heard on the way down here that there might be a delivery of bread today at the corner shop, and you can bet your life it will all be sold out in ten minutes.'

'But, Amanda…'

She was too late. After giving her a big hug, Tassie's mother bustled away, leaving Eve standing in the centre of the waiting room with a puzzled frown. A frown that deepened when Tom strode through the surgery door.

'Whatever it was, I didn't do it.' He grinned as he saw her expression.

'You obviously did something,' she observed, 'because I have just had the weirdest conversation with Amanda Lovelace.'

'Ah,' he said.

'Yes, "ah".' She nodded. 'Care to elaborate?'

'Nothing to elaborate on,' he replied lightly but when she saw a tell-tale wash of embarrassed colour begin to creep across his cheeks, she folded her arms across her chest.

'Tom, you have two choices. Either you tell me what you've done, and how it involves Amanda, or I'll go round to her house this afternoon and ask her myself.'

He sighed, then guided her towards the waiting-room chairs furthest away from the reception desk.

'You know how you and Gertie are very keen for Tassie to apply for a scholarship to go to the Lady Joan Mercer's Boarding School in Devon?' he said.

'And you're dead against it,' Eve replied.

'Not against it,' he countered. 'Just worried about the possible long-term consequences for Tassie and her family. Well, I've been making discreet enquiries about Penhally High School, and it seems to be as good a school as it was in our day.'

'And?' Eve prompted.

'I've arranged with Mrs Lovelace to pay her a monthly allowance so she can afford to allow Tassie to stay on at the local school for as long as she wants.'

Eve's mouth opened and closed soundlessly, and she finally found her voice.

'But…' She paused and started again. 'Why would you want to do that?'

'Why not?' he countered.

'Well, for a start, you don't know Tassie, or her family,' she pointed out, and he shrugged.

'No, but I do know you, and if you think the child deserves help, then that's good enough for me.'

'But, Tom, have you considered the cost?' she protested. 'If Tassie stays on at school until she's eighteen, you'll be paying for her education for the next eight years.'

'A bit longer, probably,' he said, the colour on his cheeks darkening, 'because I said I'd keep paying if she wants to go to university. Look, I can afford it,' he continued as Eve tried to interrupt. 'It's no big deal.'

But it was, she thought. It was rather a large deal, and a sudden suspicion crept into her mind.

'When did you suggest this to Amanda?' she demanded.

'Yesterday morning.' He shot her a cool look. 'Long before I told you how I feel about you so this is not, in any shape or form, a bribe, Eve.'

In truth, that had been exactly what she'd been thinking, and she felt her cheeks redden.

'I'm sorry,' she murmured. 'I deserved that.'

'Yes, you did.'

She glanced at him hesitantly.

'It's very generous of you, Tom. More than generous, in fact, though I don't know how you managed to get Amanda to agree. She may not have much money, but she's a proud woman, and I would have thought she'd have considered it charity.'

'She did at first,' Tom admitted, 'but I talked her round.'

Eve's lips curved. 'In other words, you used the famous Tom Cornish charm. Well, I suppose it's never failed you yet.'

'Yes, it has,' he said, a wry smile appearing in his green eyes. 'With one very important person.'

'Tom…'

'I won't give up, you know.'

She opened her mouth to tell him she wished he would, but she didn't get the chance to say the words. The surgery door had opened with a bang, and Dragan stood there looking dishevelled, exhausted and absolutely elated.

'I have a son!' he exclaimed. 'I have a beautiful son, and

Melinda—she was terrific—much calmer than I was—and I...'
The smile on his face widened. 'I just had to come and tell you
all.'

Hazel let out a shriek of delight, and within seconds every
member of the Penhally practice had converged on the waiting
room.

'What weight is the baby?' Kate asked, as Nick pulled the
cork out of a bottle of champagne, and began filling some
glasses.

Dragan looked comically dismayed.

'I've no idea. The midwife did tell me, but I was just so
relieved my son had arrived safely, with the correct number of
fingers and toes, I didn't take it in.'

'Have you and Melinda decided on a name?' Chloe asked,
taking the glass of champagne Nick was holding out to her, and
the Croatian doctor shook his head.

'We didn't decide on a name or buy any baby clothes either,
or a cot,' he replied. 'We felt we might be somehow tempting
the gods if we did.'

'Then you'd better start hitting the shops in Truro fast.' Eve
laughed. 'New mums and babies are lucky if they're kept in
hospital for forty-eight hours these days.'

'I hadn't thought of that,' Dragan said, aghast. 'You're right,
I'd better go shopping right away.'

'But not until we've all toasted the new arrival,' Nick said.
'I always keep a bottle of champagne in the surgery for special
moments, and I think the birth of Melinda and Dragan's son certainly qualifies as one of those.'

'Hear! Hear!' Oliver called, and everyone laughed.

'Does everyone have a glass of champagne?' Nick asked,
and, when a chorus of assent rang out, he said, 'Then I want
you all to raise your glasses to the new arrival. May he have a
long and happy life, and have inherited his mother's looks,
and—' he winked across at Dragan '—his mother's brains, too.'

More laughter rippled round the room and, as everyone raised their glasses, Tom leant closer to Eve.

'Are you OK?' he murmured so low nobody else could hear him. 'I mean, if you'd rather not be here I can cover for you.'

She looked up at him, both surprised and touched he would realise occasions like this could be painful for her, and shook her head.

'I'm fine,' she said. 'Dragan… He had so little sunshine in his life until he met Melinda, and he deserves to be happy.'

'Eve…'

'Shush,' she whispered. 'I don't think Nick's finished yet.'

'Nick could talk for Cornwall,' Tom muttered, and Eve choked over her champagne, and waved an admonishing hand at him.

'I would also like to take this opportunity to say these last few days have been very difficult for everyone,' the senior partner continued. 'We've been through the kind of flood I never want to see again in my lifetime, and lost some good, decent people, but… *But,*' Nick added with emphasis, 'in the middle of the catastrophe my staff rose to the occasion magnificently, and I just want to thank you all, and say you were incredible.'

'You were pretty wonderful yourself, boss,' Oliver observed. 'Managing to assist at a breech birth with no electricity, and damn few medical instruments, takes some doing.'

A chorus of agreement met that comment, and Nick's cheeks flushed slightly, then he held up his hand, clearly calling for silence again.

'There is, however, one person who deserves my very special thanks,' he said. 'One person who I admit I have not made welcome since he came back to the village, and yet it is that one person without whose help things would most certainly have been considerably worse, so can I ask you to raise your glasses once more, and drink a toast to Tom Cornish? Penhally's very own, home-grown hero.'

'Tom Cornish!' everyone exclaimed, but when the toast had been drunk and Dragan was, yet again, being bombarded with more questions about his son, Tom looked down at Eve quizzically.

'Did you know he was going to say that?' he asked.

'I'm as surprised as you are,' she replied. 'Considering how unfriendly he's been towards you since you came back, I'd have thought you were the last person he would have wanted to thank.'

And not just thank, Eve discovered as Nick eased his way through the throng towards them, with Kate at his side.

'I owe you an apology,' the senior partner declared the moment he drew level with Tom.

'Forget it, Nick,' Tom said, and Nick shook his head.

'I can't,' he declared. 'I know I have a brusque tongue—'

'You can say that again,' Kate murmured, and Nick gave her a hard stare.

'And sometimes speak before I think,' the senior partner continued, 'but I will be eternally grateful for everything you did for the village. If you hadn't been here, I don't know what would have happened.'

'I just wish there could have been no fatalities,' Tom observed. 'Reverend Kenner seems to have been a well-liked man, and Mrs Baxter… She and I may not have seen eye to eye, but I'm sorry she's dead.'

'Did you know that Lauren is giving Foxy a home?' Kate said as Nick walked away in answer to Oliver's beckoning wave. 'The dog knows her, you see, from when she used to do Audrey's physio, so he's not scared of her, and she actually got him to eat something yesterday which the RSPCA says is a miracle because he's point-blank refused to take food from anybody else.'

'I just wish we could find Chloe's cats,' Tom declared,

glancing across to where the midwife was talking animatedly to Dragan. 'But there's no sign of them—not even their bodies. In fact, I was wondering—'

'Tom, I think Mitch wants a word with you,' Eve interrupted, seeing the redheaded pilot hovering in the waiting-room doorway pointing silently at Tom and then at himself.

'I'll be back in a minute,' Tom said, half turning to go, then he stopped. 'Don't go anywhere. Stay here.'

'Yes, sir.' Eve laughed.

But he was going somewhere, she thought, feeling her smile slip sideways when Tom reached Mitch and the pilot ruefully handed him a sheaf of papers.

They were leaving. She could see it in Tom's face. Mitch must have received a fax from their headquarters, and they were leaving.

Well, she'd known it was going to happen eventually, she thought as she took a sip of champagne then put her glass down. She'd just hoped—stupidly—that he might have been able to stay for a few more days.

'What's up?' Kate asked, gesturing towards Mitch and Tom.

'I think Tom's just received a call from Deltaron,' Eve replied.

'But that means he'll be leaving,' Kate said with dismay, and Eve forced a smile to her lips.

'He was never going to stay, Kate. His work—his life— isn't here.'

'But I thought…'

Eve didn't give the midwife the chance to tell her what she'd thought. Instead, she made her way towards Oliver, Lauren and Chloe who were standing by the window.

'Isn't it marvellous news?' Lauren beamed when she saw her. 'Melinda and Dragan must be so happy.'

'Christenings and weddings.' Chloe laughed. 'Reverend Kenner is going to be…' She came to an abrupt halt, and bit her lip. 'Sorry. Force of habit. It's so hard to believe he's gone, isn't it?'

'How is Rachel?' Eve asked. 'I thought I might call in on her this afternoon, see how she is.'

'She's gone to Plymouth with her aunt and uncle,' Lauren replied. 'She'll come back for the funeral, of course, but I think she wanted out of the village with all its memories.'

'She's a very brave girl—braver than I would be in the circumstances,' Chloe observed. 'To be left with no mother, no father, and expecting a baby… It's going to be tough for her.'

'She'll cope,' Eve said, her eyes following Tom as he scanned the waiting room, clearly looking for her. 'We all have to cope in different ways with what life throws at us, and she'll cope.'

'I thought I told you to stay where you were,' Tom declared with a frown when he reached her side. 'Give a woman a simple order, and what does she do? Completely ignores it.'

'I can see why you've never married, Tom.' Chloe laughed, and he gazed at her severely.

'You know, for that remark, I should refuse to give you the present one of my men has just brought in for you.'

'What present?' she said, looking puzzled.

'Actually, I'm more interested in meeting the bloke who thinks he can give my fiancée presents,' Oliver said, his voice mock stern, and Tom grinned.

'It's two presents actually,' he said. 'One is ginger and has only one eye, and one is white with a black patch over its eye.'

'You've found Cyclops and Pirate?' Chloe gasped, her face lighting up.

'One of my men has. They're outside in cat boxes if you want to see for yourself.'

Chloe was already halfway out of the room, and Oliver gripped Tom's hand fervently.

'Thanks, mate,' he said. 'I owe you. I owe you big time.'

'Are you sure your name isn't actually Santa Claus?' Eve said when the couple had gone, and Tom laughed.

'I didn't find them—Gregory did. He thinks they must have

decided to take shelter on top of one of the wardrobes because they weren't even a little bit dirty or wet.'

'Lucky cats,' Eve observed.

'Eve…'

He cleared his throat, and she knew what was coming. He was going to tell her he was leaving. She could see it in his face, and she didn't want to say goodbye to him. She'd said it to him once before, and she didn't want to say it again.

'I think Nick is trying to attract your attention,' she said quickly, and, when Tom groaned, she nudged him firmly with her hand. 'Look, if he wants to thank you again, just smile and accept it with good grace.'

He went reluctantly, and she waited only until he was deep in conversation with the senior partner then quietly slipped out of the surgery. He would be angry—perhaps even upset—when he found out she had gone, but she'd much rather he just disappeared out of her life as silently as he'd reappeared in it. To say goodbye to him, knowing she would never see him again… She didn't have that much courage.

'Lovely day, isn't it?' a woman called from outside one of the shops as Eve walked quickly past.

'Beautiful, yes,' Eve managed to reply.

'You and your gentleman friend must come back once we've redecorated,' the woman continued. 'You never did get your lemon meringue pies.'

It was the woman from the café, and Eve should have recognised her immediately but she hadn't.

'We'll do that,' she said, but of course they wouldn't.

By this time tomorrow Tom would be somewhere overseas, and she would have her work, and Tassie, to fill her days, and maybe, in time, she might forget this brief interlude. Though never completely, she thought as she crossed Harbour Bridge, and heard the chug of the firemen's hoses as they continued to pump water out of the houses. No matter how hard she tried, the day of the flood would be forever etched on her memory, whether she wanted it to be or not.

But she would survive, she told herself as she headed towards the lighthouse. She had survived before, and she would survive again.

'Kate, have you seen Eve anywhere?' Tom said with a frown as he walked towards her.

'She's gone, Tom,' the midwife replied. 'While you were talking to Nick she just slipped away. I imagine she's gone home.'

'Not home, no,' Tom said thoughtfully, 'but I think I might know where she is.'

He turned to leave, and Kate put her hand out to stay him.

'I hear you're off on another mission?' she said, and he nodded.

'Earthquake in China. We're flying out tonight, but I need to return to Switzerland first to finalise a team.'

'You be careful, you hear?' Kate declared, and he grinned.

'Hey, I'm always careful,' he said, and she shook her head.

'I don't mean in China. I mean with Eve.' On impulse, Kate stood on her toes and kissed him lightly on the cheek. 'That's for luck,' she whispered, 'and now go after her.'

'You'll make my apologies to the others?' he said.

'Of course, I will,' the midwife said. 'Now, *go.*'

He did.

'First Eve disappears, then Tom,' Nick declared when he joined Kate. 'What's going on between that pair? Are they an item again, or what?'

'I think whatever Tom says to her when he finds her will decide what their futures are going to be,' Kate murmured.

The senior partner frowned as stared down at her.

'I'm sorry, but you've lost me.'

Kate smiled.

'Let's just keep your fingers crossed for them, Nick. They both deserve to be happy, and that was a very nice apology you made to Tom.'

'Well, I had to give credit where credit was due,' Nick replied, 'and I think I was wrong about him.'

'I think you were, too,' Kate replied, but as she made to move away Nick caught her by the elbow.

'Kate, on the night of the flood…' He looked uncomfortable, ill at ease, then he firmed his jaw. 'What you said—about Jem. I can't make you any promises, but I will try.'

She looked up at him, her eyes very bright, then nodded.

'That's all I want, Nick,' she said, her voice husky. 'It's all I've ever wanted.'

She should have brought her jacket, Eve thought as she sat on the grass below the lighthouse, and hugged her knees. She was wearing her cherry-red sweater and a heavy tweed skirt, but there was no denying that autumn had well and truly arrived. There was a chill in the air, a feeling of darker nights approaching, and the scent of dried leaves now mingled with the tang of seaweed.

'I could see you shivering from all the way back at the church.'

Eve glanced over her shoulder to see Tom standing behind her, and sighed. She might have known she wouldn't be able to get away from him so easily.

'How did you know I would be here?' she asked as he took off his jacket, and put it round her shoulders before she could prevent him.

'No great mystery,' he said. 'I knew you would want to think, and this is where you always used to come if you had a problem.'

'It's amazing how many unimportant things you seem to remember about me,' she replied.

'I remember everything about you—I told you that.'

She gazed back out at the sea.

'Water… It's so very beautiful isn't it?' she said. 'And yet it can be so cruel and deadly, too.'

He sat down beside her on the grass.

'Mankind thinks itself so smart, so clever,' he said, 'but it's Nature that wields the real power. It can be a horrifying power at times, a terrifying power, but Nature also has the ability to heal. I've seen whole forests reduced to a smoking ruin and yet, within a year, wildflowers will have appeared, and the first shoots of new trees.'

She picked at the grass beside her for a few moments, then took a deep breath.

'How soon are you leaving?'

'I should be on my way now, but I didn't want to leave without saying goodbye.'

She stared down at the grass again, knowing that if she turned her head slightly she would see all of Penhally Bay spread out before her. The lifeboat station, St Mark's on the hill, the houses clustered round the harbour, and the newer bungalows higher on the hill. Everything would look just the same, but not quite the same any more, and it never would be because of the man sitting beside her.

'Have you decided what you're going to do?' she asked. 'I mean, are you staying with Deltaron, or…'

'I think you're right, that Deltaron is where I'm supposed to be,' he replied, 'but only if…'

She waited for him to finish, but when he didn't she turned to face him.

'If what, Tom?'

'Before I answer that question, I have something to give you. I bought…' Awkwardly he held out the plastic carrier bag he was clutching. 'I don't know whether this will help, or if I've got this wrong again, but I was thinking about what you said yesterday, and I thought… But maybe it's not a good idea, maybe you might think…'

'Tom, what are you trying to say?' she demanded, and when for an answer he produced a small nosegay of flowers from his bag she stared at them blankly. 'You bought me flowers?'

'I bought them for her,' he said, his voice half-muffled, his head lowered as though he was afraid to meet her eyes. 'For our daughter. You said yesterday that what upset you most was there being no grave, nowhere you could go and say you were sorry. Well, I want…' She saw him swallow. 'I want to tell her I'm sorry, too. Sorry for letting her mother down, for not being there for her when she needed me.'

'Tom—'

'Eve, I want our baby to know I'm thinking of her, and I thought…' His head came up, and when his eyes met hers she saw the pain and anguish she knew were in her own eyes mirrored in his. 'I thought maybe I could put this in the sea— if you wouldn't mind if I did that—in…in memory of her.'

Tears began to trickle down her cheeks and into her mouth.

'You really want to do that?' she said, scarcely able to see him through her tears.

'She was my baby, too, Eve. My daughter, too, and maybe…' His voice broke. 'Maybe…if I do this she might know that though she's not here with me—with us—we will never forget her, and we will always, always love her.'

'Tom… I…'

Eve couldn't say another word and when he hesitantly, awkwardly, held out his arms to her, she reached for him, too, and clung to him and felt him shudder, and knew he was crying as much as she was for the child they might have had and who they would never forget.

And, when they were calmer, they walked together to the headland, and threw the little nosegay Tom had bought up into the air, watched it soar for a few seconds, a myriad of bright colours in the blue sky, then land with a gentle splash in the water, and clung to one another again and cried again.

'I know this is too soon,' Tom said with difficulty when their grief was spent. 'So much has happened—and you're fragile right now—and I...I'm pretty shaky myself—but do you think—is there any possibility—that we might start again?'

'I don't know, Tom,' she said uncertainly. 'We have so much history. Maybe too much.'

'You said...' He caught her hands, and held them tightly. 'When you first told me about the baby—you said you loved me all those years ago. Has it all gone—that love?'

'I think...' She stared up into the face she knew so well, at the lines which seemed to have become even more deeply etched around his eyes and on his forehead over the past few days. 'I think I will always love you, Tom, but I don't know whether loving you would be enough. What happened—the baby—I think it might always come between us. Not spoken about, but always there, and when we argued—and we would argue because all couples do— my fear is we'd use it as a weapon against one another.'

'I wouldn't.'

She smiled unevenly.

'You can't be sure of that, Tom.'

'Eve, no one can be sure of anything,' he insisted. 'We might have years of happiness together, or our lives could be snuffed out in a second by some pointless car crash. You said I wasn't to blame for Charlie's death, and for the deaths of those people in India, because I did what I thought was right at the time— that it was all anyone could do. Well, the decision you made about the baby was right for you at the time, it was all *you* could do, and you have to see that, accept that.'

'I hear what you're saying, Tom,' she murmured, 'and my head tells me you're right, but my heart...'

'Eve, I have loved you for so long,' he said, his voice constricted. 'I was in love with you even when we were at school.'

'No, you weren't,' she said. 'Starchy Dwyer, remember?'

'Do you want to know why I called you that?' he said. 'It was because I fancied you like mad but I was the no-hoper, Tom Cornish's son, whereas you… You were the one who always got the good grades, the one whose parents were respectable, acceptable, and I'd have looked a proper fool in front of my friends if I'd asked you out, and you'd said no, so it was easier to act like I thought you were the prat.'

'It was a pretty good act,' she said with feeling, and his lips curved into a slight smile, then the smile disappeared.

'Eve, I want to spend the rest of my life with you. Yes, we've made mistakes, and I made the biggest one of all, but I need you, Eve. It's not just the wanting—though God knows I want you so much—but…' He let go of her hands and thrust his fingers through his hair, his face taut, strained. 'I *need* you.'

'Tom—'

'No, please, let me finish,' he pressed. 'All these years I've been chasing dreams, and nothing brought me any happiness, any contentment, because you weren't in my life. When I think of all the years we could have had together, the memories we could have made and shared. I lost them. Me. Not you. Me, always on the move, thinking excitement was the answer, when all the time what I really wanted was here, in my own back yard, because, you see…' His voice cracked. 'You are my dreams, Eve, you always have been.'

There was honesty and truth in his face, and she knew she would never love anyone as much as she loved him, but so much had happened over the last few days, and she felt raw, exposed, vulnerable.

'Twenty years, Tom,' she said slowly. 'It's a lot of years to forget.'

'I'm not asking you to forget them,' he said, his voice soft with understanding. 'I know you can't, just as I know I can't go back and give myself the knowledge I have now. I wish I could. I wish I hadn't been the stupid, blind, selfish person I was then, but all the wishing in the world can't make that happen, but if we can both—somehow—forgive ourselves, then maybe we won't just have a shared past. Maybe we can have a future, together.'

'But, you're leaving,' she said. 'You're going to China.'

'Yes, I'm leaving.' He nodded. 'But what I want to know is, if I come back to Penhally, when all of this upheaval is over, would you want to see me again?'

She gazed out to sea to where the little nosegay was floating away towards the horizon, and then she looked up at him. Up into the face that had once haunted her dreams, the face she'd once loved, and then hated, and saw the entreaty in his eyes, the desperate hope, and though she didn't know what the future was going to bring she did know that the fates had given her another chance at happiness and she would be foolish to let it go.

'Yes,' she said, her voice a little wobbly, a little tremulous. 'I'd want to see you again, Tom.'

And a blinding smile illuminated his face, and he caught her hand, and pressed her knuckles to his lips.

'One day at a time, Eve,' he said. 'We'll take this one day at a time, and no matter how long it takes I will wait for you.'

And she smiled back at him, and nodded, and together they walked back down into Penhally Bay.

EPILOGUE

Six months later

DUSK. A magical time, a perfect time for a wedding. That's what any guest staying at the exclusive Lake Lausanne hotel would have said if they'd looked out of the dining-room windows onto the lawn and seen a clergyman and two other men standing beside an archway of spring blossom, clearly waiting for a bride to arrive. However, if those guests had looked a little closer, they would have seen that one of the men looked distinctly nervous.

'Mitch, are you quite sure this morning suit doesn't make me look like a complete prat?'

'Well, now you come to mention it…' the pilot began, then grinned as Tom gazed at him in dismay. 'You look fine.'

Tom tugged at his tie. 'Shouldn't Eve be here by now?'

'Tom, Eve is not going to do a runner, although I will if you keep on stressing.'

'Right. Sorry,' Tom muttered, glancing down at his watch.

'Eight minutes,' Mitch observed.

'What?'

'The ceremony is due to begin in eight minutes,' the pilot declared. 'Which is exactly two minutes less than the time was when you last checked your watch.'

'Right.'

Mitch shot Tom a mischievous glance.

'Wouldn't it just be typical if we were to get a call from Deltaron?' he said, then guffawed when Tom's mouth fell open in horror. 'Just kidding. They know you're not available. Know I'm not, too. No way was I going to miss out on being your best man.'

'I really appreciate you agreeing to do this, Mitch,' Tom said awkwardly. 'It's…well…it's very good of you.'

The big pilot looked equally embarrassed.

'Me miss out on the opportunity of seeing the head of operations at Deltaron in a complete panic? No chance.'

'I guess not.' Tom smiled, then glanced down at his watch again.

'Seven minutes,' Mitch said, 'and if you look at your watch one more time I'll ram it down your throat.'

'Amanda, are you sure we're not late?' Eve said as she glanced out of the French windows of the hotel. 'Tom's walking up and down out there like he's scared I'm not going to turn up or something.'

'Of course you're not late,' Amanda insisted as Tassie pirouetted past them, clearly revelling in her pale blue bridesmaid's dress. 'And, even if you were, it's the bride's prerogative.'

'Not this bride,' Eve said with a shaky laugh. 'This bride's been waiting twenty years for this moment.'

'No doubts, then?' Tassie's mother said, and Eve shook her head.

'None at all,' she replied, and she didn't have, not now.

Bit by bit, over the last six months, Tom had chipped away at her worries, emailing or phoning her every day, but it was when he had returned to Penhally for both Melinda and Rachel's little boys' christenings that she had finally been convinced. She knew he would never feel comfortable in Penhally, and yet he'd

come back because she'd wanted him to. Come back to make
her happy, and it was that which convinced her to say yes when
he'd asked her to marry him, and that night, after Rachel's
baby's christening…

Her face softened. She'd been so nervous and self-conscious
that night, and he'd been so gentle, so tender, making her laugh,
relaxing her, so their joining had been even more wonderful,
even more perfect, than it had been the last time they'd made
love twenty years ago.

'I still can't believe you're actually going to be living here,'
Amanda continued. 'I thought you were like me—destined
always to stay in Penhally.'

'I thought so, too,' Eve admitted, 'but it makes sense for us
to live in Switzerland when most of Tom's team have homes
here, and…' She shrugged. 'I think it's maybe way past time
I spread my wings.'

'Tassie and I wouldn't be here at all if Tom hadn't paid our
air fares,' Amanda said. 'We owe you so—'

'You owe us nothing,' Eve interrupted, putting her fingers to
the woman's lips quickly to silence her. 'We wanted you at our
wedding, and I'll be very cross if you don't use those other air
tickets Tom gave you to come and visit us regularly.'

'But—'

'No buts,' Eve insisted. 'Tassie's special, and so are you.'

'I don't know about us being special,' Amanda said, blowing
her nose vigorously, 'but you certainly look lovely today. That
colour really suits you.'

Eve uncertainly smoothed down the folds of the long crimson
skirt and matching embroidered bolero jacket she was wearing.

'You don't think it looks odd, me wearing red?' she said. 'It's
just Tom likes this colour—'

'I think you look gorgeous,' Amanda insisted. 'Like you
have a candle inside you, burning with happiness.'

It was how Eve felt as she stepped out of the French windows and saw Mitch nudge Tom, and Tom's whole face light up when he turned and saw her. It was how she felt throughout the whole ceremony as Tom repeated his vows, his voice a little husky, and she made her own pledges, her voice just as uneven, and his fingers tightened round hers as though he never wanted to let her go.

She didn't want to let go of him either. All she wanted was to be alone with him, but Mitch had organised a wedding supper for them and she knew it would have seemed ungrateful if she and Tom had slipped away the minute they'd finished eating.

Mitch obviously didn't agree. In fact, the second their plates were cleared, the pilot gave Amanda a very decided wink, then glanced at his watch.

'Half past nine already,' he said. 'I think it's time some folk should be in their beds.'

'But I don't normally go to bed until ten o'clock,' Tassie protested and, as Amanda laughed, and Eve blushed, Tom got to his feet.

'I couldn't agree with you more, Mitch,' he said, 'but there's something I want to do first.'

Eve's eyebrows rose as he strode across to the quartet who had been playing a medley of tunes throughout the evening.

'What he's up to, Mitch?' she asked and the pilot shook his head.

'Haven't a clue, love.'

Neither did she until the quartet began to play the opening bars of a tune she recognised instantly, and when Tom held out his arms to her, she had to blink very rapidly before she could walk out onto the small dance floor and join him.

'My very own Lady in Red,' he murmured into her hair as he drew her into his arms. 'And you are mine now, for always, aren't you?'

And she was, she thought as he whirled her round the small dance floor, holding her closer, and closer, moulding his body to hers, so she could feel the uneven throb of his heartbeat, could see his eyes growing darker and more intense with every passing second and, when the music ended, and he kissed her, she never wanted the kiss to end.

Neither, it seemed, did the other diners if the eruption of applause, and the sound of Mitch whooping enthusiastically, was anything to go by when they finally drew apart.

'I think maybe Mitch was right,' Tom said, leaning his forehead against hers, his cheeks flushed, his breathing uneven. 'Maybe it *is* time we go to bed before I completely forget we're not alone.'

'Definitely,' she said, chuckling shakily as the leader of the quartet shook her hand, and said something incomprehensible in Swiss, and the diners applauded again.

She thought it even more when Tom drew her back into his arms the second they reached their hotel room.

'Oh, Tom, I am so happy.' She sighed, as he slid his hands up her sides so she felt the heat of his fingers through the fine satin of her jacket. 'I keep thinking I'm going to wake up, find this is all a dream, that no one has the right to be as happy as I am right now.'

'You do,' he said, tracing the outline of her jaw with his lips. 'You deserve everything you've ever wanted, and I'm going to make it my life's ambition to ensure you get it.'

'You already have,' she said huskily. 'In fact...' She took a deep breath. 'There's something I have to tell you.'

'Later,' he said, his eyes liquid with desire as he began un-buttoning her jacket. 'Later we talk, but right now...'

She wanted the 'right now', too, she thought as he eased her jacket off, then her bra, and when he caressed her breasts with his fingers and lips she felt the heat flare everywhere. Every part of her body seemed so much more sensitive tonight, she thought as he removed the rest of her clothing, then his, and she knew why but it would keep. Just for a little while it would keep, she decided as she clung to him, revelling in his hardness as he whispered words of love, and touched her, and kissed her, telling her over and over how beautiful she was, how desirable, until she was shaking with need.

'Tom, please—*please*,' she gasped, wanting more, even more.

And he laughed, and kissed her again, and just when she thought she wouldn't be able to bear it any longer, he finally entered her, hot and slick, and she rose up to join him, wanting to give him the same joy he was giving her, and felt her heart clutch with happiness when he carried her over the edge and his cry matched hers as they spiralled and shuddered and climaxed together.

'My wife,' he said, gathering her, spoon-like, against his chest. 'You're all I've ever wanted Eve, all I'll ever need.'

She gazed down at his arms encircling her, and cleared her throat.

'Tom…do you remember when you told me how much you would like to have children?'

His grip on her tightened.

'Eve, I'm happy simply having you,' he said softly. 'I'm not saying it wouldn't be a great joy to me if we were so blessed, but…' He turned her round in his arms so he could look at her. 'For such a long time I thought I'd lost you. For an even longer time I thought I'd messed things up completely. If we should have a baby then it would be wonderful because you deserve so much to be a mother, but if we're not lucky—if it doesn't happen—you've already made my life complete, just by being you.'

'You've made my life complete, too,' she said unevenly, 'but what I meant…' She could feel her cheeks darkening which was ridiculous because she had nothing to feel embarrassed about, but she so wanted him to feel the same way she did. 'When I asked whether you still wanted to be a father I was thinking of… perhaps in about six months?'

'Six months?' he repeated with a frown. 'Eve—'

'Tom, when did we first make love again?' she interrupted, and saw his frown deepen.

'It was when I came back for Rachel's son's christening. When I asked you to marry me, and you…' He smiled. 'You said yes, and made me the happiest man on the planet.'

'That was three months ago, Tom.' He still looked confused and she chuckled softly. 'And you call yourself a doctor. Think about it. Tom. If I'm asking whether you would like to be a father in six months' time, and we made love three months ago…'

He stared at her silently for a second, then sat up so fast she had to catch hold of him to prevent herself landing face down in the pillow.

'You're pregnant?' He gasped.

'Yes.' She nodded, watching his face anxiously.

A smile tugged at his lips. A smile that grew, and grew, and tentatively he reached out and gently put his fingers on her stomach.

'A baby,' he said, wonder plain in his voice. 'We're going to have a baby.'

'Are…are you pleased?' she said, and he dashed his hand across his eyes.

'Oh, Eve,' he said, his voice husky. 'Oh, my love, my *love.*'

And he clasped her to him, his eyes as bright and shimmering as she knew hers must be, then released her abruptly, concern plain on his face, and gently touched her tummy again, and she laughed, a hiccuping laugh that was halfway towards a sob.

'Tom, I'm not made of glass,' she said. 'I won't break.'

'No, but I think I might,' he said. 'Break with happiness, and joy.'

And he drew her to him again and kissed her so tenderly, and she felt the wetness on his cheeks, knew her own cheeks were tear-stained, too, but they were tears of happiness. That at last—at long last—she and Tom would have not just a past together, but a glorious, wonderful future.

DR DEVEREUX'S
PROPOSAL

MARGARET McDONAGH

With special thanks...
To those who helped with my research on
retinitis pigmentosa – your courage is humbling
www.brps.org.uk – and on Duchenne muscular
dystrophy www.muscular-dystrophy.org.
To my fellow Medical Romance authors involved
in this exciting series.
And to the wonderful editorial team who
conceived the Penhally project – thank you
for believing in me.

CHAPTER ONE

'QUE L'ENFER?' Shocked by the sight that greeted him as his destination came into view, Dr Gabriel Devereux drew his car to a halt at the side of the cliff road and stepped out. *'Mon Dieu!'*

What had happened to the small Cornish town of Penhally Bay? His one previous visit had been in the summer when he had spent a weekend looking around and finalising details for his year-long contract to work as a GP in the local practice. Penhally had recently been twinned with St Ouen-sur-Mer in Normandy, France, where he had been filling in for the last ten months at his friend François Amiot's busy medical clinic.

As part of the twinning process, people from different occupations and ways of life were crossing the Channel, exchanging jobs and skills, building bridges and friendships, bringing the communities of the two towns together, socially, commercially and culturally. None of the other doctors in St Ouen-sur-Mer had been prepared to move their families for a year, but for Gabriel it had been too good an opportunity to miss. Taking this post in Cornwall was a heaven-sent chance to put even more distance between himself and the unresolved issues that had seen him leave Paris for St Ouen-sur-Mer in the first place.

Ruthlessly banishing any thoughts of home, Gabriel's gaze narrowed as he concentrated on the scene of devastation below him. In the summer, Penhally Bay had been an attractive, hilly, seaside town bustling with tourists and basking under sunshine and clear blue skies. The rows of houses, shops and businesses along the curving seafront, painted in an array of pastel colours, had watched over the boats that had bobbed gently in the harbour. Now… He shook his head in disbelief. This cloudy late October day, the scene could not have been more different.

When his new boss, Nick Tremayne, the senior partner at the Penhally practice, had emailed a week ago to confirm the date to begin work, he had mentioned a flash flood, but Gabriel had not fully grasped the seriousness of what had occurred. A man of few words, Nick had not gone into detail, but Gabriel could see that the event had been far more cataclysmic than that one brief email had implied.

After breathing in a lungful of fresh, salty, Cornish air, Gabriel climbed back in the car and drove down the hill to the town. He passed the promontory on which the church and the lighthouse stood, before heading along the seafront that formed a horseshoe round the harbour. At the far western end of the arc were the lifeboat station and the surgery where he would be working from Monday. Halfway around the seafront, he slowed as he neared the bridge. Here, the river Lanson, which flowed down the hill between Bridge Street and Gull Close, effectively cutting the town in two, spilled its waters into the harbour.

This central area appeared to have borne the brunt of the flooding with damage obvious to houses in Bridge Street and around the seafront. The end wall of the Anchor Hotel—on the corner of Gull Close and Harbour Road—had come down under the force of the water. Standing forlorn and closed for business, the remains of the building were shored up with scaffolding, and demolition notices warned that the property was unsafe.

Twelve days on, the waters had receded and the clean-up operation had begun, but the empty houses and shops were all too apparent, as was the debris that had washed down the angry river in full spate. Ruined and discarded belongings sat forlornly outside abandoned properties, full skips awaited collection and disposal, while redundant sandbags remained by doors and gateways.

The town bustled with life, however. These people clearly had spirit, banding together and refusing to allow the difficult circumstances to defeat them. It was past lunchtime and the Saturday market was thriving. People were shopping in the stores that had evaded damage, a few were fishing off the harbour wall or working on their boats, while dedicated parties were continuing the task of restoring order after the flood. Gabriel planned to do all he could to help in the days and weeks ahead…but first he needed to find the house that was to be his base for the next year, move in and find his feet.

As he reached the outskirts of town, his memory guiding him down a narrow, hedge-lined lane, he experienced a flicker of uncharacteristic nervousness. He hoped he would settle here, that he would be accepted…a stranger and a foreigner in this tight community. Penhally Bay was not the cosmopolitan metropolis of London where he had spent time during his medical training. Would the people here judge him on his skills as a doctor or on being different? He hoped the former…was wary of the latter.

Half a mile farther along the lane, he came to the turning he was seeking and steered the car between the twin gateposts that marked the unpaved driveway. To one side was Gatehouse Cottage, the single-storey thatched lodge which Nick Tremayne had told him belonged to the physiotherapist at the surgery. Gabriel frowned, unable to remember her name. There were no signs of life from the cottage so he hoped his arrival had gone unnoticed. The drive curved away from the lodge and fifty yards farther on the impressive but not-too-large Manor House came into view, sheltered and surrounded by mature shrubs and trees. Gabriel paused, admiring the traditional fifteenth-century building, feeling now the same contentment he had experienced when he had first been here in late July.

Symbolically, the clouds overhead cleared, and low autumn sunshine filtered down from a patch of pale blue sky, highlighting myriad colours in the old, lichen-spotted granite blocks and dark roof slates from which the Manor House was built. Instinct told him he had been right to come here. This was what he needed. A place where he could work with his customary enthusiasm for the job he loved…a refuge where he could be alone and decide what he was going to do about the rest of his life.

He parked his car at the rear of the building, out of sight should anyone approach up the drive. He had arrived a day early and planned to take time to himself before announcing his presence. After finding the keys to the house—left for him by the solicitor acting for the owners, who were working abroad long term—he collected together his essential belongings and let himself in. He knew the house had been empty since the last tenants had departed at the end of August, so he was surprised to find the air smelling fresh and the surfaces clean of dust. Someone had been thoughtful enough to make preparations for his arrival. The knowledge warmed him.

Upstairs, he selected a bedroom with a lovely view over the surrounding countryside. Whoever had taken care of the house had anticipated his choice, because clean linen was folded neatly on the huge four-poster bed and fresh towels were hanging on the heated rail in the *en suite* bathroom. Bars of unfussy, masculine soap, still in their wrappers, sat on the basin and in the generous shower cubicle. Appreciating the welcoming touches, and making a mental note to discover the identity of and thank the unknown cleaner, Gabriel stripped off his clothes and headed for the shower.

Hot water jetted down, easing the kinks out of his body, soothing his muscles and restoring his jaded spirit, making him realise how much tension remained coiled inside him.

'You're sure this is what you want?' François had asked him as he had come to see him off the day before. 'I don't want you to feel obligated to go to Cornwall because none of the rest of us are willing to uproot ourselves.'

'It's not that,' Gabriel had reassured his friend.

Frowning, François had helped him load his bags into the car. 'You're worried about interference from home?'

'Always.' His smile had been wry, hiding the inner turmoil that had plagued him for months. 'I need the distance, the space to make some decisions.'

'You know I'll watch your back. I won't be giving out details of your whereabouts to anyone. Especially now we know what Yvette is capable of to achieve her ends.'

Gabriel had nodded in gratitude. 'Thanks, *mon ami*. But you and I will keep in touch.'

'Try to get rid of me! I want regular texts and emails.'

He would miss François and his wife, having stayed with the couple for the last ten months. 'You and Celeste take care.'

'We will—and we really appreciate the way you stepped in when we needed you,' Francois had told him.

'That's what friends are for.'

After shaking hands and exchanging a brief hug, Gabriel had driven away from St Ouen-sur-Mer filled with nervous anticipation for what lay ahead. One chapter was over—a new one was about to begin.

Now, remembering that conversation, he closed his eyes and tipped his face to the shower spray. Today was the first day of the rest of his life. It was up to him what he made of it…whether he went his own way or allowed old ghosts and new pressures to trap him into something he knew he didn't want. This posting to Cornwall had bought him some extra time. Time he intended to use wisely, making the decisions that would set the course of his future.

Shutting off the water, he stepped out of the cubicle and reached for a towel, hesitating when he heard a noise downstairs. It had sounded like the front door closing. Frowning, Gabriel waited, listening. Yes, there was definitely someone moving around inside the house. More curious than concerned, he wrapped the towel around his waist and left his bedroom, moving silently down the stairs to investigate the trespass into his new domain. The noises were louder now. He tiptoed in the direction from which they came, pausing in the shadows of the unlit passageway to look through the door into a large, homely farmhouse kitchen.

A brindle-and-white greyhound lay on the stone-flagged floor, its head on its paws, solemnly watching the movements of the woman who was moving about as if she owned the place. Guessing her age to be in the late twenties, Gabriel's gaze lingered on her with as much intensity as the dog's, warmth and pure masculine appreciation spearing through him, catching him by surprise.

A bunch of home-cut flowers, dahlias and chrysanthemums amongst them, were arranged haphazardly in an old stoneware jug on the table, while several carrier bags littered the polished wooden work surfaces. Humming an unrecognisable tune, the woman busied herself stocking the kitchen cupboards with her purchases, her movements athletically graceful. Tight white jeans accentuated the length of her legs and lovingly moulded the rounded swell of her derrière. As she turned round, still unaware of his presence, he could see how the super-soft angora jumper she wore skimmed her shapely frame, outlining the curves of full, firm breasts. The lavender colour set off the natural paler highlights in her light brown hair and lent an amethyst glow to what he could see, even from this distance, were gorgeous grey eyes. Gabriel was mesmerised. Who was this woman?

Picking up a carton of milk and a box of eggs, she twirled her way to the fridge on trainer-clad feet, presenting him with a delectable view of her feminine curves as she bent over, her hips swaying provocatively to the music she heard in her head. Left loose, her wavy hair cascaded round her shoulders in a darkly golden curtain. She flicked it back with one hand as she rose and returned to the counter, still humming to herself as she delved into the carrier bags once more.

Intrigued, Gabriel stepped into the room. The dog was the first to acknowledge him. Anxious brown eyes turned his way, then the too-thin creature whined and all but crawled towards the woman, who leaned down to stroke it with gentle care.

'What's wrong, Foxy?'

Knowing whatever he did was going to startle her, Gabriel cleared his throat, announcing his presence as he walked forward. 'Hello.'

With a shocked cry, the woman swung round, the pack of pasta shells in her hands dropping to the floor. Beautiful smoky grey eyes widened between long, dark lashes as she stared at him, and lushly kissable lips parted in surprise. Her tongue-tip peeped out to moisten them as she stepped back a pace, one hand dropping to calm the fretful dog pressed against her legs, the other curled to a fist at her throat. Gabriel felt her gaze skim over his scantily clad frame and an unexpected but immediate wave of attraction crashed through him.

'I'm sorry.' He offered a smile with the apology, unable to look away from her. 'I didn't mean to scare you. I heard a noise down here and had no idea anyone was around.'

'OK. Um…hello,' she greeted after a moment, her voice melodious but with a husky undertone that appealed to him. Hell, everything about her appealed to him. 'You must be Dr Devereux. I wasn't expecting you until tomorrow,' she continued, bending to pick up the fallen pasta, fumbling briefly as she set it awkwardly back on the counter. With a sudden smile that had the same effect on him as a punch to the solar plexus, she held out her hand. 'I'm Lauren Nightingale…your neighbour at Gatehouse Cottage and also physiotherapist at the Penhally Bay Surgery.'

This was the woman Nick Tremayne had spoken of? *Ooh la la!* 'Lauren, it is a pleasure to meet you. Please, call me Gabriel,' he invited, trying to pull himself together and remember his manners.

Closing the remaining gap between them, he took her graceful hand in his. Her grip was strong, her fingers slender but capable. Looking down, he noted how much paler her warm, satiny skin was than his, how her bones were far more delicate. A jolt of electricity zinged up his arm and along his nerve endings at the contact between them. That Lauren felt it, too, was apparent by the way she bit her lip, her pupils dilating, her body momentarily swaying towards him before she caught herself and pulled back, withdrawing her hand. Gabriel released her with reluctance.

Close to, she was taller than he had realised, five-seven or -eight, he judged, and even more attractive than he had first thought. She had an earthy allure quite unlike the sophisticated, deliberate beauty of some of the Parisian women he had dated in the past but vastly more entrancing and natural. A subtle, floral scent—sweet peas, he recognised—mingled with her unique femininity, teasing and enticing him. No make-up was needed to enhance her flawless skin. Pale gold from a fading summer tan, it looked as smooth as silk. His fingers longed to touch, to discover if she was as warm and soft all over as her hand had felt in his. He struggled to rein back the runaway thoughts but it wasn't easy when every particle of his being hummed with awareness while she studied him as closely as he had regarded her.

Dr Gabriel Devereux was the most delicious surprise!

Fearing that her legs would not hold her upright much

longer, Lauren leaned against the kitchen counter and affected what she hoped was a nonchalant pose. She didn't *feel* remotely nonchalant. Any minute now she was going to do something uncharacteristically shocking, impulsive and embarrassing…like throw herself wantonly into his arms and ravish him.

Gabriel's sudden arrival had taken her off guard. She was disconcerted that she had not been aware of his presence and wondered how long he had stood there watching her. But the fact that she had not seen him in the shadows and had only formed a distinct visual impression when he had stepped into the brightly lit kitchen stirred inner anxieties she was unwilling to deal with. That he was wearing only an ivory towel was a suitable diversion, however, and she grabbed the excuse to ignore her disturbing concerns, unable to resist the temptation to observe him in detail.

She saw bare bodies, or bits of bodies, every working day, but she had never seen one that made her heart hammer, her mouth water and that robbed her of breath as Gabriel's did. Goodness! Her hands clung to the counter as she greedily inspected him. She feared she was about to melt into a puddle at his feet. Nice feet, too, she couldn't help but notice. Very nice. Like the rest of him. Her gaze slowly climbed back up his scrumptious frame.

Strong, lean legs were braced hip-width apart and the towel slung low around his hips revealed a tantalising glimpse of pleasingly muscled, hair-brushed thighs. A narrow line of dark hair in the centre of his flat stomach dipped past his navel and disappeared below the towel. She licked her lips, resisting the urge to touch as she looked over his perfect athletic body, toned abdomen, well-defined chest and broad shoulders, all supple flesh and rippling muscle. He'd clearly just stepped out of the shower as droplets of water glistened on his delicious dark caramel skin, its colour hinting at a French

Caribbean ancestry. Lauren swallowed, battling against the overwhelming desire to press her lips to that warm, damp masculine flesh. She still remembered the faint scent of him when they had been close and shaken hands...tangy citrus soap and clean male, heady and earthy and arousing.

Topping six feet, he was more than impressive. The close-cropped dark hair suited him, accentuating the classically beautiful but supremely masculine bone structure of his face, the slash of high cheekbones, the straight nose and the carved lines of his jaw. Her palm itched to smooth over his head, to feel if the razor-short hair was rough or soft to the touch. His mouth was undeniably sexy, his bronze lips sensually curved and designed for kissing. She yearned to press her own against them, to learn the shape and feel and taste of him.

Twin dimples creased his cheeks when he smiled, while laughter lines fanned out from the corners of his eyes, adding character and hinting at an active sense of humour. Finally, she looked into those thickly lashed eyes. They were the richest brown she had ever seen. As Gabriel met and held her gaze, his pupils dilated, darkening the irises to the colour of finest coffee. The flare of masculine interest was unmistakable and caused a tightening ache of want in the pit of her stomach that was so strong and so sudden she barely suppressed a gasp.

What in the world had come over her? Yes, it had been a while since she had enjoyed male companionship. She had broken up with her long-term boyfriend, Martin Bennett, six months ago, but to all intents and purposes they had been apart a long time before that. They had gone their separate ways amicably, both knowing their lingering on-again-off-again relationship had been based more on old friendship than grand passion and had been leading nowhere. Martin was desperate to get out of Cornwall, to explore and experience new things, while Lauren was content to remain in Penhally, enjoying her job, her friends and her hobbies, including her painting.

Unwelcome and worrying thoughts intruded once more. She hadn't painted much lately and she wasn't anywhere near ready to face the reasons why. Determinedly, she returned her full attention to the exquisite man before her, a quiver running through her at his thorough inspection, as if he had touched her physically.

Since midwife Kate Althorp had met Gabriel at Nick's house in the summer, she had reported that Penhally was in for a treat when the French doctor arrived in their midst. Kate's comments had caused some of their colleagues to tease Lauren about her soon-to-be neighbour. Lauren had ignored the ribbing. But now she could acknowledge first hand that Kate had not been exaggerating. Dear heaven, the man was *gorgeous*!

That Gabriel Devereux would be close by, at home and at work, for the next twelve months was wonderfully thrilling. Already the year ahead was filled with new and unexpected possibilities. Everything feminine within her stood to attention and all the hormones that had been switched off and uninterested since long before her split from Martin now started doing a happy dance like over-enthusiastic cheerleaders. She looked into Gabriel's eyes, excited by the answering desire she saw there. Oh, yes! She was most definitely interested! She just hoped he was in England alone, uninvolved, and had no wife or girlfriend tucked away at home in France.

'It is kind of you to bring things for the kitchen, Lauren,' Gabriel said, the dimples forming in his lean cheeks, his eyes crinkling as he smiled.

She could drown in that smile. And as for his accent, the way he said her name... He made her tingle all over. His English was perfect but delivered with a soft burr and all the Gallic charm imaginable. There was so much she wanted to learn about him but she reined in her rush of questions, scared that she would frighten him away before he'd even properly arrived. There would be time in the days and weeks ahead to explore the inexplicable and immediate connection she felt with this man. Or so she hoped. Better to play it cool for now.

'It's no trouble,' she answered, not sure how she managed to form any words at all, let alone sensible ones. 'I promised Nick I would make sure you had all you needed.'

Relaxed and at ease, he folded his arms across his chest, the play of muscle distracting her. 'Thank you. I am sorry I took you by surprise arriving early.'

'No problem.' Returning his smile, she couldn't prevent herself looking over his superb body once more. Oh, it was no problem at all!

'Are you also responsible for airing the house and providing the clean linen and towels?'

'Yes.' Almost overcome with nervous anticipation, she tucked some strands of hair behind one ear, her hand unsteady. 'Is everything all right?'

'Very much so. I was planning to ask the solicitor who to thank for making the house feel so welcoming.'

'I'm glad to help,' she assured him, warmed through and pleased by his thoughtfulness.

He watched her for a long moment, then glanced at the greyhound who whined and nudged against her legs. 'And who is your companion?'

'This is Foxy. He lost his owner in the flood and was found distressed after searching the rubble,' she explained, a catch in her voice as she gently stroked the dog. 'Both the RSPCA and Lizzie Chamberlain, who runs the local kennels, were overrun with extra work and animals needing help during the crisis. Foxy was always nervous of people, but he knew me and we bonded, so I was happy to give him a home. He's adjusting but still wary. At least he's started eating again. He needs time and lots of love.'

The approval and flash of admiration in Gabriel's eyes made her feel good. She held her breath as he turned his attention to

Foxy. Speaking softly, he hunkered down and held out his hand for the dog to sniff. Calm and patient, he waited for the dog to be comfortable, making no sudden moves. Lauren was surprised and delighted when Foxy inched forward and allowed Gabriel to touch him, something he had permitted few people but her to do in the last ten days. Slowly he was forming a tentative bond with her friends Chloe and Oliver. Foxy's current reaction and his instinct to trust Gabriel was more than interesting and told her much about this intriguing man.

As if satisfied with the early progress, Gabriel didn't push things, moving carefully back and rising before returning his attention to her, causing her heart to pound once more.

'Nick mentioned the flood in an email but I had no idea how bad things were. I was shocked when I drove through town.' He paused, a pout of consideration shaping his mouth and giving her all manner of wicked ideas. 'Are you busy this afternoon, Lauren? Do you have plans?'

'No. Why?' She was filled with sudden hope that she might be able to spend more time with Gabriel. She wasn't ready to leave just yet.

'I was going to make myself a late lunch. Will you join me? It would be good to talk, to learn more about Penhally and the surgery…and what has gone on in the last couple of weeks.'

Not wanting to appear as shamefully eager as she felt, she forced herself not to rush her agreement. Maybe Gabriel's reasons for asking her to linger weren't all she had hoped for, but at this point she would accept any opportunity to enjoy his company. Who knew where things might lead?

'OK.' She cursed the breathlessness of her voice but could do nothing to temper her excitement. 'I can stay a while longer.'

At Lauren's confirmation, Gabriel felt a wash of relief course through him and he expelled the breath he had not realised he had been holding. He was nowhere near ready to let her go.

This was ridiculous. He felt like some gauche sixteen-year-old boy with a crush, rather than the thirty-six-year-old man he really was. Then Lauren looked over him once more and his body instantly heated and tightened in response, as if her touch had been an actual caress. He hoped the loose towel hid the evidence of the arousing effect she had on him.

'Give me five minutes to get dressed,' he requested as he turned away and headed to the door.

'Gabriel?'

Her soft voice halted him and he glanced back. 'Yes?'

'I could prepare a quick meal while you're gone,' she offered.

'Are you sure?'

Her head bobbed in assent. 'It's no trouble. Is there anything you don't like?'

Dieu! He couldn't imagine anything Lauren could suggest that he wouldn't like, but he managed to focus his attention on food. 'Mushrooms, shellfish and red meat,' he informed her, catching her surprised smile.

'Me, too.' Mischief gleamed in her eyes. 'And I confess I'm not keen on boiled cabbage, tapioca or mushy peas either.'

'Believe me, Lauren, you are not alone!' Chuckling, he left the room.

'I certainly hope not—not any more.'

Had he really heard those final whispered words? And could they mean what he hoped they did? He was confused by his instinctive response to this woman. It was unlike him. And that was disturbing. He'd not been so spontaneously attracted to anyone for years—if ever. The timing was unfortunate. He had never considered such a thing happening to him, especially not while part of his world was in turmoil and he had decisions to make about his future. Coming here was meant to give him space to declutter his life, not add more complications to it.

But he couldn't deny the way his body had reacted to the

sight, scent and sound of Lauren Nightingale. Anxious to dress and return to the kitchen as quickly as possible, Gabriel hurried up the stairs. Had he dreamed it all? What if the sizzle of electricity between himself and Lauren had been a figment of his overactive imagination? What if it wasn't? He was here for a year. To work. To think. Did he even want to consider any kind of involvement? He hadn't been at the Manor House an hour and already he was feeling alive at an unexpected awareness, filled with a sense of wary excitement at the possibilities that might lie ahead.

Perhaps it had just been too long since he had dated a woman. After his most recent experience with Adèle, and with his mother's continued interference, he had become cautious, untrusting. But that had been a year ago. And Lauren knew nothing about his life—or his family circumstances. More importantly, Yvette, his mother, knew nothing about Lauren. If anything happened between them, it would be because of who and what they were…no ulterior motives, no deception, no scheming.

Unzipping a suitcase, he pulled out fresh clothes and dressed in record time, favouring casual jeans and a warm cashmere jumper. As he made his way out of his bedroom, tantalising aromas teased his senses and sharpened his hunger, and he increased his pace, keen to discover both the food awaiting him and the intriguing woman who was preparing it.

Lauren occupied his thoughts. He would be cautious about rushing into anything, but he wanted to spend time with her, to get to know her better. If the connection and charge of desire he had felt between them *was* real…

CHAPTER TWO

LAUREN set the plate of food she had prepared on the table in the rustic kitchen and tried very hard not to stare at Gabriel. An impossible feat. He looked almost as gorgeous with his clothes *on*…and just as impressive. The sweater he wore—over the kind of faded, body-hugging jeans that ought to be made illegal, so lethal were they to a woman's blood pressure—looked expensive, the mulberry colour warming and flattering the espresso-coffee tones of his skin.

He sat down, a quizzical expression on his face as he noted she had only laid one place. 'You are not eating, Lauren?'

'No.' The breathlessness was back in her voice—an uncharacteristic reaction that seemed to afflict her at every sight and sound of Gabriel Devereux. 'I met up with friends in town. We had soup and sandwiches at the farmers' market.'

'But you will join me here, yes?' He drew out the chair nearest to him before extending a hand and inviting her to sit.

Gratified by his suggestion to be near him, Lauren hastened to take her seat, hoping she looked far less flustered than she felt. 'Thank you.' For goodness' sake. She was a thirty-year-old woman, not some blushing schoolgirl!

'Forgive me tucking right in, I'm hungrier than I thought.' The appreciative look he sent her, and the readiness of his

smile, heated her right through. So much for cool, calm matu-
rity. 'This looks and smells wonderful.'

Cooking was not her greatest talent, but Gabriel gave every
evidence of liking her food. She'd made him a simple omelette
with cheese and chives, serving it with a warmed granary roll,
plus a tomato, rocket and watercress salad…all fresh ingre-
dients she had picked up on her shopping trip that morning.
He was eating with relish, his enjoyment making her smile
with relief. And she had even more to be grateful for, she
admitted to herself—she'd not had any accidents or set fire
to the kitchen which, given her current run of clumsy *faux pas*,
was a major achievement.

Foxy, having quenched his thirst from the bowl of water
she had set down for him, now sprawled his long, too-skinny
body beside her chair, his paws twitching in his sleep, blissfully unconcerned by the electrically charged atmosphere
crackling between the two humans. Lauren couldn't help but
be aware of it. Aware of Gabriel. She was glad she had made
herself some tea. It gave her something to do with her hands.
Anything to avoid the temptation—the compulsion—to touch
him. She cupped the mug, watching from beneath her lashes
as he finished his meal. When she raised the mug to her lips
and took a sip of her drink, she looked up to find mocha eyes
watching her intently, and a fresh dart of feminine recognition zinged through her body.

'That was delicious.' Gabriel's smile and sexy accent undid
her every time. 'Thank you, Lauren.'

'My pleasure.'

After taking a drink from his glass of water, he turned so
he was facing her, giving her his undivided attention. She
could feel fresh heat tinge her cheeks. 'It seems a long time
since breakfast.'

'Did you come over from France this morning?' she ventured,
struggling to appear cool and composed.

'I took the chance of an earlier ferry from Cherbourg to Poole yesterday, then I stayed the night with an old friend in Bournemouth before driving down here today.'

A bleakness shadowed his eyes, so fleeting it was gone before she could be sure. But she was left with a sense that there was more to Gabriel's departure from France than he had let on. She wondered what had happened, and whether there was a woman involved.

Instead of satisfying her curiosity and asking outright, she endeavoured to be more subtle. 'Wouldn't getting a ferry to Plymouth have been easier?'

'Not really. Cherbourg is only about thirty or forty minutes from where I was based in St Ouen-sur-Mer. If I had gone to Plymouth, it would have meant a long drive through France to Roscoff and almost twice as long for the Channel crossing.' His eyes twinkled as he sent her a wry smile. 'I am not the best traveller on ferries! And I prefer to be in control of my own destiny. Besides, the drive down from Dorset to Cornwall today gave me the opportunity to reaccustom myself to English roads.'

'How did you come to take this job?' she asked, propping her chin in one hand as she looked at him.

'I volunteered.' Pushing his empty plate aside, he leaned closer and rested one forearm on the table. 'I was only working in St Ouen-sur-Mer on a temporary basis to help out a friend from medical school. François is head of the clinic and his wife, Celeste, is also a doctor there. Another of the partners, Marianne, had a baby last Christmas and was on maternity leave. Then, in early January, François badly broke his leg in a skiing accident. He was having trouble finding a replacement doctor, so he called me. As I had reason to leave Paris for a while, I was happy to provide cover. I've been there ever since. But now François is back on his feet and Marianne is ready to return to work. It was time for me to move on.'

'I see,' Lauren murmured, toying with the handle of her mug. Clearly Gabriel was loyal to his friends and ready to help in a crisis, but she wondered what had made him so eager to leave Paris in a hurry at the start of the year. He had sounded relieved to have received François's initial call…and now to be in Cornwall.

'When the position came up to work here for a year, I was interested in taking it,' he continued, and she lost herself in the sound of his huskily accented voice, captivated by the way he looked at her, maintaining eye contact as though she was interesting and important to him. 'I speak English—'

'Perfect English,' she interjected, halting his explanation.

An amused smile curved his mouth at her praise. 'Thank you, *chérie*.'

'Sorry, I interrupted you.' She smothered a groan of embarrassment.

'That's all right.' Her skin tingled as Gabriel briefly reached out and whispered his fingertips across the back of her hand. She sucked in a shaky breath and struggled to concentrate as he continued to speak about his reasons for moving to Penhally. 'I was the only doctor at the clinic who was single and without commitments…the others did not want to uproot their families to come here. And I've worked in England before—in London. I enjoyed it, but I was eager to experience small-town, rural medicine, too.'

Again Lauren thought there was more to the story than he had told her, but she was exceedingly glad he was here. She had also noted with a shiver of hopeful anticipation his comment that he was single and had no commitments. Surely that was a good sign? She had no idea why, but she had felt a deep connection with and recognition of this man from the outset.

'So, Lauren, tell me about the flood.' Gabriel broke the silence, drawing her from her thoughts. 'What happened?

How much damage has there been? You said Foxy's owner was tragically killed but was anyone else hurt?'

Lauren huffed out a breath, taking a few moments as she wondered where to begin recounting the events of that never-to-be-forgotten and emotional day.

As Gabriel waited for Lauren to speak, he resisted the fierce urge to keep touching her, remembering how silky her skin had felt beneath his fingers. Instead, he reflected on what he had told her about himself and his reasons for coming to Cornwall, hoping he had said enough to curb her interest without giving away any of his secrets…or his inner turmoil.

It was true that the request from François in January to help out in his clinic on Normandy's west coast could not have come at a better time. He had been deeply sorry for the injury that had caused François so many problems, but his friend's need had provided Gabriel with the chance to leave Paris—and Yvette—far behind. Time away to come to terms with all he had suddenly learned about his family, and to put space between himself and home, had been exactly what he had needed. But that space had not proved great enough, so the offer to work in Penhally Bay had been even more welcome. The width of the English Channel would surely be a suitable barrier. Here in Cornwall he felt he could breathe again and hear himself think.

His early departure from France had been sparked by another summons from home—one more demand, one more threat he had chosen to ignore. Things were increasingly strained with his mother. Not that Yvette Devereux had ever been particularly *motherly* towards him, he reflected with a cynical twist of his lips. She had never been the warm, nurturing and understanding type, but always stiff, distant, with her rigid view of duty and propriety. Now he knew why.

A light touch on his arm startled him from his disturbing

thoughts and he glanced up to find Lauren watching him with a frown on her face.

'Are you all right, Gabriel?'

'Yes, of course.' His skin felt warm and alive long after her fingers had been withdrawn. He managed a smile, grateful for the interruption and thankful to push family troubles to the back of his mind again. 'I was miles away. Please, you were going to explain the events of the last couple of weeks.'

'You hear about these things happening, but you never expect them to affect your own community,' she began, a serious tone to her voice. 'We had no warning. The sky went black, there was thunder and lightning, and the most torrential rain I've ever seen or heard. It poured off everything. Combined with the run-off inland, something collapsed upstream and the deluge swelled watercourses, causing a flash flood that swept away everything in its path. The river Lanson burst its banks, funnelling massive amounts of earthy-black water laden with debris down through the centre of Penhally, hitting us full force.'

'What happened to you?' Gabriel asked with concern, noting how Lauren shivered, rubbing her forearms in reaction. 'Were you caught out in it?'

'I was lucky. I was visiting a patient at the time. The power went out, the telephone lines were down and mobile phone coverage was patchy, but I received a message to go to one of the two evacuation points. I spent the rest of the time at the school, helping out.' She raised her gaze to his, her eyes registering grief. 'It was really frightening. People were missing, we didn't know what had happened to friends. There were a number of minor injuries, some more serious ones…and two people died.'

Gabriel listened to Lauren's explanation of the disaster with shock. '*Dieu.* I had no idea things were so bad,' he murmured, taking one of her trembling hands in his, needing to comfort, to touch her. 'I am so sorry. It must have been horribly traumatic and such a loss for the whole community.'

'Yes, it was. Is.' Hearing the waver in her voice, he tightened his hold on her hand, linking their fingers and brushing the pad of his thumb across her wrist. 'Audrey Baxter was one of our regular patients at the surgery. Elderly and with health problems, she was a bit of a busybody but she meant well. She had recently taken Foxy in as a companion from the rescue centre and having him helped her emotional well-being considerably. They helped each other, I suppose. Anyway, Audrey was caught outside when the flash flood came. She never stood a chance with that wall of water. The local vicar, Reverend Kenner, plunged in to try to save her, but he was lost, too, when the end of the Anchor Hotel collapsed on them. He was such a good man. He did a great deal for this community. And it was tragic for his daughter, Rachel. She's just a teenager, and with her mother dying a few years ago her father was all she had. They were very close. Now she's pregnant and alone. Her aunt and uncle in Plymouth are caring for her.'

'Lauren,' he murmured, wishing he had the words to ease the pain and horror of what she and the rest of the town had been through.

'It's all so unfair!'

'I know.' He stroked her arm, aware of the softness of her skin and the beat of her pulse. 'Sometimes it is impossible to understand why these things happen.'

Her fingers returned the pressure of his and she looked at him with a sorrowful smile. 'That's the truth.' She shook her head, a sigh escaping.

'Thank goodness you had such excellent rescue aid or things could have been even worse for the town.'

'Yes, we were very grateful. I think people are finding it hard to accept we've been affected like this again. It's not that long since Penhally's last great tragedy. The big storm ten years ago took many lives, including those of Kate Althorp's husband James and Nick Tremayne's father and brother.'

'How are people coping now?' Gabriel asked after a short silence, one that saw them both lost in thought.

'A lot are still displaced after the flood. The caravan park above the cliffs on Mevagissey Road has taken in several families, while others are staying with relatives and friends or renting temporary accommodation.'

'It looked as though much has been done to begin clearing up.'

Lauren nodded, her voice stronger again now. 'Everyone has worked very hard. It's amazing the mess and damage water can cause. I think it will be months before some of the homes are fit to be lived in again.'

'Many of your patients must be needing extra care and understanding,' Gabriel allowed, looking down at their joined hands, thankful that Lauren had not pulled away.

'Yes, there's been trauma and anxiety. And it's hard for some to come to terms with losing irreplaceable and senti-mental possessions. We also had to be careful because of things like polluted water and so on as some people failed to heed the safety advice in the aftermath.'

Gabriel watched as she tucked a couple of wayward strands of hair behind her ear. Adjusting his hold on her hand, he played with her fingers and traced a circle on her palm with his thumb, aware of the growing connection between them.

'So, tell me about your regular patients,' he suggested after a few moments, relieved to see a lightening of her expression.

He listened with interest as Lauren talked of little Timmy Morrison, nearly five months old and diagnosed at birth with cystic fibrosis, of eleven-year-old Paul Mitchell, coping spir-itedly with Duchenne muscular dystrophy, and of older patients like Harry Biscombe in sheltered accommodation at

Gow Court, with osteoporosis, whom she had been visiting when the flood had hit, and Stella Chamberlain, currently in the Harbour View Nursing Home with Parkinson's disease.

'Stella's desperate to go home but it's becoming impossible for her daughter Lizzie to cope. It's very sad. We're all doing the best we can to find the best solution for both Stella and Lizzie.'

Every word Lauren spoke, both about the regulars she visited at home and her more mobile and short-term patients who came to the surgery, revealed how dedicated she was and just how much she cared about each and every person. Minute by minute Gabriel was more impressed with Lauren Nightingale. Her natural beauty had first appealed to him and he had been unable to ignore the sparks of attraction that had crackled between them from the first moment. He had only just met her and yet the more he knew about her, the longer they talked, the more he respected and admired her as a person. She was funny, intelligent and caring. Genuine, without any airs or graces.

Meeting Lauren put an interesting and unexpected slant on his time in Cornwall. Her eyes reflected a feminine interest she made no effort to hide and he felt the answering response rise within him, one he had not felt in a long time. This might well turn out to be an even more interesting year than he had ever imagined.

'I'm not sure which patients you'll be seeing,' Lauren told him now, explaining about the staffing at the surgery and how GP Dragan Lovak was taking time off to be with his wife after the recent birth of their baby boy. 'I expect Nick will suggest you spend time with one of the other doctors this week—if you are lucky, it will be Oliver Fawkner.' The affection in her voice as she mentioned the other doctor brought a flash of unexpected jealousy. 'If Nick agrees, it would also be good if you could come out on house calls with various members of staff.'

'Including you?'

'Probably.'

His gaze caught hers. 'I hope so.'

'Me, too.' She bit her lip, her eyes widening as she realised she had spoken aloud. He felt the kick of her pulse beneath his fingers as she hurried on. 'There have been some changes due to the surgery expansion—you'll see those when you look around on Monday. Immediately after the flood, Nick asked us all not to go out on calls after dark unless it was an emergency, because of all the debris and possible danger of unsafe buildings and falling masonry.' Gabriel nodded, knowing it made sense not to put more people at risk than necessary. 'That ban has been lifted since the clean-up started,' Lauren continued. 'But I've kept to the new schedule. It works for me and my patients now we have the new physiotherapy room. With Nick's agreement, I do house calls that are required in the mornings and see patients at the surgery in the afternoons.'

'So I'll keep at least one morning free to go on visits with you.'

Gabriel's statement brought fresh warmth to her cheeks. 'OK,' she agreed, already eager for the time they would spend together, even if it was work related. That he was so keen and interested in her patients and the work she did brought her a glow of pleasure.

He asked more questions about the surgery, staff and the town in general, and she was happy to answer them, to help him fit into his new role in a different country. They had clicked from the first and got on so well she felt she had known him for ever. Yet all the time there was the undercurrent of sexual tension, the hum of desire between them, and excitement bubbled inside her at what might happen.

She had not forgotten for a moment that her hand was still in his, their fingers entwined, but she had no desire to let go until he did. They talked about local activities and their hobbies, discovering shared interests in books and music. They both loved sport, but while Lauren was keen on running, swimming and cycling, Gabriel favoured team sports like football. She could listen to him for ever with that sexy accent and soft huskiness edging his voice.

'So you jog every morning?' he asked now, pulling her from her thoughts.

'Yes, I try to do between three and five miles a day.'

'I can see it keeps you fit.'

The knot in her stomach tightened as he looked her over, the expression in his melting brown eyes letting her know that he liked what he saw. 'I try.' She swallowed the restriction in her throat, a tingle running through her as his thumb began to brush across her palm and wrist once more. 'I've done a few triathlons in the past but I don't get the chance to compete much these days.'

'Do you prefer to run alone, or do you enjoy company?'

'Company is good,' she murmured, hoping that meant he might join her one day. 'If you still play football, you should talk to Oliver. He's organising a charity match next weekend to raise money for the flood relief fund.'

'That's an excellent idea, I'll do that. Lauren—'

Whatever Gabriel had been about to say was halted by the sudden beep of her mobile phone announcing an incoming text message. Lauren jumped at the intrusion, disappointed when her hand was released. Already she missed the contact between them. Beside her, Foxy stirred at the noise, stretching and yawning before rising to his feet and nudging her leg. Absently, she stroked his head with one hand while rummaging in her bag with the other to find her phone.

'Sorry about this.'

'Don't worry,' Gabriel reassured her, but he looked as regretful for the interruption as she was.

Sighing, Lauren tilted the phone, frowning as she concentrated on reading the message, aware it was harder to see the small letters illuminated on the screen than it had once been. Again, she pushed the concern away, unable to face the implications. The text, she discovered, was from her friend Chloe MacKinnon.

'Worried you aren't home yet. Any problems? Oliver says supper ready in an hour. Love C x'

Shocked, Lauren looked towards the windows and saw how dark it was outside. She glanced at her watch, stunned to discover the time. 'Oh, my gosh!'

'Everything all right?' Gabriel asked.

'I'd no idea it was this late. I'm so sorry, I've taken up all your afternoon!'

Laughing, his hand brushed her arm. 'I've enjoyed every moment with you, Lauren. Thank you. I am the one who should apologise for detaining you.'

'It's fine. I just didn't say I was delayed. I was expected home ages ago.'

'I see.' Gabriel moved back from her, disappointment dulling his eyes.

Her breath caught as she realised what he thought. 'I've told you about my friends Chloe and Oliver, midwife and GP at the surgery?' she asked, and he nodded. 'They're engaged and Oliver's been living at Chloe's cottage in Fisherman's Row since the end of July. They were flooded out and have been staying with me since then,' she rushed to explain, gratified to see relief lighten his expression.

'So there's no boyfriend waiting for you?'

'No. There's no one.' She responded to his blunt question with equal clarity. 'But I'd better get back.'

'Of course.'

Reluctantly, she rose to her feet, unhooked her bag from the back of the chair and looped the strap over her shoulder. 'Is there anything else I can do? Do you have all you need?'

She looked around the kitchen, hoping she had remembered everything.

'It's fine, Lauren. You have done so much and I appreciate it.'

'If you think of anything…'

'I'll let you know,' he promised with a smile.

'I wrote out some phone numbers for you.' Including her own, she added silently, pointing to the fridge where a piece of paper was held firm by a colourful Penhally magnet. With nothing else to prevent her leaving, she slipped on Foxy's lead and turned towards the door. 'I'd better go, then.'

She was acutely conscious of Gabriel following close behind her as she walked out of the kitchen. Pausing a moment, she formed a picture in her mind of the dim, unlit hallway and the route to the front door, trying to remember if there was anything in the way. She didn't think so…provided she avoided the bottom tread of the stairs that stuck out a few inches on her left. Anxiety gripped her as she was faced with her failing night vision. She could fumble for an unseen light switch and risk drawing attention to her problem, or take a chance the hall was clear. She chose the latter.

A short while ago she had breezily told Gabriel about her altered working hours. What she had not told him was how she had used the cover of the flood disaster and completion of the new physio room to make her changed schedule permanent. A flicker of guilt assailed her for the deception and for hiding her real reasons from Nick and everyone else. She was afraid to venture out after dark and, with each passing autumn day, dusk was falling earlier. The only journey she felt able to make at night was from the surgery to her cottage, a route she knew so well she could cover every inch of the short distance with her eyes closed. Which was how it had felt lately in the dark. She was scared what it meant, but was unable to face the fact that something strange was happening to her sight. At some point, if it got worse, she would have to. She would never put other people in danger. But for now she could still cover it up.

After she had negotiated the hallway slowly but safely, Gabriel reached round her to open the door, momentarily bringing their bodies into close proximity and firing her blood once more. Before he could put on the outside light, she moved forward, missing her step, unable to see. For a second, she teetered off balance, then Gabriel's arm was there to steady her. The light came on and she blinked, disoriented for a second, aware, when her vision sharpened, of the frown on his face.

'Are you OK?'

'Yes, fine,' she assured him breathlessly. With caution, she stepped out of his hold and down the steps to the gravel drive. Needing to disguise her latest mishap, she turned back to smile at him. 'There is something you should know about me before you hear it from anyone else.'

The wariness returned to his eyes and she could sense his tension. 'What's that?'

'I'm renowned for being impossibly clumsy.' She managed a passable laugh, trying not to think of her catalogue of stupid incidents. Unfortunately they seemed to be happening more and more often, her most recent examples being the moment she had inexplicably reversed into a parked car at the church after Jack and Alison's wedding, and the way she had stumbled and fallen in the rubble the day after the flood. 'Everyone teases me for being an accident waiting to happen.'

'I'll consider myself warned,' Gabriel replied, his answering laugh not completely masking his confusion.

Eager to leave on a more positive note, Lauren lingered. 'If you have nothing else planned, would you like to come for lunch tomorrow? You can meet Chloe and Oliver…get to know them before work on Monday.'

'I'd love to.' A teasing glint flickered in his eyes. 'Not the roast beef?'

'No! Chicken and all the trimmings. And Chloe is doing one of her special puddings,' she told him, laughing back.

'What time?'

'About noon?' She tried to sound casual, but already she was brimming with excitement at seeing him again.

'I'll be there,' he promised, making her pulse race. 'Would you like me to walk you back?'

She would, but she didn't want him witnessing her tripping again. 'Thanks, but there's no need.'

'Until tomorrow, then.' His voice dropped to a rough murmur. *'Au revoir, chérie.'*

'Bye.'

She felt him watching her as she walked carefully down the drive, Foxy well behaved at her side. Silently, she counted her steps, having made this journey before. She knew that when she reached the curve, the lights in her cottage would guide her home, but the knowledge that she was seeing less and less at night filled her with silent fear. How long could she hide her secret?

A sigh of relief escaped when her cottage came into view and she picked up her pace, more sure of herself, keen to tell Chloe and Oliver about the exciting new doctor. It was awful that the flood had driven her friends from their home. Chloe had been more upset at her missing cats, but one of the members of the rescue team had found Pirate and Cyclops unscathed on top of a wardrobe upstairs as the waters receded. In the days since they had moved in, Foxy and the cats had negotiated a cautious stand-off.

Until Chloe and Oliver found a suitable new home, Lauren was happy for them to stay with her. She enjoyed their company. But she wondered if things might get a bit awkward should anything develop between herself and Gabriel. There was plenty of time to worry about that, she reassured herself, knowing she shouldn't get too excited even though their first meeting had left her in no doubt about the connection between them. However foolish, she sensed that something unusual and important could evolve in the days and weeks ahead.

'We were going to send out a search party!' Chloe teased when Lauren let herself in, took off Foxy's lead and walked into the living room.

Her friend was cuddled up in Oliver's lap on the sofa in front of a roaring log fire. It didn't take a genius to know from their rumpled clothes and tousled hair what they had been doing with their extra time alone. Lauren was delighted for Chloe but it was ironic that her friend—who had suffered an abusive past at the hands of her brutal father, and who had remained a virgin until Oliver had come into her life—had enjoyed a more varied and extensive sex life in three months than Lauren had in ten years. She didn't begrudge Chloe her happiness and pleasure for a moment, but she wouldn't half mind being as lucky.

An image of a certain scrumptious French doctor filled her mind. Oh, yes! Now, there was a man with va-va-voom, one who would surely know how to make a woman feel special. Unable to stop smiling, Lauren sank into an armchair. Her heart was still pounding.

'Sorry you were concerned. I got held up. Dr Devereux had just arrived when I took the shopping up to the Manor House. I stayed for a chat.'

'Some chat,' Chloe commented with a meaningful grin that had Oliver laughing and Lauren's cheeks warming. 'Come on, tell us what happened.'

Nothing…and yet everything. But Lauren didn't know how to explain that. 'We talked about the surgery, Penhally and the flood. Gabriel's coming here for lunch tomorrow. I told him about your football match, Oliver, and he's keen to play.'

'Great! Thanks, Lauren. Nick has suggested that Gabriel shadow me next week, so it will be good to meet him in advance.'

'But what's he like?' Chloe persisted.

Lauren leaned back and sighed, unable to keep her smile from broadening. 'Absolutely *divine*.'

No way was she going to last out Gabriel's time here without being a *very* bad girl.

Hopefully.

CHAPTER THREE

'THANKS again for coming in early this morning, Gabriel. I think we've covered everything,' Nick Tremayne decided, leading the way back to his consulting room after a tour of the revamped surgery. He returned to his chair and rubbed his hands together. 'Do you have any other questions?'

'Is the expansion work nearly complete?' Gabriel had been impressed with the improvements that had taken place since his previous weekend visit in July.

'It won't be long now. Hopefully no more than a week. My daughter Lucy originally worked on the plans for the changes and devised a way to use the dead space we had here to make more room. We've rearranged the layout, adding extra facilities as well as increasing consulting-room availability upstairs and down,' Nick explained. 'There are a few minor jobs to finish, mostly outside, but we've been very lucky...the builders have worked around us so that patient disruption has been kept to a minimum.'

'The new X-ray and plaster rooms on the ground floor must make life much easier.'

'Indeed,' Nick agreed. 'It means we can handle the less serious breaks and injuries here now, rather than having to send everyone on the half-hour journey to the hospital in St Piran. It benefits the hospital, the patients and ourselves. As does having the new physiotherapy room for Lauren,' he added. 'Our workload is increasing all the time—and not just during the tourist season—so your presence here is even more welcome.'

'Thank you.'

Nick shuffled some papers on his desk. 'I've arranged for you to spend a few days working with Oliver Fawkner. You can take your own consultations, of course—we've assigned you one of the new rooms next to Lauren's—but Oliver will help you learn your way around the district. Is that all right with you?'

'But, yes, I appreciate it. I have already met Oliver, Chloe and Lauren—we had lunch together yesterday.'

'Good, good. I'm sure you'll get on well.' Nick nodded with approval, then handed over a sheet of paper. 'Here is this week's roster. We take turns doing out-of-hours cover so no one is unduly burdened, but we won't expect you to do your own evening and weekend calls until you are settled in. Again, as Oliver is temporarily living so close to the Manor House, you can share duties with him for a week or two before we add you to the list to do calls alone.'

'That sounds fine. Maybe I could also make some visits out with other staff?' Gabriel suggested, following up on the idea Lauren had given him.

Nick glanced up, an eyebrow raised in question. 'What did you have in mind?'

'I would be interested in learning how the various disciplines interact here. And it would give me a chance to meet some of the regular patients. Maybe if I spent a morning with the nurses, and also go out on a few home visits with Chloe and Lauren during my first couple of weeks?'

'An excellent idea,' his new boss agreed. His smile of approval stripped some of the characteristic sternness from his face. 'The more familiarisation you can gain, the better. I'll leave you to arrange the details with the staff concerned. You can sort things out to fit your own schedules. I'll mention it when we all meet and—' The phone buzzed and Nick frowned, momentarily distracted. 'Excuse me,' he murmured. 'Yes? Of course, Hazel. We'll be there directly.'

Gabriel visualised Hazel, the practice manager, whom he had met a short while ago during his wander around with Nick. The older woman had been polite while giving him the once-over but appeared to be reserving her judgement about him. He could understand that. Hopefully he would pass muster with her, and the rest of the staff, in time. He was thinking of all he had been told about his new colleagues when Nick set down the phone and reclaimed his attention.

'Pretty much everyone on duty is here now. Come on up to the staffroom, Gabriel, and I'll introduce you,' he invited, rising to his feet.

Glad that their chat had gone well, and looking forward to starting work, Gabriel followed Nick towards the stairs. Although reserved and serious, the senior partner had been welcoming, their discussion informative. Even so, Gabriel was thankful to have had the chance to meet Oliver and Chloe in more informal and relaxed circumstances at Lauren's cottage the previous day. He had thoroughly enjoyed himself. They had lingered over a delicious lunch and talked long into the afternoon. It had been dark by the time he had walked the short distance back to the Manor House feeling content and more comfortable about his new job.

With dark hair and green eyes, Chloe was kind and gentle, as dedicated to her role as a midwife as Lauren was to hers as a physiotherapist. As for Oliver, dark-eyed and with over-long dark hair, Gabriel had liked him from the first, forming an instant friendship with the handsome, charismatic doctor. Oliver was only three years younger than himself and they had quickly established that they shared many interests in common besides their careers, especially a love of sport. Gabriel did not share Oliver's and Chloe's love of motorbikes, however. It hadn't needed Lauren to tell him that Oliver and Chloe were a couple…that they were madly in love was obvious to anyone who saw them together.

And then there was Lauren herself.

She had been a complete surprise to him and he had not been able to stop thinking about her since finding her in his kitchen on Saturday afternoon. He'd been intrigued to learn she was an accomplished artist. There hadn't been an opportunity to look around her studio the day before but he had seen a couple of her landscapes hanging in the surgery's reception area during his tour with Nick. He had found himself drawn to the paintings even before he had realised they were Lauren's. She had real talent. He was looking forward to working with her—and to getting to know her better socially. Only his early meeting with Nick had prevented him from joining Lauren for her morning jog. There would be time for that in the days ahead. And, he hoped, for much more. He still intended to be cautious, but any resolve to remain uninvolved had wavered on Saturday and melted entirely on Sunday.

The sound of chatter coming from the staffroom became louder and drew him from his thoughts. As Nick led the way inside and an anticipatory silence descended, Gabriel's nervousness at the prospect of meeting his colleagues returned. He'd never experienced this self-doubt about acceptance until recently—until his world had turned upside down after his father's death and things he had thought he had known about his life, his family, his very identity—had proved to be a lie. Gabriel swallowed the rush of emotions, forcing his private issues to the back of his mind. It was good to know there would be at least a couple of familiar faces here. A quick glance around the room told him that Lauren had yet to arrive and he struggled to mask his disappointment. However, Oliver and Chloe were there, their smiles reassuring him.

Uncomfortable at being the centre of attention, he hoped

his own smile was natural and that he came across as being more relaxed than he felt under the scrutiny he was being subjected to. Thankfully the atmosphere was welcoming, although he imagined some people had similar reservations to those Hazel had exhibited earlier. He remained silent as Nick made the introductions and turned to draw him forward.

'Come on in and join us. Everyone, this is Gabriel Devereux.' His manner benevolent and paternal, Nick gestured around the room. 'You already know Oliver and Chloe. And you remember Kate Althorp, our other midwife, from your visit in the summer?'

'But of course. It's good to see you again, Kate.' As the older woman rose to greet him, he gave her a Gallic kiss on both cheeks. 'How is your son Jem?'

Kate's smile revealed her pleasure. 'He's well. Thank you, Gabriel. Welcome back to Penhally Bay! We are so pleased to have you with us.'

'I am excited to be here.' He smiled back, grateful for Kate's warm approach.

Nick made the other introductions and Gabriel shook hands with the rest of the team. When the formalities were over, Gabriel sat on an empty chair opposite Oliver and Chloe, and accepted the mug Eve Dwyer, one of the practice nurses, handed him.

'We usually start the day with a coffee and a chat,' she explained, her manner friendly. 'Milk and sugar?'

'Just a dash of milk, please.'

As Eve added the milk to his mug and then turned to replace the carton in the fridge, a crash sounded out on the stairway, followed by a string of muffled curses. Gabriel looked round in time to see Nick shaking his head and moving towards the door.

'That must be Lauren.'

Everyone laughed in response to Nick's wry comment, but

the amusement was affectionate, Gabriel realised with some relief, already feeling protective of Lauren. Then he noted the concern on Oliver's face, along with the way Chloe's smile dimmed when she exchanged a glance with her fiancé. Gabriel shared a look with Oliver and as a silent acknowledgement passed between them he felt a shiver of unease. He had known Lauren less than forty-eight hours, but it appeared he was not alone in his impression that something more might lie behind her clumsiness. Gabriel filed the moment away. He would keep his own counsel for now, but Oliver could be the man to talk to if his initial worrying suspicions came to anything.

Looking adorably flustered, and dressed in a uniform of navy blue tunic and trousers, her hair tied back in a ponytail, Lauren hurried into the room. She was carrying a haphazard stack of files and balancing a round tin precariously on top.

'Sorry I'm late. I was delayed downstairs talking with a patient on the phone,' she explained, sounding a touch breathless. 'The waiting room is starting to fill up early—the usual collection of post-weekend crises, no doubt. Hazel is holding the fort and says to carry on without her.'

'Are those some of Hazel's biscuits?' someone asked.

Gabriel watched as Lauren awkwardly juggled the files and manoeuvred the tin so she could prise open the lid. 'Her Cornish fairings,' she announced once she had peeped inside. A twinkle of mischief in her smoky grey eyes, she offered him the tin. 'All Hazel's home-made food treats are favourites here, Gabriel, so I advise you to take what you can before the rest of this unruly lot devour them.'

'Thank you.' It was a bit early in the day for him, but Gabriel accepted one of the biscuits to please Lauren. He tried it with his coffee, surprised how much he enjoyed the ginger-flavoured local delicacy. 'They're excellent.'

'Tell Hazel that and you'll be in her good books for life.' Kate laughed.

'Come on, Lauren, don't hog the tin. I missed breakfast and I'm starving,' GP Adam Donnelly called, growling in mock complaint as others grabbed their share of the biscuits before the tin reached him.

Gabriel was gratified when Lauren chose the chair next to him, her smile and the look in her eyes setting off the zing of awareness he felt every time he saw her.

'A word of warning, Gabriel,' one of the district nurses joked. 'Make sure you park your car well away from Lauren's—if you want to find it in one piece when you go back to it!'

As the tale of her reversing into a car at a recent wedding was recounted, Lauren smiled, taking the ribbing in good part, but Gabriel could see the flash of hurt and worry in her eyes. The belief that there was something more than Lauren just being clumsy nagged at him but he hadn't yet put his finger on what it was that disturbed him. Frowning, he remembered her uneasiness leaving the Manor House on Saturday night and the way she had tripped in the dark. She had explained away her stumble by telling him how accident prone she was, but he had sensed she was covering up for something else. More than once in their short acquaintance he had noticed the way she squinted at her mobile phone screen, tilting it around before reading the message. Then there were the moments she displayed an apparent lack of spatial awareness and misjudgement of distances.

As Nick reclaimed the attention of those in the room, the teasing ceased and Gabriel had to set his considerations about Lauren aside. Instead, he listened with interest as the discussion turned to items of surgery business and any noteworthy out-of-hours incidents with patients. Adam had been called out the previous day to a thirteen-year-old girl with appendicitis who had been admitted to St Piran Hospital, while Kate had attended a mum-to-be who had reported some abdominal pain.

'I'm convinced it is nothing serious but, given her level of anxiety, I've arranged for her to see the consultant at the hospital today instead of next week.'

'Better to be safe than sorry,' Nick remarked, to murmurs of agreement.

Gabriel watched the interaction between Nick and Kate with interest. The tension between the two had been glaringly apparent during the barbecue at Nick's house back in July. He had no idea of their history but he thought it went beyond the doctor-midwife dynamic. Thankfully, the atmosphere between them today was less fraught.

'Gabriel is going to be shadowing Oliver this week, especially on home visits and out-of-hours work,' Nick outlined as the patient reviews came to an end. 'I've also supported his request to spend some time with other staff and will leave you to organise convenient days between you...Lauren, Chloe and the district nurses in particular. Gabriel, enjoy your time here and speak up if you have any queries. I am sure everyone will do all they can to make you welcome and help you settle in for this year-long stay with us.'

Smiling his thanks, Gabriel's attention lingered on Lauren beside him. She had done more than anyone to make him feel comfortable, both at home and work, and her insights and advice had been invaluable. As everyone rose to their feet and began to file out, heading off to attend to their respective duties, Oliver hung back with Chloe.

'We can do a joint list this morning, Gabriel. And when we come back from the house calls, we'll get you set up in your own room. You can take your own surgery slots from this afternoon if you'd care to,' his new friend suggested.

'That suits me.'

'Great.' Oliver smiled and ushered Chloe ahead of him. 'I'll see you downstairs in a few minutes, then.'

Left alone in the staffroom, Gabriel felt Lauren's hand slide into his. Palm to palm. A perfect fit. Delicate yet strong.

And her skin was satin soft. Not at all sorry to be touching her but surprised by her actions, he looked into warm grey eyes.

'Lauren?'

'I just wanted to wish you an enjoyable first day.' Her fingers squeezed his before letting go. He felt the loss of their contact. Then she caught him unawares again, leaning in to press a gentle but all-too-fleeting kiss on his cheek. 'Good luck, Gabriel.'

His skin prickled from the brush of her mouth. Unable to let her go, he caught her hand as she drew away. Her thoughtfulness and caring touched him on an emotional level, while inflaming the physical desire he had felt from the first moment they had met. His body tightened with need for her. He wanted to haul her into his arms and kiss her senseless. Unfortunately he didn't think Nick would be impressed to find the new doctor passionately making out with the physiotherapist in the staffroom on his first day at work!

'Thank you, *chérie*.' He cupped her face with his free hand, relishing the feel of her and the instinctive way she pressed her cheek to his palm. He grazed his thumb across her parted lips, the pad briefly catching on the fullness of the lower one. Her breath hitched, and he watched as her eyes darkened, the desire in them unmistakable. 'I'll see you later.'

'Yes. OK,' she agreed, the husky edge returning to her voice.

He regretted letting her go but he had to. If he kissed her now he wouldn't want to stop. Oliver and their patients were waiting for him downstairs. It was time for him to start work. Time to concentrate on the first day of his new job and think about something other than Lauren…before he lost his head entirely.

Come Friday, Lauren was convinced her lips were still tingling. She licked them, sure she could taste a hint of the masculine tang of Gabriel's skin even now. He'd felt so good. And had smelt delicious, too…earthy and citrusy and all male. She had never been so drawn to and aware of a man before.

The attraction was fierce. Immediate. Scary but incredibly exciting in its intensity.

On Monday morning, dressed in a dark suit, crisp white shirt and ocean-blue tie, Gabriel had looked as if he had just stepped off the catwalk—a star model for the finest Parisian fashion house. She hadn't thought he could look any better than he did in his figure-hugging jeans—or that ivory towel— but suited up for work he'd taken her breath away all over again. He had an aristocratic bearing, one that hinted that he had origins in wealth and status, yet he was completely natural, down-to-earth and unpretentious.

Gabriel's reaction to her good-luck gesture had taken her by surprise. She could still feel the warmth of his palm cupping her face, the stroke of his thumb across her lips, the desire that had flared in his eyes as he had looked deep into her own. She desperately wanted to know what it would be like to kiss him. It was all she had thought about for days. How would it feel? How would he taste? She wanted to touch him. Wanted to feel his hands on her body.

It had been such a hectic week that she hadn't seen Gabriel anywhere near as much as she had hoped to. Not alone, anyway. He had joined her for her morning jog before work on a couple of occasions and he'd come to Gatehouse Cottage for an evening meal some nights. But Oliver and Chloe had been there, too, and there had been far too much talk about work for Lauren's liking. Tomorrow, Saturday, marked the first-week anniversary of when she had met him. Gabriel had morning surgery and then was on call with Oliver for the rest of the day, so there was not going to be much chance for her to see him then. And Sunday was the day of the charity football match. Yet another missed opportunity for some time alone with him. She knew she was behaving like a foolish, thwarted schoolgirl, but she couldn't seem to help herself.

'Are you all right, Lauren?'

Embarrassment made her cheeks turn pink as Mike Trevellyan's voice jolted her from her thoughts. 'I'm so sorry, Mike, I was…distracted.' Guilt surged through her because she had been daydreaming about Gabriel instead of focusing on her patient.

'So I gathered.' Amusement shone in his eyes. 'Anything to do with the new French doctor I've been hearing about?'

'Why would you think that?' Goodness, had the rumour mill started already?

'Kate has mentioned Dr Devereux to Fran several times since meeting him in the summer. She said Penhally was in for a treat when he finally arrived here to work,' Mike explained, his tone teasing. 'And there's been some envy that you are his nearest neighbour. The whisper has gone around that he's impressed many people during his first week here.'

'Gabriel is an excellent doctor,' she allowed, trying to keep her comments professional and hide the pride she was experiencing at the news.

'I'm not sure his medical skills are what interests most of the ladies!'

A wave of possessiveness surged through her. She was unaccustomed to jealousy, but she felt territorial and protective of Gabriel, and she didn't want to think of other women lusting after him. Refusing to react to Mike's comments and add more fuel to fire any possible local gossip, she forced a smile and got them back to the matter at hand.

'Now then, how are things going with you, Mike? How is your leg?'

'I've been doing all the exercises you gave me. Mostly the ankle is fine, although I do get some pain at times,' he admitted grudgingly.

Lauren nodded, knowing what a rough time Mike had been through and how important it was for him as a busy farmer to keep mobile and working. 'No doubt you've been overdoing things, though.'

'I've tried to increase my workload slowly, but I can't do as much as I'd like. There is still a bit of weakness and stiffness in the ankle.'

'That's to be expected,' she reminded him.

Lauren ran through some of the exercises and checked his range of movement. The offending leg bore the marks of the breaks and subsequent surgery he had sustained when part of a tree he had been cutting with a chainsaw had fallen on him, pinning him to the ground.

'Any problems from the bruised ribs?'

Mike shook his head. 'Not any more. The doctors tell me I healed quickly.'

'Just not quickly enough for you,' she filled in with an understanding smile. 'I know it seems a long haul, Mike, especially when you're used to physical activity. You've done so well. We don't want any setbacks. Let your brother help you.'

'Joe's picked up enough of the slack. But you're not alone...Fran tells me I'm too impatient,' he conceded wryly, speaking of his wife with affection.

'Thankfully you didn't tear the ligaments, but the two fractures to your fibula—one above the ankle and one at the bottom, the lateral malleolus, where it joins the tibia—were serious. As you well know from your time in a cast after the operation to fit the plates and screws.' She gave him a sympathetic pat on the shoulder. 'You've worked hard to build up the strength in the muscles and to remobilise the joint. It must be frustrating, but keep up the exercises, don't try to do too much too soon, and you'll continue to improve.'

Mike nodded his agreement. 'Thanks, Lauren. I'll do my best. I've got so much to be grateful for.'

'You have indeed!' While he put his socks and shoes back

on, she reflected on how delighted the whole of Penhally had been at the news that Fran Trevellyan was expecting naturally after a previous miscarriage and an unsuccessful attempt at IVF. 'It's so exciting about the pregnancy. When is the baby due?'

'Late spring.' Mike positively glowed with joy. 'We're just praying everything goes without a hitch this time.'

'I'm sure it will,' she reassured him, happy for the couple.

'Things definitely seem different with this pregnancy. It's nearly November now, past the danger point in terms of the number of weeks when we lost the baby before. Kate is keeping a close eye on Fran and she says everything is fine.'

'So we have to make sure you are fit to run around changing nappies and chasing after an active toddler!' Lauren teased. 'Come back and see me in a month, Mike, but phone any time if you have questions, swelling or discomfort.'

After showing Mike out, she welcomed her next patient, a woman in her late forties who had presented with pain and associated symptoms in the C5 and C6 region of her neck. The classic 'poking-chin posture' evident at their first appointment had been caused by over-activity in the levetator scapulae and stermocleidomastoid muscles, along with a weakness of the cervical flexor muscles. This was Zena's third visit and she was showing excellent signs of improvement in her range of movement and her posture.

'The pain and stiffness are much less and I've had no more headaches or dizziness,' Zena reported, her relief evident. 'I'm finding the exercises easier now.'

'That's great.' Lauren was pleased that the combination of manipulation therapy she had used at the surgery and the corrective exercises Zena had done at home had resulted in the woman's progress. 'We'll make another appointment, but keep up the programme. It's helping correct your posture as well as increase your range of movement and strengthen the muscles.'

Happy that Zena was following her advice and had no more questions, Lauren sent her on her way and welcomed patient number three of the afternoon.

It turned out to be a busy Friday clinic, one that overran as she had a couple of new cases and time was needed to make a thorough assessment and take a complete history. Consequently it was late by the time she had finished her list. When her last patient had left, she sat down and adjusted her desk light so she could see more clearly to type up all her case notes and make comprehensive profiles of her new patients. She didn't anticipate being able to leave for home any time soon. Stifling a yawn with one hand, she switched on her computer and set to work, ignoring the noises coming from the workmen who were putting the finishing touches to alterations outside the building.

She was engrossed in updating her files when all the power suddenly went off, shutting down her computer and plunging her room into darkness. Losing any unsaved work was the least of her problems. Disoriented, she sat still, but her eyes didn't adjust to the gloom. She could see nothing. This was the realisation of one of her worst fears. Her heart started thudding under her ribs and she felt tense, her throat tightening. After sitting in the dark for a while, increasingly concerned, Lauren rose gingerly to her feet and, one hand extended out in front of her, slowly, awkwardly edged her way towards the door, thankful that her mental map of her new room was accurate. Judging each step with care, she found the door without bumping into anything, but opening it brought no relief.

It was pitch black throughout the whole surgery.

She strained to hear, but no sounds came. How late was it? Had everyone else gone home? She didn't recall hearing the workmen for a while. Pulling out her mobile phone, she tried to read the time on the screen, but the luminous glow provided scant light and failed to aid her vision. Increasingly alarmed, she pressed herself against the wall, not wanting to lose her bearings.

What should she do? Wait a bit to see what happened? Or call someone? She clutched her mobile phone tighter in her hand. How could she ring without alerting the person to her predicament? She wasn't ready to face the issue of her diminishing night vision herself, let alone confide in anyone else. Fear chilled her at the knowledge that she might not be able to ignore or hide the subtle but insidious changes to her sight for much longer.

A noise from upstairs made her jump. Her pulse throbbed.

'Hello?' Was that her voice sounding so uncharacteristically shaky and feeble? She hated this. What was happening to her? Silence descended again, enveloping her. Cursing herself for being feeble, battling the inner panic rising within her, she raised her voice. 'Is anyone there?'

Several moments later, footsteps sounded on the stairs. 'Lauren?'

'Gabriel!' Relief flooded through her and she blinked back a stupid threat of tears.

'Where are you, *chérie*?'

She pressed a hand to her chest, trying to calm her ragged breathing. 'Outside the physiotherapy room.'

'Stay there.' Gabriel's accented voice calmed her nerves. 'I'll find you.'

Seconds later, Lauren squinted at a pinpoint of light wavering in the darkness. Sensing Gabriel's nearness but misjudging the distance, she stepped out from the wall and bumped into his solid frame.

'Oomph!' she gasped.

His hands came out to steady her. 'Are you all right, Lauren?'

'Yes.' She was now. 'Thanks.'

It was brazen but she couldn't help snuggling closer, welcoming the feel of his arms coming around her. She absorbed his strength, scared of her lack of vision but unable to explain to him.

'I finished my surgery half an hour ago and Nick had just

called me up to the staffroom to talk about my first week when the power went off,' he explained, one hand soothing as it stroked up and down her spine.

'What's happened, do you think?'

'The contractors were finishing off some work outside and one of them cut a cable by mistake. Nick has gone to see them. I knew you were still here and was coming to find you when you called.'

Reassured by his presence and the knowledge he had thought of her, Lauren allowed herself to relax, some of the tension draining from her.

'Come and sit in my consulting room while we wait.'

'Um…' Lauren hesitated. Unfamiliar with the layout of his room, she didn't want to fall over anything or make even more of a fool of herself in front of him. How could he see with just a penlight? Had he guessed her problem? Not wanting to alert his suspicions by asking if they could just stand where they were, she reluctantly agreed to his suggestion. 'OK.'

His arm around her made her feel safe as he led her back down the corridor to the next doorway. Unable to see him, all her other senses seemed heightened, and his warmth wrapped around her like a comfort blanket in the dark. The citrusy male scent of him was familiar and exciting. Putting her trust in him, she was thankful that he guided her to a chair without any fuss. She sat down, disappointed when he released her. But then she heard the sounds of him dragging another chair closer, and he sat beside her, taking her hand in his, linking their fingers. She tried not to cling too tightly and reveal the extent of her unease.

'I want to thank you for all you have done helping me to fit in and making me welcome in Penhally,' he told her with warm sincerity.

'I don't think I'm responsible for much, but I'm glad that

you've settled so well. Word is you've made a great impression.' She wished there was enough light for her to see his face.

'I just want to be a good doctor for the people here,' he responded with simple but genuine modesty. 'Perhaps we can arrange a morning next week for me to come out on your home visits?'

'Yes, of course,' she agreed, delighted at the prospect.

Gabriel's thumb stroked across the inside of her wrist, making her shiver. 'Oliver and Chloe plan to go to Plymouth next weekend to see Rachel Kenner. Will you spend some time with me while they are gone? We can be alone…get to know one another better.'

'I'd like that.' Which was a massive understatement! She felt breathless with anticipation. The week ahead would be a long one…waiting. 'Gabriel—'

Before she could speak further, the lights flashed back on. Startled, Lauren blinked several times, her eyes taking a few moments to adjust and refocus. Then the fog cleared and Gabriel's gorgeous face swam clearly into view. She noticed his look of concern as he watched her, then he smiled, dimples creasing lean cheeks, and her stomach turned over.

'Lauren? Gabriel?' Nick's voice sounded from the front of the surgery.

With a wry grimace, Gabriel squeezed her fingers before he released her and stood up. Moving to the door, he called out to Nick, and a few moments later the older man arrived in the room.

'Here you both are.' Looking harassed, Nick ran a hand through his hair. 'I'm sorry about the disruption. I've been assured the problem is now resolved. Gabriel, perhaps we can have our informal debrief over a drink and something to eat?'

'Of course.' Gabriel's consent and smile were polite, but Lauren sensed his reluctance.

Nick turned to her. 'Are you heading home now, Lauren?'

'Yes, I am.' She could finish updating her computer files from her written notes another time, she decided, disappointed that she wouldn't be seeing Gabriel again this evening.

'Good. Right, then.' Nick rubbed his hands together and smiled. 'I'll meet you out front in a few moments.'

When he had gone, Lauren rose and walked towards the door, pausing to look at Gabriel. 'Thanks for being here.'

'No problem. If I don't catch up with you tomorrow, I'll see you at the football on Sunday.'

'All right.' She returned his smile, warmed through by the huskiness of his voice and the promise in his eyes. 'Goodnight, Gabriel.'

'Goodnight. Sleep well, *chérie*.'

After a short but tense and cautious drive, the lights of her cottage welcomed her home. The cars outside announced that both Oliver and Chloe were in, and she parked her own with extra care not to hit anything. As much as she loved her friends and valued their company, it was someone else who dominated her thoughts and whom she wished she was with right now.

Sleep well, Gabriel had said…

As had been the case every night since she had met him, she knew her sleep would be filled with dreams of a sexy Frenchman.

CHAPTER FOUR

SUNDAY dawned a perfect warm and sunny autumn day. The whole of Penhally had turned out to support the charity football match, along with many outsiders and autograph-hunters who had been drawn by the impressive number of sporting and television personalities in attendance. The media were also out in force, capturing the action from the school playing fields. Given the size of the crowd, plus the interest in the snap auction of items donated by the celebrities, there was going to be a very healthy sum of money added to the relief fund.

Kate didn't want to think about the flood. Almost three weeks on and the memories of being stuck in an upstairs flat in Bridge Street with Nick, the water rising beneath them, still left her feeling shaky. They had struggled successfully to deliver Stephanie Richards's breech baby, and then had come the frightening experience of being winched up to the rescue helicopter. Kate shivered despite the mild temperature.

'Are you all right, Mum?'

'Yes, my love. I'm fine.' Smiling, she ruffled Jem's hair. He'd found her at half-time and was taking advantage of the refreshments she'd brought. 'Are you enjoying yourself?'

'It's cool! I've got some great autographs,' he added, pointing to all the signatures he'd collected on his football jersey, then his eyes went round in alarm. 'You won't wash them off, will you?'

'Never, I promise.' She hid her amusement as she reassured him, watching as he drained his fruit drink and wiped the back of his hand across his mouth.

'It was good of Uncle Nick to arrange for me be a ballboy.'

Uncle Nick. Pain lanced through her. Jem had no idea that Nick was his natural father. Would the man she had loved for ever one day claim his son? Or were old hurts and the weight of guilt too much to be overcome? While they had been trapped during the flood, they had talked about that long-ago night when they had lost their heads...a night of great stress and emotion that had resulted in Jem's conception. Nick had promised to try to make an effort to come to terms with the situation, and at least be more attentive to Jem, even if he couldn't go as far as making a public declaration of fatherhood. Kate wasn't holding her breath that anything would come of it but she could not help but hope—for Jem's sake if not her own. So far Nick had kept his word and things were less tense between them.

'The second half is starting soon. Will you come and watch me?' Jem asked, returning after throwing the empty drink carton into a nearby litter bin.

'Of course, my love.'

He caught her hand and tugged. 'Come on, then.'

Kate allowed her son to lead her towards the touchline, pleased that he was so happy. Nick had already returned from the half-time break, acting as team doctor for the celebrity side. Jem released her hand and ran to him. Kate saw Nick's guarded smile as he greeted the boy and heard the modulated tones of his voice.

'Back to help again?' he asked, and Jem nodded enthusiastically. 'Good lad.'

Sharing a look with the most enigmatic of men, Kate

mouthed, 'Thank you,' understanding how difficult it was for
Nick to confront his own demons. Not wanting to push things
or make a scene in public, she saw Lauren and Chloe returning to the side of the pitch and went to join them.

'Everything OK, Kate?' Chloe asked.

She nodded in response to the gentle query, seeing the
understanding in the younger woman's green eyes. Her
fellow midwife was one of only two other people, besides
herself and Nick, who knew the secret about the identity of
Jem's father.

'It's been an excellent day and Jem is having fun being part
of it.' Again, Kate's gaze strayed to where her son waited impatiently for the game to restart. Nick was watching him, too,
and she wondered what was going through his mind. Aware
she was on dangerous ground, she turned her attention back
to her two colleagues. 'Oliver did a brilliant job organising
this. It's a huge success.'

Chloe glowed with pleasure at the praise for her fiancé. 'I
know. He worked so hard. Jack Tremayne helped, too. Both
of them were able to call in favours from their days in London,
securing the support of several national celebrities as well as
the Cornish ones.'

'Everyone's really got behind the event,' Lauren added
with approval. 'Despite the arrival of his baby boy, Dragan
worked hard behind the scenes for today.'

'I think he would have liked to play, but it's understandable that he and Melinda wanted to keep out of public view
after the press intrusions last spring,' Chloe pointed out, and
Kate nodded in agreement, remembering what it had been like
in the village when Melinda had been identified as a member
of European royalty.

As both sets of players jogged out for the second half,
cheers echoed around the playing fields.

'Gabriel has been a star, jumping in to give support the

moment he arrived here,' Kate commented, glancing at Lauren. 'He scored an excellent goal, too.'

'All our guys have been great.'

Kate smiled at Lauren's reply, noting the wink Gabriel sent the young physiotherapist as he ran past and the flush that warmed her cheeks in response. It was clear where those two were heading! And Kate couldn't be more pleased for them. Her smile broadened as Oliver detoured to give Chloe a kiss. Leaving the two friends to focus on the match—and the men who held their interest—Kate wandered farther along the side of the pitch so she could keep a better eye on Jem.

The flood had been terrible for the whole village, causing physical and emotional trauma. The damage to property would take many months to overcome, while the loss of Audrey Baxter and Reverend Kenner was a tragedy never to be forgotten. But the aftermath, including the mass support for today's event, showed what could happen when the community pulled together.

Penhally's previous disaster, the big storm a decade ago, had been the catalyst that had caused the moment of madness between herself and Nick which had led to Jem's existence. Maybe the flood could have done some good if it sparked a turning point for the future…if Nick found a way to move on from the past and accept his son.

'You really like Gabriel, don't you?' Chloe asked Lauren as Kate walked away from them.

Lauren nodded, although 'like' was an insipid word to describe the complexity of her feelings and the extent of her attraction. 'I do.'

'The electricity the two of you generate when you're together could power the whole of Cornwall,' her friend proclaimed, giving her a quick hug. 'I hope everything works out. I want you to be as happy as I am—and around Gabriel you look how I feel when I'm with Oliver.' She hesitated a moment, then added more soberly, 'I know we rarely mention it, but I'll never forget all you've done for me, Lauren.'

Chloe was such a sweetheart. That she was now blossoming was wonderful. Lauren still vividly recalled the state in which she had found Chloe eleven and a half years ago when the girl, then sixteen, had been beaten by her father. She had helped Chloe get away that night and was so proud of the success she had gone on to make of her life. Even so, for a long while Chloe had shut herself off from love because of her past—until Oliver had arrived. The perfect man to be understanding, gentle and loving, he'd taught Chloe all about being a woman in the fullest sense of the word.

'You've come such a long way and I'm so delighted for you,' she said, hugging Chloe back.

'Thank you. Ooh, sorry, I didn't mean to get all sentimental!' Chloe's smile was wobbly, her eyes bright with a suspicion of tears. Doggedly, she changed the subject. 'Can you believe Vicky taking off like that after the flood?'

Lauren had been friends with Vicky Clements since junior school. They were close but she acknowledged Vicky's faults—primary amongst them being her propensity for gossip. Vicky didn't mean any harm, but she often hurt people's feelings and said thoughtless things she shouldn't. And working at her mother's hair and beauty salon, Vicky heard a lot of tales she was only too keen to pass on. They'd had a lot of fun together over the years, and Lauren enjoyed the flighty woman's company, but it was to Chloe that Lauren turned for advice and to share confidences. Chloe was discreet and kind and totally selfless.

'It will be a while until the salon is up and running again after the flood damage. Vicky's mother is going to keep up her regular clients by doing home visits until the salon can reopen,' she explained now. 'Vicky's been restless since embarking on her hot new romance with the guitarist of that up-and-coming band she met in a nightclub in Rock. When the band asked her to go with them on their world tour, to do all the styling and hair for them and the backing singers, she felt it was too good an opportunity to miss.'

'A real adventure, for sure,' Chloe agreed.

'Vicky's never been so committed to a man before...maybe this will change her.'

'It'll seem quiet around here with her gone.' A twinkle of mischief appeared in her friend's green eyes. 'At least Vicky is too busy with her own love life to gossip about or interfere in ours!'

'Amen to that.'

Lauren remembered how Vicky's tactless meddling had caused problems—thankfully temporary ones—for Chloe and Oliver back in the summer. It was a good thing that Vicky was away for the next few months, she decided. She didn't need her nosy friend making wisecracks or involving herself in what Lauren hoped was her own budding new relationship with a certain sexy French doctor.

'The second half is about to start.' Chloe's comment drew Lauren from her thoughts. 'It's been competitive but friendly so far—I hope no one gets hurt.'

'Me, too.'

The famous, top-flight referee, who had agreed to officiate for the charity match, blew his whistle and the game began again in earnest with the celebrities leading the locals by four goals to three. Lauren, as Penhally team physio, was kept busy as the game went on, with various muscle pulls and a couple of sprains. Then Jack Tremayne received a nasty cut to his knee, one that was suspiciously shaped like a stud mark from a misplaced football boot.

'You need stitches in this,' Adam Donnelly declared, examining the wound and stemming the bleeding.

'It can wait until after the game.' Jack ignored the combined medical opinion and insisted on rejoining the fray once he had been bandaged up. 'If we win, I'll let you at me with a needle.'

Adam turned away with a good-natured grin. 'Gee, thanks. Perhaps I'll misplace the local anaesthetic. That or sew your lips together,' he called back, making everyone laugh.

The game continued and the goals kept coming for both sides. Lauren cheered loudest of all when Gabriel scored another spectacular goal to put the home team in the lead with only ten minutes left to play. Standing on the sidelines, enjoying the action, she couldn't stop watching Gabriel. He had a wonderful physique, strong but leanly athletic, and his sleeveless top—part of the players' kit donated by a national sportswear chain for the occasion—showed off the roped, corded muscles of his arms to perfection. Oliver had a good body, too, but looking at him did nothing for her in terms of attraction. Neither did any of the other men here. Only Gabriel. Just one sight of him stole her breath and set a fire of need smouldering inside her, clenching her stomach and leaving her giddy with excited anticipation.

Watching him so closely, she was aware the instant something went wrong. She was already reaching for her bag when Gabriel collapsed as if he had been poleaxed. Seeing him fall scared her witless. Then she was running towards him, even before the referee had given her permission to cross the pitch. Gabriel needed her. Her heart in her mouth, Lauren dropped to her knees beside the prone figure on the ground.

'Gabe, what's wrong?' Her voice shook with emotion and she didn't consciously realise she had shortened his name. 'Where are you hurt?'

'Cramp,' he managed through teeth gritted with pain.

His right leg was rigid with vicious spasms. Lauren got to her feet and grasped his ankle, holding his leg up straight and

pushing back against his foot to try to ease the locked muscles.
By the time the referee, Oliver and a few of the other Penhally
players had jogged across to see what was going on, some of
the knotted tension in Gabriel's leg was beginning to dissi-
pate.

'You'll have to carry out any other treatment off the pitch,'
the referee insisted, for all the world like this was a major professional match rather than a fundraising one.

'I can play on,' Gabriel insisted, trying to get to his feet.
'There's not much longer to go. I want to see it out.'

Lauren held on to him as he took a few faltering steps only
for his leg to give out and cramp up again. 'Gabe, you can't.
We need to get you rehydrated and your leg dealt with.'

'She's right, my friend.' As Oliver backed her up, she sent
him a grateful smile. 'Let Lauren take care of you.'

'You've given your all and scored two goals,' she reminded him.

Coffee-coloured eyes, threaded with pain, looked into hers.
After a moment, he nodded. 'All right.'

'Thank you.' She turned to Oliver. 'I'll take him down to
the treatment room.'

'Good idea. We'll ferry down any other walking wounded
when we're done.'

As Oliver went to organise a substitute for the last part of
the game, Lauren grabbed her bag with one hand and slid her
free arm around Gabriel's waist, helping him balance as he
limped to the sidelines. He put an arm around her shoulders,
accepting the support, and she welcomed the weight of it.
Even given the circumstances, she couldn't help but be aware
of how it felt to be so close. She could feel the heat of him
and scent his earthy maleness.

Chloe and Kate awaited them on the touchline, looking
worried.

'Is there anything we can do?' Kate asked.

'Can you keep an eye on him while I get my car?' She hated to leave him but no way could he walk all the way to the car park. 'If you have water or a sports drink, Gabriel needs them.'

'Of course.'

Knowing Gabriel was being cared for, Lauren ran for the car. Soon she was driving as close as she could to the pitch, pleased to find that Chloe and Kate had helped to guide Gabriel to her through the crowds. She jumped out and hurried round to open the passenger door, noting the tension on his face as his leg tightened again when he sat in the restricted space.

'Thanks.' She smiled at her friends and slid back behind the wheel, grateful it was only a very short distance to the surgery.

She threw him a quick glance, pleased to see he was continuing to drink. His eyes were closed and he was stretching out his leg as much as the confines of the car would allow. 'Are you OK?'

'I'm getting too old for this,' he joked. 'Don't worry, *chérie*, the cramp will ease.'

It certainly would once she had a chance to work on those calf and thigh muscles. But she made no comment as she parked outside the surgery, unlocked the door and helped Gabriel inside. The problem with her plan only hit her once they were in the physio room.

Alone.

And Gabriel had gone behind the curtain to take off his football boots, socks and shorts.

Oh, sweet mercy.

Now he was lying face down on the treatment table. True, he was still wearing his football top but the towel covering his lower half reminded her of the day they had met. Lauren swallowed. She was a professional. She could do this. She could put hands on Gabriel's scrumptious body and give him a therapeutic massage without thinking about or acting on any of the salacious and erotic fantasies running through her mind.

Of course she could. And would. If she kept telling herself enough, she might even believe it.

Ignoring the way her hands were shaking, she took out a bottle of the embrocation she favoured for working on tired, cramped muscles and approached the table. Biting her lip, she pushed the hem of the towel up to mid-thigh. His legs were beautifully sculpted, all toned muscle and supple, dark skin.

'L-let's get these knots sorted out,' she murmured, cursing her lack of control. 'Ready?'

'Do your worst, Lauren.'

'Right.'

She poured oil into her hands and rubbed them together to warm it, telling herself to forget all the 'worst' things she really wanted to do to him and focus on the professional massage. Sucking in a steadying breath, she touched him for the first time. Her hands settled low on his calf, feeling the tightness of the muscles in spasm as she pressed upwards with deft strokes to the back of the knee. She forced herself to concentrate on what she was doing. She couldn't allow herself to dwell on how wonderful it was to touch him, or let her gaze to move any farther up to where the towel brushed his thighs and draped across the enticing shape of his rear.

Gabriel groaned as her thumbs circled deeply into his flesh. '*Mon Dieu*, that feels good.'

The sultry roughness of his voice shimmered to every nerve ending. *He* certainly felt good, his skin warm and male beneath her fingers. She worked slowly up his leg, relaxing the muscles of the calf and thigh, feeling his tension ease while her own magnified. No matter how hard she tried to remain professional, to keep her touch neutral and impersonal, she had never been so intensely aware in her life. She wanted this man as she had never wanted anyone before. The temptation to caress, to glide her hands higher and allow her fingers to explore his body was overwhelming.

Lauren was relieved that Gabriel didn't talk. She didn't think she could. Indeed, he seemed unaffected, his head turned to one side, resting on his crossed forearms. His eyes were closed, and he gave every impression of being relaxed and at ease, while she was on red alert, aroused and aching. It was mortifying.

'Turn over now, please,' she directed, injecting as much calm unconcern into her voice as she could manage.

'Lauren…'

She reached for the bottle of oil. 'Hmm?'

'I think it is fine now, *chérie*,' he stated, sounding oddly wary.

'Nonsense,' she riposted briskly. If he could do this without batting an eyelid, so could she. 'I haven't finished massaging the leg.'

'But—'

'Please, Gabriel.'

He huffed out a breath, and she frowned, wondering what the problem was as he continued to hesitate. She waited endless moments before he slowly rolled over. Her pulse rate rocketed and her throat closed as the reason for his reticence became apparent…the tented towel gave evidence to the fact that the extent of his arousal matched her own. She couldn't look away. Her stomach knotted with an ache of need, her heart pounded, and she could feel her nipples pucker even further in response, sensitive against the lacy fabric of her bra.

Gabriel sat up and swung his legs off the table. 'Lauren.' His hands cupped her face, raising it until she was looking into eyes so dark and hot with desire she felt singed from the fire.

'Gabe…'

His name had barely whispered from her lips before his mouth met hers, firm, demanding, delicious. The plastic bottle she was holding fell forgotten to the floor, her fingers trailing up the leanly muscled contours of his arms before clinging to the strength of his shoulders. She had longed for this moment.

Had yearned to taste him. And now, at last, she was. There was no hesitancy, no awkwardness of a first kiss. It was as if their mouths, their bodies, already knew each other.

Her lips parted in welcome and she moaned as he accepted the invitation with barely restrained hunger, sweeping inside, taking and giving, stroking and sliding. One arm wrapped around her waist, pulling her closer, and she stepped up between his thighs. The fingers of his other hand sank into her hair, tilting the angle of her head to deepen the contact between them. His touch was electric, his kiss explosive. Lauren felt as if all the cells and molecules in her body bonded with his, their genes homing in on each other.

The kiss melted her, stealing her reason. Her legs threatened to give way and she tightened her hold, leaning into him for support. She had never felt like this before. The intense, thorough kiss was even more than she had imagined and dreamed about in the time she had known him. She met and matched Gabriel's every move, never wanting this to end. Her tongue twined with his, and she sucked on him, excited when he nibbled at her lips, teasing and tormenting before deepening the kiss again and sucking back at her. She wanted more, needed everything, revelled in his immediate response, the passion between them intensifying.

Gabriel lost himself in the sweet heat of Lauren's kiss. The firm softness of her breasts pressed against his chest and he could feel the hardened crests of her aroused nipples through the thin barrier of their clothes. His hand grazed down her back to cup the enticing swell of her rear, and he shaped her, pulling her tighter, swallowing her involuntary whimper as she met the fullness of his erection. An answering groan escaped him as she wriggled closer, rubbing herself against him.

He'd never felt this out of control from a kiss, but the wild chemistry between them had him on the ragged edge already.

A kiss was never going to be enough. He wanted her. Wanted her as he had never wanted any other woman in his life. Needed to see her and touch her and taste her all over. Couldn't wait to unite their bodies, to possess her fully, to lose himself deep and tight inside her. Lauren and this incredible passion they shared could make him forget all about the problems awaiting him back in France.

A loud knock on the door brought them sharply back to reality. They broke apart, panting for breath. How could he have forgotten where they were? Lauren's eyes opened, dark grey and smoky with unfulfilled passion, her regret at the interruption matching his own. They stared at each other and he watched as she stepped back a pace, raising shaky fingers to lips that were moist and plump from the incendiary kiss that had taken him to paradise. He could see the pulse beating wildly at her throat, mimicking the way his own heart pounded a frantic rhythm beneath his ribs.

'*Damnez-le,*' he cursed, drawing in a ragged breath. 'Wrong time, wrong place.'

'Yes. Gabe…'

No one had ever shortened his name before. He liked it. Liked it that Lauren was the only one who used it, who spoke it with such husky intimacy. Renewed heat prickled through him as they looked at each other, her eyes dark with an answering desire and need. Another knock at the door had Lauren moving farther away, adjusting her clothes and smoothing down the hair he had tousled.

'Just a minute,' she called out, her voice sounding shaky and rough.

He licked his lips, still able to taste her. Her subtle sweet-pea scent had invaded him, familiar, arousing, sensual. His whole body was charged with excitement. There was bitter disappointment that they'd had to stop, yet raging anticipation at the thought of how explosive the experience of making love was going to be for them when the time came. As it inevitably would.

'I'd better get that.' She forced the words out but they sounded hoarse.

Knowing he couldn't delay things now, Gabriel sighed. 'I know.'

He retreated behind the curtain, listening as she opened the door and had a conversation with Adam.

'Sorry to bother you, Lauren. I hope Gabriel's OK. We've brought down two more team players needing treatment,' Adam explained. 'I'm just going to stitch Jack's cut—we won, so I'm at him with the needle!—and Dan Somers has pulled his hamstring. It looks a bad one so he's going to need follow-up treatment. Can you see what you can do for him?'

'Of course.'

Gabriel heard the thread of reluctance at being interrupted mingle with genuine concern in her voice as she agreed. The son of one of the local farmers, Dan had played for the Penhally team and Gabriel had met him for the first time that day. Hurrying so as not to embarrass Lauren in any way, Gabriel pulled on his shorts then sat down to sort out his socks and football boots. Once he was done, he drew back the curtain in time to see Lauren glance over her shoulder at him, her expression flustered.

'We're just about finished here,' she told Adam. 'Give me a few moments to make sure Gabriel is all right and I'll be happy to help Dan.'

'Thanks, Lauren. He's in the waiting room. We'll help him through.'

When Adam had gone, Gabriel moved up behind her and, hidden by the door, turned her to face him, cupping her cheek with one palm, enjoying the feel of her warm, soft skin.

'I'm sorry,' she whispered, and it was an effort to drag his gaze away from the temptation of her mouth.

'It's not your fault. Next weekend we'll have some privacy. I don't want to rush things and have to steal odd moments like this.' He felt the tremor run through her in response to his words. 'Thank you for making my leg feel so much better.'

Her smile held a spark of mischief and he chuckled, not sure if it was the expert massage or the fiery kiss that had most eased the pain in his cramping leg. Hearing people approaching along the corridor, Gabriel released her and stepped back, allowing her to open the door again so that Adam and Oliver could assist Dan Somers into the room.

'How are you feeling Gabriel?' Oliver asked as Lauren and Adam settled Dan on the treatment table.

'Like a new man, thanks to Lauren.'

Gabriel noticed the warmth bloom on Lauren's cheeks as she rejoined them. 'He should be fine,' she said.

'I'm heading home with Chloe,' Oliver continued, apparently oblivious to the charged atmosphere. 'Do you want a lift as Lauren's going to be busy for a while?'

'Sure. Thanks, Oliver.'

'Thank *you* for all your help. The match was a huge success. And we won—thanks to our secret weapon in our French star!' Oliver smiled, his humour infectious.

'We'll leave you to get on, Lauren,' Adam decreed. 'I have an appointment with Jack and a needle!'

Lauren walked them to the door, and Gabriel hung back, allowing Adam and Oliver to leave ahead of him. He paused, leaning in to whisper in her ear. 'Later, *chérie*. Next weekend we'll have time for us,' he promised, gratified by the flare of desire in her eyes.

Filled with impatience at the wait and disappointed to be leaving her, Gabriel walked away. The time until they could be alone together with no threat of interruptions couldn't come soon enough.

* * *

The frustration and anticipation was every bit as bad as he expected as the following week unfolded and he had little time alone with Lauren. One bright spot on the horizon was the arrangement to spend a morning accompanying her on her home visits. He was happy to give up his time off on Thursday because it meant being with her.

Finally it was Wednesday. His late-afternoon surgery was typically mixed, with cases including a young man with psoriasis, a fifty-two-year-old woman with menopausal symptoms, a teenage girl with a nasty stye, who needed some antibiotic eyedrops, an elderly man with signs of blood in his urine, who needed further tests to rule out infection and determine the source of the bleeding, a toddler with earache and several cases of colds, sore throats and influenza.

'You done for the day?' Oliver asked, tapping on the open consulting-room door and stepping inside.

'Yes.' Gabriel smiled, waving Oliver to a chair and saving the notes he had written up on his computer to back up his handwritten ones. 'What can I do for you?'

'I hear you are going out on home visits with Lauren tomorrow.'

And the time couldn't come soon enough, Gabriel thought, nodding at his friend. 'That's right.'

'You'll be visiting one of our regular patients, Gertrude Stanbury. She's quite a character, as I am sure Lauren will explain to you!' With a bad-boy smile, Oliver sat back in the chair and hooked one ankle over the opposite knee. 'Would you mind giving her a flu jab? I found out today that the district nurses missed her off their schedule by mistake, and I'm not due to see her for a fortnight. I don't want her to wait that long. I'd go myself, but I have a full list tomorrow and I'm off on Friday. I could get one of the nurses to fit her in, but as you'll be there anyway…'

'No problem, Oliver.'

'Great. Thanks. Chloe's free on Friday, too, so we're planning to get off early for our weekend in Plymouth.'

'I hope Rachel Kenner is coping.' Having heard the full story of how the troublesome youth Gary Lovelace had targeted the vicar's daughter so cruelly, he felt sad for the girl. 'I'm sure she will be delighted to see you.'

Concern shadowed Oliver's expression. 'Chloe is fretting about her. It will set our minds at rest if she's settled in as happily as possible with her aunt and uncle, as well as managing her pregnancy. Goodness knows how she is dealing with all that on top of losing her father.'

'Grief affects people in different ways.' Realising that his tone of voice had revealed more than he had intended and had roused Oliver's interest, Gabriel cleared his throat and changed the subject, unwilling to think of home and family. 'Don't worry about anything here. I'll see to Ms Stanbury's flu vaccination tomorrow. And I know Lauren will take care of the cats for Chloe while you are gone.'

A knowing gleam shone in Oliver's dark eyes. 'Somehow I doubt that you and Lauren will be sorry to have us out of the way for a while. We've cramped your style a bit, having to move into Gatehouse Cottage after the flood.'

'It's fine.'

'You look much more relaxed than when you first arrived,' Oliver continued after a moment.

Gabriel nodded. 'I feel it. It's been enjoyable and I've learned a great deal. I'm glad I came here.'

'Moving to Penhally Bay certainly changed *my* life.'

'How so?' he prompted, interested to know more about the man who had become a close friend in such a short time.

'I was dissatisfied with my life in London and knew I wanted something different. I'd planned to take time to settle in and establish myself before I started thinking about the future and a family. But then I met Chloe. I knew from the first moment that she was the one for me.' He glanced across with a smile that was both reminiscent and wicked. 'It took me a while to acknowledge the truth of it to myself—and a bit longer to persuade Chloe I was serious. She's the best thing that's ever happened to me. I've never been this contented.'

'I'm pleased for you. Anyone can see how great you are as a couple.'

'I hope Penhally will bring you the same contentment.'

Gabriel hesitated a moment, finding it surprisingly easy to share confidences with Oliver—something that was uncharacteristic for him. 'I have issues to work out from home... things to consider about my future. And a year here in which to decide on the direction of my life.'

'Penhally is a good place to think. If you want to talk, I'm here. And there's Lauren,' he added, a teasing glint in his eyes. 'The sparks between you are obvious. I hope you'll find your time in Cornwall brings you the same happiness and direction it gave to me.'

'Thank you, *mon ami*.'

Gabriel wondered the same thing. Would his time in Penhally not only lead him to some answers about his family dilemma but also open up a whole new world of opportunity with Lauren? Their friendship had established and deepened from the first moment. It had happened quickly, but there was no denying the connection between them. The heightened awareness and desire fizzing through him whenever he so much as thought of Lauren could not be ignored.

He was looking forward to finding out what the next weeks and months held in store for him.

CHAPTER FIVE

'WE JUST have Gertrude Stanbury left to visit,' Lauren informed Gabriel as she steered the car away from the Mitchell family's home and headed towards Trelissa Road.

Despite hearing good things from others, this morning was the first time she had seen Gabriel in action as a doctor for herself. She was even more impressed than she had anticipated. He had an innate warmth that set people at their ease and evoked their trust. He was interested and genuine, compassionate without being patronising. Combined with everything else she knew about him, it made her admire and care about him even more.

'Paul Mitchell is an inspiring youngster,' Gabriel said, and Lauren smiled.

'He is. I always feel humbled by his bravery,' she admitted, shaking her head at the way the eleven-year-old coped with the limits Duchenne muscular dystrophy placed on his life. 'Paul's faced each new challenge and stage of the disease with good humour and fortitude, although he hates having to use the wheelchair now. He loves school but doesn't attend full time because of the difficulties, so has some lessons at home, like today. Thankfully he's a genius with a computer…it's his pride and joy. The family don't have much materially but they do all they can to meet Paul's needs with home adaptations and equipment. They are very close and wonderfully supportive of each other, not to mention grateful for whatever back-up we can give them.'

Gabriel nodded, his admiration evident. 'They are certainly devoted to Paul and take his exercise regime seriously.'

'Paul's willingness to keep trying, to do the stretching exercises for his muscles and the breathing ones to keep his lungs clear, expel the mucus and reduce the risk of infections, makes my job much easier. He's determined not to let it beat him. And we are all determined to work as a team to ensure that Paul has the fullest and most enjoyable life possible.'

'I think you are amazing.' Gabriel's compliment warmed her inside. 'I've seen you today helping a variety of people—Harry Biscombe with his osteoporosis, Edith Jones with her minor stroke, the after-effects of her broken knee and assorted health problems, Stella Chamberlain with her onset of Parkinson's disease, the Morrisons with young baby Timmy's cystic fibrosis, and now Paul.' He paused and she could feel his gaze on her. 'You have a special rapport with your patients, Lauren. You give so much of yourself. It's not just a job to you.'

His praise touched her, his opinion mattering a great deal. But his own dedication and giftedness as a doctor was unsurpassed. 'You're the same. Medicine—caring for people in need—is part of the very fabric of who you are.'

'Yes.'

There was a thread of sadness and confusion in his voice, along with a weary sigh. She glanced at him, wondering what lay behind his change of tone. Did it have something to do with why he had been so keen to leave France? There was so much she wanted to discover about this man.

'Gabriel—'

'Tell me about Gertrude Stanbury,' he suggested, interrupting her. 'Oliver tells me she is something of a character.'

Reluctantly, Lauren allowed the change of subject...for

now. 'You can say that again. Gertrude is retired now but she was an institution as long-time headmistress at the secondary school here in Penhally. She has a bungalow in Gull Close and suffers badly from arthritis, especially in the knees and hands, although other joints are becoming affected more seriously. She had her first knee replacement recently but is still not very mobile. Her recovery wasn't helped by the flood, but at least she was safe. Thankfully one of the young local girls, Tassie Lovelace, was visiting her at the time, and as the water started coming in she was able to encourage Gertrude into the attic, from where they were rescued by one of the helicopter crews.'

'How on earth did Gertrude manage to get up there?'

'I've no idea, but it didn't do her joints much good.' Lauren shook her head, pausing a moment as she parked in Trelissa Road, taking extra care to make sure she didn't have a repeat of reversing into anything…not with Gabriel as a witness. 'Until her home is fit to live in again, Dr Tom Cornish has insisted she live in this house—it used to belong to his father and Tom inherited it. A former Penhally resident, he happened to be here, dealing with the house, when the flood hit. He's head of Deltaron, the international rescue agency, and his team were marvellous during the emergency.'

Gabriel unclipped his seat belt and glanced at the house. 'Why would Dr Cornish loan Gertrude his house?'

'Apparently Tom was a bit wild when he was young and, although a formidable adversary, Gertrude always believed in him. Tom was glad to help her now and repay her faith in him.' She chuckled at her own memories of the feisty woman who had watched over the school and its pupils with an all-seeing eye. 'She scared the life out of most of us!'

'I shall look forward to hearing all about your misspent youth!'

Lauren laughed. 'The trouble is, Gertrude will be all too keen to tell you.'

'Now I'm even more intrigued.' He smiled back at her, and she felt the faint wash of pink that tinged her cheeks.

'Just don't believe everything you hear.'

'Maybe that depends what *everything* is.'

His teasing deepened her blush. She was aware of him following close behind as she walked towards the house and opened the front door with the spare key they kept at the surgery. Rotund, white-haired Gertrude was propped up on pillows in a comfortable recliner in the living room. Age and crippling arthritis had brought an end to her working life, but had done nothing to dim the sharp expression in her steely grey gaze or take the edge off her shrewd watchfulness. A sense of humour and keen interest still lurked behind her outward bark and bluster.

'Oh, it's you, Lauren. Come in, then, if I have to be poked and prodded,' she grumbled, a sparkle dancing in her eyes as she took her first look at Gabriel. 'Who is this handsome creature?'

'I've brought Dr Devereux to meet you, Ms Stanbury.'

Lauren introduced them and watched with amusement as the elderly lady regally extended her hand, a pink glow washing pale, papery cheeks at Gabriel's gallant greeting. She was surprised, however, when Gertrude began speaking rapidly to him in his own language.

'I'd forgotten that you used to teach French, Ms Stanbury.'

'I did have a life before becoming a headmistress, you know,' she barked in response.

Lauren saw the laughter in Gabriel's eyes and struggled to contain a giggle. 'How have you been since I last saw you? Have you been managing the exercises I gave you?'

'Pure torture, they are.'

'I'm sorry to hear that.' Lauren smiled, not fooled for a moment by Gertrude's mock complaints. As she carried out a gentle examination and encouraged her to try a few more movements and exercises, both standing and sitting, she could see the improvement in the knee that had been replaced. 'You are doing so well, Ms Stanbury. Once your other knee is done, you'll find your mobility will be much better. How are your hands? Are you finding the new combination of pills Dr Oliver put you on helping at all?'

An affectionate expression crossed the elderly lady's face at the mention of Oliver, for whom it was well-known she had a soft spot. 'These pills are an improvement.'

'I'm so glad. We'll run through a few more gentle exercises to keep you moving, then Dr Devereux is going to see to your flu jab.'

A groan greeted the news and Lauren shared another smile with Gabriel. When she had finished, she sat back on her heels and packed away her things while Gabriel dealt with the vaccination and chatted with Gertrude in French. Lauren didn't catch much of the conversation, but hearing the names of Martin and her parents mentioned, she smothered a groan of her own. Maybe it was a good thing she couldn't remember much of her schoolgirl French or she would likely be mortified at whatever Gertrude was telling Gabriel. The former headmistress possessed an encyclopaedic knowledge about her past students and embarrassing moments were recounted with glee. Feeling Gabriel watching her, she looked up. The interested speculation evident in his mocha-brown eyes made her wonder what questions she would face once they were alone.

'You didn't understand much of that, did you, Lauren? You would remember your French had *I* been your teacher,' Ms Stanbury rebuked, reverting to English, mischief in her eyes. 'As I recall, it was always art and sport with you. When you weren't tripping over and dropping things. Still,' her tormentor continued, her knowing gaze moving from Lauren to Gabriel and back again, 'it seems to me that your interest in things French has increased considerably of late.'

As Gabriel chuckled, Lauren fought another blush. The

woman was a menace! Fortunately, they were soon able to escape. Unfortunately, her time with Gabriel was over for today and she dropped him back at the Manor House.

'Gertrude Stanbury was everything I expected and more,' he teased, silencing her grunt of disgust with a parting kiss that left her breathless. He drew back and stroked the fingers of one hand down her cheek. 'Thank you for this morning, *chérie*. I learned a lot.' Lauren feared he had learned rather more than she had intended, thanks to Gertrude's runaway tongue. 'We'll talk at the weekend.'

With his enigmatic promise ringing in her ears, Lauren returned to the surgery for her afternoon list of appointments, wondering what the weekend held in store and if, once finally alone, they would succumb to the charge of desire that hummed between them.

Today had been his most enjoyable day in Cornwall so far, Gabriel reflected, lingering over coffee after the meal he had cooked and shared with Lauren in the kitchen at the Manor House on Saturday evening.

The weather had continued to be kind and they had spent the day exploring, Lauren showing him Bodmin Moor and parts of the coast. They had also indulged in a number of increasingly heated kisses that had whetted his appetite for more. From the look in her eyes and the responses of her body, he was pretty sure Lauren felt the same. Foxy had accompanied them on their walks, growing in confidence all the time, and the sleek greyhound now lay asleep in the basket Lauren had brought up for him. Returning from their outing as dusk had descended, they had stopped off at Gatehouse Cottage to check on and feed Chloe's cats.

He had noticed once again Lauren's nervousness and caution in the dark, the care she took, the way she sometimes counted to herself as if she was measuring her steps because she couldn't see. He wasn't even sure she was aware of the habit. Once the lights went on, she reverted to her usual self. Again, her actions puzzled and concerned him, but he was wary of mentioning anything to her until he had a clearer idea if there was, indeed, anything wrong…and until she knew him well enough to trust him. Was he making something out of nothing? Maybe, if everyone else accepted her as clumsy and she had always been this way, he was seeing something that wasn't there and Lauren just had bad night vision. Gertrude Stanbury had confirmed Lauren had been renowned for being accident prone even in her schooldays. He planned to keep a watch on her until he was more certain of the facts.

Looking at Lauren now, Gabriel marvelled again at her natural beauty. Her skin glowed with freshness, her hair, left loose around her shoulders, shone with life—myriad shades of light browns and golds—and her womanly figure was shown off to perfection in dark jeans and a lilac button-through top that hugged the fullness of her breasts. Long, sooty lashes rose and beautiful grey eyes stared into his own.

'What?' she asked, her voice husky, rosy lips parting slightly as her tongue-tip peeped out to moisten them, tightening his gut with need.

He edged his chair closer and reached out to take one of her hands in both of his, holding her palm up in one hand and stroking her soft skin with the fingers of the other, feeling the way her flesh quivered in response to his touch.

'I had a great time today, Lauren.'

'Me, too.'

He forced himself to look away from the temptation of her mouth for the moment. They had talked about so much today but had not touched on any of the things that were contentious or difficult, like family and past relationships. Gabriel thought of all the well-meaning but meddling gossip Gertrude had told him on Thursday. Knowing how he felt about having his own privacy invaded, he didn't want to pressure Lauren, yet he knew they had reached a point where an exchange of confidences was needed if they were to take the simmering passion that only grew hotter and more intense between them to its logical conclusion.

'Will you tell me about Martin?' he asked after a long moment of silence. He watched Lauren carefully but saw nothing in her reaction to worry him, no sign she was still in love with the man Gertrude had mentioned.

'Martin and I had an on-off relationship for a long time,' she explained, no inflection in her voice. 'We grew up together, went out as teenagers, then broke up when I went away to do my physiotherapy training. I had a couple of casual boyfriends while we were apart and I know Martin dated other people. He stayed in Penhally, apprenticed to his father's construction business, but he was never happy there.' Gabriel waited when she paused again, welcoming the way she twined her fingers with his. 'When I moved back here to work, neither of us were involved with anyone and we started seeing each other again. I suppose we drifted into it for lack of other options. That sounds bad, but we were good friends first and foremost. We just became comfortable with each other, like an old habit. Things were wrong for a long time but neither of us faced up to what was happening.'

'And what did happen?'

'Martin became increasingly restless and withdrawn. He felt stifled by a job he hated, a town he wanted to escape from and a relationship I'm sure he knew deep down was going nowhere. I was settled—I love my job, my friends, my hobbies. But he needed to go off and explore new things and places. And to find someone he could share more than friendship with.'

She sounded understanding and not too sorry that things had ended, Gabriel thought. 'So he left.'

'It was the right decision. We were both relieved.' She smiled, her expression clear. 'A lot of people were shocked— a few had presumed we would marry. That was *never* on the cards. We didn't even live together. It was only once we'd made the final break that I realised how dull and predictable and restricting things had become, and how long it had been since we had been together in any real sense of the word. Our friendship was important but anything more was wrong for us both. Martin needed to leave. We couldn't provide what each other wanted.'

Smiling, she rose to her feet and began to clear the table, moving to the sink to wash up the plates. Thoughtful, understanding the rut she had found herself in, Gabriel drained the last of his wine and crossed the kitchen to join her, working silently by her side for a moment. The atmosphere was thick with the ever-present awareness and desire that rippled between them.

When the last plate had been washed and dried, Gabriel turned her to face him. 'And what did you want, Lauren, that you never got from your relationship?'

Gabriel's smoky, accented voice sent shivers down Lauren's spine. Did she dare admit her secret yearnings? She sensed that with Gabriel she could experience all the things she now knew she had been missing. His compelling gaze drew her in, mesmerised her. The last two weeks had been leading up to this point and they both knew it. Taking her courage in both hands, she looked into his eyes, holding nothing back.

'I wanted things to be more passionate, more spontaneous, less boring.'

'You'd like to be adventurous, *chérie*?'

'Yes,' she whispered, her own voice low and throaty in response to the dark sensuality lacing his.

He didn't move. He wasn't touching her in any way but it

felt as if he was. 'You want to experiment, to be fully satisfied.' It was a statement, not a question, and Lauren swallowed, a shiver of desire skimming down her spine.

'Yes.' The admission was torn from her.

'You want a partner to be your equal, to explore the full scope of your sexuality, to surprise you and challenge you. To give and to take. To break rules and test boundaries.'

Speech was now impossible. He was seducing her with his words, his voice, the promise that remained as yet unspoken. Excitement fired her blood. The wicked glint in his sexy dark eyes made her breathless. She had no doubt that making love with Gabriel would never be boring or predictable or lacking in passion. Her heart pounded beneath her ribs. Unable to wrest her gaze from his, she nodded her answer, aroused beyond bearing, unable to look away from the flare of desire that turned his brown eyes almost black.

He stepped closer, reaching out to take her hands in his. It was their only point of contact and yet her whole body vibrated with sensation. His arms encircled her, his fingers linked with hers so that their joined hands fisted at the small of her back. The movement caused her body to arch and press against his. Every thud of her heart sounded loud in the silence of the kitchen and her breathing sped up, matching the uneven rate of his.

A gasp escaped unchecked as his lips whispered over hers, the tip of his tongue teasing as he circled it round the outline of her mouth, pausing to stroke each corner. It was incredibly erotic. She moaned, opening involuntarily, seeking closer contact, her lips clinging to his as he gave her what she needed. From the first second the kiss flared out of control, deep and demanding as they all but devoured each other, exploring, tongues duelling and entwining. His teeth nibbled at her, inflaming her senses. He pulled on her lips, then sucked on her tongue, drawing her into him. She couldn't get close enough, intoxicated by the male taste of him and his warm, citrusy, masculine scent.

The next moment, she found both her hands restrained behind her by one of his, leaving his other hand free to explore her. And explore her he did. His fingers trailed her face and down her throat, setting little fires wherever he touched, making every particle of her skin tingle. She whimpered when his mouth abandoned hers. Forcing heavy lids to open, her eyes focused to find him watching her, following the path of his fingertips over her flesh. As he bent her back, his palm splayed over her skin, stroking across from one collar-bone to the other before slowly grazing lower. Lauren held her breath as his thumb dipped down her cleavage, tantalisingly brushing against the swell of her breasts, setting her aflame, making her ache for a firmer touch.

'Gabe…'

Her breath rasped out again as his fingers went to work on her buttons, peeling back her top and freeing one breast from the confinement of her lacy red bra. The sight of his darker skin against her paler tones enthralled and excited her. Her nipple, already peaked and flushed with arousal, tightened further under his hungry gaze. She quivered as the pad of his thumb brushed around the outside edge of her areola before gliding once over the proud crest, making her cry out at the sweet ache. After an agonising delay, when she thought she would die of anticipation, his palm cupped the firm fullness of her breast, shaping, testing, before plumping it up as his head lowered. She tried unsuccessfully to free her hands, desperate to touch him, but he kept her captive to his will. Her knees turned to jelly as the moist warmth of his mouth closed over her swollen flesh and he suckled her deeply.

'Oh, my!' She sobbed, shocked by the powerful sensations crashing through her, more intense and incredible than she had ever felt before. Her body arched further in response to his sensual caresses, the rhythmic, hot, heavy pull of his mouth at her breast spearing a devastating ache of need straight to her womb. 'Please. Gabe, please!'

He finally released her hands and she clutched at his shoulders to keep from melting to the floor. Cupping her rear, his fingers flexing, shaping her through the denim as he sank to a chair, he drew her down so she was straddling his lap. Swiftly he dispensed with her shirt and bra. He arched her back, supporting her spine with one hand as the fingers of his other hand traced her skin, learning the contours and textures of her body.

'*Tu es parfait, ma belle,*' he praised huskily, his accent more pronounced. 'Perfect.'

His mouth moved to lavish attention on her neglected breast, bringing the nipple to an aching ripeness to rival its twin. Lauren wriggled on his lap, making him groan as she rubbed herself against the hard thickness of his arousal. She glided one hand up his neck to the back of his head, holding him to her. His close-cropped hair tickled her palm, feeling softly spiky to her touch. Unable to wait any longer to see him, to feel more of him, her fingers tugged at his cable-knit jumper, and he drew back just long enough for her to wrench it over his head. As her fingers traced his upper arms, he returned his avid attention to her breasts, driving her insane with the devastating skill of his hands and mouth, tormenting with his lips and teeth before salving with his tongue. Again he suckled strongly, taking her flesh deep inside, rolling her swollen nipple against the roof of his mouth with his tongue. She cried out, already on the ragged edge, shocked by the urgency of her need.

'I can't bear it!'

He chuckled, the huff of his breath against her over-stimulated flesh nearly sending her past the point of no return. She had never responded to any man the way she did to Gabriel.

He only had to look at her to arouse her. One touch and she was primed, ready. Now she was a whisper away from climaxing and they still had most of their clothes on!

'Hold on, *chérie.*'

Taking her by surprise, he stood up, lifting her with him. She curled her legs around his hips and her arms around his neck, as he headed out of the room towards the stairs. She wanted this with a fierceness that shocked her. They had been heading here since the first moment they had seen each other. Excited anticipation rippled through her. Her hands explored his shoulders and back, delighting in the smoothness of his warm supple skin, the feel of hard muscles rippling beneath.

The rest of the house was in darkness and she pressed her face to his neck, not wanting to acknowledge how little she could see. Instead, she lost herself in his scent, the feel of him, the rightness of her body against his. His hand on her rear tightened, one finger wickedly dipping down to stroke the seam of her jeans over her most sensitive flesh. She moaned, her body reacting instantly, and she wriggled, trying to assuage the terrible ache, desperate for release.

When they reached his bedroom, he set her on her feet, keeping hold of her as he leaned over and switched on the twin bedside lights, casting their welcome glow in the room, easing her anxiety and helping her to see.

He cupped her face with his hands, his expression serious. 'Things in my life are unsettled at the moment, Lauren, and I need to make decisions about my future.'

'Is this about why you left France?' she ventured, nerves tightening her insides.

'Yes. There are family issues.' He hesitated, his uncertainty evident. 'I'm not ready to talk about it. When I am, it will be to you.'

She nodded. 'I understand.' And she did. She wasn't ready to get into her whole family situation either, or face the scary subject of her changing sight. No way would she push him but she would be there if and when he needed her.

'I hadn't planned on or expected to get involved in anything here.'

Terrified he was going to call a halt, she began to protest. 'I—'

'However…' The pad of his thumb pressed gently against her mouth and silenced her. 'I cannot deny the connection that sparked between us from the first moment, or the attraction and longing I have for you. I want you…badly.' Her body tingled, her legs felt weak, and hopeful excitement stirred within her. 'I've not dated at all since my last relationship ended a year ago.'

She was surprised. 'Because you still love her?' she dared to ask.

'No. I didn't love her.' Gabriel smiled and she read the truth in his eyes. 'Like you and Martin, Adèle and I had no grand passion. One day I'll explain, but it ended because of deceit and manipulation. I was angry. It's made me cautious, and I have not been interested in a woman since. Until you.' He paused a moment, then continued. 'I can't make any promises at the moment, Lauren. I—'

'Let's not worry about the future or waste time assessing what this is. I'm not expecting anything or asking for commitment, Gabe, but I don't do one-night stands.'

'Neither do I. I don't embark on things lightly.' His thumbs brushed across her cheekbones. 'I can't give you any guarantees now but this is a hell of a lot more than one night for me. If that's what you want, too.'

'It is.'

Lauren knew the decision had been made the instant she had met him. She meant what she said. She wasn't holding him to anything, but she couldn't deny the hope flaring within her or quell the sense that the chemistry between them was special. She planned to explore it to the fullest and see where this exciting journey took them.

'Why don't we enjoy what we have and see what happens down the line?' she suggested. It had been a long time for her—for him, too, apparently—and she craved Gabriel with an intensity that was almost scary. 'Later will take care of itself.'

'I agree. We live for the here and now.'

She sucked in a breath as his touch became caressing and the flare of sultry desire returned to his eyes. His fingers whispered down her throat, stroking her skin as they trailed between her breasts, neglecting for the moment the flesh that most craved his caresses. Instead, he journeyed down, over and around her navel, making her muscles clench, before grazing down to the waistband of her jeans and working all too slowly to unfasten them.

Lauren was glad he had left the light on. She wanted to see him, to experience everything of their time together. Heat flared inside her as his fingers slid inside the loosened waistband of her jeans, moving down to cuddle her rear. Her own hands settled against his bare chest, enjoying the freedom to touch him. She wanted to linger, to learn every inch of him, but she was too impatient, too needy. She ran her nails lightly over his bronze nipples, smiling at his reaction as he groaned, his body trembling. Moving closer, she set her mouth to him, nipping, licking and teasing, heady from the male taste of him.

Gabriel fisted a hand in her hair, drawing her mouth away from his chest, his eyes dark with a hunger that drove her wild. She sought his kiss, but he denied her, kneeling in front of her to remove her ankle boots and strip off her jeans, revealing the French knickers she favoured, the red lace matching her discarded bra.

'Very nice,' he murmured, nuzzling against her, taking her back to the edge of reason.

Oh, so slowly, he eased the lingerie away. His fingers tor-

mented her, skimming up the backs of her legs, stroking her
inner thighs, withholding the touch she most needed. Instead
he set his mouth to her navel and used his lips, teeth and
tongue to drive her crazy with want.

Just as her legs became too shaky to hold her upright any
longer, Gabriel swept her off her feet and tumbled her to the
huge four-poster bed that had featured in so many of her
dreams in the last two weeks. Dreams that were becoming a
reality. She lay there, breathless with expectation, watching
hungrily as he kicked off his shoes then took off his faded
jeans and black briefs. The breath locked in her lungs as she
took in his wonderful physique, the blatant, beautiful maleness of him, her stomach tightening and her mouth watering
as she looked at his impressive erection.

'All right?'

Way more than all right. She nodded at his husky query,
involuntarily licking her lips. *'Magnifique,'* she whispered
with anticipatory delight.

Smiling, he took an unopened box of condoms from a
drawer and put them on the bedside chest after ripping off the
outer plastic covering. Then he unsnapped the watch on his
right wrist and set it aside. Unable to wait any longer, she held
out her hand and he took it, joining her on the bed, drawing
her into a deeply intense and arousing kiss. Gabriel rolled
them over until she was beneath him and she welcomed the
weight of his body on hers. She lost all ability to think as his
hands and his mouth laid claim to her body, rapidly taking her
to a fever-pitch of need.

'Please,' she demanded, uncaring that she was begging.

'All in good time.'

'Now!'

Gabe chuckled at her plea, sending another stimulating
huff of warm air across her taut nipple. 'There's no hurry.'

'There is,' she whimpered, part of her craving release at

once, part of her never wanting the delicious torture to end. 'Gabe, I can't.'

'Trust me, you can…and you will.'

'Wait until it's your turn,' she threatened, making him chuckle again, the throaty, seductive sound tightening everything feminine inside her.

'I'm looking forward to it, *chérie*. Now be still and let me enjoy you.'

No way could she be still! Her body arched and bowed and writhed to his intensely sensual and skilful caresses as he journeyed slowly down to settle between her thighs and use his mouth to take her to paradise. She was the instrument and he was the virtuoso musician and conductor, orchestrating her downfall, playing her to a shattering orgasmic crescendo. Gabriel unleashed a depth of passion and sexuality from within her that she'd had no idea was there. She had enjoyed making love in the past, but she had never experienced this all-consuming, out-of-control explosion of earthy desire and searing need before.

She had barely re-established a tentative grip on reality when he eased two fingers inside her, setting up a rhythmic stroking that threatened to turn the aftershocks still rippling through her into an earthquake of unprecedented proportions. Her heart pounded, her lungs burned, and every nerve ending zinged with sensation. She couldn't bear it. It was incredible, terrible, wonderful. Far too much and yet nowhere near enough. Shaken by her total abandonment, she tried to rein in the litany of cries and moans and whimpers clamouring for escape. She'd never been noisy before. Now, on the point of another explosive climax, she pressed a hand to her mouth to bank down the uncharacteristic scream rising inside her.

'No. Let it go, *ma belle*,' Gabriel demanded huskily against her ear, his tongue teasing her before he sucked on her lobe.

Her hand dropped away as he encouraged her, pushing her to shed any remaining inhibitions. 'Gabe!'

'I want to hear your pleasure.' His fingers intensified their erotic torment, joined by his thumb that circled her clitoris, sending her shooting back into orbit, his rough, accented voice urging her for more. 'That's it. Again. Come for me.'

Gabriel relentlessly took her from peak to impossible peak. Just as she was sure she was totally spent and satisfied, he protected them with a condom, then his hands found hers, their fingers linking, grasping, holding on tightly as he finally united his body with hers. Any remaining breath she had struggled to maintain was stolen as she cried out at the blissful reality of his slow, deep, total penetration.

Lauren couldn't look away from him, trapped by the searing heat in his eyes. She had never felt so taken, so possessed, so complete. Had never shared such intense intimacy—laid bare, as if he could see into her soul. For endless moments he remained still and she savoured his delicious invasion. But she didn't want him to wait. He *had* to move. *Now.* Her hips lifted and rotated in encouragement, demanding a response, and he needed no further invitation. As he slowly withdrew, only to return with more urgency, laying claim to her in a way she had never experienced before, her grip tightened on his hands. His fingers returned the pressure of hers and they anchored each other, swept along on an unstoppable tide.

Lauren surrendered herself totally to Gabriel and the unparalleled joy of making love with him. The friction and pressure were exquisite, the sense of fullness unbelievable. She drew her legs higher, wrapping them around him, taking all of him, drawing him deeper still. He groaned, his control slipping as his movements intensified, harder, heavier, faster.

'Yes, yes.' She sobbed, matching his rhythm, losing all sense of reality as the unimaginable pleasure built wave after wave, threatening to swamp her. 'Please, Gabe. More.'

He gave everything, took everything, demanded everything. She did the same. Together they drove each other higher and further, caught in a raging firestorm of passion that engulfed them and carried them over the edge, consumed by the flames, surrendering to the ecstasy, tumbling into oblivion.

They collapsed together, fighting for breath, their hearts thundering in unison. As Gabriel released her hands and wrapped his arms around her, Lauren clung to him, shaking, shattered, rapturous, scared to let go in case she never found her way back to earth again. An aeon later Gabriel eased his weight from her. She protested, not wanting him to go, but he drew her with him, pulling her even closer and burying his face in her neck. Lauren tightened her hold, inhaling his scent, stunned by the incredible experience they had shared.

'*Mon Dieu.*' Gabriel's voice was throaty and raw. He sounded as overwhelmed as she felt. Slumberous dark eyes looked into hers, his fingers shaking as he brushed damp tendrils of hair back from her cheek. 'Are you all right?'

Lauren licked lips still plump and tingly from his deliciously erotic kisses. 'I don't know. You?'

'Not sure.'

'That was…' Still dazed, she searched for the right word. 'It was…'

'Wow,' Gabriel volunteered huskily, cradling her against him.

That pretty much covered it in any language, Lauren decided. 'Exactly.'

She was never going to get enough of this man. He did things to her she had never imagined, made her feel things she had never thought possible and took her to places she had never been before. She had no idea what the future held in store for them beyond his stay in Penhally, but she wanted Gabriel to be part of her days…and her nights…for as long as possible.

CHAPTER SIX

THE weeks leading up to Christmas sped by and Gabriel had never felt so content…settled both at work and in his private life. Being with Lauren was the most amazing thing that had ever happened to him. A smile curved his mouth just thinking about her. The first patient for his Saturday morning surgery having cancelled, he had a few moments before the next person arrived, so he leaned back in his chair, his hands linked behind his head, and thought back to that first night he and Lauren had spent together.

He had known from the moment that they had met that there was an inexplicable and special connection between them, one that transcended the undeniable physical attraction. The first time they had made love had proved him right. He'd never experienced anything like it before. Incredibly, it had just got better and better since…not only in the intensity of their passion but in the deepening of their close bond and instinctive trust. In bed they matched each other in adventurousness, pushing each other to explore the boundaries of their desire and sensuality. Their rapport and innate friendship meant they were perfect companions personally and fully supportive and complementary colleagues professionally.

The only subjects that remained taboo were their family histories—his in particular—and Lauren's sight. A frown creased his brow. After lingeringly making love a second time that first night, they had fallen into an exhausted sleep, only for him to wake in the early hours when Lauren had slipped out of bed. Unknown to her, he had watched as she had tried to find her way to the bathroom through the unfamiliar room, one hand extended out in front of her, feeling her way in the dark, taking cautious, baby steps, bumping into things. He'd waited until she had been in the *en suite* before switching the bedside lamps back on, noting the way she hesitated when she came out, looking uncertain. Not wanting to spoil things or to confront her about the issues with her vision, he had smiled and pulled back the duvet.

'I missed you, *chérie*.'

More sure of her footing with the lamps casting a glow in the room, she had hurried back to bed and he had given himself up to the blissful magic of her mouth and her hands on his body. But the incident had convinced him that Lauren was exhibiting night blindness. There had been several more moments over the weeks, little things he had noticed but which Lauren had brushed aside, and he had not found the right moment to talk to her about it. In truth he was scared of saying or doing anything to spoil what they had, so he kept putting it off, telling himself he would wait until something happened that could not be ignored. But Lauren's problem nagged at him. Had she always been lost in the dark? Was there some simple cause? Or was her night blindness a symptom of something more serious?

His fears had been compounded following a conversation with Chloe last week. Worried about Diane Bailey, one of her mums-to-be, Chloe had asked for a doctor to accompany her to the woman's home and, with Oliver unavailable, Gabriel had been happy to help. Having had a terrible time delivering her first baby, the young mother had been understandably terrified at facing the birth of her second child. She was determined to have a home birth, refusing to go to St Piran's for the delivery in case she suffered as she had at another hospital whose overstretched staff had failed to give her proper care and consideration. Between them, he and Chloe—the best midwife he had ever worked with—had allayed many of the woman's fears and promised to work together as a team to give her the safest birth possible and ensuring her their constant support.

On the way back to the surgery Chloe had surprised him by pulling over to the side of the road. 'Gabriel, can I talk to you for a moment?'

'Yes, of course.' Concerned, he'd turned to study her. 'Is something wrong?'

'Lauren saved my life,' she had told him softly after a long pause.

Gabriel had listened in horror as Chloe confided in him about her past with her abusive father, her green eyes shadowed with remembered pain as she had told him of the last beating and how Lauren had rescued her and helped her escape. '*Mon Dieu*, Chloe. I am so sorry. I had no idea.'

'No one but Lauren and Oliver know the full story. And now you.'

'Your secret is safe with me,' he'd assured her.

'She saved my life back then…now Oliver is teaching me to live it to the fullest. I'd do anything for her.' She paused a moment, nibbling her lower lip in indecision. 'Gabriel, have you noticed anything, I don't know…*off*…about Lauren?'

He felt his own guard slipping into place. 'What do you mean?'

'I'm probably being silly.'

'Go on,' he encouraged when she hesitated.

'Everybody has always teased Lauren because of her clumsiness, her habit of doing daft things and having minor accidents. She has terrible hand-eye co-ordination.' Anxiety and confusion had replaced her earlier indecision. 'The incidents seem to be happening more often these days. When Oliver first came here in June, he didn't know of Lauren's reputation for mishaps and I had the feeling he believed there was more to what was happening than her just being clumsy. He wouldn't say more and I'm scared to bring the subject up again. It's just…' Again Chloe paused, her worry for her friend evident.

'Just what? Tell me.'

'I don't know how to explain.' Sighing, she shook her head. 'Spending more time with Lauren at Gatehouse Cottage because of the flood damage to my place in Fisherman's Row, I've noticed little things I'd never been aware of before. Odd things. And then there's her painting. She's so talented and she loves her art. In the summer I bought a picture for Oliver's birthday present and was looking around her studio—it was the first time I'd been there in a while. I noticed subtle differences in her newer works, less detail, more fuzziness, but Lauren denied it. Shortly after that she stopped painting altogether. I tried to ask her about it and she got defensive, made excuses.'

She looked away from him for a moment and took a deep breath before rushing on. 'Plus she seems reluctant to go out at night. Not that we've had many opportunities lately with the other girls in our circle of friends busy with new babies and husbands, Vicky away and myself being with Oliver. But Lauren doesn't even seem keen on going to the cinema now.'

'Is that new? Has she been confident in the dark until recently?' he probed, concerned that Lauren's lack of night vision was not a long-standing issue after all.

'I've never noticed that nervousness in the dark before. It's like the way she used the chance to change her work hours so she does her home visits in the mornings. I sense something is wrong, Gabriel, but I don't know what to do. I'm so delighted you and Lauren are together…' she flashed him a sweet smile '…but I wondered if you saw whatever Oliver did, what the rest of us who have known her for years have missed because it's always been there or worsened slowly.'

'Chloe, I—' He broke off, unsure what to say.

She rested a hand on his arm. 'I don't want to put you in a difficult position. But I care about Lauren and I *am* worried. Can I just ask that if you have any doubts or concerns in future, you'll talk to Oliver to see if you both think the same and if there is anything you can do to help her?'

'I can promise you that, Chloe, yes.'

He would keep the promise he had made but not yet. Not until something more specific happened that gave him real evidence of a problem. Part of him was relieved to know he was not alone in noticing the odd, erratic and worrying things about Lauren's poor night vision. But the rest of him was wary of invading her privacy, unsure how to get Lauren to talk about something she had so clearly not even acknowledged for herself. He *would* talk to Oliver—if and when the time came that he had to intervene.

In the meantime, scared about Lauren driving at night— even though the only time she took the car out after dark was for the short drive home from the surgery—he had managed to contrive a new routine. They now went home together, leaving her car at work where it was ready for her morning house calls. He wasn't sure how long he could get away with it without arousing Lauren's suspicions.

Since their first night together Lauren had virtually moved into the Manor House with him, leaving Oliver and Chloe at Gatehouse Cottage, although they got together often for meals and the occasional trip out when they were all off duty at the same time. At work he and Lauren were totally professional, keeping their private life separate from the surgery, but their relationship had never been a secret. Without exception, everyone had accepted them as a couple and were happy for them, especially Oliver, Chloe and Kate. Even Hazel had warmed to him.

As the days and weeks went by, they had enjoyed time alone as well as taking part in community events. They had been to the local firework display on Guy Fawkes night, eating toffee-apples and cuddling up in front of the bonfire to keep warm. They had explored the local environment, walking with Foxy who was growing more confident all the time. They had jogged, listened to music, spent time with Oliver and Chloe, and had talked for hours about everything and anything but their taboo subjects. Most of all, they had made love…everywhere, every way and as frequently as possible. A smile replaced his frown. By rights he should be worn out! But he was energised, happier than he ever remembered being. Any doubts and worries about what was going to happen when his time in Penhally was over, he forcibly set from his mind.

The ringing of the telephone brought an end to his reverie and he leaned forward, reaching for the receiver. 'Yes, Sue?' he asked of the head receptionist.

'Adrian Westcott is here, Gabriel,' the friendly, efficient woman informed him. 'He's a few minutes early but I thought you would like to know—it isn't every day we're ahead of schedule.'

Gabriel chuckled. 'Indeed not. Thanks, Sue. Please, send him through.'

After hanging up, he pulled the notes out of the tray and had a quick glance at them before rising to greet his patient. In his early forties, with thinning blond hair and pale blue eyes, the man looked tired and dejected.

'Hello, Adrian,' he said, shaking the man's hand. 'Please, take a seat.' He waited a moment as Adrian made himself comfortable. 'What can I do for you today?'

'It's about my tinnitus, Doctor. It's worsening all the time, as is my hearing, and affecting my work. Things are really getting me down.'

'What work do you do?'

'I'm a teacher at the secondary school.' Adrian grimaced and shook his head. 'I love my job but it's harder to cope with the noise levels or several people talking at once, not to mention making sure I'm hearing my students properly.'

Gabriel glanced again at the notes to see what history and previous advice had been recorded. 'You saw a specialist ten years ago and you were told you had otosclerosis?'

'That's right. I lived in the north of England then. I moved here for the job with my family eight years ago. No one really explained what it meant to have otosclerosis, just that I had to live with the tinnitus, that there was nothing much to be done.'

'Tinnitus is a symptom that has many causes and is experienced in different ways. For most types there isn't a cure. Otosclerosis means that the bones in the middle ear harden and this affects the hearing as it prevents the bones vibrating. It can lead to deafness. What kind of noises do you hear with your tinnitus?' he asked, making notes as his patient explained.

'It's a whooshing noise but throbs and thumps like my pulse, as if I'm hearing my heartbeat all the time. I've had it for fifteen years or more. For a while I tried to follow the advice to cover up the sounds, but it's progressively got worse, to the point I can't ignore it. And my hearing is diminishing.' Adrian paused, a deep sigh escaping. 'One on one with people I'm not too bad, I'm learning to lipread, but in a gathering or with other noises, it's becoming impossible. My wife encouraged me to come, to try again, even though I doubt there is much you can do.'

Gabriel considered the options, feeling for the man and his situation. 'What you describe is pulsatile tinnitus. It's many years since you saw the specialist and things may have changed since then, so I'd like to refer you to a consultant at the audiology department at St Piran's. He'll do a thorough reassessment.' He paused a moment, not wanting to give any false hope. 'There is an operation that works for some sufferers of otosclerosis that involves removing the stapes and replacing it with an artificial plastic bone. It's high risk and carries a chance of deafness during the operation, but if successful it gives improved hearing and a reduction in the tinnitus. They do the worst ear first. But all this is dependent on what the surgeon has to say when he sees you—and on what risk you want to take.'

'I certainly want to find out about it,' Adrian enthused, looking much happier than he had when he'd arrived.

'I can't promise that you will qualify, or that it would work.'

The man nodded at the warning. 'I understand. But it's worth exploring…better than doing nothing and just going on as I am. You live with something for so long and the changes creep up on you slowly, so you learn to live with it. Often it's only when something unusual or big happens that you realise just how bad things have become and how much you have deteriorated,' he added and Gabriel frowned, thinking of Lauren and what could be a similar pattern with her sight.

'I'll write to the consultant and arrange for him to see you,' Gabriel reassured him, focusing back on his patient. 'I'm not sure what the waiting time is but we'll get things moving as quickly as we can in the new year.'

As Gabriel rose to show Adrian out a few moments later, the man turned at the door and shook his hand. 'Whatever happens, I can't tell you what a difference it makes to have someone understand and take me seriously. Thank you so much, Dr Devereux.'

'No problem. Call me any time if you need anything explained or have any problems.'

His appointments continued smoothly for the rest of the morning and, after tackling some of the mountain of paperwork, he was able to leave and meet up with Oliver for a pub lunch. Lauren had gone out with Chloe for the day to do some last-minute Christmas shopping. He couldn't wait for her to come home.

It was the last weekend before Christmas and the shops in Newquay had been manic. Thankful to escape the crowds, Lauren wedged her purchases with Chloe's in the back of her friend's car before sinking thankfully into the passenger seat.

'Oh, boy, my feet are killing me.'

'Tell me about it.' Chloe slid behind the wheel and sighed. 'I can't believe we got everything done.'

'I don't want to see another shop or hear another tinny carol ever again.'

Chloe chuckled, steering the car out of the parking zone and heading out of town towards home. 'You'll get a second wind. Let's hope Oliver and Gabriel have managed to pick out decent trees. Do you think we were right to entrust the job to them?'

'They'll be fine.' Lauren wasn't so fussed about all the Christmas paraphernalia as Chloe but she kept her thoughts to herself, knowing how miserable Chloe's childhood had been and how much she wanted this first Christmas with Oliver to be perfect. 'That set of baby clothes you got for Rachel Kenner's little boy are so cute.'

'Thanks. I can't wait to see him. I'm just so relieved both she and the baby are well after the birth. Rachel's naming the baby Daniel after her father,' Chloe added, a wobble in her voice.

Lauren smiled in sympathy. 'She's been through so much, the poor girl, but she's remarkable, the way she's handled everything.'

'She is. And her aunt and uncle have been wonderfully supportive.'

Dusk was falling as they arrived back at Gatehouse Cottage and Lauren wasted no time in switching on plenty of lights as soon as she went inside. Foxy greeted her enthusiastically. After she and Chloe had unloaded the car and hidden away their packages, they sank down for a reviving cup of tea while they waited for Gabriel and Oliver to come back. Foxy laid his head on her knee and she stroked him.

'Lauren?'

'Hmm?'

'I want to tell you something.'

Alerted by the uncertainty mixed with excitement in her friend's voice, Lauren opened her eyes and looked over at Chloe. 'Is anything wrong?'

'Nothing, it's just…' A blush pinkened Chloe's cheeks.

'You're pregnant!'

'No! No, that's not it.'

'Sorry.' She sent Chloe a rueful smile. 'Everyone in Penhally seems to have been breeding like rabbits this year! I wouldn't have been surprised.'

'I know! And I do want children one day. We both do. For now all this is so new to me and I just want time to be alone with Oliver, to enjoy being a couple,' she explained, her blush deepening.

Lauren fought a grin. 'Of course you do.' Chloe was such a sweetheart and it was obvious that she was more than well loved—and satisfied—thanks to Oliver. As she deserved to be.

'The thing is…' Chloe's green eyes sparkled with delight. 'This is a secret and you can't tell anyone. Except Gabriel.'

'OK, I promise,' she agreed, reaching for her tea.

'Oliver and I are eloping.'

'What?' Lauren nearly dropped her mug she was so surprised at Chloe's rushed announcement. Setting it safely on the table, she faced her friend. She felt Foxy's tension at her sudden movements and soothed him. 'You're eloping? When?'

Chloe positively bounced with excitement. 'Over Christmas. But we don't want to spoil anything for you.' Worry momentarily dulled the gleam in her eyes. 'Gabriel isn't going back to France for the holiday, is he?'

'I don't know. We've not discussed it,' Lauren admitted with a frown.

'Well, I know it's an awful cheek, but Oliver's asking Gabriel today if he'd mind covering for him. Kate knows I'm taking my remaining week's holiday, but not why. We're hoping not to have to tell Nick. You know he can be a bit starchy about things.'

'He does have set ideas,' Lauren agreed. 'It's so exciting, but why all the cloak-and-dagger stuff?'

It was Chloe's turn to frown. 'We're getting a lot of interference from Oliver's family. It's well meant,' she hastened to explain, 'but neither Oliver nor I want some huge fuss and production made of it. And with Reverend Kenner gone and no permanent replacement here in Penhally, I'd feel weird getting married in the local church,' she finished, and Lauren felt a shiver of empathy.

'I can understand that. So what's the plan? Can you tell me?'

'Oliver has a friend he trained with in London who has a glorious cottage in southern Scotland. He's loaning it to us. We found out all about it three months ago and got the necessary permissions. We've sent the papers back to the registrar and we're getting married at Gretna in the traditional Old Blacksmith's Shop! We'll be back the day after New Year,' she confided, bubbling over with happiness.

Chloe's enthusiasm was infectious and Lauren was thrilled for her. 'How romantic!'

'I can't wait! I hope everyone will understand. We plan to have a party for all our friends later in January.'

'Do what's right for you and don't worry about anyone else,' Lauren urged, reaching out to take her hand. 'You know I'll support you. I just want you to be happy—and I know Oliver is the man for you. It's wonderful seeing you together.'

Tears shimmered in Chloe's eyes. 'Thanks.'

As they talked more about the secret wedding plans it was impossible not to share Chloe's excitement. Although nothing had been said about Christmas and New Year, Lauren was certain Gabriel would do all he could to cover for Oliver. She'd miss her friends over the holiday, but the thought of being alone with Gabriel held its own appeal. The man was amazing! His dimpled smile pulled at something inside her. And she could listen to him for ever. That softly husky voice with the delicious accent always made her stomach turn over and sent a tingle of awareness down her spine.

The bond had formed quickly between them. Friendship, respect and trust mingled with instant attraction and high-octane passion deepening and swelling her swiftly growing feelings for him. She tried to live every moment, as they had agreed, and not think about what was going to happen in the future, but it was impossible to imagine not having Gabriel in her life.

He was a wonderfully inventive lover, exciting, erotic, wicked, challenging her to really let go and experiment. She had never experienced such pleasure, such closeness, such utter bliss as she did with him. He brought all her secret fantasies to life. The desire and passion between them seemed to increase, not diminish, blazing ever hotter with every passing day.

The only black moments came as she tried to cover up her increasingly scary sight problems. The night blindness was now a major and permanent problem. She was pretty sure that Gabriel had noticed her difficulties, her clumsy moments when her sight failed her, but he'd not brought the subject up and she was grateful. Equally grateful that they had fallen into going home together most nights so she didn't have to drive. She suspected Gabriel was doing it on purpose but she was too thankful to make an issue of it.

That Chloe and Oliver were aware of some changes was obvious. Several times Chloe had mentioned painting and Lauren hadn't been able to explain why she had stopped the thing she had loved so much for so long. In the summer Chloe had noticed changes in the new paintings, changes Lauren herself didn't want to face up to. When her sight problems had been confined to the dark, she had been able to pretend it didn't matter, but in the last weeks she had noticed that it took longer for her eyes to adjust to changing light, and it was starting to become difficult to distinguish contrasts, even in daylight or under bright light indoors. In the last few days she'd had odd moments when she'd thought her peripheral vision wasn't as sharp as usual. She was frightened, unsure what to do.

'You are the only one, apart from Oliver, I can confide in like this,' Chloe said, and Lauren tried to push her own worries aside. Her friend paused a moment, nibbling her lower lip, the expression in her green eyes serious. 'You know you can always talk to me about anything, too, don't you, Lauren?'

She forced a smile and kept her voice steady, unable to speak aloud the fears that grew more troublesome as the weeks went by. 'Sure.' How much longer could she pretend that nothing was wrong?

Thankfully, Gabriel and Oliver arrived back then, a blast of wintry air sweeping through the cottage as they propped the door open to wrestle a huge, sweetly scented pine tree into the cosy living room. Diverted from her questions, Chloe jumped to her feet, hovering eagerly as the tree, already potted, was positioned, then she threw herself into Oliver's arms.

'Hi, babe,' he welcomed her, enfolding her in a hug. Lauren saw him glance at Gabriel before he looked at her. 'Have you told Lauren?'

Beaming, Chloe nodded. 'Yes.'

'Gabriel's happy to help out and he's going to cover my

shifts for me the week we're away—and look after Pirate and Cyclops,' Oliver informed his bride-to-be, laughing as she rushed to hug Gabriel, too.

'Thank you so much!'

'My pleasure, Chloe,' Gabriel reassured her.

Lauren stroked Foxy before she, too, rose to her feet. 'Congratulations, Oliver.' Smiling, she kissed his cheek. 'I'm so happy for you both,' she added, hugging Chloe.

After enjoying a celebratory glass of wine, Lauren happily agreed when Gabriel suggested they return to the Manor House. 'I'm sure you and Chloe would like some time alone and I still have another Christmas tree to wrestle with,' he joked.

'Do you want me to come and help?' Oliver offered, walking with them towards the front door, Foxy trotting ahead.

'We'll be fine.'

It felt odd, standing in the small hallway of her own house, leaving her friends there, as if she were the visitor, and going back with Gabriel to the Manor House where she felt so right and content. She was about to step outside, grateful the lights were illuminating the short pathway, when Oliver stopped her.

'Sorry, Lauren, I forgot. There's a pile of mail for you,' he told her, handing her a stack of envelopes held together by an elastic band.

'Thanks.'

Once at the Manor House, Lauren switched on the lights downstairs and settled Foxy in the kitchen with his food while Gabriel managed to manoeuvre a beautifully shaped tree that smelled as delicious as the one Oliver had bought, into the living room. Lauren joined him. While she may not be as excited about the festivities as Chloe, she was looking forward to decorating the tree with Gabriel and to them spending time together. She thought of the presents she had bought him, now hidden safely away until she had some time alone to wrap them, and hoped he would like them, that she had found the right balance and hadn't gone too over the top.

'I didn't see the elopement coming.' Kneeling on the floor to light the log fire, Gabriel chuckled. 'Did you?'

Lauren sat on the sofa, the pile of unopened mail in her lap. 'No. But I'm not surprised. In fact, I'm delighted for them, they're so perfect together.'

'Indeed.'

'You're sure you are OK with taking on the extra shifts? You weren't planning to go back to France for the holiday?' she probed cautiously.

'Hell, no.' Gabriel paused, glancing over his shoulder. 'I know I've been close-mouthed about it, but I'm not in any hurry to go home.'

Unsure of the issues but having every faith that he not only had his reasons but had done nothing wrong, she placed a hand on his shoulder. 'It's OK. I'm certainly not complaining about having the chance to spend the holiday with you— even if we are working for part of it.'

'There's no one I want to spend Christmas with but you, *chérie*.'

The husky words warmed her right through. Smiling, Lauren watched for a moment as Gabriel turned back to tend to the fire, putting some larger logs on as the kindling took hold. She turned her attention to the mail and sorted through the mixture of bills, letters and cards, including an oversized postcard of Cologne cathedral from Vicky, full of excited news and typical Vicky-isms. Her smile faded, to be replaced by a knot of tension in her stomach when she recognised the Australian stamps and familiar handwriting on an air-mail envelope. For a moment she sat and stared at it then, fingers shaking, she forced herself to open it. A stupid threat of tears pricked her eyes as she looked at the plain card. There was no accompanying letter and nothing written on the inside but two names.

'I know we've avoided talking about our families, Lauren, mine in particular,' Gabriel said, but she barely heard him, focused as she was on the card. 'Lauren?' She jumped when Gabriel's hand settled on her knee and looked up, finding him watching her with concern. 'What is wrong, *ma belle*?'

'You said we avoided families—perhaps that's because family often isn't all it's cracked up to be,' she whispered, sucking in a breath and handing him the card.

Gabriel opened it, then glanced at her with a frown. 'Who are John and Betty?'

'The people I called Mum and Dad for the first twenty-five years of my life.' She managed to say the words without betraying the emotion roiling within her. 'They became John and Betty the moment they told me I was adopted and the pretence of being my parents ended.'

Gabriel cursed, taking one of her hands in his. 'You had no idea until five years ago?'

'No. Don't get me wrong, they were always kind to me. I had everything I needed in terms of a safe and secure home, guidance, the freedom to go my own way…'

'But not the love and cherishing,' he suggested when her words trailed off.

She sighed and ran the fingers of her free hand through her hair. 'I never felt as if I belonged. Like a cuckoo in the nest, I didn't fit. I still don't understand why they waited so long to tell me. Worse was the realisation that had they known they could have their own children after all, they would never have adopted me. I was always second best. Clive was born after I had been with them for two years and they couldn't exactly give me back.'

Gabriel swore again, his fingers linking with hers. 'That's horrible. It must have been a huge shock and very confusing.'

'Yes.' She'd been so unsettled, so angry and hurt when the truth had come out. Yet it had explained so many things. 'I was three months old when they adopted me as a last resort, believing Betty couldn't conceive. It was a big surprise to them when she fell pregnant. They doted on Clive. He was terribly spoiled. We never got on. He knew he was the favourite, the golden boy who could do no wrong. I envied him his special place in their lives, unable to understand what was wrong with me. I think I sensed even at a young age that I was less somehow.'

'Lauren—'

'No, really. All Clive's needs came first. Everything was geared to him and his success. He went off to Australia seven years ago and settled there, marrying a local girl and starting a family. Two years later, wanting to be near their grandchildren, my parents—' she stumbled over the words '—decided to take early retirement and emigrate. Before they left, they told me the whole story, explained their need to go and gave me Gatehouse Cottage as a gift, a pay-off to salve their consciences and feel they had done right by me, I guess.' A part of her, a part of that child she had once been, craved to be loved for herself…to be really wanted. But she didn't say that aloud. 'Fortunately, I'm happy here—I love my friends and my job.'

'So they just cut you loose? They left you alone to deal with the shock, having told you the truth about your life?' Gabriel protested, his anger on her behalf clear.

'Yes.'

He shook his head and huffed out a breath. 'Do you know anything about your birth parents?'

'Only that they died in an accident shortly after I was born. There weren't any grandparents or siblings to take me in…' not who wanted her, anyway, she added silently '…so I was taken into care and put up for adoption.'

Gabriel didn't say anything for a few moments but Lauren hardly noticed as she was lost in thought. There was so much she wanted to know about the family she had originally come from, not least details of her medical history. Was there any clue among her birth relatives that could explain the weird things happening with her eyesight?

'I understand how disruptive and unsettling learning the truth about your identity can be, Lauren.'

Startled from her reverie, she looked up and saw that the pain in Gabriel's eyes matched that lacing his voice. 'You, too?'

'Yes.'

Hurting for him, she returned the pressure of his fingers. 'Can you tell me now?'

The only sound in the room was the crackling of the flames as they ate into the wood in the fireplace. Lauren held her breath. Was the time right for Gabriel to open up and trust her with the demons that had driven him from his home?

CHAPTER SEVEN

'You are not alone in learning late on that everything you thought you knew about yourself, your family, your life is a lie, Lauren. Or in wondering where you fit in.'

As he spoke the words, Gabriel found it easier than he had imagined to confide in Lauren. He had been so contented these last weeks in Penhally Bay that he had largely succeeded in pushing France and the unresolved issues there from his mind. The approach of Christmas had brought them to the fore again. At least this year promised to be more settled and happier. Last year had been the first Christmas without his father, bringing back the pain of his loss and the anger and uncertainty at the secrets that had come to light after his death, leading to a widening of the rift with Yvette and the row about his future.

Lauren had shared her background with him and he more than understood how shocked and hurt she must have felt, learning about her adoption in such a way and then being cut off by the couple who had raised her. The strength of his desire to have been here to support and protect her through such a difficult time took him by surprise and made him realise just how involved his feelings for her had become. He knew with utter conviction that he trusted Lauren completely. Without giving himself any more time to consider his actions, he sat back on his heels in front of the fire and told her things he had never shared with anyone else, laying bare the skeletons in the Devereux family cupboard.

'My father, Pierre, died twenty months ago. He was fifty-eight. It was sudden and unexpected...a big shock. We were very close,' he explained, shying away from the knowledge that his father had kept such an important truth from him. 'I was working at a practice in Paris at the time, in an area that served a poor community and a large immigrant population.'

Lauren edged closer and he was happy to let her take his hand in hers to return the understanding and comfort he had tried to offer her a short while ago. 'Gabe, I'm so sorry about your father.'

'Thank you. The trouble began shortly afterwards.'

'Trouble?' Lauren queried with a frown.

'The exposing of family secrets and lies.' He stared into the flickering flames of the fire and sighed. 'I have always had a difficult relationship with Maman. She was cold, unforgiving, dictatorial, and mostly I was raised by a nanny. I spent a lot of time with Papa, but never with Maman. Now I know why. And why my skin is darker than most of the other members of the family. Yvette Devereux is *not* my mother. She did not give birth to me and she resented it that she had to raise me.'

'Oh, Gabe... How could she?'

He shot Lauren a quick glance but saw nothing but concern and understanding in her slate-grey eyes. 'I only have her side of the story—a story she took vicious delight in telling me after the funeral. Part of me feels betrayed that my father never explained to me himself but, despite that, I did know him and love him and the things Yvette said just don't make sense. I have the feeling she has embellished the truth at best and lied at worst to serve her own ends.'

'What was her explanation?' Lauren asked, encouraging him to talk it out.

'She said that my father had an affair with a lowly woman from Martinique, a *servant*—it infuriated me the way she used that word. He took me away from this woman and demanded Yvette bring me up as her own, using her obsessive sense of duty and fear of sullying the family name to force her to agree. Now she expects me to pay her back for all the years she had to be humiliated and put up with me.'

'That's absurd,' Lauren exploded, gripping his hand. 'You are not to blame for anything. Whatever the truth of your birth, your father—who must have been very young at the time—took you, loved you and raised you. Yvette had choices of her own. Choices that are not your responsibility. What does she expect you to do?'

'The first demand is that I stop playing at being a doctor and—'

'Playing?' she interrupted with outrage.

'To Yvette my career and lifestyle are not good enough for the family name and she sees it as my duty to take my father's place in the running of the family estates, safeguarding her position. She doesn't feel secure that the decisions and the control of finances are left in the hands of my uncle's side of the family, despite the provisions made for her in my father's will.' His cynicism deepened as he thought of Yvette's other plans for him. 'She also expects me to marry someone socially acceptable of her choosing.'

Lauren stared at him, wide-eyed. 'No way. That's archaic and ridiculous.'

'Exactly. But so determined was she that she sent Adèle to Paris to lure me.'

'Lure you?'

'Yes. We went out for a while, but then I found out about the deceit, that Yvette had set me up and was using Adèle to try to ensure I gave up medicine and returned home, especially that I left what Yvette considered an unacceptable job. She made a lot of trouble for me at the practice. Adèle was to be handsomely rewarded with my name…plus the family money and standing, of course, which interested her far more than I did.' He sighed before continuing. 'That's why I needed the space away. First in St Ouen-sur-Mer and now here in Penhally Bay. No matter what levels of guilt my mother tries to lay on me, I have no intention of marrying for convenience.'

'Nor should you. And you can't give up medicine either. It's your *life*.' Lauren squeezed his hand, her gaze earnest. 'You are an amazing doctor, Gabe. You have to live your own life in whatever way is right for you. Don't let Yvette's schemes and any misplaced guilt force you into something that would make you unhappy and change the person you are.'

It felt amazing to have someone believe in him. Cupping her face, he kissed her before drawing her close and wrapping his arms around her. 'Thank you. I think Yvette is bitter that she could never have children of her own and give my father a legitimate heir. Not that I believe theirs was ever a love match—she was as distant to my father as she was to me. She's an attractive woman in a polished, icy kind of way. Everything was, and remains, about duty and appearances to her.' He slid Lauren off the sofa and nestled her more snugly into his embrace, breathing in her scent. 'What hurts is that Papa never explained any of this. I don't know his side of it, what is the whole truth and what is exaggerated. He wasn't a man to avoid anything, no matter how awkward, which makes me more confused that he kept it from me. I thought he approved of my career, that he was proud of me.'

'Of course he was proud of you,' she protested heatedly. 'How could he not be?'

Lauren's loyal support and fierce protectiveness eased some of the tension inside him and he found it easier to continue his story. 'My father and his brother inherited a big estate that includes a vineyard, a farm and assorted business holdings, all funded by my ancestors who made their fortunes in the Caribbean. I find it hard to come to terms with that part of my family history. I feel ashamed that my family's money and success was built on the disenfranchisement and misery of others, even if it was generations ago. I had so many privileges and took them for granted, not knowing it was based on the hard work and sacrifices of those who'd had nothing, often not even their freedom,' he told her, his emotions scarcely held in check.

'You are not accountable for the actions others took years ago. Many businesses and families today are founded on regrettable things from times past. What matters is how *you* act and what you do with those things in your own control.'

'Logically I know that, but…' He hesitated, brushing his free hand over his face. 'It's just been a confusing time with much to try to come to terms with. The identity of my birth mother explains my darker skin—something I share with a couple of distant cousins, which was explained away by the past involvements and dalliances of my great-grandfather and grandfather in the Caribbean. Nothing was said about my father. I want to learn more about my true heritage and find out more about my real mother, but I don't even know her name.'

Lauren's arms tightened around him. 'So many things go through your mind, so many questions that have no answers.'

'Yes.' He stroked her hair, knowing from what she had told him of her own adoption and family circumstances that she understood the sense of rootlessness and uncertainty. 'I never questioned my ethnicity and very identity before. Now…'

An aching vulnerability laced Gabriel's voice, cutting Lauren deep inside. She felt his pain and confusion, knew exactly where he was coming from, and wished she could do more to reassure him and help him find a solution, a *resolution*, to his past. She'd had five years to get her head around who she was and how her perceptions had changed. Gabriel had known for less than two years. And she had not suffered a bereavement. He had lost the father he had loved and who he now questioned. That had to be impossibly hard. If there were things she needed to know, she could ask—it wouldn't be pleasant, but she had the choice. Gabriel didn't. She wished she could ease his heartache, make things right for him, but all she could do was be there to listen and comfort and understand.

As well as mourning his father and dealing with the revelations about his true birth mother, Gabriel still had Yvette to contend with. The woman sounded awful. It was bad enough that she had been emotionally cold to a child in her care, worse that she wanted to change Gabriel and tie him to something so wrong for him. But to insinuate a woman into his life, one who cared nothing for him, with the purpose of influencing him, lying to him, deceiving him was unforgivable. No wonder Gabriel was loath to return to France or have contact with Yvette.

'Never before has the colour of my skin been an issue.'

Startled from her thoughts and shocked by Gabriel's words, Lauren frowned, pulling back to look at him, seeing the shadows dulling his eyes. 'What do you mean?'

'I never questioned my ancestry. If anyone mentioned my skin colour, it didn't bother me. Now comments about it make me feel uncomfortable.'

'Why would anyone mention it? No one in Penhally has said anything, have they?' she asked, unable to imagine anyone being so narrow-minded.

'One or two. Not in a prejudicial way,' he added, and Lauren tamped down her anger on his behalf. 'But I'm conscious of being different…the cuckoo in *my* family, to follow your analogy. That's probably because of the derisive way Yvette spoke of my birth mother, as if the woman was beneath contempt, as if I was worth nothing.'

'Your father didn't think so. He cared about your mother and he loved you.'

'I think so. I hope so. I wish I knew the circumstances, how Papa really felt, if he *did* have feelings for my mother or if I was a mistake,' he murmured.

'I understand the need to uncover your missing roots, to find answers to your questions, but *you* are the same person you've always been.'

As Gabriel released her and moved to put another couple of logs on the fire, Lauren's heart cried out for the uncertainty he was feeling. She studied his handsome profile, the leanly sculpted body outlined under his shirt by the flickering flames, the play of muscle along hair-dusted forearms.

'What?' he asked, a quizzical smile on his face as he turned back to her.

She shook her head, raising a hand to cup his jaw. The end-of-the-day stubble there prickled against her palm, reminding her how exciting and arousing the rasp of it felt on her body as he caressed and explored her with his mouth. Realising he was waiting for her answer, she returned her gaze to his.

'The colour of your skin is not what I see when I look at you.'

'What *do* you see, Lauren?' he asked huskily, taking her hand and moving it so he could kiss her palm, his tongue tracing teasing circles, igniting the fiery need for him that always simmered inside her.

'I see *you*. All that makes you the man you are. An excellent doctor…one who shows great care and consideration for his patients, and…'

He nibbled on her fingers, momentarily stealing her breath and her words as he slowly sucked each one in turn into his mouth, distracting her. 'And?'

'And,' she continued, trying to force the words past the constriction in her throat, every part of her trembling with desire, 'I see a gorgeous man who is warm and intelligent, funny and generous. A man who is great to be with, who is a loyal friend, who makes me feel good…and who is incredibly sexy.' Her breath ragged, her voice rough with emotion, she looked deep into his eyes, seeing how they darkened with answering passion. 'Gabe, you are beautiful just as you are.'

She gasped in surprise as he caught her to him, one hand threading through her hair to hold her still for his inflaming, hungry kiss. Kneeling in front of him, she opened her mouth hotly in welcome. His free hand slid down her back to shape her rear and pull her against him, leaving her in no doubt of his growing arousal. With Gabriel she felt truly alive, aware of every sensation. The fierceness of his desire was a powerful aphrodisiac, heightening her own. He made her feel whole, complete, and so wanted. Needing to make him feel the same way, to reassure him and prove to him how special he was, she took over, pushing him back until he was lying on the floor beneath her.

She sat up and went to work on his clothes, glad they had left lamps on in the room so she could see him as she slipped each button free before he impatiently pulled off his shirt and tossed it aside. Bending to him, she took her time working down his torso with her mouth and fingers, lingering over his nipples, then his navel, his muscles rippling and tautening, before licking down to the waistband of his jeans.

'No. Let me,' she demanded, pushing his hands away when he moved to undo his belt.

With a groan, Gabriel surrendered to her and she teased him, fondling the hard length of him through the soft, worn denim. 'Lauren,' he growled in warning.

Smiling, she unfastened his belt, then unsnapped the jeans and lowered the zip as slowly as she could, her own aching desire increasing with every moment. He raised his hips to aid her as she skimmed down his jeans and briefs. Once he was naked, she revelled in enjoying his body, in bringing him pleasure, encouraged by the sounds he made, the way his body shifted restlessly beneath her.

'Lauren…'

This time her name was a plea on his lips as she took him to the brink of his control. Nuzzling against him, she breathed in his warm, earthy male scent. She wanted to savour him for hours, as he did with her, but already she was as impatient as he was and could no longer deny herself. She needed him so badly. Hastily dispensing with her own clothes, she took the condom he'd carried in the pocket of his jeans, controlling her eagerness long enough to torment him as she rolled it on, earning herself another threat of retribution. The kind of sensual threat she loved. Sliding over him, she wasted no more time and welcomed him fully inside her.

His hands stroked her with a reverence and tenderness that brought a rush of emotion, making her acknowledge how deep her feelings for this special man had become. Taking her by surprise, Gabriel sat up, pulling her close. Sitting in his lap, she wrapped her legs around his hips, pressing her body against him. They rocked together, sharing slow, deep kisses, their hands caressing. The firelight flickered over their joined bodies as they moved in unison, their rhythm increasingly urgent. When, eventually, they drifted down from the giddying height of passion, reaching a new pinnacle of pleasure, they remained locked in each other's arms, cuddled up in front of the fire under the fleecy throw Gabriel had pulled off the sofa to cover them.

The evening had been the most intimate she had ever known, not only in the intenseness of their love-making but in the sharing of confidences and baring of souls. They had each revealed a part of themselves in a way they had never done with anyone else, which said much about the level of trust between them. She had told people about the adoption thing, it wasn't a secret, but she had never discussed her innermost feelings about it, not even with Chloe. Only with Gabriel.

Holding him tight, she nestled against him, turning her face into his neck. She had never felt closer to him than she did at this moment. Gabriel cared about her, she knew that, but she could no longer pretend to herself that her own feelings stopped there. She loved this man, totally and completely. Knowing what he faced in France, what decisions he had to make about his future, troubled her...both for his own peace of mind and for whatever might lie ahead for them as a couple.

But she couldn't afford to think about that now. She had agreed the terms. No commitments. Live for today. And she would. She loved him, would cherish every moment with him, would show him in every way she could without words what he meant to her, but she couldn't and wouldn't put pressure on him for more than he could give. For now they had the promise of Christmas alone together and she planned to make it as special and unforgettable as possible. She could only wish with all her heart that the new year and beyond would bring hope and happiness.

Christmas Day brought winter sunshine, pale blue skies and cool temperatures. Kate stifled a yawn and took a sip of strong coffee, hoping it would help her wake up. Jem had been on the go for ages. Although he no longer believed in Father Christmas, he still had all the youthful enthusiasm for the day and had opened his presents with breathless excitement. Fearing her son was missing out without his father—and maybe salving her own inner guilt over his true parentage— she tended to spoil him at this time of year, no matter how hard she tried not to overdo it.

Having wolfed down his breakfast, Jem had raced upstairs eager to try on the new football shirt of his favourite Premiership team that Oliver and Chloe had given him. Kate smiled. Her friends were so generous and always remembered Jem, usually giving him books and CDs which he enjoyed immensely. Her smile faded as she thought of Nick. So far he had not given Jem anything. Not that he was obligated to do so, of course, but she had hoped the effort he had been making to be more friendly to Jem since the flood would continue.

She knew that the whole Tremayne clan were getting together for a big family Christmas this year—the first for a long time. With Jack and Edward now back in Cornwall and settled with their respective partners, and with Lucy and Ben celebrating Annabel's first birthday over the holiday, it was a special time for the Tremaynes. Had it only been a year since she had helped deliver that precious baby in difficult circumstances in a deserted barn during a snowstorm?

A wave of sadness swept through her. She wished Jem could be a part of all that Tremayne love and laughter. But she doubted it would ever happen. If only Nick would acknowledge Jem she would be content. She would even be able to force herself to ignore her own needs, her loneliness, the unrequited love she had harboured for Nick for so many years—as long as her son was happy and secure.

This morning, the plan was for a walk along the beach as Jem was eager to fly the Rhombus Entry stunt kite she had bought him, an inexpensive but longed-for item that had been top of his Christmas wish list since they had watched a display in the summer. The fliers doing elaborate stunts and tricks had allowed Jem to have a go and had recommended the Rombus as an excellent beginner's kite.

Kate was about to go upstairs to get dressed for their outing when the doorbell rang. Puzzled as to who would be calling on Christmas Day, she tightened the belt of her robe, pushed some wayward strands of hair back from her face, and left the kitchen. Chloe and Oliver were away—if her suspicions proved correct, Kate believed they would return with some exciting news—so she was on call for any midwifery emergencies over the holiday. But that would entail a phone call, not a visit to her house.

'Nick!' she exclaimed, shocked to discover who awaited her when she opened the door. She could feel the blush warm her cheeks and cursed herself for responding like some flustered teenager to the very sight of him. It didn't help that she was still in her robe. 'Sorry, I wasn't expecting anyone. Merry Christmas.'

'Good morning, Kate. Merry Christmas to you, too.'

Noting the wrapped gifts he held, she moved back. 'Would you like to come in?'

'Please.' He stepped into the hallway and she closed the door. 'I hope I'm not too early. I wanted to call in before going to Lucy and Ben's.'

'Not at all. Jem's been up for hours, excited to open his presents.'

A smile softened the characteristic sternness on Nick's face. 'I imagine. I hope you don't mind. I've bought him a couple of things.'

'No. That's lovely. Thank you.' Surprised and delighted that Nick had unbent enough to remember his son and think to bring him gifts, she led the way to the kitchen. 'Would you care for a cup of coffee? I'll run upstairs and fetch Jem.'

'All right.'

Her pulse racing, Kate hurried upstairs and dressed hastily, pausing a moment to brush her hair and apply some lipstick and mascara before going to Jem's room. She found him wearing his new red-and-white Arsenal top, absorbed in the football annual that had been a present from Lauren and Gabriel.

'Jem, we have a visitor,' she told him with a smile. 'Can you come down, my love? Then we can take your kite and go for our walk.'

'OK.'

Downstairs, Kate smiled at Jem's excitement when he discovered the identity of their guest and the unexpected presents that awaited him.

'Uncle Nick!'

'Hello, Jeremiah.' Setting down his mug of coffee, Nick held out two neatly wrapped parcels. 'These are for you.'

'Gee, thanks!'

A lump lodged in Kate's throat as man and boy exchanged smiles and she noticed the similarities between them. The same eyes. The same shape to the mouth. The same frown of concentration. Would those likenesses become more pronounced as Jem grew older? Would people begin to suspect who his real father was? Hiding her concerns, she watched as Jem tore off the paper to reveal a fun book of science facts and two of the latest computer games.

'Wow! I love them. Thanks, Uncle Nick,' he gushed, taking the older man by surprise and giving him a hug.

'Happy Christmas, Jem.'

Nick's voice was hoarse as he responded to his son's engaging and instinctive reaction. Looking stiff and uncertain, he rested a hand on the boy's head for a moment, and Kate met his gaze, her own eyes stinging with unshed tears at the confusion and emotion in Nick's. This was more than she had expected and she knew it was greedy of her to wish for more.

'Do you have to leave already?' Jem asked with disappointment as Nick rose to his feet.

'Yes, I'm afraid so.' Nick cleared his throat . 'Um… We're having a get-together at my house on New Year's Eve,' he announced after a moment. 'It will be family and a few friends, including children, so it won't be a late night. If you and Jem would like to come, Kate, you'd be welcome.'

Her heart fluttered at the surprise invitation. 'We'd love to, wouldn't we, Jem?'

'Yeah, that would be great!'

Walking with Nick to the front door a few moments later, Kate hesitated and looked up at him, unable to read the expression on his face. 'Thank you, Nick,' she said, fearing the welter of emotions *she* was feeling were all too apparent.

Nick nodded and stepped outside. Kate tightened her hold on the door as she watched him climb into his car, not looking back before he drove away to be with his proper family. He'd thought of Jem, had made him happy, she told herself as she closed the door. That was the important thing to remember right now.

Half an hour later, they had walked around the harbour and reached the nearly deserted beach. While Jem concentrated on sending his colourful delta-wing kite soaring into the sky for the first time, Kate's thoughts remained grounded and on Nick. He had thought to include them in his gathering to mark the end of a year that had been eventful personally, professionally and for the town as a whole, and for that she was grateful. What, she wondered, would the new year hold for them all?

'Lauren?'

Receiving no answer when he walked into the Manor House shortly after midnight, Gabriel headed to the kitchen, washed his hands and then poured himself a glass of water. Reflecting on the last couple of hours, he gave a rueful shake of his head. This had not been the way he would have chosen to spend New Year's Eve.

His first callout had come late in the evening to a four-year-old girl who had experienced her second severe acute asthma attack in less than a week. Her breathing had finally been eased with the administration of oxygen, nebulised salbutamol and oral prednisolone but, given the child's distress, along the frequency and severity of her symptoms, he'd arranged for hospital admission.

He'd only just arrived home when he had been asked to attend an emergency at the Penhally Arms on the harbour front, where a fight had broken out between two groups of revellers who'd had too much to drink. Taunts had turned to threats and, uncharacteristically for Penhally Bay, a running battle had ensued in the street when the guilty parties had been evicted from the pub. Several people had suffered minor injuries, while two had received more serious stab wounds from broken glass. It had taken a while to sort everything out and to stabilise one of the patients, who had lost a great deal of blood and gone into hypovolaemic shock, for ambulance transport to hospital in St Piran. Gabriel had been thankful to come home and leave the police to handle the aftermath of the trouble.

As promised, he had stopped off at Gatehouse Cottage on the way back to check again that the cats, Cyclops and Pirate, were fine. Oliver and Chloe—who had rung a couple of times during the week, sounding blissfully happy with married life—were due back in a couple of days, ready to face the music about their secret wedding. Gabriel felt sure that everyone would be delighted for them.

Foxy, who was curled up on his beanbag by the range in the Manor House kitchen, stretched and snuffled in his sleep. Gabriel washed up his glass, checked all was secure downstairs and that the log fire had safely burned down with the guard around it before he jogged up the stairs in search of Lauren. Light spilled out from his bedroom across the landing, drawing him onwards. His heart swelled and emotion gripped him at the sight he found when he walked into the room.

Dressed in lilac French knickers and matching camisole— the satin and lace creations far more alluring and feminine in his view than blatant, obvious items like G-strings—Lauren was sprawled face down across the four-poster bed. The lavishly illustrated book he had given her on her favourite artist, Claude Monet, and his stunning garden at Giverny in France, was open in front of her. Smiling, he recalled her reaction when she had unwrapped the book on Christmas morning and discovered the promise that had accompanied it...

'What's this?' she had asked, holding up the sticky note he had stuck on the front with 'IOU' written on it.

'Do you have a valid passport?'

A frown had creased the smoothness of her brow. 'Yes, I think it has another two or three years before it's due for renewal. Why?'

'Maybe we could have a long weekend away together in the spring.' Grey eyes had widened with surprised delight at his suggestion. 'I want to take you to see Giverny for yourself.'

'Do you mean it?'

'Of course, *ma belle*. I've been once. It's beautiful.' It meant returning to France far sooner than expected, but it would be worth it to make Lauren happy, and he wouldn't be near the family home. 'I want to share it with you. We'll go when the gardens reopen in April.'

Tears shimmering in her eyes, she had thrown herself into his arms. 'Thank you, thank you, thank you! It's the best gift ever!' She'd kissed him...then shown her gratitude in wickedly enjoyable ways.

Now he crossed slowly to the side of the bed and discovered that she was fast asleep. She looked adorable. Gently, he eased the book out from under her outstretched hand, marked her page and set it on the bedside chest. He hesitated, looking down at her, loath to wake her but needing her with as much desperation as ever.

She had made this Christmas so special for him. Aside from the Monet book, they had exchanged several gifts, each of them finding a mix of things that were either funny, touching, saucy or thoughtful. But it was the time with Lauren, her warmth, her understanding, her passion, her generosity of spirit, that had been the greatest gift of all. The issues with Yvette, his heritage and his future remained unresolved, but some of his heartache had eased by sharing his fears and his hurt with Lauren.

Turning off the main light, leaving the room illuminated by the rosy glow of the bedside lamps so Lauren could get her bearings, Gabriel stripped off his clothes and returned to the bed. Desire rippled through him as he began kissing his way softly up her silky smooth legs, whispering along her calves and lingering at the back of her knees before skimming over her creamy thighs. Lauren murmured, moving gracefully under him as she gradually came awake. He allowed her to roll over and, sleepy-eyed, she looked up at him with a smile…a smile that was so beautiful, so welcoming and so sexy it almost overwhelmed him.

'Gabe.'

'Hey, sleepyhead,' he whispered, his voice rough with emotion and arousal. 'Sorry I was so long.'

'Are you all right? Was it bad?' she asked, her concern evident.

'It wasn't pretty but I'm fine.'

He sat back on his heels and indulged himself, running his hands up and down her body, his fingertips catching on the lace covering nipples that peaked to his touch. Lauren pulled him back down to her, her kiss hot and intense, matching his own hunger. Her hands glided over him, her touch tender, reverent, setting him on fire. He forced himself to slow down, concentrating on removing her camisole and French knickers, kissing each fragment of flesh he exposed. He felt as if he was unwrapping the most precious gift he had ever been given.

'Please,' she begged, moving against him. 'I want you.'

'Soon.'

He nuzzled against her, wanting to take his time and cherish every inch of her but as needy and impatient as her. The subtle, flowery scent of sweet peas, mingled with her own womanliness, intoxicated him. She was so responsive to his touch. Her body quivered beneath his lips and fingers, and the little purring sounds of pleasure in the back of her throat drove him crazy with want.

'Now, Gabe…'

Succumbing to her pleas, unable to resist her or deny her anything, he gave himself up to the magical passion that grew more intense and fiery and special every time they came together.

An age later, sated and relaxed, Gabriel held Lauren close, arms and legs entwined, as she slept. They had gone into this with the pledge of no ties and no commitments. At one time he would have felt relieved that a woman made no demands, but with Lauren he was disappointed and felt a flicker of unease. He had not been looking for any kind of relationship when he had come to Cornwall but what he'd found with Lauren was unique, and he very much feared that nothing between them was ever going to be as simple as they had both vocalised at the start. Instead, he had the sense that he was at a crossroads in his life and what happened here was going to be far more important and life-changing than he could ever have foreseen.

Each day he fell more in love with her. But he hadn't told her. She'd made it clear there were no expectations and she'd given no indication that what they shared meant any more to her, that she felt more for him. He had ten months left in Penhally…ten months to convince Lauren that they were right together. But before he could pledge himself to her, he needed to settle the family issues that dogged him, as well as decide what to do about Yvette and her demands.

Confiding in Lauren, knowing she believed in him and supported him, had helped him rationalise that he could never give up medicine. She had told him about her adoption but he needed her to show the same level of trust, to face up to the problems with her sight and share it with him. Could she ever do that? Would she?

Hugging her tighter, he let out a shaky breath. As they headed into a new year, filled with new hopes and endless possibilities, he vowed to show her in every way how much he loved her. One day, when the time was right, he would tell her how permanently he wanted them to commit to each other. Until then he could only pray that the future would be kind to them and that Lauren would come to love and trust him, too.

CHAPTER EIGHT

LAUREN stood on the pavement by the construction site where the demolished Anchor Hotel was in the process of being rebuilt and gave her details to the policeman beside her. How did her voice sound so calm when inside she was shaking? She looked at her beloved Renault as it sat by the kerb, the driver's side dented and crumpled. A few yards farther along Harbour Road was another car, its front caved in, its angry and foul-mouthed driver arguing with two other policemen.

'I'm sorry about this,' she murmured as the constable put his notebook away.

'It's not your fault, Ms Nightingale, not according to all the witnesses.' He gestured to the gathered crowds and then to the young man who had hit her. 'Luckily there was an off-duty policeman on the scene or the other driver would have driven off. Turns out he has no insurance and was driving while disqualified.'

Lauren didn't know what that would mean in terms of a claim to repair or replace her car, but apparently everyone was satisfied that she had not been to blame for the accident. Everyone but her. She had finished her morning home visits— her final appointment having been with Harry Biscombe at Gow Court, whose osteoporosis was increasingly trouble-some—and had been returning to the surgery for lunch before her afternoon clinic when the crash had happened. Having stopped at the junction of Bridge Street and Harbour Road, she had pulled out into a gap in the traffic, only to have an oncoming car plough into the side of her. Apart from a few bruises she was unharmed but shaken...and she felt impossibly guilty.

The witnesses all attested to the fact that the young man had been speeding and driving erratically, having almost hit a pedestrian and a parked car farther along the seafront before colliding with her. What Lauren hadn't said, but could not ignore, was the simple fact that she had never seen the car at all. It had come out of nowhere and sideswiped her. Her explanations had been silenced by the behaviour of the young man, his unsuccessful efforts to flee the scene and the discovery that he had no business driving at all taking precedence with the police.

'Lauren!'

Hearing her name and the sound of running feet, she looked round to see Gabriel and Oliver hurrying towards her. Someone must have phoned the surgery, she realised, stifling a groan. The last thing she needed was to have people fussing over her and asking her more uncomfortable questions. However, she couldn't deny how comforting it felt to be enfolded in Gabriel's embrace, and she allowed herself a few moments to lean against him and absorb his strength.

These first months of the new year had been the happiest she had ever known. Everything would have been one hundred percent perfect if only she hadn't had to hide two things...how much she loved Gabe and how frightened she was that her sight was deteriorating further. The night blindness she had managed to excuse and cover up, but the fuzziness, the blind spots and decreasing peripheral vision that had begun to occur in recent weeks terrified her.

'Lauren, *ma belle*, what happened? Are you all right?'

Gabriel demanded, holding her slightly away from him so he could look her over, one hand stroking her hair before his fingers trailed down her cheek. He tilted up her chin and looked into her eyes. 'Are you hurt?'

'I'm fine.'

Gabriel frowned, clearly disbelieving her, and glanced over his shoulder. 'Oliver?'

'Here.' The smile curving Oliver's mouth failed to mask the concern in his brown eyes as he stepped forward. 'Hi, Lauren, how are you?'

'She says she's fine,' Gabriel answered for her, increasing her annoyance.

'I'm perfectly all right and able to speak for myself.'

'OK.' Oliver smiled, but she wanted to stamp her foot as the two men shared a glance before Oliver eased Gabriel aside. 'Let me take a look at you to be sure.'

'For goodness' sake,' she muttered ungraciously, aware that the shock of the crash and the fright about her eyes was making her uncharacteristically grumpy.

'Did you bump your head at all?' he asked her.

'No.'

With a gentle but impersonal touch, Oliver carefully checked her neck for any pain or stiffness. After assessing her pulse and her breathing, he cupped her face and she noted his slight frown as he studied her. What had he seen? She bit her lip to keep from asking, not ready for the answer.

'Do you have any discomfort with this bruising?' Oliver queried, moving on to check her arms and discovering the marks beginning to colour along her right forearm that had taken the brunt of the bang as the driver's door had distorted inwards. 'Any nausea or dizziness?'

'Nothing, really. My arm isn't even sore. Honestly, I'm OK. I was just a bit shaken up.'

'I'm not surprised.' Gabriel stepped close again and slid an arm around her waist, his angry gaze on the young man who was being arrested and put into a police car. 'I'd like a few moments with that driver myself.'

Oliver rested a hand on Gabriel's shoulder. 'Let the police take care of him. There are enough witnesses to make sure he doesn't get away with it and from what I hear, he has no licence or insurance, so he will definitely be charged.'

'I should hope so. He could have hurt or killed someone.' Gabriel drew her closer and she could feel the tension in him. 'Come on, I'll take you home.'

'No, it's OK. I need to go back to the surgery,' she insisted, determined to carry on as if nothing had happened.

Gabriel turned her to face him. 'Lauren, be sensible, you've had a shock. You need to rest, *chérie*—'

'What I need,' she stressed, her anger mounting as she pulled away from his hold, 'is not to be babied and told what to do. I make my own decisions. And I'm going back to work to attend to my patients.'

'Lauren…'

Aware that Gabriel and Oliver were staring after her, she picked up the belongings that had been rescued from her car and walked purposefully along the pavement towards the surgery. She was not yet ready to deal with the consequences of what had happened today—or to face the horrifying truth that the problems with her eyesight were getting worse.

'Leave her for a while,' Oliver advised.

Angry, confused and scared, Gabriel wanted to shake off his friend's hand and rush after Lauren, needing to cuddle her and satisfy himself that she was really all right. The rational part of him accepted the sense of Oliver's words, so he fell into step with him and followed Lauren back to the surgery at a discreet distance. At least he was keeping her in sight.

Her outburst had been so unlike her. She had been genuinely irritated by his concern, while all he had wanted to do
was take care of her. The day was mild and the March
sunshine gleamed off the lighter streaks in her hair as she
moved on ahead of them. Another three weeks and they would
be in France for their long weekend. He couldn't wait for them
to be alone, away from the usual distractions and demands on
their time and energy.

Professionally, things had been hectic since the new year,
with the surgery busier than ever. Oliver and Chloe had
returned from Scotland to much fuss and celebration of their
marriage. Only Nick had displayed any sign of disapproval
about the elopement, not that anyone had taken much notice
of him because it was clear to everyone how happy the couple
were and how perfect for each other.

Some of the pressure had been taken off for all the doctors,
the workload easing, especially for out-of-hours and weekend
calls, with Dragan Lovak back from paternity leave. Gabriel
admired the calm, quiet Croatian and was enjoying getting
to know him.

Adrian Wescott, the local schoolteacher with long-term
tinnitus, had seen the specialist at St Piran and had been
declared a suitable candidate for surgery. The operation to
remove the stapes and implant an artificial plastic bone
was scheduled for the Easter holiday when Adrian would
have time off school to recover and, if all was successful,
to accustom himself to his altered hearing before the new
term began.

Personally, things between himself and Lauren had been
just as blissful as they had at the end of the previous year. If
anything they were even closer physically, their relationship
more intense, but still neither of them had spoken of the future
or their feelings, and Gabriel was becoming edgy as almost
half his time here in Cornwall was already over. He'd noticed

more small moments of concern with Lauren's sight but she refused to confide in him and that lack of trust hurt.

Gabriel thought back to his talk with Chloe in December and her request that he talk to Oliver if he became worried about Lauren. He'd been worried for a while but... He let out a rough sigh. Maybe now was the time to consult his friend and get some advice.

'Did you notice Lauren's eye?'

Oliver glanced at him. 'The right one?'

'Yes.' Gabriel paused, a frown on his face as he watched Lauren disappear through the entrance to the surgery a few yards ahead of them. 'What did you see?'

'Her eyelid was a bit droopy and I thought I detected a squint I'd not noticed before,' Oliver admitted, his voice serious and concerned.

As if by mutual consent, they slowed their pace, coming to a halt outside the car park and turning to look out over the harbour. 'But you've noticed other things before—about Lauren's sight, I mean—since you've been here?' Gabriel asked, sliding his hands into his trouser pockets.

'Nothing I could be definite about, Gabriel.' Oliver sighed and leaned against the wall. 'As an outsider coming in, I was suspicious about Lauren's supposed clumsiness. Everyone laughed at her mishaps and said she had always been that way. I had a hunch there was more to it...but no facts.'

'Me, too,' Gabriel agreed. 'From the first day I met her I knew she was having trouble with her night vision, but I didn't know if it was a long-standing problem or a symptom of something else.'

'And now?'

Gabriel shook his head. 'I'm still worried. She's definitely night blind but copes well and manages to cover it. I'm sure that's why she changed her work hours. And she never drives after dark now. There have been a few other incidents lately and over the last couple of days I saw what you did with her right eye.' He hesitated but decided to keep his nagging suspicions about today's accident to himself.

'Have you spoken to her about it?' his friend asked, meeting his gaze.

'No. Once or twice I've tried to mention the night blindness, as well as the fact that she's stopped painting, but she gets defensive and changes the subject.' Shifting with restless impatience, he let out a shaky breath. 'I'm scared of rocking the boat, Oliver, of pushing her away if I press too hard. I have a feeling that Lauren is increasingly worried but she's not facing up to the problem.'

Oliver gave his shoulder a reassuring pat. 'I never said anything either, even though I noticed that Lauren didn't judge distances well, that she tripped on kerbs and didn't see things in shadow. I didn't know that had progressed to such serious night blindness, though.'

'So should I wait a while longer?' He looked up and saw the answering worry in Oliver's eyes, as if neither of them wanted to voice out loud the various and increasingly frightening explanations that could be the underlying cause of Lauren's sight problems. 'You think it's right that I don't confront her about it?'

'Until Lauren admits it to herself, she's not going to appreciate or accept anyone else challenging her on it. Especially you.'

'Would *you* try to talk to her?' he asked, knowing he was expecting a lot of his friend.

Letting out a heavy sigh, Oliver ran his fingers through his hair and moved away. 'Damn, Gabriel.'

'Please. I'm worried about her.'

'If the opportunity presents itself, I'll see what I can do,' he agreed with evident reluctance, a warning in his eyes when he turned back to face him. 'But I have to tell you, Gabriel, that if Lauren confides in me as a doctor, I'm not going to break her trust and divulge anything if she asks me not to. Not even to you.'

Gabriel felt rigid with tension, his hands clenched to fists. He wanted to argue, but he knew Oliver was right, knew he would do the same if the situation were reversed—their oath allowed them no other option. 'On a personal level I don't like it, but I understand. And I'd just be relieved to know that Lauren was getting some help.'

'I know it's difficult.' Oliver's smile was sympathetic. 'If the chance arises, I'll be advising her to talk to you—count on that.'

'Thanks.'

Knowing there was little more he could do right now, Gabriel tried to be satisfied with the progress he had made. At least now he had voiced his fears to Oliver and he knew his friend would do his best. But knowing he wasn't alone in recognising Lauren's problems was a double-edged sword—while it confirmed it wasn't his imagination, it increased the real possibility that there was, indeed, something wrong. Filled with a mix of emotions, he walked back into the surgery with Oliver, planning to check on Lauren before taking his afternoon appointments. For now his most important job was to be there for her, to love her…and hope that she would trust in him.

Lauren hesitated outside Oliver's consulting room, her hand poised to knock on the closed door.

It was early Friday evening at the end of March and the surgery was quiet. Most of the staff were having a farewell drink with practice nurse Eve Dwyer, who was leaving not only the surgery but the country, too, and heading out to Switzerland to marry Dr Tom Cornish. Lauren didn't know the whole story but apparently the couple had been reunited at the time of the October flood and had spent the last few months rekindling their relationship. Now they were getting married in Tom's adopted country where he was based for his work with the international rescue organisation, Deltraron.

Lauren had been for a drink and had said her goodbyes. Oliver, too, had been at the pub but had returned to the surgery to finish some paperwork while waiting for his wife. Chloe was out with Gabriel attending Diane Bailey, the mother-to-be who had been under their joint care since the autumn and who was determined to have her baby at home—a baby that was now on its way. It was the perfect time to see Oliver alone and confide in him. If she could pluck up the nerve.

It was two weeks since the car accident. Two weeks in which Gabriel had been supportive, caring and concerned. He hadn't pressured her at all, had asked no questions, but she feared he suspected things were not right. It had made things tense between them. Physically things were as wonderful as ever, but she'd been more reserved, concerned about what was wrong with her and trying hard to hide it. She felt guilty. Gabriel would be hurt if he thought she didn't trust him. It wasn't that. It wasn't him. She was scared…terrified. How long could she continue to deny the problems with her sight? It was one thing to fool herself, quite another to put other people at risk.

The young driver who had crashed into her was being prosecuted. Not only had he been driving while disqualified and without insurance, but it turned out he had taken the car without permission. Crashing into her had been a minor sideshow compared to the other charges against him. Her car had been towed to a garage and, as nothing vital had been damaged with the chassis frame or alignment, it was being repaired. While she waited for the work to be done, the insurance company had arranged for a rental car for her.

Although the days continued to lengthen and the nights became shorter, she refused to venture out after dark. During daylight hours, she had been too nervous to do more than the basic local travel she needed to see those patients who relied on her for home visits. Even then she was taking extra care and time. It was an impossible situation and one she knew could not continue.

However scared she was, she had to talk to someone—a doctor—and find out once and for all what was wrong with her eyes. She admired Nick, but she couldn't feel comfortable seeing him and discussing something like this. Dragan and Adam were delightful colleagues, but she knew it would be Oliver to whom she would turn. She trusted him. Despite being aware she was putting him in a difficult position, she knew he would not tell Gabriel, Chloe or anyone else anything she told him in confidence.

She was still undecided what to do when the door in front of her suddenly opened and she stepped back with a gasp of shock, her hand dropping to her side and her startled gaze clashing with Oliver's.

'Hi, Lauren. Were you coming to see me?' His easy smile faded as he looked at her. 'Is something wrong, sweetheart?'

Much to her dismay, she felt an uncharacteristic welling of tears. She *never* cried. What was the matter with her lately? 'No, I— Sorry…' Horrified, she heard her voice break and felt the moisture on her cheeks.

'Come here.'

Oliver gently drew her inside his consulting room and closed the door. He led her to a chair and sat her down, pulling another up so he could sit beside her, his arm around her shoulders as he held her close. After pressing a tissue into her hand, he waited in silence while she gathered her composure.

'Sorry,' she whispered again.

'There's nothing to apologise for.' He took her hand, making her feel comforted, safe, less lonely. 'Lauren, anything you tell me in this room is strictly between us.'

His reassurance gave her the courage to speak up, but

also alerted her to the fact that maybe she hadn't hidden her problems as well as she had thought. 'You know why I'm here.' It was a statement, not a question, and he met her gaze steadily.

'I think maybe you are ready to talk about your eyes.'

The words were gentle but she flinched nonetheless. 'How long have you known?'

'I suspected when I first came here last summer that there was more to your mishaps than clumsiness.' He paused a moment, his touch gentle as he brushed her hand. 'There was nothing I could put my finger on at the time.'

'Does everyone else know?'

'I very much doubt it. No one has said anything...except Gabriel,' he added, watching her.

Lauren swallowed against the sudden restriction in her throat. 'What did he say?'

'Just that he'd noticed a few things, including how you have trouble seeing in the dark.' His expression was sympathetic, understanding. 'He's worried because he cares about you, but he knew it would be wrong to pressure you, that you needed to come to terms and ask for help yourself.'

'I see.'

She pulled her hand away and looked down at her lap, toying with the damp tissue. Part of her was relieved, grateful that Gabriel had given her space and not nagged her, but the knowledge that he had guessed all along, had apparently spoken to Oliver about her, made her uncomfortable.

'Gabriel didn't betray any confidences, Lauren. It was a one-off conversation after your crash when we both noticed that your right eye appeared...different.'

'Different how?' She remembered the way Oliver had looked her over, his frown when he had studied her face. At the time she hadn't wanted to know—now she did. 'What did you see?'

'Your eyelid was unusually droopy and you had a squint.'

'Do you think it was caused by the accident?' she asked after a short pause.

Oliver shook his head. 'Gabriel said he had seen it a few days before.' Sitting forward, he rested his forearms on his knees. 'He also knows that, should you ever decide to speak to me, I would never break my word to you, as a doctor and a friend, and tell him anything you asked me not to. Are you going to talk to me, Lauren? I want to help if I can,' he told her, his voice encouraging, cajoling.

'Yes,' she whispered, knowing she had little choice but to see this through. 'But I'm scared.'

'I'm sure you are, sweetheart, but we'll take things a step at a time together. OK?'

She nodded. 'OK,' she agreed, barely managing to get the word out.

'Good girl.' Oliver's smile carried both relief and gratitude for her trust. He crossed the room, returning after a moment to hand her a glass of water before sitting down again and picking up a notepad and pen. 'Now, in your own time, tell me what's bothering you and what's been happening with your sight.'

After taking a few sips of water, Lauren leaned back in the chair and drew in a steadying breath. 'I don't know exactly when I started to notice things or to equate being clumsy with vision problems. It happened so gradually that it crept up on me over years,' she explained, finding it easier to talk as she found her stride and released so many things she had bottled up and hidden for so long.

She was grateful for Oliver's patience. He listened without interrupting, silent yet supportive, as she recalled her clumsiness, her lack of hand-eye co-ordination, which had made her bad at team sports at school, and how the visual problems had grown worse in the last few years, how it was only in recent months that the night blindness had deteriorated so disastrously and how she had stopped painting since the summer when Chloe had noticed differences in her work.

'I couldn't even see it at first.' A fresh wave of emotion hit and she took a few moments to regroup. 'It was only in good light when I really studied the pictures that I saw the new ones were less sharp, less detailed, that I'd missed things not in the centre of my vision, and that there were subtle changes in depth perception.'

'And you can't see anything in the dark now?' Oliver prompted.

'No. It's becoming difficult in shadow, too, even during the day, and my eyes take a while to adjust to sudden changes in light. Even some colours of text on certain backgrounds are hard to distinguish, including the display on my mobile phone.'

He nodded, resting a hand on her arm and giving her a gentle squeeze. 'Can you tell me what it's like now? What can you see? How do the visual disturbances happen and affect you? Are they there all the time?'

'Not all the time. Things come and go, but gradually worsen.' She frowned, trying to explain, to put the vague impressions into words. 'Sometimes it's like a hazy veil is slowly closing in from the sides and I can't detect things on the periphery of my vision. Things are fuzzy at the edges. The central area is really clear, though, and I can see perfectly. I went to the optician last year and things were fine—but he only checked the basic things like reading the charts and I didn't mention the other problems I was having. I know it was silly but I was in denial.'

'Did he check the pressures in your eyes?' Oliver queried, making a few notes.

'Is that the little puff of air that makes you jump?'

Oliver chuckled. 'Yeah. It's a weird feeling, isn't it?'

'Yes, it is.' Grateful for the easing of the tension, Lauren smiled back. 'He said the pressures were normal.'

'Right. That's fine. And these changes you've noticed have been happening over a long time?'

Lauren nodded in confirmation as they recapped. 'For years the differences were so tiny that they scarcely registered and I guess I deceived myself into believing nothing was wrong. And I found ways of working around things, made excuses for misjudging distances or bumping into things. But I'm worried, Oliver. I can't keep ignoring it. I'm frightened I'm going to make mistakes.' She paused and bit her lip. 'Having found out recently that I was adopted, I have no family medical history to draw on. I don't know what's happening to me or what I should do,' she finished, her voice breaking again as she battled a new threat of tears.

'It's all right, sweetheart,' Oliver soothed, drawing her close for a hug. 'You've taken a huge step, and a very brave one, by admitting it and talking about it. You are not alone in this, I promise. We'll find out what's going on.'

'What do you think it is?' she asked, voicing the fearful question.

Oliver hesitated a moment, raising her concern it might be serious. 'It could be one of several things, so let's not get ahead of ourselves. I'm going to refer you to an excellent consultant at St Piran. Professor Murchison is one of the best. He'll talk things over with you and then he'll do some tests and assessments. When we know what he has to say, we can discuss it again and decide what to do. All right?'

'All right.' She accepted a fresh tissue and blew her nose. 'How long do you think it will be before I can see him?'

'I'll arrange it as soon as possible, but the appointment won't be until after your holiday.'

Lauren bit her lip. 'We're meant to leave next Thursday, but—'

'I know it's difficult when you're worried, and you can't

forget about your eyes, but I want you and Gabriel to go to Giverny and have a wonderful, relaxing time,' Oliver insisted.

She wanted that, too, so she nodded her agreement. 'I'll try. Are you sure you and Chloe don't mind looking after Foxy?'

'Of course not. He's much more comfortable with us now,' he reassured her with a smile. 'And he'll be on familiar territory, too. I know none of us meant for our stay at Gatehouse Cottage to last for so long, but it's worked out well so far. You just tell us if you want your space back.'

'No, it's fine. I know all the repair and renovation work after the flood is taking ages, but we agreed it was important to get those in temporary accommodation at the caravan park back into their homes first.'

'Not to mention people like Gertie Stanbury,' Oliver added with an affectionate grin.

Lauren smiled back. 'Yes. She's done well at Tom's place but I know she'll be much happier when she can return to her bungalow.'

'I hear it should be ready in another couple of weeks.'

'Good.' She paused a moment. While not regretting a moment of her time with Gabriel, living with him at the Manor House meant she had seen less of Chloe and Oliver at home. 'There's no hurry on my account for you to move on. I know the cottage in Fisherman's Row won't be habitable for a while yet.'

'I'm not sure we'll move back there. It's a bit small. But we've not found anywhere else we like. We're just very grateful to share with you.'

'Well, I've rather neglected you,' she admitted, colour staining her cheeks.

Oliver chuckled. 'With good reason. Both Chloe and I are delighted to see you and Gabriel so happy.'

'Thanks.' But mention of the man she loved brought a

return of her anxiety. 'You won't tell him anything about my eyes or the appointment, will you?'

'No, of course not.' Frowning, Oliver closed his notebook. 'You have to decide what is right for you but, for what it's worth, my advice is to confide in Gabriel. I know you care about each other. He's already worried and he'll want to support you. You need that support, sweetheart.'

But what if there was something seriously wrong? She and Gabriel had made no commitment to each other and she didn't want him feeling trapped. He had worries of his own, decisions he had to make about his future, and she couldn't add to his burdens.

'Lauren?'

'I'd rather wait, Oliver. Please. I need to have all the facts first, to know where I stand, before I decide what to do.'

'If that's what you want,' he allowed, but she could tell he was disappointed and that he disagreed with her decision. 'I'll contact the consultant on Monday and make the arrangements for you to be assessed as early as possible. As soon as I have a date, I'll let you know.'

A sliver of fear iced her spine. 'OK.'

'The appointment and tests might last a while, so you should be prepared to be at the hospital for a few hours. You'll likely have some drops in your eyes that could temporarily affect your vision, so you shouldn't travel alone.' He paused a moment, watching her. 'If you haven't told Gabriel or Chloe by then—but I hope you will—I'll come with you to the hospital myself. You don't have to handle this on your own.'

What had she done to deserve such wonderful friends? 'Thank you, Oliver—for everything.'

CHAPTER NINE

'IT'S even more amazing than I ever imagined! I can't believe I'm really here!' Spinning round, a huge smile on her face, Lauren launched herself into Gabriel's arms and he caught her in a tight hug. 'Thank you *so* much for this.'

'My pleasure.'

And it was. Seeing Lauren so relaxed and happy and engaged was all the reward he needed. With reluctance, Gabriel released her, contented to follow when she took his hand and led him off around Monet's famous garden. This was her moment, her day, and it was a joy to share it with her.

They had flown from Bristol to Charles de Gaulle airport in Paris on Thursday morning. After spending a couple of hours in the city so Lauren could enjoy some of the sights, they had driven their hire car north-east to the hotel where they were staying for their long weekend. Situated in a stunning eighteenth-century chateau an hour from Paris and twenty minutes from Giverny, the hotel was in a beautiful and peaceful setting, the staff friendly and discreet.

Today, Friday, with the weather exceptionally mild for early April, they were enjoying their visit to Claude Monet's home. Parts of the restored pink-painted house with its green shutters had canopies along the veranda covered in swathes of lushly leaved climbing roses that would look spectacular when in flower. The main gardens were full of spring colour, the borders packed with tulips, narcissi, forget-me-nots, aubretia, fritilaries and pansies, with irises, geraniums and other perennials coming through, along with the soon-to-flower wisterias, clematis, rambling roses and yellow laburnums, which draped over arches and pergolas. Cherry and crab-apple trees were also in bloom and looked magnificent.

Lauren chattered freely and he was happy to listen, to live the experience through her. As she made notes and sketches and took endless photos on her digital camera, he indulged himself and watched her, unable to banish his concern about her behaviour since the crash. Physically she appeared fine, but... He frowned. She'd been different these last days, distracted and distant.

Things had been hectic at the surgery. He'd been out almost all night the previous Friday, missing Eve Dwyer's farewell as he and Chloe had worked together to bring Diane Bailey's second daughter safely into the world. He'd arrived home in the early hours to be welcomed to bed by Lauren who had made love to him with an almost frantic urgency. He still sensed that desperation and restlessness in her and he hoped their few days away would enable him to get to the bottom of what was driving her.

'Can we go and find the Japanese water garden?' Lauren asked, pausing to consult her map of the site.

'Of course.' He brushed a few strands of caramel-coloured hair—the natural blonder streaks shimmering under the spring sunshine—back behind her ear, then dropped a quick kiss on her smiling mouth. 'We have to go through the underground passage to the other side of the road.'

'Great!'

Her enthusiasm was infectious and her delight at finding the famous waterlily pool with its weeping willow trees and the graceful wooden bridge, so familiar from Monet's paintings, filled him with warmth and love.

'It's a shame we're too early for the waterlilies themselves, but it's just magical here, Gabe,' she murmured, awe in her voice as she snuggled close to him.

'We can come again at a different time of year.'

She didn't respond to the promise with the pleasure he expected. Instead, he felt her tense. She withdrew, using the pretext of taking more photos, but he experienced a real sense of fear, an inner chill, that in some intangible way he couldn't understand, Lauren was slipping away from him.

Giverny was as magical as Lauren had imagined it would be and it was even better to be sharing the experience with Gabriel. He was puzzled by her, she knew, and she tried her best to hide the fact that she was distracted by following Oliver's advice to make the most of this short holiday and set her worries to one side. It wasn't easy.

How ironic that she should be here at this time. The place inspired her to paint but her nerve had failed her because of her vision problems and she had made excuses not to pick up a brush since the previous summer. For the first time, faced with the reality that she might never paint again, she felt grief at the loss of the activity that had been such a part of her. And yet Monet, one of the world's greatest artists, had produced some of his best and most well-known works while living here amidst this landscape he had created and when he'd been suffering from his own loss of sight.

Aside from never-to-be-forgotten memories, she took endless photographs which she would download to her computer so she could share them with Chloe, who was excited and envious of her trip. She would also email some to Vicky, who was currently in California, the latest stop on the band's tour. Not that Lauren had divulged much to her curious and gossipy friend about Gabriel and, with the worrying issue of her eyes coming to the fore, she was even more glad now that Vicky was away and otherwise occupied.

The whole weekend was wonderful. They breakfasted on chilled fruit juice and fresh warm chocolate croissants at the hotel, and she wondered how many miles she would have to jog to burn off all the extra calories when they went back home.

On Saturday they went to the nearby town of Vernon. As well as visiting the museum, which held some of Monet's paintings as well as many other interesting exhibits, they also enjoyed seeing the old mill on the Seine and Bizy castle.

While she savoured every moment of being with Gabriel, exploring the local area or relaxing at the hotel, and making love with fervour every night, Lauren couldn't shake off her edginess. She was aware all the time of the sword of Damocles hanging over her. When she returned to Cornwall on Tuesday, this special time out of time would be over and she would have to face reality…the appointment with the consultant which Oliver had scheduled for the end of the week. An appointment which could reveal the true state of her visual problems.

She loved Gabriel so much, but she couldn't tell him so until she knew what was wrong with her and what, if anything, she had to offer him. For now she would not burden him with her worries and confusion. Not until she knew exactly where she stood and what the future held for her. What if she had some kind of tumour or something? If things were bad, she knew he wouldn't desert her, but that was part of the problem. She wouldn't want him to stay for the wrong reasons, couldn't bind him to her out of pity. Despite how her feelings had changed, they had made no promises to each other and were taking things one day at a time until his contract in Penhally Bay came to an end. *If* her situation proved to be bleak, she would have to set Gabriel free. He had his own issues to face. But the very thought of him no longer being in her life, of never being able to touch him, kiss him or make love with him again, was too painful to contemplate.

On Monday morning, after a lingering shared shower, they were enjoying a walk in the hotel grounds before breakfast and discussing their plans for their last full day in France when Gabriel's mobile rang. Lauren noted the frown on his face when he took out the phone and looked at the display.

'It's François,' he explained, surprise evident in the huskily accented voice that still sent tingles down her spine. 'Sorry, *chérie*, I'd forgotten I had left the phone on. Is it OK if I speak with him?'

'Of course.'

She knew the two men kept in touch but it was unusual for his friend to call at this time of the day, especially when François knew they were having a few days away. Despite Gabriel teaching her some French these last months, she didn't follow much of the conversation, but the changing expressions on his face made it clear that whatever news his friend was imparting was unexpected and of some importance. A flicker of unease rippled through her.

'Is everything all right?' she asked as he hung up but remained rooted to the spot, looking stunned. Closing the gap between them, she took his free hand. 'Gabe?'

He shook himself, his fingers linking with hers as if he needed the contact. 'I don't know what to say,' he murmured, sounding shaken.

'Come and sit down.' Concerned, Lauren led him to a rustic seat on the edge of the woodland path. 'What's happened?'

'I had not told anyone but François my address in England. As you know, I needed space from Yvette and her scheming,' he explained and Lauren nodded, still gripping his hand. 'François had a letter this morning from the firm of solicitors in Paris who did work for my father. They have been trying to find me.'

Lauren frowned. 'Does François know why?'

'Yes…in part.'

'And?' she whispered, the tension growing with every passing second.

Dark eyes focused on her and she saw the whirl of emotion in them. 'And they have found something I should have received two years ago. It was mislaid.'

'Mislaid?' Lauren swallowed, barely managing to force the words out. 'What is it?'

'A letter—to me—from Papa. He didn't forget me, Lauren.'

His shaky smile and the roughness of his voice undid her, and she wrapped him in her arms, holding him tight, hoping and praying that his father's last words would help to ease the pain inside him and provide answers to some of his questions.

'Are you sure you don't mind doing this?' Gabriel asked for the umpteenth time.

They sat in the foyer at the solicitors' office in Paris. He shifted restlessly, anxious about what was to come yet filled with gratitude for Lauren's support. From the moment he had received the news from François, she had been adamant that they change their plans and return to the capital straight away. After a hasty breakfast, they had packed their things and settled their bill with the chateau owner, apologising for their premature departure.

'I don't mind at all. This is important, Gabe,' she reassured him now, her hand resting on his thigh. 'We've had a wonderful time and now we need to be here.'

The sudden events had distracted him from his worries about Lauren, the feeling he had that something was wrong and that, despite their physical closeness, she was emotionally withdrawing from him.

'Dr Devereux?' The receptionist, a trim brunette, claimed their attention. 'Monsieur Picard will see you now. You go up the stairs and take the second door on the left.'

'Thank you.'

'Do you want me to wait here?' Lauren asked.

Feeling uncharacteristically vulnerable and uncertain, he shook his head. 'I'd like you to come with me.'

'No problem.' Rising to her feet, she slipped her hand into his and gave an encouraging squeeze. 'Let's go.'

All too soon they had reached the designated room and were greeted by Monsieur Picard, a dapper man in his early sixties, who welcomed them with a gracious smile, switching to English with ease when Gabriel informed him that Lauren's French was not proficient.

'Please, sit down and make yourselves comfortable. Can I offer you some refreshment?' the man enquired as he took his own chair behind a vast leather-topped desk laden with folders.

'No, thank you.' Gabriel hoped Lauren wouldn't mind him speaking for them. He felt on edge, wanting only to take possession of his father's letter. 'It is pure chance that I happened to be in France when the message came through. I understand you have something that belongs to me.'

The solicitor's expression turned grave with apology and discomfort. 'Yes. And I cannot say how sorry I am. The fault was entirely ours. The envelope was misfiled and only came to light in the last week. We did not have your current address on file, hence the further delay in contacting you,' the man explained.

'And this letter...it is from my father?' Gabriel asked, cursing the unsteadiness of his voice but drawing strength from the way Lauren's fingers tightened on his.

'Yes,' Monsieur Picard continued, opening the file in front of him and withdrawing a white envelope. 'This was meant to be given to you in the event of your father's death.'

Gabriel's hand shook as he took the envelope the solicitor handed to him. 'Thank you.'

He looked down at it, saw his name typed on the front, and

was filled with a mix of fear, hope and curiosity about what it might contain. The next moments passed in a blur. He signed a release form, then Lauren handled the pleasantries of departure before guiding him out of the building and encouraging him on the short walk back to the hotel they had booked into for their final night in France. Once there, Gabriel sat on the bed and stared at the envelope in his hand.

'Would you like me to leave you alone for a while?'

'No!' Surprised by Lauren's question, he looked up at her and shook his head. 'Please, stay.'

With care, he finally slit open the sealed envelope and withdrew several sheets of thick cream paper. His heart lurched at the sight of his father's familiar large, sweeping handwriting in the dark maroon ink he had always favoured for his fountain pen. A few photographs fell out and he picked them up, shocked to find himself staring at an attractive young woman with long dark hair, a laughing face and wide dark eyes. He turned one over and read the note, name and the date written on the back before passing it to Lauren.

'My mother,' he managed, staring at the other pictures of the same woman with his father as a young man.

'She's beautiful, Gabe.' Lauren's whispered words and the emotion in them brought a lump to his throat. 'You have her eyes…and her smile.'

Scared he wasn't going to hold things together, he sucked in a steadying breath, returned his attention to the letter and read it through. By the end, he was feeling awed and immensely grateful, as well as emotional. He looked back at Lauren, saw the concern and care in her grey eyes, and desperately needed to share with her, and her alone, what he had just learned about his father and himself.

'It's in French,' he told her. 'I'll translate it for you.'

'If you're sure.'

He just hoped he could reach the end without making a fool of himself. 'I am.' That said, he read the letter again, this time aloud...

'My dear son,
'If you are reading this, I am gone, and I did not find the courage or right time to explain things to you in person. I regret that more than words can say.

'Whatever you may have heard by now from Yvette, I hope you will read my side of the story and find it in your heart to forgive me. I loved Angelique, your birth mother, with all my heart. We were so young, barely twenty, yet she was everything to me. She truly was my angel. Despite all the obstacles my family put in the way, we married as soon as we knew you were to be part of our lives. I would have given up everything for Angelique but she died just days after you were born. I refused to lose you, too, but I couldn't manage alone.

'Beside myself with grief, I stupidly allowed my family to take over and railroad me into marrying Yvette—a good business and social match. Yvette promised to raise you as her own in return for the wealth and position the marriage afforded her. There is enough mixed blood in our ancestry that no one questioned your skin being darker than ours. Your grandfather and some of your cousins carry the same Caribbean heritage, as you know.

'The family placed a condition—you were not to be told about Angelique. I was uneasy but weak. I agreed...but have long wished I had not. Yvette was never a good mother and I am so sorry for her coldness to you. She resented you, hated me and the situation. She will try to use my death to tie you to a life not of your choosing. Do not yield, my son. You are a doctor through and through. The estate will survive well in the hands of your cousins and Yvette's welfare needs are guaranteed for life.

'Please…follow your heart. Do not repeat my mistakes and be bound by a false sense of duty to something that will never make you happy or fulfilled. Live your life your way. You have my love and my blessing always. You have so much to give to the sick who need you. Medicine is your destiny.

'Enclosed with this letter are details about Angelique and her origins, as well as some photographs. Although she had no immediate family left when she came to France, I am sure you will wish to learn more of your heritage and that side of the family. She was an amazing young woman, full of goodness and love. We both wanted you desperately.

'There is much of her in you. I am so proud of you, Gabriel, and Angelique would be, too. Be true to yourself, my son, and be happy.

'Love always, Papa'

His voice cracking, Gabriel set the letter aside and looked up to see tears streaming down Lauren's cheeks. She rushed across the room and wrapped her arms around him. Taking her down with him to the mattress, Gabriel held on tight, burying his face in her hair, breathing in her scent, giving thanks that she was here.

He felt a huge weight lifting off his shoulders and a new sense of freedom welled within him, a peace he had not known for a long time. It was nearly two years since his father had died, two years in which he had struggled to come to terms with all Yvette had told him. Now he knew the truth. His father had not had an affair. He had loved Angelique. Both his natural parents had wanted him. Thanks to his father's loving words, the road ahead was clear to him. Being a doctor was a fundamental part of who he was. His father had known that, had released him from any misplaced family duty and urged him to follow his own path.

Despite Yvette's belief, family responsibility was not something he took lightly. He valued his upbringing, the benefits he'd enjoyed, his father's love. Learning that his father had been proud of him and respected his choices brought a rush of emotion to his heart. His father had known what would happen, had wanted to prepare him, to protect him in death, as he had in life, from Yvette's bitterness and spite.

Thank goodness Lauren was here with him. Natural, earthy, intelligent and genuine, she had given him so much in every way. And she responded to his touch like no other woman he had ever known. She shifted, pulling back to meet his gaze. Touched by her concern for him, he brushed away the tears that showed how much she cared. He loved her so much and valued her opinion above all others. She accepted him for who and what he was, the whole person, not his family name or his bank balance or the ancestral estate. From the first he had sensed Lauren was a kindred spirit. It had been like a meeting of souls.

'I'm so glad for you, Gabe,' she told him, her voice thick with emotion. 'Listen to your father—and to your heart.'

It was good advice. And he planned to follow it. 'Right now my heart is telling me to take you to bed,' he murmured huskily, delighting in the way her eyes flared with answering desire.

Late that night, cocooned in the privacy of their room, the noises of the city filtering up from the streets below, Gabriel held Lauren close, their bodies tangled together, limbs entwined. It had been an unforgettable day…a day in which he had been given a new lease of life and had recaptured his true memories of his father.

His thoughts turned to Lauren. Their love-making remained as passionate and explosive as ever and yet he still sensed that new desperation in her. He needed to tell her how special she was and how much she meant to him. He had held back for so long, scared to push too soon or too hard—in the same way he had given her space to come to terms with the problems with her sight.

Stroking her satiny hair, breathing in her scent, he tightened his hold. 'I love you, Lauren, *ma belle*,' he whispered against her skin, knowing she was not yet asleep.

He fought against the heartache that gripped him when there was no response to his admission bar the tensing of her body. Fear clenched his stomach. Today Lauren's support and reactions had proved that she cared, too, and yet she refused to acknowledge what was between them. Why? What was holding her back? For days he had sensed the times when she had been distancing herself, backing off from him emotionally, and he didn't know how to stop it.

He couldn't force her to trust in him, to love him, but he wanted so much more than the commitment-free relationship they had discussed at the beginning. He *wanted* commitment, *needed* Lauren in his life—for ever. How ironic that at the very time he should have rediscovered his father and be in a position to not only understand his mother's heritage but to be free to plan his future, the one person he wanted most to share it with him was slipping out of his reach.

Lauren sat in Oliver's car on the journey back from St Piran Hospital on Friday afternoon frozen with shock and despair. She bit her lip, trying not to think of the last hours and all the tests she had undergone—a battery of assorted eye-function tests and examinations, including visual field, acuity and colour assessments. There had been a blood test, an electro-retinograph—which determined the function of the photoreceptors in the eye—and endless questions. Unfortunately, due to her adoption, she had not been able to provide any details of her family medical history.

Oliver had reassured her several times about Professor Kieran Murchison's reputation and the rotund, balding and jovial man had lived up to his billing today, showing a kindness that matched his thoroughness. Yet he had held her fate in his hands and she had felt sick to her stomach when he had finally delivered his verdict.

'I'm sorry to keep you waiting so long, my dear, but I wanted to be very sure of the results,' he had told her when she had been shown into his office, leaving Oliver—who had stuck with her throughout and had borne the delays and boredom with amazing fortitude—sitting outside in the waiting area.

'But you have the results now?' Her voice had wavered alarmingly. 'What's wrong with me?'

His expression serious, the professor had looked down at her notes before speaking. 'I'm afraid you have a condition called retinitis pigmentosa.'

'What does that mean?'

'It's a group of related, inherited disorders—a genetic disease of the retina—the majority of which have no known genetic cause. The most common cases of RP result from abnormalities of the photoreceptors—the rods and the cones,' he had explained. 'The presentation of your symptoms suggests that you have autosomal dominant RP, which means that you fall into the group who have rod-cone dystrophy, affecting the rods more than the cones. This explains the problems you have reported, including those with your night vision, peripheral vision, bumping into things, slow adjustment to light and so on.'

Struggling to take it all in, Lauren had forced herself to ask the next question. 'What about treatment?'

'There is much we can do to help you manage the condition, and to prepare and cope for the changes that lie ahead. There are various genetic and stem-cell studies ongoing around the world which might have positive results in future, even a bionic eye project. For now, though, Lauren, there is no treatment and no cure. Progression of RP is different for everyone. Yours has been slow so far. Hopefully it will continue to follow the same pattern. You have a challenging time ahead, but it's not a death sentence. And it's not going to happen overnight. So much will still be open to you.'

The words rang in her ears even now. She had a whole stack of advice leaflets to read, a list of recommended books and website addresses to gain further information, but the appalling and impossible truth could not be ignored. Retinitis pigmentosa was a progressive disease. She would continue to lose her vision and, ultimately, could become totally blind.

Her mind in turmoil, she leaned back and closed eyes still blurry from the drops Oliver had warned her would be administered. Aside from the utter terror of today, of facing up to the reality that all was not well with her eyes, she couldn't get Gabriel out of her thoughts. France had been amazing, she'd loved her time away with him. The icing on the cake had been learning about the letter and seeing the difference his father's words, love and pride had made to him, to his sense of identity and his thoughts for the future.

On Monday night in Paris she had frozen when Gabriel had told her he loved her. She had wanted to turn in his arms and kiss him, to shout from the rooftops that she loved him, too, but instead she had pretended to be asleep and had ignored his longed-for words. If only they had come at a different time and not while she'd had this problem hanging over her and had been rigid with fear for her future. A future that now stretched ahead of her, painful and lonely, because Gabriel could not be part of it.

He had been hurt by her silence and there had been an uncharacteristic tension between them on their journey back to Cornwall the next day—a tension that had continued throughout the rest of a busy week. No matter how much she told herself she was doing the right thing, guilt weighed heavily upon her. She hated deceiving Gabriel and keeping things from him. He'd be so upset if he knew where she had been today. And he'd believe she'd kept it from him because she didn't trust him. Which wasn't true. Far from it. She was just so terribly scared about what was happening to her and devastated now that the diagnosis confirmed the worst.

'Lauren? Talk to me,' Oliver cajoled, taking her ice-cold hand in his as he drew the car to a halt outside Gatehouse Cottage. 'What do you want me to do?'

'I don't know. I can't think at the moment.'

His fingers squeezed hers and she heard the shock and upset in his voice. 'I'm so sorry, sweetheart. I'm here for you. We all will be…if only you will let us.'

'I need some time to decide what to do,' she whispered after a long, uncomfortable pause. 'Promise me that you won't say anything to anyone. Not even Chloe. Especially not Gabriel.'

'I've already told you I won't break your confidence, Lauren. But I have to say I think you are wrong to shut out those who care so much about you,' he advised gently.

Shock, anger and fear made thought and reason impossible. Withdrawing her hand from his, Lauren gathered up her things and reached to open the door. 'I can't thank you enough for all you have done for me. I'm more grateful than you can know. But I need to handle this my own way, Oliver,' she told him, her voice quiet but firm.

'All right.' He sighed, running his fingers through his hair, his frustration and concern clear. 'You can always come to me at any time if you want to talk about things, or if there is anything at all I can do. Promise me that much.'

'I know. I promise.'

'I don't like to leave you alone,' he protested, his voice

heavy with worry. 'But Adam swapped with me and I have to get back to the clinic to take evening surgery.'

'Go. Please. I'll be fine. I need to read up, to absorb all the professor said,' she reassured him, holding on to her composure by a tenuous thread.

After Oliver had finally been persuaded to leave, Lauren went inside and wandered around the cottage that no longer felt like home. Home was with Gabriel. A place she could no longer be. She sat down on her bed, Foxy's head in her lap, the booklets describing her disease spread around her, and cried for all that was lost. Everything seemed too monumental to cope with. How long could she continue to do her job? What was going to happen to her one, five or ten years down the line? Would she be totally blind?

The first most pressing and impossible thing she had to do was to distance herself from Gabriel, to begin the terrible process of withdrawing and ending their magical relationship. Even thinking about it brought more pain and sadness than she had ever known. It cut deep inside her. But she had to do it. For his sake. Because he deserved someone who could be his equal, someone with whom he could have a family. With her condition, genetic testing might show she could never risk having children of her own.

Hearing Gabriel's car going past in the drive, Lauren left Foxy behind at Gatehouse Cottage and walked slowly to the Manor House. For endless moments, scared of what was to come, she hesitated on the steps, shivering despite the mildness of the late afternoon. Finally, unable to delay the inevitable, she rang the doorbell. After a few moments, she heard Gabriel's steps jogging down the stairs, then the front door swung open. All the breath left her lungs in a rush at the sight of him. He was so gorgeous. More than anything she wanted to throw herself into his arms, confess all, tell him she loved him, but it wasn't fair to him.

'*Chérie*, what are you doing?' he asked with a laugh, reaching for her. 'Did you lose your key?'

Evading his touch, she stepped back and shook her head. 'No. I—' She broke off before her voice cracked, seeing the smile leave his face, doubt and fear dimming the light in those glorious dark eyes.

'You are scaring me, Lauren. What is it?'

'I need some space—some time to think,' she began, cursing her lack of decisiveness.

Gabriel frowned. 'Space?'

'Yes.' Wringing her hands together, she took another step away, trying to find the strength to do what she believed was right.

'To think about what?'

'I'm going back to the cottage, Gabriel. We've had a great time, but we said no promises, no ties, and I think we need to cool things. You've sorted the situation out now about your father,' she rushed on, her heart breaking at the hurt disbelief on his face. 'You're free to plan your future, to find out about your mother's heritage, to go where you like with your work. The last thing you need is to be shackled to anything or anyone.'

Anger mingled with the pain in his eyes as he looked at her, roughly thrusting his hands into his trouser pockets. 'Don't make this about me, Lauren. Don't make excuses. You had to know how much more this had become. It was never some casual fling. Not for me. I had thought not for you either,' he challenged, his accent more pronounced with his hurt disappointment. 'Or have the last months been nothing but a game to you?'

'No, but…' He had cut her to the quick and she had no way to defend herself so she fell silent.

'I love you, Lauren. I want to make a commitment to you, to marry you. But that clearly means nothing to you and you don't feel the same for me. You've been pulling away emotionally for days. Just have the guts to say so.'

'OK.' She swayed, fearing she was going to collapse in a pit of pain. Nothing had ever been this difficult and she couldn't bring herself to look him in the eye. 'You're right. I can't commit like that.' Her voice wavered as she told that fragment of truth. She couldn't commit but she couldn't tell him why…because she loved him heart, body and soul and couldn't burden him with a blind wife. 'I'm sorry.'

'You're sorry? Is that meant to make this right?' he demanded with an anger she had never heard from him before.

Tears stung her eyes. 'No.'

'You've made your decision, Lauren. There's nothing else to be said.'

Rigid with tension and with a quiet dignity that cried out with his pain and twisted the knife inside her, Gabriel closed the door, shutting her out of the house and his life. The tears fell then, hot and heavy. Selfishly, she wanted to call him back, to pound on the door, to tell him it was all a mistake and explain everything. She needed him, wanted him, couldn't face this without him—but she couldn't manipulate him that way, not after all he had been through with Yvette.

She thought of all he had said, words that should have made her joyous, not despairing. Gabriel loved her. It was what she'd wanted most. But for his sake she had had to reject that love—the most precious of gifts. She didn't deserve him. Pressing a hand to her mouth to mask the sound of the sobs that racked her body, she turned and stumbled back down the driveway, praying that Oliver and Chloe would not be back yet.

She had achieved what she had set out to do. Now her future stretched ahead of her—cold, dark and full of fear. A future that was going to take her sight, her job, her hobbies, her independence. Even that didn't seem to matter as much as what she had already lost. Gabriel…the only man she had ever loved.

CHAPTER TEN

'I'M GOING for a walk,' Lauren announced, unable to bear the atmosphere in the cottage any longer and needing to be alone with her thoughts. 'I'll take Foxy down to the beach.'

'Whatever.'

Chloe's response, while not unfriendly, left Lauren in no doubt that she remained in her friend's bad books and was not to be forgiven any time soon. Smothering a sigh, knowing it was her own fault for not following Oliver's advice and confiding in the people who cared for her, she attached Foxy's lead and let herself out, the Saturday morning sunshine failing to raise her spirits.

She had no idea how she had lived through the last week. Nothing had been this painful and no matter how much she told herself that hurting Gabriel now was better than condemning him to a hopeless future with her, it didn't help. She couldn't sleep, couldn't eat. People were shocked and surprised by the break-up. However many times Lauren trotted out the same excuse—that things had run their course and she and Gabriel had decided to go their separate ways—the telling never became easier, the lie sticking in her throat, multiplying her agony.

She couldn't avoid contact with Gabriel at the surgery. The sight of him, proudly dignified yet so obviously unhappy, ripped at her shredded heart. How she was going to bear the situation for the remainder of his time in Penhally she didn't know—seeing him every day, not being able to touch him, barely speaking unless it was with strained politeness about work. But the very thought of him leaving for good, of never seeing him again, or hearing his softly accented voice and rumbly laugh, was impossible to contemplate. No matter how much she kept convincing herself she was doing the right thing for Gabriel's sake, the temptation to be selfish and go to him to confess all never diminished. Indeed, it increased with every hour that passed.

Desperate to escape the pain of losing Gabriel and the anxiety over her diagnosis, she had thrown herself into her work, all the time wondering how long she would be able to do her job and how soon she would have to stop driving completely. Yesterday she had taken Paul Mitchell and his mother on their once-a-month trip to a local private spa that made their hydrotherapy pool available by appointment for patients with special needs. The water-based exercise she was able to do with him was good for Paul with his Duchenne muscular dystrophy.

Some long-term patients she had seen during the last twelve months had been signed off, Mike Trevellyan among them. As well as cases which turned around fairly quickly, like Zena with her sore neck and Dan Somers with his hamstring injury, she had all her regulars, including Harry, Edith and baby Timmy Morrison. Stella Chamberlain's Parkinson's disease was still keeping her in the Harbour View Nursing Home, while Gertrude Stanbury was looking forward to returning to her bungalow in Gull Close in the next week. Neither the anticipation of going home nor her painful arthritis diverted Gertrude from commenting on what she viewed as Lauren's stupidity in letting Gabriel get away.

At home she had Chloe on her case and she recalled her

friend's initial reaction when she had learned of the break-up. 'You said to me in the summer to grasp what I had with Oliver, that something that special, some*one* that special, doesn't come along often in life. You and Gabriel are special, Lauren. He loves you, and I'm sure you love him. Why are you throwing it all away?'

'You don't understand.' And she hadn't been able to explain.

'No, I don't. Neither does Gabriel. He's confused and distressed. You've really hurt him. You owe him more than that.'

Lauren had spent as much time in her room as she could, avoiding Oliver and Chloe. She'd studied the leaflets the professor had given her, looked up information on the Internet and read a couple of biographies written by people who were living with retinitis pigmentosa. It was all depressing but moving. She hoped she could be even as fractionally as brave and resourceful as those whose stories she had read—stories which had scarily mirrored many of her own experiences. With time she hoped to come to terms with it, to make plans, to find some courage to cope with whatever was thrown at her, but the shock still lingered, as did the gut-wrenching ache of missing Gabriel every minute of every day.

Leaving the quiet country roads, she headed down through the town towards the harbour front. All she could do was tell herself she was making the best choice for Gabriel in the long run. He'd had enough of manipulative women in his life. She couldn't tie him to her out of duty or because he felt sorry for her. But it was almost impossible to let go. Nothing had hurt this much. When his time here was over, he would go back to France and no doubt settle down one day and have a family of his own. She couldn't allow him to take on a wife who was slowly but surely losing her sight, who might be a genetic risk and unable to have children, and who, at some time down the line, could be blind and dependent in more ways than she could bear to comprehend.

Despite feeling as if she was slowly but surely unravell-
ing, somehow she had to try to survive this torment. One day
at a time.

With one more house call left to make on Saturday morning,
Gabriel sat in his car outside the patient's home, his arms
folded on the steering-wheel, his head resting on them. A
week and a day on and he had still not recovered from the
shock of Lauren's words. One day he had been given the gift
of his father's love and approval, the identity of his birth
mother, and had felt his life was finally getting back on track
again, but shortly afterwards Lauren had dropped her bombshell, rejecting his love and breaking his heart in the process.

What had he done wrong? Had he taken Lauren for
granted? Had he been mistaken that she returned his feelings?
He still didn't understand how she could have walked away
as if there was nothing at all between them. It hadn't been just
sex. Lauren could deny it all she liked but he wouldn't,
couldn't, believe she felt nothing, that all they had shared had
been meaningless fun. He was sure he hadn't misjudged
things that badly. What they had was special, explosive, a
once-in-a-lifetime connection…a connection that had hit
them both the moment they had met. He had never felt like
this about anyone else. Had never hurt so much. He couldn't
sleep without Lauren in his arms, couldn't eat, was barely
getting through each day.

Even the letter from his father had failed to distract him
for long, despite the searches he had done on the Internet to
learn about Martinique, where his mother had come from.
One day he hoped to go there, to find out more about his roots,
but he couldn't get excited about it now, could do nothing but
yearn for Lauren.

With a deep sigh, he climbed out of the car, collected his
medical bag, and walked to the front door, reviewing what he

knew about the woman he was going to see. Delia Rocco was only thirty-two and had suffered a serious stroke ten days ago. She had been discharged from hospital the previous day and he was doing a follow-up visit to ensure she and her husband were coping. He hadn't wanted to leave them all weekend without support, and he needed to discuss Delia's needs—which would include physiotherapy and necessitate him facing Lauren. His gut tightened with pain.

Delia's husband, Neil, answered the door and invited him in, a tired smile on his face. 'Thanks for coming, Dr Devereux.'

'No problem. How are you both doing?' he asked, knowing that Neil was going to need as much understanding and support as Delia. 'Relieved to be home?'

'Very. But it's scary, too, not having the nurses on hand,' the man admitted.

'That's understandable, but I'm sure you'll do fine, and don't forget you have the doctors, district nurses and physiotherapist from the surgery willing to step in whenever you need us.'

Looking reassured, Neil relaxed. 'Thank you. Well, I expect you want to see Delia first?'

'Yes, please. Then we can have a chat.'

Talking with and examining Delia revealed that she had been left with weakness and reduced movement down one side of her body and her speech was slurred. Given the severity of her stroke, she had done well to make so much improvement so quickly, although she had a long haul ahead of her. She was brave but clearly bewildered at having been struck down at such a young age, scared about what the future would hold for her. Gabriel determined to do the best he could for the couple to ensure they had something positive to look forward to.

'I'm just so grateful Delia is still here and recovering,' Neil said a while later, holding his wife's good hand. 'Life without her would be intolerable. She tried to send me away, of course, but I wasn't having any of it.'

Puzzled, Gabriel frowned. 'Sorry? Send you away?'

'I was so scared, so confused. I got it into my head that Neil would be better off without me, that I would be a burden to him and prevent him having a normal, happy life,' Delia explained, taking time to try to enunciate each word.

'She said she didn't love me any more, that she didn't want me,' Neil confirmed with a rueful smile. 'I almost believed her at first, I was under so much stress and so worried about her, but thankfully I saw through what she was doing.'

With a start, Gabriel sat back, his thoughts on Lauren. Frowning, he thought over the sudden way she had ended things with him. Was there more behind it than he was seeing? Unsettled, he began packing his things away and returned his attention to Delia and Neil.

'I'll see you again next week. But call any time if there is anything you need,' he advised them. 'Our physiotherapist, Lauren Nightingale, will come to see you on a regular basis and work out an exercise and therapy schedule with you.'

'Thanks. How is Lauren?' Neil asked.

Pain lanced through his heart. 'Fine, as far as I know. She's an excellent physio, so you'll be in good hands.'

'Oh, I know that,' Delia confirmed with a lopsided smile. 'I was a couple of years ahead of her at school. She was always very caring to people.'

'I was just concerned because I saw her at St Piran Hospital last week when I was waiting for Delia. Lauren didn't see me, but she looked upset,' Neil clarified.

Lauren had been at the hospital? Upset? Every part of him went on high alert. 'When was this?' he asked, trying to keep his tone casual.

'Last Friday afternoon. They'd taken Delia down for some

eye tests,' he added, clearly unaware of the turmoil Gabriel was experiencing.

Dieu! Why hadn't he considered it before? He thought of the timing. Lauren had been to the hospital and that same night she had broken up with him. What on earth had she found out? Fear gripped him. Had Lauren reacted to the shock as Delia had, pushing away those close to her because she felt she would be a burden? He had to know, had to find out.

Taking his leave of the Roccos with as much speed as was polite, he rushed back to the surgery where Oliver was taking the Saturday morning clinic. Hippocratic oath or no Hippocratic oath, he was going to get some information from his friend.

'Is Oliver still with patients?' he asked Sue when he arrived back at the surgery and handed over his tray of patient notes.

'No, the last one left about five minutes ago,' she confirmed. 'Everything OK?'

'Mmm? Oh, fine. I need to see Oliver.'

Leaving a surprised Sue behind him, he hurried to his friend's consulting room. The door was closed, so he knocked and waited impatiently, just in case Sue was wrong. Despite his urgency, he wouldn't embarrass or upset a patient.

'Come in.'

Oliver was alone, he discovered, writing up his notes. He swung his chair round, a wary expression on his face as Gabriel closed the door and crossed to the desk.

'I know you can't break a confidence, Oliver, but I want to know what's going on with Lauren,' he began, pacing out his frustration. 'I love her, I want to marry her. When she broke things off, it nearly killed me. Someone told me they saw Lauren at the eye clinic last week. That same day she told me it was over. I don't believe that's a coincidence.' He paused, considering how much to tell Oliver. 'It's taken a while to get my head together but I think she has some mis-placed idea she's going to be a burden and has to let me go.'

'Gabriel—'

'I *know*,' he cut in with irritation, rubbing a hand across the back of his neck, feeling the tightness of the tension gripping his muscles. 'I know you can't tell me outright. But you can give me a clue.'

Oliver regarded him for a few moments in silence. 'For what it's worth, I've tried several times to get Lauren to confide in both you and Chloe, but I have to respect her wishes.'

'Whatever it is, however bad, I'm not leaving her, not giving up on her. Am I on the right track? Or does she really feel nothing for me? Give me something to work on. Please.'

'You don't make things easy, Gabriel.'

'How would you feel if it was Chloe?' OK, he wasn't playing fair, but he was desperate. 'If Lauren thinks she's doing this for my benefit, she's wrong. If she cares about me, she'll thank you in the long run.'

Oliver closed his eyes and sighed, running his fingers through his over-long hair. 'I can't give you any details, but you're right, Lauren's pushing everyone away because she thinks it's the right thing to do.'

Sitting down because his legs felt too shaky to hold him up, Gabriel met Oliver's troubled dark gaze. 'She's not dying? It's not a tumour?' He forced the words out, the relief inde-scribable when his friend shook his head. Sucking in a steady-ing breath, he pressed a hand over his sternum as he acknowledged how frightened he had been. 'OK. It doesn't matter what it is, I want to be there for her. I just wish she had told me so she hadn't had to face all this alone.'

'She wasn't alone,' Oliver admitted after a moment.

Gabriel glanced up, a mix of emotions rushing through him—disappointment and annoyance at being shut out, but gratitude to Oliver for being such a good friend. 'You went with her?'

'Yes. I thought it was the lesser evil. Lauren refused to tell you or Chloe and I knew none of us would want her to go on her own.'

'Thank you for being there for her. Now, it's time I found her and discussed a few things,' he finished, rising to his feet.

'Good luck.' Oliver's smile was wry. 'She can be stubborn when she sets her mind to something.'

'So can I. And now I know what she's up to, I'm not going to let her sideline me again.'

He left the surgery for home, needing to change clothes and then track down Lauren. A shiver went through him as he imagined all she had been through this last week or more. He realised now that the worry of facing up to her sight problems had led to her withdrawal, to her being distracted and to her urgency for physical closeness—especially if she'd feared things would be over when she had a diagnosis. While it pained him that she hadn't spoken to him about it, he understood how fear and anxiety could affect someone's decision-making. Thinking of her frightened and confused and alone brought a lump to his throat. He wished more than anything that he had been there to help her through what must have been a shocking and scary experience. His heart ached for her.

Lauren touched something deep inside him, filling an empty space he hadn't realised he'd had until he'd met her. She grounded him, made him laugh. The last months with her had been the happiest of his life—breaking up more painful than anything he had ever experienced. But now he knew what lay behind her actions and her misguided thoughts he wasn't letting her go—not while he had breath in his body.

'I can do all kinds of tricks with my kite now, Uncle Nick.'

'I'm sure you can,' Nick responded, voice gruff. 'Show me some of them.'

Kate smiled as Jem rushed ahead of them on to the surfing beach below the cliffs and beyond the promontory on which the lighthouse and the church stood. She glanced back at the latter building, wondering what the new permanent vicar would be like, an appointment finally having been made. Whoever took up the role next month would have a difficult act to follow. Reverend Kenner was still much missed.

It was a perfect spring morning, sunny and with a hint of freshness in the air. Nick's suggestion of a walk on the beach had been a pleasant surprise and she had been happy to put off her visit to the Saturday farmers' market so that the three of them could spend time together. Since Christmas, and the successful New Year's Eve party at his house, Nick had made a real effort to play a part in Jem's life. For that Kate was grateful. That he'd made no mention of claiming his son still pained her, but she tried not to be impatient.

They stood side by side, watching in silence as Jem skilfully had his kite soaring into the sky and began performing some stunts.

'He's good,' Nick commented after a while, an enigmatic expression on his face, his hands buried in his trouser pockets.

'Yes.' Kate pulled her gaze away from his profile and looked back at her son with pride. 'He took to it straight away. I'm thinking of getting him a more advanced kite for his birthday.'

'Good idea.'

Nick's tone was cool and she worried that mentioning Jem's birthday had touched on forbidden ground and brought back memories of his conception. She sighed, weary of having to be careful what she said in case Nick took exception to it. Before she could decide whether to call him on it or change the subject, they were approached by an older couple.

'Are you folks local?' the woman asked with a broad smile, her American accent thick with Deep South tones.

'We are.' Aware of Nick's reserve, Kate smiled back. 'Can we help you?'

'Would you be kind enough to take a photograph of us with the lighthouse in the background?'

'Of course.'

Kate was surprised when Nick stepped forward and took the digital camera. While he snapped a few photographs, the man chattered about the legend of the wreck of the seven-teenth-century Spanish treasure ship, the *Corazon del Oro*, which lay off the rocks to the north of the lighthouse. Keen not to be left out, Jem ran up to join them just as Nick handed back the camera.

'Thank y'all so much! What a cute family you make,' the woman gushed, beaming at them as she linked arms with her husband. 'Why, the little man is just the image of his daddy!'

The American tourists left and Kate smothered a groan as she glanced at Nick and saw him stony-faced and rigid with tension. Jem, however, laughed.

'She thought you were my dad, Uncle Nick,' he joked, oblivious of the atmosphere as he picked up his kite and prepared to run off again. 'Cool, or what?'

Anxiety gripped her at Nick's expression. She sucked in a breath. 'Look, Nick—'

'No.' He held up a hand and backed away. 'I'm sorry, Kate. I tried. But I can't do this. It's too much.'

Tears stung her eyes, pain lancing through her as he turned and strode off in the direction of his house, leaving her and Jem alone. Again. All the progress of these last months, the new closeness, the joy for Jem, had been stolen in an instant by a stranger's unwitting comments. Clearly Nick wasn't ready. Maybe he never would be.

The knowledge tore at her heart and made her unutterably sad for herself and deeply hurt and angry for Jem, who had asked for none of this. How could Nick reject the boy? She wanted to chase after Nick and make him see reason, but she knew him of old and he wouldn't change his view unless he wanted to. Pushing him further would get nowhere. He had to come to terms and make the decision for himself. And if he didn't? If he could never accept Jem and have any kind of role in his life?

If that were the case, maybe the time had come for her to make a complete break, to think about leaving Penhally Bay and the man she had secretly and hopelessly loved for so long. For Jem's sake she couldn't risk Nick flitting in and out of his life as the mood took him. It would be too confusing for her son. And unfair. Maybe she should admit defeat and make a new life for herself and Jem elsewhere. A life without Nick. As he disappeared from view, her heart ached, and she feared this might well be the end to all her hopes and dreams.

A familiar car drew her attention as it approached the church and parked. Gabriel climbed out and she watched as he walked towards the solitary figure sitting hunched and alone on the rocks by the lighthouse at the end of the promontory. Lauren. With all her heart Kate prayed that the young couple, so right for each other, could find a solution to whatever had caused them to part last week. Their hurt had been palpable. She sent up a wish that Lauren and Gabriel could enjoy the kind of happy ending and life-long love that she herself had been denied.

Her mind full of the tough decisions that lay ahead, Kate turned and went to find her son.

Lauren sat on the rocks by the lighthouse—a favourite place she had often come to paint—and stared sightlessly out to sea. She wore sunglasses, as advised by the professor, to protect her eyes from damaging UV rays…eyes currently blurred and puffy from her tears. She despised self-pity, but she felt so overwhelmed at the moment and liable to cry at the merest provocation. It was very unlike her. But the future seemed so scary, so lonely, so bleak. She was worried about her eyes, about how she would cope when she could no longer work or maintain her independence. And her heart ached for Gabriel and what could never be.

Foxy sat beside her and she hugged him close. When he began whining and struggling against her hold, she pulled back in puzzlement. He strained at his lead, panting as he stared fixedly at something behind her. Lauren glanced round, a gasp of shock escaping, her heart lurching and her body tensing as she saw Gabriel striding towards her. He looked impossibly sexy in well-worn, figure-hugging jeans and his mulberry jumper. The lead slipped through her suddenly nerveless fingers, and Foxy's paws scrabbled for purchase on the rocks as he charged to greet the man whose every step inexorably closed the distance between them.

She watched as Foxy greeted Gabriel with enthusiasm. Clearly the dog had missed him as much as she had. Gabriel hunkered down and she could hear his huskily accented voice, if not his words. She saw him stroke the smooth brindle-and-white coat and her stomach clenched as she vividly recalled what it was like to feel those hands caress her bare skin.

Unable to bear it, she stifled a sob and swung round to face the sea again, trying to tune out Gabriel's voice by focusing on the sound of the waves against the rocks. But the sea was fairly calm today, providing poor entertainment for the surfers and failing to distract her from the man she could sense approaching. She stiffened as he sat beside her, far too close, far too tempting. What was going on? Why had he sought her out?

'Hi. Chloe said you might be here.'

His voice betrayed none of his previous anger and hurt. Indeed, he seemed impossibly relaxed. The same could not be said for herself. She was too aware of Gabriel. His earthy, citrusy fragrance tantalised her. Even across the small gap that separated him she felt the warmth of his body—a body every fibre of her being longed to hold again. Gabriel knew just where to touch, to stroke, to lick to send her to madness, as she did with him. Her heart yearned for what she could never have. Shifting restlessly, she kept her gaze averted, watching as Foxy turned a couple of times and lay down on a rock in front of them, dozing in the sunshine. She jumped when Gabriel reached out and captured one of her hands in both of his, panic rising as he refused to allow her to pull free.

'It's not going to work, you know, *chérie*.'

The sound of his voice tightened her insides with longing and his touch made her shiver. Her control deserted her. 'W-what isn't?'

'You…trying to push me away,' he told her, his tone calm and conversational. 'Pretending you don't feel the same as I do about what we have.'

'You don't understand. I can't offer you anything,' she whispered, failing once more to remove her hand from his, his touch setting of ripples of sensation, weakening her resolve.

'I understand more than you think. And you can offer me everything, *ma belle*, if only you believe and trust me.'

'Gabriel…'

'It took me a while to work out what you were doing.' He raised her hand to his mouth, his lips whispering over her skin, stealing her breath. 'This has been the worst week of my life. I cannot describe how much I have missed looking at you, talking with you, making love to you, holding you in my arms as I sleep.' His tongue-tip teased circles on her palm and she bit back a whimper, fighting with everything she had to hold on to her resolve. 'I'm not prepared to be without you for another minute.' He took off her sunglasses, dark mocha eyes gazing deep into her own. 'Look at me and say you don't love me. I know you think you're doing the right thing.

but you're not. Tell me the truth, Lauren, once and for all. Lay it on the line.'

Every part of her was shaking and a tear breached the barrier of her lashes and trickled down her cheek. His thumb caught it, brushing the salty wetness away. It had been impossible enough to end it and send him away that evening outside the Manor House. There was no way she could force the lies out a second time. She felt trapped, desperately wanting to avoid this confrontation but unable to escape.

'I'm losing my sight! Is that what you want to hear?' she cried, all the fear, anger and despair welling up inside her and seeking release in an unstoppable tide. 'I have retinitis pigmentosa. I'm going blind, Gabe.'

'Shh. Come here, *mon amour*.'

Turning to face her, he pulled her close and she collapsed into his arms, sobbing as she buried her face against him. His warm strength enfolded her and she breathed in his scent. One arm held her tight while his free hand stroked her hair, his soothing words calming her. Weak, she allowed herself a few moments to believe everything could be all right, but reality intruded and she pulled back. He allowed her some space but he didn't let her go.

'Gabriel, we can't do this. I—'

'Yes, we can,' he interrupted with steely determination, his fingers gentle as they wiped her cheeks. 'I've known from the first that there was something wrong. The way you walked into things or missed what was in shadow right in front of you. How you unconsciously count your steps in the dark. You stopped painting, sought routines that were familiar, had trouble judging distances.'

'Why didn't you say anything?' she challenged, shocked and upset.

He frowned, a furrow creasing his brow. 'Because I didn't want to lose you by nagging. And you had to come to terms yourself, to recognise and accept, to ask for help.'

'But—'

'Lauren, it doesn't change how I feel about you. It matters to me in the sense of what it means for you and your joy in life, but not for any of the reasons you think.' He cupped her face, forcing her to look at him, to see and hear his sincerity. 'I don't feel pity or duty. Far less trapped. I love you, *ma belle*, no matter what. As the vows say…in sickness and in health, in good times and in bad, for better and worse.'

'You can't want me! I can't let you be burdened with this,' she cried.

For the first time a thread of anger returned. 'What gives you the right to make my decisions for me? To take away my choices? I'm an adult, Lauren, and capable of knowing my own mind.'

'I can't ask you to be tied to this. To me.'

'You are not asking. I am choosing. Of my own free will. Because I love you.' He paused a moment, watching her, considering, thoughtful. 'If it was the other way round, what would you do?'

Lauren licked lips that felt dry and struggled to find her voice. 'I don't understand.'

'If I were the one who faced some kind of illness or had RP, or if I had an accident and faced the rest of my life in a wheelchair, would you walk away and leave me? Would you stop loving me?'

'No!' she exclaimed, fury rising within her. 'Of course not.'

'Then do not expect that of me.'

Her heart stopped. With those words, she truly understood. 'Gabe…'

'I can no more live without you than I can without oxygen,' he told her huskily, drawing her back into his arms. 'You give meaning and joy to my life. You're my friend, my confidante, my lover. I will always love you, no matter what, and I will *not* walk away from you.'

'I don't know what's going to happen to me,' she sobbed, fresh tears threatening.

'I know you are frightened. And angry. It's all so new and confusing and scary. That is normal, human,' he reassured her, hugging her close. 'But I also know your courage and humour and intelligence. Your spirit will see you through. And you won't be alone, *mon amour*. We'll face this together. And together we can do anything.'

She cried again then, releasing all the tension and the fear and loneliness of the last days and weeks as she clung to him. 'RP is degenerative and incurable.'

'No one knows what the future holds. Already there are advances, possible new treatments, encouraging research with stem cells, even prosthetic retinas. However bleak things seem now, a few years down the line it may be different, there may be much that can be done to save, maintain or even improve sight for those with RP. But whether or not that happens, we have our love, our passion, our friendship. Life waits for no one, Lauren. We grasp what we have. We've been blessed to have each other.'

Accepting a tissue, she blew her nose and allowed him to cradle her against him. 'What about a family?' she asked, broaching a subject that disturbed her greatly. 'Professor Murchison said I could have genetic screening but what if the results show I can't risk having children? I don't want you to give things up for me.'

'We'll cross each bridge as we come to it, *chérie*,' he encouraged, and she marvelled at his calmness, his acceptance. 'You are the person who matters most to me. If we can't have children, so be it. If you wanted to, we could consider adoption—and do it properly so any child knows he or she is loved and all about their roots.'

'I really don't deserve you,' she whispered, overwhelmed by his love and understanding and innate goodness.

With a mock growl he gave her a gentle shake. 'Don't say silly things like that. You are the best thing to ever happen to me.'

'But what about your search for your own roots, Gabe? You can't give up on that, on finding out more about your mother,' she insisted, knowing how important it was to him. 'I don't want to hold you back. And don't you want to go back to France? What about your work?'

'Stop inventing obstacles,' he chided with the kind of rumbly chuckle that warmed her right through.

'I—'

His fingers stroked her face as he hushed her. 'I'm still going to research my mother. I've not decided what to do when my contract here ends, but we'll make that choice together. There are all kinds of options. I just heard this week that Lucy is about to give birth again,' he informed her. 'She wants to stay at home with the children and may not come back to work at the surgery for some while, and then only part time. Maybe I can stay on in Penhally.'

'Really?'

'I love it here.' He dropped a kiss on her forehead. 'The solicitor says that the Bartons have decided not to return to England after all. They are going to put the Manor House on the market when my tenancy ends. We could buy it—leaving Oliver and Chloe to buy Gatehouse Cottage, where they are happy. There are a range of possibilities, Lauren. We can do whatever we want.'

Filled with new hope, she pressed closer to him. 'I don't care where we go or what we do—as long as I'm with you. I'm sorry, Gabe. I thought I was doing the right thing. I love you so much and I thought it was unfair to trap you, that you would have a better life without me being a burden and dependent on you. You'd already been so manipulated by Yvette, I didn't want to do the same thing.'

'I know. You temporarily lost your judgement,' he teased,

nipping her earlobe. 'But I forgive you. We put that behind us now and move on. OK?'

'OK.' A rush of peace flowed through her and she allowed herself to believe that maybe it was going to be all right.

Gabriel smiled and drew her to her feet, taking Foxy's lead in his other hand. 'Good. Now, come with me.'

'Where are we going?'

'Home. To bed. We have a week of loving to catch up on and I intend to make the most of every moment.' The sensual promise in his sexily accented voice sent needy desire coursing through her. 'When we come up for air,' he continued with a wicked smile, 'we can start planning our wedding. We can elope like Oliver and Chloe or we can have a big shindig. Whatever you want. Just so long as it is soon.'

'Is that a proposal, Dr Devereux?'

'It is, Ms Nightingale.' He sent her a mock glare in warning. 'And I don't plan to take no for an answer.'

'Just as well I'm going to say yes, then.'

He caught her to him and swung her round, tangling them up with Foxy. Lauren laughed through her tears—happy tears—beyond grateful that Gabriel loved her, believed in her and hadn't given up on her. The fingers of one hand sank into her hair, tilting her head for his kiss. A hungry, deep, thorough kiss that was full of the passion and desire that had flashed between them from the first moment and the love that had grown with each day that had passed.

Gabriel broke off, his breathing as ragged as hers. She could feel his heart thundering as madly as her own. She could also feel the effect their kiss had had on him as she rocked her hips against his. Sweet mercy she had missed this…missed him…so much.

'Home,' he growled with pleasing desperation.

She wasn't at all sure she could wait to get back to the Manor House. Excitement fired her blood and an ache of need clenched deep in her womb. Some time in the next decade or two she might even manage to breathe again. Filled with the same urgency that drove him, she allowed Gabriel to take her hand, linking their fingers, as they all but ran back to his car.

Anticipation clamoured inside her. How could she have gone from despair to blissful joy in such a short time? The sexual tension crackled between them as they drove back through town—a town that had been through so much in the last year or two but which had only grown stronger and more together because of it.

Just like Gabriel and herself.

The future of her eyesight was uncertain, but with Gabriel by her side and secure in their once-in-a-lifetime love, she would no longer be afraid. Wherever they went, whatever they did, together they had everything they would ever need. Each other…united in body, heart and soul.

THE REBEL OF
PENHALLY BAY

CAROLINE ANDERSON

PROLOGUE

HE WASN'T concentrating.

If he'd been concentrating, he might have seen it, but he wasn't. He was miles away, in Cornwall, thanks to his mother and the letter he'd just been handed on his way out of the hospital.

It was all the usual blah.

Hope you're well, Jamie's done well in his exams, goodness knows how, he's so idle, who does that remind you of? Oh, well, if he turns out as well as you he'll be all right but why you want to bury yourself in Africa, goodness knows. I wish you were here, you could keep him in order…

Fat chance of that. They were like peas in a pod, and the only thing that would keep Jamie in order was Jamie, as Sam very well knew.

But then the letter changed.

I've seen Gemma again, by the way, and she asked after you. I can't believe it's ten years since you had that fling with her. You've hardly been back since, but maybe you'll come now, with her here. Bit of an incentive for you—more interesting than your boring old mother. She's a brilliant practice nurse, and still single, though I can't imagine why when she's so gorgeous, but there doesn't seem to be anyone else around for her and she seemed very keen to hear all about you. You missed a chance there, Sam. Maybe you should come home and take up where you left off…

He hadn't read the rest. He'd screwed it up, hurled it into the bin and stalked out into the sun. Damn. He'd meant to leave before dawn, but what with one thing and another, and now the bloody letter…

The bike was loaded, stocked up for the run to the makeshift little clinic thirty miles away, and he had enough to do without distractions. He really—*really*!—didn't need to be thinking about Gemma, or that summer all those years ago. Ten, for God's sake. A whole decade. Ten long, lonely years. And he hadn't *missed* his chance, he'd had it snatched away from him—

'Oh, dammit to hell.'

He kicked the starter viciously, dropped the bike forwards off the stand and straddled it while he fastened his helmet. Why the *hell* was she back in Penhally? And why, more to the point, was she working as a practice *nurse*? So much for her dedication to medicine—but that was just par for the course, really, wasn't it? After all, she hadn't stuck to him, either.

He twisted the throttle, listened to the feeble sound of the little engine and mourned his old bike. Gemma had loved his bike, and they'd gone everywhere on it. They'd been inseparable for a year, every time she'd come down from Bath with her parents to their holiday cottage, and they'd had so much fun.

Not that her parents had approved of him, but, then, they wouldn't, would they? Not with his bad-boy reputation, and they'd had to do a fair amount of sneaking around to be together. But that second summer she'd come down alone after her final school exams, for the last summer before uni, and instead of it being the end, in a way it was to be the beginning—the beginning of the next phase of their lives. They'd got places at the same medical school in Bristol, and everything was panning out perfectly.

So he'd asked her to marry him and crazily, unbelievably, she'd said yes, so on a glorious day in early August they'd made their vows—vows he'd really meant, vows from the heart—and they'd honeymooned in the tumbledown little wooden shack on the beach that was his home for the summer, a retreat from the demands of home, a haven of tranquillity at first and then, with Gemma, a place of paradise—until her parents had come down from Bath and found them there.

They'd gone crazy, and Gemma had been in floods of tears, but she'd stood her ground, told them they were married and he'd shut the door in their faces and held her while she cried.

And then just days later, she'd left a note to say she'd changed her mind about them, and about going to uni. She wasn't sure if she wanted to read medicine after all, and she was deferring for a year and taking time out to think about things, going travelling—Gemma, who'd already seen the world with her wealthy parents—and going alone. She didn't want to see him again. And she was gone, she and her parents who'd obviously meant more to her than he had, their holiday home empty, closed up for the winter.

He'd never seen her again. Not a word, in all these years, all the time he'd been at med school in Bristol, keeping an eye on his family from a close distance and waiting and hoping for her to change her mind—he'd even been to see her parents, but they'd told him she didn't want to see him, and he wasn't going to beg.

So he'd given up on her and finished his degree, then moved to London, trained as a GP, then done a surgical rotation, and now here he was ten years down the line, working for an aid agency in Africa, and still she was following him in his head, in his heart, eating holes in him like some vile flesh-eating bug that wouldn't leave him alone. Asking after him, of all things!

How dare she? How *dare* she ask after him?

And he'd dream about her again tonight, he thought bitterly as he let out the clutch and shot off down the dirt track on the start of his journey. Every time she was mentioned, every time he thought about her, which was pretty much daily, she haunted his sleep, the memory of her laughter, her smile, then those few days and nights they'd had together, so precious, so tender, so ab- solutely bone-deep *right* that he'd just known she was the only woman he'd ever love—the memories were enough to drive him mad.

As mad as his mother, if she thought he was ever going back to Penhally to expose himself to that again. No way. It would kill him. But just to see her again—to touch her—to hold her in his arms, to bury his nose in her hair and smell the warm summer fragrance that was Gemma…

So he wasn't concentrating when he swerved off the

road to avoid the broken-down car. He wasn't thinking that it was strange for the car to be there, that it was possibly a booby trap. He wasn't looking out for the rebels who'd left it there to trick him into going onto the verge.

He was thinking about his wife, about the soft sighs, the taste of her skin, the sobbing screams as she came apart in his arms.

And then he hit the landmine.

CHAPTER ONE

'HERE'S trouble.'

Gemma looked up from the paperwork she was sorting and saw old Doris Trefusis jerk her head towards the door. And her heart hiccuped against her ribs, because there could be only one person she was talking about, and she wasn't ready!

How silly. She'd thought she was prepared, but apparently not, if the pounding of her heart and the shaking of her legs was anything to go by.

Since his mother's stroke yesterday evening, she'd been psyching herself up for Sam coming down from London, but nothing could have prepared her for the emotional impact of her first sight of him in years. Ten years, nine months, two weeks, three days and four and a half hours, to be exact.

Long, lonely years in which she'd ached for him, hungry for any scrap of news, any snippet that would tell her what he was up to. Then last year his distraught mother had told her he'd been hurt in a stupid bike accident and she'd misunderstood and thought for a fleeting second that he'd died. Not for long, but it had devastated her, the pain of loss slamming through her and bringing home to her just how much she still loved him.

But that was ridiculous, because she didn't know him, not any more—if she ever really had. They'd been little more than kids, but he wasn't a kid now. Lord, no.

Not that he'd really been one then, at nineteen, but he certainly wasn't now, she thought, her heart lurching as he came into view. She was standing in the shadows at the back of Reception and she watched spellbound as he sauntered in, tall and broad, more solid than he had been in his late teens, but every bit as gorgeous. A slight limp was the only sign of his injuries, if anything only adding another layer of attraction, and that cocky smile flickering round his mouth was tearing her composure to shreds. But it wasn't for her. He hadn't seen her yet in her shadowy corner, and his smile was for Mrs Trefusis.

'Morning, Doris!' he said, and his deep, husky voice, so painfully familiar, made her heart turn over. 'How are you? Looking as young and gorgeous as ever, I see!'

Their diminutive and elderly cleaner put the magazines she was tidying back in the rack and looked him up and down, her mouth pursed repressively even though her eyes were twinkling. 'Good morning, Dr Cavendish.'

Gemma saw his mouth twitch and his eyebrows shoot up. '*Dr Cavendish*? Whatever happened to young Samuel? I get the feeling I'm still in trouble with you, Doris—or does it have to be Mrs Trefusis now?'

Doris tutted. 'You can hardly expect a warm welcome, Samuel. You've been gone so long, and your poor mother—'

He snorted. 'My poor mother has had my support

continuously since my father walked out seventeen years ago, as you very well know.'

'From a distance. You should have been here, Sam,' she chided gently.

Did his smile lose its sparkle? Maybe, although it didn't waver as he went on, 'Well, I'm here now, so you can start by offering me a cup of tea. I'm as dry as a desert.'

Doris sniffed. 'I'm not sure you deserve one.'

He grinned and gave her a slow, lazy wink. 'You're just saying that. You love me really,' he said, and Gemma watched old Doris Trefusis melt under the megawatt charm.

'Go away with you,' she said, blushing and flapping her hand at him. 'I'll bring it in—Dr Tremayne's half expecting you. I might even be able to find you one of Hazel's fairings if those doctors have left you any. She made an extra batch specially when she knew you were coming home.'

'What, to help lure me back in?' he said drily, glancing at Hazel Furse, the practice manager, with a wry smile. Then, as if he'd only just become aware of her presence at the back of Reception, he turned and met Gemma's eyes, his face suddenly expressionless.

'Gemma.'

That was all, just the one word, but it stopped her heart in its tracks. *Oh, Sam. Were your eyes always so blue? Like a Mediterranean sky at night, cobalt blue, piercing through me.*

'Hello, Sam.' Her voice sounded forced, and she had to swallow the sudden lump of emotion in her throat. 'Welcome home.'

His jaw tightened, and he nodded. 'Thank you.

Hopefully it won't be for too long. Mrs Furse, would you be kind enough to tell Dr T. I'm here, please.'

'Sam! Good to see you! I saw you drive up. Come on in. Doris, I don't know if you could rustle up some tea…'

'It's all in hand, Dr Tremayne. Kettle's already on.'

Without another word to her, Sam turned his back on Gemma and limped into Nick's surgery, the older man's arm slung round his shoulders, and the door closed behind them.

She let her breath out then, unaware that she'd been holding it ever since he'd come in, holding back a part of herself that was too vulnerable, too tender and delicate and scarred to let him see.

He was back. Sam was back, but not the way she'd always dreamed of, had waited breathlessly for ever since she'd returned to Penhally last year in the hope that he might find out she was here and come back to her. Instead he'd come back for yet another family crisis, another duty visit, another call on his endless good nature and sense of responsibility that nobody else ever seemed to recognise.

But he hadn't come back for her, and she realised now, after seeing him, after the way he'd looked at her, that he never would. And the pain was devastating…

'Are you all right?'

She opened her eyes and saw Kate Althorp, one of their midwives, watching her with concern in her all-too-intelligent eyes.

'I'm fine, Kate.'

'Are you sure? You look a little pale.'

'I'm fine,' she said again, more firmly, because if Kate didn't let her go and get on, she was going to do something stupid like burst into tears in Reception. And there was no way she was letting anyone see her show so much as a flicker of emotion.

Even if her heart was being torn in two…

Sam stood at the window and stared back along Harbour Road at the devastation left behind by the flood last autumn, putting Gemma's face out of his mind. 'What happened to the Anchor Hotel?' he asked, although in truth he didn't care. It and its patrons had never appealed to him, and he was sure it had been mutual.

'It's been demolished—the new additions that were never properly built—and they're rebuilding it. There were a lot of properties damaged around the bottom of Bridge Street and Gull Close. There are lots of people still out of their homes.'

'It must have been quite something.'

'It was. It's a miracle the bridge survived. The noise was tremendous.'

'I'm sure. I missed all the news, I'm afraid—I was in hospital.'

'Yes, I know, your mother said you'd had an accident on your bike. I see you're still limping a bit. How are you?'

'Really?' He shrugged. 'Better. Frustrated by the slow progress, but better. So—I gather your crew are all married now?' he said, changing the subject to one he was more comfortable with, and Nick smiled, his lean face relaxing slightly.

'Yes, they are. And Jack and Lucy have both got families. In fact Lucy's decided she doesn't want to come back, so there's a job here if you're at a loose end…'

Sam snorted softly and shook his head at his old friend and mentor. 'I owe you a great deal, Dr T., but not that much.' Not while his wife was working here. 'Anyway, I'll be busy.'

'Yes, of course. How is your mother? She was pretty bad when I saw her yesterday evening, on her way in, but I phoned this morning and they said she's doing well.'

'Yes, she is, thanks. They've got her in the specialist stroke unit, and they scanned her straight away and put her on mega clot-busters, and she's improving already.'

'That's excellent. We're lucky to have the stroke unit. It's a real asset, but she'll still need some support for a while. Is that going to be a problem for you?'

'Not really.' He'd spent the last few months torn between physio and a desk job he loathed, trying to earn his keep at the charity he'd been working for when he'd been blown up and wondering where the hell to go from here. Next to all of that, this further infringement of his personal choice was small potatoes.

But his mother's life—well, that was certainly going to change, and if she had her way, change his with it. 'She's OK,' he said, trying to sound convincing. 'It's her left side, mostly her hand and her face, but that's just the visible stuff. I have no idea what else might have been affected or what she'll get back with this intensive treatment. Hopefully she'll make a full recovery, but I expect the full extent will reveal itself in time. I would have thought there are bound to be some after-effects.'

'Any idea of the cause?'

He shook his head. 'Not as yet. They're looking into it—she's having an echocardiogram and a carotid scan, and she's on a monitor, but so far they've drawn a blank. Her blood pressure's dreadful, too, and she's put on weight. Her diet's always been atrocious—she's addicted to chocolate, always has been, and the only reason she isn't enormous is that she hardly eats anything else. God alone knows what Jamie's been surviving on, there's no food in the house to speak of, and she's obviously depressed.'

'We'll sort her out, Sam, once she's home. Don't worry. And how's your brother coping?'

Sam turned away from the window and eased into a chair with a sigh, toying with one of Hazel's biscuits. 'By running away from it, I think, but he's been worrying her for a while. He's a nightmare. It's all too familiar, I'm afraid. Been there, done that, as the saying goes. I gather he's in trouble with the police as well, just to add insult to injury.'

'He is. He's got in with a bad crowd—Gary Lovelace amongst others.'

Sam frowned. 'Lovelace?'

'Yes—do you remember him? Proper little tearaway as a child, and he's no better now. He's a year older than Jamie, I think.'

He trawled his brains. 'I remember the name—probably the father's. Always in and out of the slammer for one thing or another. Petty stuff mostly, if I remember. So Gary's leading my little brother astray, is he? Damn.'

'I think he's willing to be led,' Nick said wryly. 'I've tried, Sam. I can't get through to him. I don't know him like I knew you—because my children have all grown up now, I hardly see his generation, whereas you were always in the house—usually in the kitchen eating us out of house and home or getting up to mischief in the garden. I can remember a few spontaneous bonfires…'

He gave Nick a crooked grin over the rim of his mug. 'Hmm. My "SAS" phase. Sorry about that.'

'Don't be sorry. You never really did any harm, and you were always welcome. Annabel had a really soft spot for you, you know.'

He met Nick's eyes with a pensive smile. 'I was very fond of her. You must miss her.'

'I do. She was a good woman. She used to worry about you, you know, and how your mother relied on you so heavily. It was no wonder you went off the rails. You had more than enough on your plate.'

'Yeah, well, that doesn't change, does it? I can't believe I'm back picking up the pieces all over again.'

'I can. You were a good boy, and you've turned into a good man, just as I knew you would.'

'Oh, that's just so much bull, Nick, and you know it. I wouldn't be here at all if I had the slightest damned excuse to get away.'

'Yes, you would—and your mother needs you. She misses you. Lots of people do.'

He gave a wry snort. 'Hardly. They all remember me as a hell-raiser. Even Doris Trefusis tore me off a strip on the way in, and I have no doubt Audrey Baxter won't waste a moment telling me I'm not welcome home.'

'Ah, no—you'll be spared that one. Mrs Baxter died in the flood.'

'Really? Poor woman.' He gave a wry smile. 'Not that she'd say that about me. She was always horrible to me—she made damn sure everyone knew everything I ever did, to the point that I used to do things in front of her and place bets with myself that my mother would know before I got home.'

'You were just misunderstood.'

He wasn't so sure about that. He grunted and looked around, not wanting to get into the past he was so keen to avoid. 'So—what's going on here? It looks a bit different to the last time I saw it. I haven't been in here since I did work experience when your brother was the GP.'

'Well, it's certainly changed since then. We reopened it five years ago.' He paused, his face troubled, and Sam realised he looked suddenly a great deal older. As well he might. Then he seemed to pull himself together and stood up. 'Come and have a look round. I doubt if you'll recognise it now. We've extended out the back, built a new minor injuries unit and X-ray and plaster rooms, but we're also planning to build another extension on the side into what used to be Althorps'. The boatyard burned down in September, and it worked in our favour because we were able to buy part of the site—do you remember Kate Althorp? James's widow?'

'Vaguely. I know the name and I remember James dying in the storm.'

A quick frown flitted across Nick's brow. 'Yes. Well, her brother-in-law wanted to sell up, and without the income Kate's half was redundant, so they cashed in on the insurance and sold the site. We bought enough land at the side of the surgery to extend it further, and to provide some more consulting rooms so we can extend the facilities offered by the MIU, which will give us a much better use of our space here. Come and see. You'll be impressed, I hope.'

He was—but he wasn't fooled. Nick was angling, but Sam wasn't biting. Under any other circumstances—but they weren't. They were what they were, and what they were was too damned hard to contemplate. They were standing at the top of the stairs discussing Nick's vision for the future of the surgery as a multi-disciplinary health centre with dental and osteopathy services when Nick was called to the phone, and he left Sam there and went into a consulting room to take the call.

And Gemma, who'd been the one to find Nick and tell him he was wanted on the phone, was left standing there with Sam, her soft grey-blue eyes wary, her body language defensive. As if he was in some way a threat.

That was a laugh. She was far more of a threat to him than he would ever be to her. She was the one who'd walked away.

He held her eyes, hardening himself to the expression in them, refusing to be drawn in. 'My mother said you were back.'

'Yes, I've been working here for a year now. How is she, Sam? Nick said she was improving.'

'Doing really well. Rather shocked, I think. We all are. She's only fifty-seven.'

'I know, but she's had high blood pressure for years, and her diet's a bit lacking.'

'What, in anything other than chocolate?' he said with a wry grin, and then felt his heart turn over when she smiled back. Oh, God, he wanted her—wanted to haul her into his arms, up against his chest and bury his nose in that thick, soft waterfall of hair, to breathe her in and see if she still smelled the same.

'She said you're still single,' he told her with an edge to his voice, and the smile faded instantly as she looked away.

'Well, we both know that's not true,' she said under her breath.

'I never could work it out. All this time, and you haven't asked for a divorce. And I wonder why not.'

'Well, you haven't, either.'

'No. It's not really been an issue. I've been busy.' Busy trying to forget her, busy pretending to himself that he didn't need a social life, that his marriage was just on hold and one day…

'I gathered. In Africa, saving the world. So how did you fall off this bike?'

'Oh, you know me—always taking risks, pushing my luck, playing the fool.'

'You're thirty, Sam. Isn't it time you grew up and stopped worrying your mother sick?'

He swallowed. Oh, he was grown up. He'd grown up the day he'd come home late from work with a bunch of flowers for her and found her letter.

Nick returned from taking his call. 'Sorry about that. Right, where were we?'

'I'll leave you to it. Send Linda my love,' Gemma said, and fled back into her room, her heart pounding, her legs like jelly and her stupid, stupid hormones racing through her body and dragging it from an eleven-year slumber into vibrant, screaming wakefulness…

'So—what do you think of the set-up?'

Nick had concluded his guided tour after a walk through the minor injuries suite downstairs and a quick chat with Lauren, the physio, a local girl whom Sam vaguely remembered, and they were back in Reception when Nick asked the question, his expression hopeful despite the simple words.

Except of course there was nothing simple about them, and it didn't take a genius to read the sub-text.

'Excellent—but I'm not falling for it, Nick,' Sam said softly. 'I don't want to work here.' Not with Gemma.

'Why? You need a job, we need a doctor. Your mother and brother need you and, frankly, looking at you, I reckon you need us. Can't I talk you into it—at least for a few weeks until we can get someone to take over? We'd be hugely grateful, and it would give you something productive to do while your mother recovers.'

'I've got plenty to do. The garden can't have been touched for years—'

'Gardening leave?' Nick said softly, his eyes mocking. 'At least think about it. Maybe it's time to come home, Sam.'

But then Gemma came downstairs again, and their eyes locked and pain lanced through him.

'I don't think so,' he muttered, and, turning on his heel, he crossed the reception area in two strides and slapped the swing door out of his way.

Then and only then did he breathe again...

She didn't know how she got through the rest of the day.

Sam had left the building, but his aura hung in the air, his presence filling every corner and bringing a huge lump to her throat every time she allowed herself the luxury of thinking of him.

Not that she had much time, because she had a busy afternoon surgery and afterwards she was due to go up to the high school for a careers evening. And on her way home to change, of course, she had to drive past his mother's house, and his car was on the drive. At least she assumed it was his car, because it had a hire-car logo in the window.

Oh, why was she so fixated on him? She couldn't afford to let herself do this. He was passing through, doing what he'd done over and over again, coming back only for long enough to do what was necessary and this time, just for good measure, tearing the scab off her wounded heart.

If she let him. She didn't have to, of course. She could keep him firmly at a distance. She'd heard Nick ask him to stay, seen him leave the building as if it were on fire.

Sam wouldn't be staying.

And she wouldn't be letting him into her heart.

'Sam! Hello, darling, I hoped you'd come.'

'Hiya. How are you? You sound better—your speech is much clearer. That's fantastic.' He brushed a kiss over his mother's drooping cheek—was it less noticeable?—and eased himself down into the chair beside her bed. 'I've brought you some grapes.'

'Not chocolate?'

He gave a short laugh. 'No, Mum, not chocolate. Grapes are good for you and, besides, I like them.' He helped himself to a handful and settled back in the chair, one foot crossed over the other knee. 'Anyway, I want to talk to you. About Jamie.'

'Oh, Sam, where is he?' she slurred, her eyes welling. 'I thought you'd bring him.'

'No, sorry, I had to walk the dog, and when I got back he'd gone out—he sent me a text, though. He had to be at school, he said.'

'He doesn't want to see me.'

He didn't tell her that the thought had occurred to him, too. 'No, it's legit. I rang the school—it's a careers evening and he's apparently volunteered to help out. I'm going over there as soon as I leave you to make sure he's there and talk to the staff.'

'Oh, dear,' she said ruefully.

'Mmm. I'm sure they'll have lots to say, but so have I. Don't worry, I'll sort Jamie out. You just concentrate on getting better.'

She gave a funny little laugh, then her face creased. 'How's Digger? Does he miss me?'

Sam smiled. 'I think he does, but he's enjoying his walks. We had a lovely run on the beach this morning at dawn.' Down to the other beach, to sit on the stumps of the old cabin and torture himself with the memories...

'Don't let him off the lead. He'll go down a hole.'

Sam laughed softly. 'I do remember you telling me how he got his name. I'll keep him on the lead, don't worry.'

'So—did you go to the surgery?' she asked after the slightest pause, and he braced himself for the inevitable questions.

'Yes, I saw Nick.'

'And Gemma?'

He felt his mouth tighten and consciously relaxed it. 'Yes, I saw Gemma. She sends her love. She seems to know you quite well.'

'Oh, she does. She runs the cont...'

She trailed off, exasperated by her uncooperative tongue, and Sam put in, 'The continuing care clinic?'

'Mmm. She does my blood pressure. She's beautiful, isn't she? Pretty girl.'

'I didn't notice,' he lied. 'I was a bit busy.'

God, it was a wonder his nose wasn't longer than Pinocchio's! He put the grapes back on his mother's bed table before he crushed them all inadvertently, moved her newspaper and picked up her weakened left hand.

'Come on, let's do some physio. We need to keep these fingers moving.'

She shook her head. 'They just won't.'

'They will. Keep trying. Here, come on, I'll help you,' he said, and, taking her fingers in his, he started working on them, giving himself something to do apart from conjuring Gemma's image into his crazed mind.

But it didn't work, her image was still there larger than life, her soft, wounded, wary eyes torturing him, so after a few minutes he put his mother's hand down and stood up. 'Right, I'm off to the school to sort out young Jamie. I'll see you tomorrow. Be good.'

'What else?' she said sadly, and her eyes filled again, ripping at his conscience. 'Bring him—come for longer. I miss you, Sam. You don't know…'

His conscience stabbed him again, and he sighed softly. 'I do. You tell me often enough. But my life's not here, Mum.'

'Could be.'

'No. No, it couldn't. Just the moment you're better and I'm given the all-clear by the physios, I'm going back to Africa.'

Her fingers tightened on his, her right hand clutching at him in desperation. 'No, Sam! Don't! You can't go back!'

That was probably true, although not the way she meant it, but he wasn't giving in. Not yet. 'Mum, I have to go,' he repeated, and, freeing his hand, he dropped a swift kiss on her cheek and walked out.

'Sam! I didn't expect to see you here. It's the last place!'

'Well, ditto,' he said, and his smile looked strained. 'Have you seen Jamie?'

'He's here somewhere,' Gemma said, trying to control her see-sawing emotions. 'Doing the name badges and the drinks for the parents? He will have done the careers thing last year, so he's only helping. I don't like to be unkind, but it doesn't sound like him.'

'Maybe it was just a reason not to go and see Mum. He hasn't been in yet. I think he's scared, but while I'm here I need to speak to his teachers and find out what I can about him hanging around with Gary Lovelace.'

'Well, Lachlan D'Ancey's here, he'll fill you in. He's Chief Constable now, but he just comes to support the school and sell the police force. Nick Tremayne's here, too. If Lachlan's busy I expect Nick could use some help, there are always lots of people thinking of studying medicine.'

He shook his head. 'I don't think the school would be interested in my support. I wasn't exactly their star pupil.'

'That's rubbish, Sam, you got four As at A level!'

'Only because I was constantly being grounded.'

She smiled slightly, remembering the tales of how rebellious he'd been, how he'd pushed everyone to the limit of their patience, worried his mother senseless and alienated half of the town.

Which, of course, had only made him even more attractive.

She dragged her eyes from Sam and looked at the girl who was hovering behind him. 'Hi. Did you want to see me?'

'Um—yes, please. I'm thinking of going into nursing, and I wondered if you could tell me about it.'

Out of the corner of her eye she saw Sam lift his hand in farewell as he walked away, and she stifled a sigh of regret.

Foolish, foolish woman. It's over. Forget it.

But she couldn't, and for the rest of the evening her eyes were constantly searching for him, and every time they found him, her silly, stupid heart would lurch against her ribs.

It might be over, but apparently she couldn't forget it. Not for the last nearly eleven years, and certainly not now, with Sam right here under her nose, his presence reminding her of everything she'd lost…

CHAPTER TWO

'SAM—good to see you.'

He stifled a wry grin at the blatant lie from the man who'd had altogether too much to do with him in his youth. 'Hello, Lachlan. How are you?'

'Very well. Great, actually. Married again.'

Sam hadn't known he'd got unmarried, but he wasn't surprised that yet another thing had happened in Penhally without him knowing. He'd done his best to distance himself, so it was hardly rocket science, and he made some trite and socially acceptable remark and then Lachlan brought the conversation, not unexpectedly, around to Jamie.

'Your brother's getting himself in a bit of bother these days,' he murmured. 'You want to have a word with him. He's going to end up with a criminal record if he goes on like this, and it's a crying shame because he's a good lad really. Sharp as a tack, which is half his trouble, of course, like it was yours. What he needs is a good role model.'

'Well, don't look at me,' Sam said with a low laugh. 'I'm the last person to give him advice.'

'I disagree. You're just the person—he reminds me a lot of you.'

'What—loud and unruly?'

'No—lost,' he said, and Sam looked away, uncomfortable with Lachlan's all too accurate interpretation of his youthful emotions. 'You need to get him out of the influence of that young Gary Lovelace. He's a nasty piece of work—God alone knows what Jamie sees in him, but he's leading your little brother into all sorts of mischief.'

Sam straightened. 'Not drugs?'

'Not that we know of, but I shouldn't be surprised. But Gary's a thief, and a bully, like his father and his little brother, and you need to get Jamie away from him before something bad happens.'

Sam sighed inwardly. This was the last thing he needed.

'So how's your mother? I was sorry to hear about her stroke—she seems far too young.'

'Yes. But strokes can happen to anyone, from tiny babies upwards. She's making great progress, but we just need to know why it happened to stop it happening again.'

'You ought to speak to Gemma. It was Gemma who found her. She went round after work and checked up on her because she was worried.'

'Did she?' he said softly, wondering why Gemma hadn't mentioned it. Because she didn't want to talk to him any more than she had to? Very likely. He didn't really want to talk to her, either, and so far all their exchanges had been carefully contained, with all hell breaking loose just under the surface—at least, on his side. But if Gemma had found his mother, she could easily have been responsible for saving her life, and at the very least he ought to thank her. Not even he was that churlish.

'I'll go and have a word. Thanks, Lachlan—and if you hear anything I need to know about Jamie, let me know.'

'Will do. And you do the same.'

'Sure.'

He went back towards Gemma, but there was a crowd of young girls around her, so he wandered over to the desk where Jamie was handing out name tags and soft drinks to parents.

'Checking up on me?' Jamie said, his mouth set in a defiant line, and Sam just smiled.

'No. I don't need to, I've got the rest of Penhally doing that, by all accounts. How long are you going to be here?'

'Another few minutes, then I'm going out with my friends.'

Sam frowned. 'Why? It's a school night. You've got your exams in a few weeks, you should be working.'

'Nah. I've got it all under control, Sam. You don't have to come home and play the heavy brother with me.'

'That's not what I'm hearing.'

'Well, tough. What do they know?'

'Well, I gather Mr D'Ancey knows quite a lot about you—probably rather more than is healthy.'

Jamie's eyes slid away and his face took on a defensive cast. 'Whatever. I'm out tonight. My work's up to date, I've got nothing outstanding—and don't even think about suggesting I tidy my bedroom. All I hear from Mum is that I'm just like you.'

Sam stifled a smile and gave up—for now. 'OK. But not late. Ten.'

'Ten-thirty.'

'Ten-fifteen—and if you're so much as thirty seconds late, you're grounded for a week.'

'What? Where do you get off—?'

'Suit yourself. Ten-fifteen or you're grounded. I'll see you later.'

And without giving his brother a chance to argue any further, he walked away. Gemma was free now, and he crossed to her quickly before another wannabe nurse appeared. 'Can we talk?'

Her eyes widened with alarm, and he realised she'd misunderstood. Or maybe she hadn't, not really, but he wasn't getting into all that now. He could barely keep a lid on his emotions as it was. The last thing he needed was to have a deeply personal conversation in public with the woman who'd shredded his heart. 'About my mother,' he added, and saw the alarm recede.

'Sure. When are you thinking of?'

'After you finish? I haven't eaten yet, I don't know if you have, but I thought we could go up to the Smugglers' and have something there while we talk.'

She nodded slowly. 'That would be fine. Give me another few minutes, and if nobody else comes, we can go.'

'Fine.' He gave her a brisk nod, and walked off to find Nick.

'Ah, Sam, just the man. This is Dr Cavendish—he's been working in Africa with an aid agency—was it Doctors Without Borders?'

'No, but it's similar,' he said. 'Why?'

'Young David here is considering medicine and wants to work in that field. Can you give him some advice?'

He dredged up a smile for the youngster. 'Sure. What do you want to know?'

'Sorry about that, I got caught up.'

'So did I. Nick found me a young lad with a death

wish. He wants to work in Africa—he's talking about doing a gap year with an aid agency before he goes to med school.'

'So what did you say?'

'Don't do it. Are you all done now?'

'Yes.'

'Then let's get out of here—have you got your car?'

'Yes. Shall I meet you up at the pub?'

'Good idea.'

He followed her down past the surgery to the harbour and turned right along Harbour Road past the shrouded site of the Anchor Hotel, over the River Lanson at the bottom of Bridge Street and along to the end, past Nick Tremayne's house and his mother's house next door, then up the hill, past the little church on the left with the lighthouse beyond it on the headland, and then over the rise to the Smugglers' Inn.

The place was doing well, if the number of cars outside on a week night was anything to go by, and he parked in the last space and got out, breathing deeply and drawing the fresh sea air into his lungs.

God, that smelt good. It was one of the few things about Penhally that he missed—apart from Gemma, who was walking towards him now, her eyes unreadable in the dimly lit car park. Her hands were stuffed into the pockets of her coat, and she looked wary and uncertain, as if she was regretting saying yes.

She didn't need to. He wasn't a threat to her. He had no intention of getting into any personal territory at all. Not even slightly.

'Lots of cars,' he said, aiming for something neutral. 'Do you think we'll get a seat?'

She looked round and shrugged. 'I don't know. We

could always sit outside on the terrace,' she said doubtfully.

Hell, no. They'd spent whole evenings on that terrace, and it was the last place he wanted to go. 'It's not warm enough, the food might get cold.'

'There might be room inside.'

'We'll see.' Oh, God, endless pleasantries, and all he really wanted to do was touch her, thread her hair through his fingers, feel her body soft against his...

He yanked open the door of the pub and ushered her in, and as they walked into the bar, a hush fell.

'Well, by all the saints, young Samuel. Come home to cause havoc, have 'e, lad?'

'Ignore him,' Gemma muttered, but he went over to old Fred Spencer and shook his hand.

'How are you, Mr Spencer?'

'Better'n you, by all accounts. Why you limpin'?'

'Fell off my bike,' he said economically. 'And don't say it.'

'Well, I 'spect it *was* your fault.'

'Why not? It always was, wasn't it?'

The old man cracked a laugh and turned back to his companions. 'Always had to have the last word, young Sam.'

Only not always. Not with Gemma. There'd been no chance to have the last word, to talk things through, to get to the bottom of it—and he wasn't starting now.

Leaving Fred with his mates, they went over to the bar and ordered drinks and scanned the specials board.

'The steak's still good,' Gemma said. 'I think I'll have that—just the small one.'

'Rare?'

She nodded, surprised and yet not that he would have

remembered. They'd always had the steak frites in here, and it had always been good, and she'd always had it rare.

Listen to her! Always, indeed. What was she thinking? It had only been—what? Ten, maybe twelve times in all, over more than a year? But it was all the time they'd had together, and it had been precious, every last second of it.

He ordered the steak for her, but to her surprise he ordered beef Stroganoff for himself—just in case she thought it was all too cosy down Memory Lane? She wasn't sure, not sure at all, about any of it, and she didn't really have any idea what she was doing here with him, tearing herself apart, when she could have been safely tucked up at home.

'Ah, there's a table here,' he said, and led her across the room to where a couple were just leaving. He held the chair for her to sit down, and as he did so, his hand brushed her arm.

Dear God, he thought, desperately resisting the need to touch her again, to reach out and let his fingers linger over that soft, slender arm, to run them over her shoulder, to slide the lightweight jersey top aside and press his lips to her skin…

He retreated to the safety of the other side of the table and sat down opposite her, flicking his eyes over the menu even though he'd already ordered, staring out of the window as she shuffled in her seat, organising her bag, placing her drink carefully in the centre of the beer mat with great precision.

And then, once they were settled and there was nothing left to fidget with, there was a silence that was so full of unspoken words it was like a roar in his head. And he had to break it or go mad.

'So—you came back to Penhally,' he said, trying to find something neutral to talk about and failing dismally at the first hurdle.

She glanced away, but not before he'd seen a shadow in her eyes. 'Yes. I love it here.'

Especially when he wasn't there. His mouth tipped in a mocking smile. 'I thought it was too small for you? Too pedestrian. Too provincial. Wasn't that why you left to see the world and didn't come back?'

Hardly. It was the place where her heart was, where she'd found a love she'd thought would last forever, but she couldn't tell him that or she'd have to tell him why she'd gone, so she just gave him a level look and lied in her teeth.

'You know why I left—to go travelling while I considered my career options. And you can talk about leaving to see the world, Sam. It's me who's living here now. You've hardly been home.'

'*Et tu, Brute*? Isn't this where you tell me that I've failed my mother and failed my brother and ought to move home like a good little boy? Well, news flash, Gemma. I've got a life now, and it's not here. And it never will be.' Thanks to her. His jaw tightened, and she felt a stab of pain for him, and for herself.

'I'm sorry,' she said softly. 'It's none of my business. But for what it's worth, I don't think you should come home for your mother or your brother. You did more than enough for them, Sam, and you've got two sisters who don't live a million miles away who could be putting more into this than they are. But maybe you should think about coming home for you.'

'Oh, for God's sake, what *is* it about Penhally and everyone telling me what to do?'

'I wasn't telling you—'

'Weren't you? Well, it sounded like it from where I'm sitting.'

Or maybe that was his conscience, he thought, guilt racking him yet again for the hurt look he'd put in her eyes.

'I don't want to go into this. I brought you here to talk about my mother's stroke, not me,' he said after a moment in which they'd both taken a deep breath and regrouped. 'I gather you found her last night?'

She met his eyes squarely, her own still reproachful. 'Yes—she came in the day before yesterday to see me for a routine blood-pressure check, and she mentioned that she'd noticed her heart doing something funny in the evening a couple of times. I had a word with Adam—Adam Donnelly, one of our doctors—and he suggested we should do an ECG and then refer her to St Piran for some tests.'

'And?'

'I did the ECG yesterday, and there was nothing out of the ordinary at all, but I was just a bit worried about her. Her blood pressure was up again, and—I don't know, she just didn't seem right. And she looked a bit strained around the eyes. So after work I popped in. There was no reply to the doorbell, so I went round the back and opened the door because I could hear Digger whining, and I found her at the kitchen table, looking chalky grey and sweaty and feeling terrible. And she had a killer headache, apparently, and she said she'd had some kind of convulsion, but I noticed her mouth was drooping a bit and then she just lost her speech. It was a classic stroke, so I called Nick and got the ambulance on its way, and alerted the specialist unit, and—well, I don't know how she is now. I went in with her last night because Jamie wasn't around and I didn't want her to be alone, but I haven't had time to get up there again. I was going to go and see her in my lunch break but I thought you might be there, and then there was the careers evening so I just haven't had a chance. So how is she? Really? She must have been so frightened.'

He nodded slowly. 'I think so. But who wouldn't be? It's a really big thing, isn't it, and it could have been so much worse if you hadn't checked on her. I hate to think what would have happened if you hadn't. It sounds as if your prompt action's made a huge difference to the impact of her stroke, and if you hadn't gone in—well, talking to the staff it's clear that without immediate help she could easily have died, so thank you. She sends you her love, by the way. She seems very fond of you.'

Gemma gave a soft, wry little laugh. 'I can't imagine why. I bully her dreadfully.'

'She needs it. So—about this heart thing…'

'Mmm. I mean, obviously it hasn't been investigated properly yet, but I was wondering—do you think she could have some kind of AF?'

'Atrial fibrillation? Could well be. It would fit. I just can't understand how she hasn't felt it in her chest before, if she's got AF and it's sustained enough that she's forming clots. You'd think you'd feel it if your heart's not beating right.'

'Not everyone does feel it, though, and atrial fibrillation is notoriously tricky to control.'

'Especially if you OD on stimulants like tea and coffee and very dark chocolate. It's always given her the odd palpitation, and maybe it's just accustomed her to a funny heartbeat from time to time, and then the AF doesn't feel so very different—'

'Steak frites and beef Stroganoff?'

'Thanks, Tony,' Sam said, leaning back so the landlord could put their plates down. He paused to welcome Sam back.

'Good to see you again. How are things? Sorry about your mother.'

'Thanks,' he said, feeling a little awkward because clearly everyone knew about her, recognised him and also recognised the fact that he'd been notable by his absence. Then he chatted to Gemma for a few moments, and while he listened to them, Sam watched her, her face attentive, her eyes crinkling with humour when Tony made a joke, and all the time her lips were moving, soft and warm, bare of lipstick but moist from the occasional flick of her tongue, and it was getting increasingly difficult to sit there and pretend that he felt nothing for her, this woman who'd torn his heart apart.

His wife, for heaven's sake.

Then Tony moved away, and he turned his attention to his food, and for a while they were both silent. Then she lifted her head and said, 'You know you made that remark about David having a death wish because he wanted to go to Africa? What did you mean?'

He shrugged. 'It was just a joke.'

'No. You meant something, and you said you'd told him not to go, and when you were talking to Fred just now about the accident—what happened, Sam?' she asked softly. 'Did you really just fall off your bike?'

He sighed and set down his fork. 'Really? In a manner of speaking,' he said, and then bluntly, because he still wanted to lash out, he went on, 'I hit a landmine.'

Her face bleached of colour, and he caught her glass just as it slipped through her fingers. 'Careful, anybody would think you still cared, and we all know that's not true,' he said with bitter irony.

She sat back, her eyes filling, and closed them quickly, but not quickly enough because a single tear slipped down her cheek and that old guilt thing kicked in again. 'Actually I was thinking of your mother—how she would have coped if…'

'If I'd died?' he prompted, trying not to look at the tear, and she sucked in a tiny breath.

'Don't.' She swallowed and opened her eyes, reaching for her glass. He still had it in his hand, and as he passed it to her, their fingers met and he felt the shock race through him again.

Damn. Still, after all these years…

She took a sip and put it down, then met his eyes again. 'So what really happened, Sam? With the landmine?'

He made himself concentrate on something other than the little trail the tear had made on her cheek. 'There was a booby trap—a car in the road. I swerved round it, not paying attention, and the back wheel caught the anti-personnel mine and it hurled the back of the bike up into the air. Luckily the panniers were rammed with equipment, which protected me from the blast, but the force of the explosion threw me forwards onto the ground.'

'And?'

'And I broke my collar bone and my ankle,' he told her, grossly oversimplifying it. 'Oh, and tore the rotator cuff in my left shoulder.'

She nodded slowly. 'I've noticed you don't use your left hand very much.'

'Got out of the habit,' he lied, and turned his attention back to his food, leaving her sitting there in silence, struggling with the image of him being hurled through the air and smashed into the ground.

She felt sick. It could have been so much worse, she thought, and set down her knife and fork, unable to eat while her emotions churned round inside her and the man she loved was just a foot away, his eyes fixed on his plate, obviously in a hurry now to finish his meal and leave. He'd only wanted to thank her for finding his mother, and he'd done that, and now he just wanted to go.

Fair enough. So did she, and she was about to get up and leave when Tony stopped by their table.

'Everything all right?' he asked, and she nodded and smiled at him and picked up her knife and fork again, forcing herself to finish her food before it was not only the flavour of sawdust, but stone cold with it.

'So how long will she be in?' he asked the registrar the next day.

'Just a few days. We want to get her anticoagulation sorted and then she can be discharged.'

He felt a flicker of fear, the tightening of the noose of responsibility, and consciously slowed his breathing down.

'Surely she can't come home until she's able to look after herself?'

'But I gather you're at home now, so that's not a problem, is it?'

He arched a brow. 'You want me to look after my mother? Attend to her personal care?'

'Why not? You're a doctor.'

But she's my *mother*! he wanted to scream, but it was

pointless. She would have done the same for him, and it was only because it made him feel trapped that he was so desperate to get away. And last night, with Gemma— well, it had been an emotional minefield every bit as dangerous to his health as the one he'd encountered on the bike, and he hadn't been able to get away from the pub quick enough.

He'd used Digger as an excuse, and he'd gone back to the house, collected the dog and taken him for a long walk along the beach in the moonlight, right down to the far end and back while he thought about Gemma and how he still wanted her so badly it was tearing holes in him.

He couldn't do it—couldn't stay here. He just wanted to get away, to go back to Africa and lick his wounds in peace. Well, not peace, exactly, but ano- nymity, at least, without the benefit of the residents of Penhally telling him he'd deserted his mother and let his brother run wild and failed them both, with Gemma in the background reminding him that he'd failed her, too, or why the hell else would she have left him when ev- erything between them had seemed so incredibly perfect?

But he couldn't go back to Africa, because he couldn't operate, because his collar bone hadn't just broken, it had shredded his left brachial plexus and damaged the sensory nerves to his left hand, and his shoulder was still weak from the tear to his rotator cuff when he'd landed on it, and his leg—well, his ankle would heal slowly and improve with time, unlike his hand, but in the meantime he'd struggle to stand for hours operating, even if he could feel what he was doing with his hand, which he couldn't, and he couldn't ride a bike, not with his left arm so compromised and his ankle inflexible, so it was pointless thinking about it and tormenting himself.

And his mother aside, there was the problem of Jamie, who had come in last night at seventeen minutes past ten. Late, but not so late that he was going to say anything, and so they'd established an uneasy truce.

But the need to get away was overwhelming, and after he left the hospital he drove up onto Bodmin Moor and walked for hours with Digger over the rough grass and heather until his ankle was screaming and he wasn't sure how he'd get back, his mind tortured with memories of Gemma, lying there with him in the heather and kissing him back for hour after hour until he thought he'd die of frustration.

Huh. No way. He'd discovered through painful and bitter experience that you didn't die of frustration, you just wished you could, because that would bring an end to it at last.

He sat down on a granite outcrop with the panting Jack Russell at his feet and stared out over the barren, wild landscape while he waited for the pain in his ankle to subside. He could see a few sturdy little ponies grazing and, in the distance, a small herd of Devon Red bullocks turned out for fattening on the spring grass. But apart from that and the inevitable sheep dotted about like cotton-wool balls in the heather, there was nothing there but the wide-open skies and the magical, liquid sound of the curlews.

And gradually, as the warmth of the spring sun seeped into his bones and the bleak, familiar landscape welcomed him home, he accepted what he had to do— what he'd known, ever since he'd had the phone call about her stroke, that he would have to do.

He didn't like it—he didn't like it one bit—but he had no choice, and he would do it, because that was who he was. He would stay at home and look after his mother until she was better, he'd get his brother back on the rails, and then he'd look at his future.

Always assuming he could get off this damned moorland without calling out the Air Ambulance!

'Lauren?'

The physiotherapist looked up and smiled at him a little warily. 'Oh, hi, Sam. How are you?'

He pulled a wry face. 'Sore—that was what I wanted to see you about. I don't suppose I can book myself in for some physio with you, can I? I overdid it up on Bodmin this afternoon and I could do with a good workout. Maybe after you finish one evening?'

Her face clouded. 'Oh. Um—evenings aren't good for me. I've got RP—retinitis pigmentosa…'

She was going blind? 'Hell, I'm sorry, I had no idea.'

She shrugged. 'It's fine, Sam. It's progressing slowly, but I'll take it as it comes and in the meantime—well, I can still do practically everything I did before, but I only work daylight hours now. I can't see very well when the light fades, but I'm more than happy to fit you in at lunchtime—or if Gabriel's not working late so he can get home for the dog, I can do it then if you don't mind giving me a lift home?'

'Of course not—but lunchtime's fine if it suits you best. It's just my ankle.'

'Not your hand and arm?'

He hesitated, glancing down at it and wondering if it was so damned obvious to everyone.

'I noticed you don't use it,' she said gently, 'and you

don't use your shoulder much, either, but it's not obvious, Sam. It's my job—I ought to be able to tell. But it doesn't matter now. Just come and we'll go through it all then, see what I need to do for you. Say—one tomorrow?'

He gave her a fleeting smile. 'That would be great.'

'Can't you keep away, Sam?'

He straightened up and stepped back out of Lauren's doorway, and met the older man's eyes. 'Hi, Nick.'

'So, have you changed your mind? I sincerely hope so. We're so damned busy it's ridiculous. Dragan's out today because the baby was ill and Melinda's had a foul cold and he thinks he's going down with it, too, just to add insult to injury, and everyone in Penhally seems to have realised it's coming up to the spring bank holiday weekend so they're trying to get in quick, and I'm desperately trying to find time to organise the lifeboat barbeque for Saturday. So if you want a job…?'

'Organising the barbeque?' he asked, surprised, but Nick gave a short laugh.

'No, you don't get off that lightly—the locum job.'

He sighed and rammed a hand through his hair. 'Nick, I—'

'Please?'

'I'm out of touch.'

'Rubbish. What the hell do you think you've been doing in Africa?'

He laughed. 'Taking out an appendix under local? Trying to rehydrate a tiny child with boiled river water with some salt flung in it? Lancing an abscess the size of a football? Not juggling someone's drugs to get the best result from their blood-pressure medication, or advising some spoilt middle-aged woman to drink more water, get off her backside and take some exercise if she wants to get rid of her constipation, that's for sure! Hell, Nick, I can't do this any more.'

'Of course you can. Compared to Africa it'll be a walk in the park.'

He shook his head. 'I don't want this, Nick. Don't ask me, please.'

'Why not? It's a great practice, and if you wanted to come back permanently, with Lucy gone I'm sure we can find a slot for you here.' His voice changed, becoming deeper, huskier, and he looked exhausted. 'We're desperate, Sam. We've been struggling without Lucy for weeks, keeping the job open for her because we couldn't get a locum, but now—well, we need to advertise the post and that takes time, and frankly we're all at the end of our rope. We need you.'

Them and everyone else, it seemed. He sighed again and turned away, but there was nowhere to go, because Jamie was running wild and his mother was in hospital and needed him for weeks, if not months, and he couldn't just sit on his backside and watch the world go to hell while he twiddled his thumbs, it just wasn't in his nature. But...

'The people here don't want me, Nick. I was a nightmare.'

'You were a boy. You're a man now. And people forget.'

'Not in Penhally, they don't. They're all bloody elephants.'

Nick chuckled, but his face was still hopeful and he could feel the staff behind the reception desk all holding their breath for his reply.

He shook his head slowly, feeling the ground crumbling beneath his feet. 'OK. I'll help you out—but just the odd day here and there. Nothing drastic. And don't go getting ideas about me coming back in a full-time, permanent post or anything like that, because it just won't happen.'

Nick smiled, slapped him on the shoulder and led him over to Reception. 'Of course not. Hazel, sign him up for locum duty, please. And start booking him in for as much as you can talk him into. I haven't had a day off in four weeks and I'm tired. He can cover Dragan's surgeries tomorrow. Oh, and schedule a practice meeting for the morning—I'll introduce you to everyone, Sam. I'm sure they'll all be delighted you've agreed to join us.'

'Temporarily.'

'Of course, of course,' Nick agreed, but there was something in his voice that wasn't in the least reassuring.

Sam shut his eyes and sighed. Damn.

Damn, damn and double damn.

Why the hell had he said yes?

And then he opened his eyes and saw Gemma staring at him with a stricken look, and if there'd been any way out, he would have taken it.

But there wasn't, and he wasn't any more delighted than she was.

CHAPTER THREE

How on earth was she going to work with him?

She hadn't spoken to him since she'd left the Smugglers' on Wednesday night, and her heart hadn't settled back into a normal rhythm since he'd been back in Penhally. But work with him, having to talk to him about patients, going into the staffroom and finding him sitting there and having to exchange polite conversation when all she wanted to do was turn back the clock and—

What? Not have married him? Not have spent that wonderful, idyllic time with him that fate had so savagely cut short? It would have been kinder, but not to have had that time—even the thought was unbearable. And anyway, she had married him, and for the last nearly eleven years he'd hated her, and then suddenly, because he'd taken the locum job, they were going to be thrust together and she couldn't understand why he'd agreed.

She hadn't slept all night for thinking about it, and now she was in the crowded staffroom perched on the edge of Lauren's chair with Chloe balanced on the other arm, and all the doctors and reception staff were crowded onto the other seats or clustered round the tea and coffee pots as they waited.

And then Nick strode in, followed by Sam, and she felt his eyes on her instantly.

'Morning, everyone!' Nick said, smiling broadly and rubbing his hands together. 'I'm sorry about the early start, but I wanted to introduce our new locum Sam Cavendish to you. I know some of you will recognise him—Lauren, Chloe, you were probably at school with him—but I'd just like to run through everyone and their jobs, to help you find your feet, Sam. Now, from left to right, Gemma Johnson and Lara Mercer are our practice nurses—Gemma, I know you met many years ago.'

Met? *Met*? Gemma nearly laughed out loud, but the tears were too close to the surface to let go that much. And Nick was still talking.

'Hazel's now our practice manager but I don't know if you've met Sue Gunnell, our head receptionist, then Kate Althorp you remember—she and Chloe are midwives, Rebecca Grey is one of our district nurses, and Lauren, as you know, is our resident physio.

'As for the medical team, we've got Adam Donnelly, who's another local you may remember, Dragan Lovak who's off sick today, Oliver Fawkner, and Gabriel Devereux who's on loan from France and who we've just persuaded to stay. And that's pretty much us. Sam, do you want to introduce yourself?'

The handshaking over, Sam grunted softly and looked around. 'Yeah, hi, everyone,' he said, his voice soft. 'I do know quite a few of you, certainly by sight, and I wish I could say it was good to be back, but you'll all know my mother's had a stroke and that's why I'm here, so I've agreed to fill in for Lucy just until my mother's recovered, and then I'll be going back to my real job, so for those of you who're having heart failure at the thought of a Cavendish having anything to do with your nearest and dearest, relax. I'll be out of here just the moment I can. In the meantime, I'll do what I can to help, so please, just ask.'

It was said with a smile, and it was greeted with a warm ripple of laughter, but it made Gemma's heart ache. Why was he so sure he wasn't welcome, when it was clear to her, looking around at them, that they were all more than happy to have him back in the fold?

Well, almost all. She couldn't count herself in their number, but her reservations were entirely different, and had things not been the way they were, her life, and Sam's, would have been very different too. But at least she had a life, and if he decided to stay, if in the long term his mother's problems were resolved and he was here by choice, then maybe then she might be able talk to him, tell him why—

'Could I just mention something?' Kate Althorp said. 'I know Sam's stepped in, and we're all very grateful because it means the doctors will have less to do and so Nick might not be so crabby all the time…'

They all laughed—even Nick, she noticed—and then she went on, 'It's become apparent, talking to the mums, that losing Lucy—or more specifically losing our only woman doctor—wasn't universally welcomed, because many of them would rather see a woman for some of the problems that they encounter. Now, Sam is only going to be here for a short while if everything with Linda progresses well, and for her sake I hope it does, but I've heard on the grapevine that Polly Carrick is looking for a change of direction and may be looking for a job—some of you may remember her, very quiet, soft-spoken, nice girl. She used to be Polly Searle. Lauren, she's a little younger than you.'

'I remember her,' Sam said. 'She had her nose in a book all the time—we met at a few careers things for wannabe doctors, and I was surprised at that. She was so quiet—tiny little thing. Bit of a mouse, really.'

'That's her. Well, she's a GP now, in London, but as I say, she might be on the move. And, yes, she is my goddaughter, but she's also a wonderful doctor—and a woman, of course. She's a fantastic listener, and I think she'd be brilliant. Just a thought to drop into the mix, if we find ourselves in a position to employ another doctor at any time. And I don't even know at this stage if she'd be interested, but I think we should consider the issue of having a female doctor on staff very seriously.'

Nick straightened, obviously keen to get on. 'Right. Thank you for that, Kate. We'll bear her in mind. OK, if there's nothing else, I'd like to welcome Sam again and I'm sure you'll find that everyone does what they can to make you feel at home. If it helps, I'm sure some-one'll take you under their wing for the day to show you the ropes. Gabriel, perhaps, if you wouldn't mind? And now I'm going to sort out the barbeque or we'll all be eating raw sausages tomorrow. You can get me on my mobile if you need me. Kate?'

The meeting broke up, Kate raising her eyebrows and following Nick with a resigned look on her face, and then as Gemma stood, she found herself hard up against a solid and still achingly familiar body.

'Sorry. I was just coming over to talk to you,' Sam murmured, stepping back hastily, but she could hardly hear him for the roaring in her ears and the thundering of her heart.

'That's fine. Sorry. Um—so what did you want?'

'A quiet word?'

Damn. She didn't want a quiet word with Sam. She didn't want any words with him—unless they were words that would take her back into his arms, and she didn't think those words had ever been invented…

'Not now. I've got a clinic.'

He followed her to the door of her room and stood just inside it, his voice low. 'I'm not going to hold you up. I just wanted to say that I know this situation isn't ideal, but I don't want to make things difficult for you and I'll keep out of your way as much as possible. It's not for long, and nobody knows about us, not really, so I'd like to keep it that way. Less complicated all round.'

And God knows, there are enough complications, she thought sadly. 'Sure,' she said, swallowing and wishing he'd leave her alone, and then there was a tap on the door and Gabriel came and rescued her, taking Sam off to his consulting room on the ground floor to shadow him for the day and leaving her in peace to start her clinic.

'Right, I've spoken to Mike Trevellyan and he's going to deliver the meat tomorrow morning, and they're also donating some ice cream and the vending cart for the day. Have you sorted out the rolls and sauces and so on?'

Kate gave a quiet sigh at Nick's typical need to micromanage everything. 'Yes. The supermarket's delivering everything in the morning, and lots of people have volunteered to bring salads and side dishes, so all we have to do is fire up the barbeque and we're done.'

'Excellent. I've got to pick the oil drums up from Ben and Lucy's barn, and we need charcoal. Shall I do that?'

'If you've got time. Your car's bigger than mine. And we need the tables picked up from the church hall, while you're at it. There'll be someone there from three.'

Kate watched Nick as he jotted down a note to himself, and then when he looked up, she said carefully, 'Do you think it's wise, asking Sam to do the locum job?'

Nick looked startled. 'Well, of course it's wise! For God's sake, Kate, if I can't have a bit of faith in the lad, who can? I've known him all his life—'

'It's not Sam I'm worried about, Nick. It's Gemma.'

'Gemma?'

He looked utterly confused, and for the hundredth time Kate wondered how he could be so incredibly obtuse and emotionally inept. 'Yes, Gemma. Well, Sam and Gemma, to be absolutely accurate.'

'What about them?'

She shrugged. 'I just wondered if it would be difficult for them.'

'Difficult? Why on earth should it be difficult? They had a little fling eleven years ago. Why would that make any difference to them now? It's in the past, Kate.'

'Because they're not over it? You can feel the tension coming off them in waves. It may be in the past, but it's far from over, if the look on Gemma's face is anything to go by, and when she's in the room Sam doesn't know where to look. And just because something's in the past doesn't mean it's resolved,' she added pointedly.

He met her eyes then, a flicker of guilt in them. 'Kate, I don't want to talk about this.'

'I know. You never do. But that won't stop Jeremiah being your son, Nick, and one day you're going to have to accept that, because one day I'm going to have to tell him before he finds out from somebody else.'

'Who?' he snapped sharply. 'Who knows?'

'Well, virtually no one—unless you count the tourist who pointed out how alike you are.'

A dull run of colour stained his neck as he turned away. 'I can't deal with this now.'

'You never can, Nick—and I'm beginning to wonder if you ever will until it's thrust on you by circumstance. But you need to know that if Jem ever asks me, I won't lie to him. I *will* tell him the truth. And he'll have a right to know why his own father wouldn't acknowledge him.'

And without another word, she walked out, head held high and her heart pounding. She was sick of it. Sick of beating her head against a brick wall, sick of Nick stonewalling her on the subject, sickened by everything that had happened that summer—the same summer that Sam and Gemma had had their fling that was so obviously not forgotten.

She just hoped that they had more luck resolving it than she'd had.

To Sam's surprise, remarkably few people commented on his presence in Gabriel's surgery. There was a sign up in Reception telling the patients that he'd be covering Lucy for a while, and far from dragging him out into the car park and setting fire to him, they either smiled politely or ignored him.

That was fine. He didn't want or expect a rapturous welcome. He just wanted to do his job, and by eleven he was clawing the walls.

And Gabriel must have realised it, because in the next gap between patients he pushed back his chair after the last patient and smiled at him.

'OK. You don't need me showing you how to do

this. You can take over from me here now so I can go and do my calls, and Oliver's around if you have a problem. I'll be in this afternoon doing a surgery, so if you think of anything else you need to know, just buzz through and ask one of us, and we should get through the list nice and quickly. Which means I can get home and walk the dog in daylight!'

'Lauren mentioned you've got a dog. I'm babysitting my mother's—I'll have to look out for you on the beach.'

'Maybe we can meet up and sniff tails!' he said with a laugh, and stood up. 'Right, I have to get on, I have calls to make and then I need to amuse myself until afternoon surgery. I gather my fiancée is going to see you at one.'

'Yes. Sorry. I didn't mean to disrupt your lunchtime routine—'

'*Sans fait rien*, it's not a problem. You go and let her torture you, and I'll wander into town and find us a sandwich from the shop when I've finished my calls. Tell her I'll see her later.'

He went out, and Sam carried on with his clinic, surprised at how easily it all came back to him. And how much he was enjoying it, although it was all a little cosy and he had no doubt at all that after a few weeks it would drive him absolutely mad.

His last patient had just left when Hazel buzzed through. 'Sam, I've got a gentleman here who needs to be seen this morning, and you're the only doctor left in the surgery. Would you mind awfully taking a look at him?'

'Of course not,' he agreed, sighed quietly and wondering if he'd find time for lunch before he saw Lauren. Breakfast seemed to have passed him by and he was getting very hungry. Maybe there'd be a biscuit or two left in the staffroom.

There was a tap on the door, and a man in late middle age came in and sat down.

'Hello, Sam.'

He frowned. There was a not-too-distant memory of some washing tied to the top of a tree, and he gave an inward groan. 'Mr Reynolds.'

'I see you haven't forgotten me, then?'

'Indeed not. Apparently it's mutual.' He gave a slight smile, and Mr Reynolds smiled back.

'I didn't expect to see you back here. I'm sorry about your mother.'

'Thank you,' he said for what must have been the hundredth time since he'd come back. 'So what can I do for you today, Mr Reynolds?'

'It's my angina. I just can't seem to get on top of it today, and I've been puffing away on the old GTN and—well, I don't know, it doesn't seem to be making any difference.'

'Just slip your jacket off, let's check your blood pressure,' Sam said. 'Have you been overdoing it?'

'I did a bit of gardening this morning, but I don't know if it was a good idea.'

'Well, your blood pressure's a little high, and I can see you're on medication for it, and you're on a statin. Can you describe your symptoms?' he asked as he took off the cuff and made a note of the reading. And what he heard, he didn't like at all.

'OK, I think just to be on the safe side I'm going to give you a little aspirin—you don't have asthma, do you? No? OK, just chew this up and we'll get a nurse to run an ECG on you—no, stay there, don't get up.

I'll go and find someone. I just want to make sure nothing's going on.'

He left the door open and asked Hazel if there was a nurse free, just as Gemma came downstairs. 'Do you want something done?' she asked, and he nodded.

'Please. An ECG for Mr Reynolds. His angina's bothering him.'

He lifted a brow, and Gemma nodded her understanding of the urgency. 'I'll get the ECG machine. His angina's a bit unstable.'

She came into his room wheeling the machine a few moments later, just as Sam had settled Mr Reynolds on the couch.

'Hello, Ron, what've you been up to? I bet you've been gardening, haven't you?' she asked, peeling the backing off the electrodes and sticking them on Mr Reynolds's hairy chest.

'How did you guess?'

She smiled, and Sam's heart turned over. No wonder Mr Reynolds's angina was unstable! 'Ah, well, a little bird told me the family were coming for the weekend. I hope you're all coming to the barbeque tomorrow.'

'Wouldn't miss it, Gemma. Never have.'

'Excellent. Right, just lie still while I run the printout, and while I've got you there, I'm going to give you a little lecture about your diet, because I can see from your tummy that you've been down to the chippy a few times too many, haven't you?'

'Nothing gets by you, does it?' he said with a little smile, and Gemma chuckled.

'Not much, not in this village. And anyway, I saw you and Doreen sitting on the harbour wall eating them last Saturday. So it'll be low-fat sausages for you at the barbeque tomorrow. I'll get Dr Tremayne to buy some specially.'

But just then the ECG trace began to flutter, and he pressed his hand to his chest and groaned.

'Well, that'll save worrying about the low-fat sausages,' Sam murmured in her ear, and she stepped aside, raising the backrest as Sam took over and sat their patient up to ease the load on his heart. 'I think you might be having a little heart attack, Ron, so I'm going to send you off to St Piran's to get checked out.'

'Are you sure? You do know what you're doing, don't you?' he said with a wry grin. 'Only I wouldn't have wanted you to miss the lecture on heart attacks— Aaah!'

'Just sit back and try to relax, and I'll give you some painkillers. That should make it a bit easier. Gemma, could you ask Hazel to call the ambulance and his wife and then draw me up some diamorphine—ten milligrams, I think. Thank you. And you just lie there and thank your lucky stars I attended that lecture, Ron, and don't you worry about a thing. It's all under control.'

And less than fifteen minutes later he was off to hospital, and Sam left Gemma tidying up the ECG machine.

'Right, I'm sorry, I'll have to leave you to it, I'm supposed to be seeing Lauren at one and I'm already late,' he said, and with a resigned sigh Sam crossed the wide corridor and tapped on Lauren's door.

It opened instantly, and she came out with a smile. 'Hi, Sam. Come on in.'

He shut the door, then hesitated. Did he strip off to his boxers, or wait for her to take a history? 'I'm sorry I'm late, I got held up with a patient.'

'Don't worry. Just peel your things off behind the screen and I'll take a history as we go along. Maybe I'd better have a look at all your injuries today, and we can sort out a treatment plan.'

'Well, good luck with that,' he said with a dry chuckle, and dropped into the chair behind the screen while he took off his shoes and socks and unbuttoned his shirt. He really, really didn't want to do this, but if he ignored the problem it would get worse, and he couldn't expect to make progress if he neglected his physio. No gain without pain and all that, but he'd frankly had it with the pain and it was growing old very quickly.

'OK, let's go through this from the top because we've got no notes on you, of course. So—what exactly happened?'

'Oh, no.'

She picked up the specs off the desk and hefted them in her hand. Sam was bound to be going in to visit his mother later, and he'd just popped in for a chat with Lauren, presumably about another patient. She'd give them to him, he'd be able to take them to Mr Reynolds.

And then she'd go for a walk along the harbour, maybe pick something up to eat on the way. Anything rather than sitting around in the staffroom and waiting for Sam to come in, and as long as they were both in the building, she'd be on edge.

She tapped on Lauren's door and stuck her head round without waiting for a reply, knowing that Lauren was free because Gabriel was out and her patients had all gone, but to her horror she wasn't free. Not free at all, and the patient lying propped up her couch, wearing nothing but snug jersey boxers, was Sam.

'Well, come in,' he said drily, and she felt hot colour scorch her cheeks.

'I'm sorry, I didn't realize…' She trailed off, her eyes taking in the still-purple scars that slashed across his chest and shoulder, then sucked in a breath as she saw his leg. The skin must have been torn as he'd slid along the ground, because the outside of his left thigh was a mess. He'd had skin grafts, but they could never cover it completely, she knew that. It would always leave a nasty, disfiguring scar. And lower down, on his shin, were the marks of an external fixator, and on the outside of his ankle further evidence of surgery.

Dear God. He must have been through hell—was still going through it, if the faint sheen of sweat on his skin was anything to go by, and Lauren was standing there holding his foot in her hand and quietly waiting for Gemma to free herself from her trance and either say her piece or leave.

'Sorry, I'll—I just wanted to give you these. Mr Reynolds's specs. I thought you could drop them into him at the hospital while you're visiting Linda,' she croaked, and, dumping them on the desk, she fled out of the room and ran out of the building, all thoughts of lunch forgotten, driven out by the image burned on her mind—the image of Sam, so severely wounded yet so dismissive of his injuries that she'd had no *idea* they had been so bad, or that he must have come so very, very close to death…

She crossed the road and sat on the harbour wall, her shaking arms wrapped round her waist as she stared out over the muddy harbour where the fishing boats were stranded by the low tide, and tried to see something other than that image of his broken, damaged body on Lauren's couch.

And all the time she'd been staring at him, she realised, he'd been smiling a wry, bitter, twisted little smile that tore her heart in two.

Something wet landed on her arm, and she looked down. Another drop landed, and this time she'd felt it sliding down her cheek.

Stupid. So, so stupid. He didn't want to know her. He'd promised to keep out of her way, had said he wanted to keep their relationship quiet. He sure as hell didn't want her tears.

But still they fell, as fast as she could swipe them away, and in the end she got off the wall and ran down beyond the lifeboat station to the rocks on the headland and sat hugging her knees until the shock had receded and she felt she'd regained her composure enough to go back to the surgery and face him.

Then, and only then, did she stand up and turn round—and saw Sam, just a few feet away, perched on a rock and watching her with guarded eyes.

'I'm so sorry I barged in,' she began, but he just arched a brow.

'You need to learn to wait when you knock.'

'I know. Believe me, I wish I had.'

'What—too shocking for you, was it? A little bit too real?'

She felt sick. 'Sam, don't be horrible. You know it's not that.'

'Do I? I'm not sure what I know any more. And why the hell are you so upset? You walked away, Gemma. You didn't want me then—so what's changed enough now to make you cry?'

Nothing. Nothing had changed. She'd always loved him—always wanted him, always missed him. And that was why she'd left him, why she'd gone away and done what she'd had to do alone, so that if the worst came to the worst, he could move on with his life without her.

Except he hadn't, apparently. Like her, he'd been in limbo. And like her, he'd almost died.

She held his eyes. 'Nothing's changed, Sam. It was just the shock—I didn't realise you'd been so badly injured. The other night, you gave me no idea it had been so bad.'

He shrugged. 'It was just one of those things. You get on with it, don't you? I mean, you can't change it, so what's the point of bleating about it?'

He walked slowly up to her, moving carefully over the rocks, and lifting his right hand he brushed away the tears that still stained her cheeks. Apart from the one tear the other night in the Smugglers', he'd only ever seen her cry right at the end, when her parents had found out they were married and had said terrible, cruel things to her. And he hated to see her like this.

'Don't cry for me,' he said gruffly. 'I'm all right, Gemma. It's over now, there's no need to cry. I don't need your pity, I'm fine.'

But the tears were still leaking slowly from her eyes, welling up and sliding down her cheeks, glistening in the sunshine, and he couldn't help himself. He tried to stop, tried to hold himself back, but somehow his lips were there, on her cheek, kissing away the tears.

And then not just the tears. His mouth found hers, just lightly brushing it, their breath mingling as they took tiny, shallow gasps of air, little shuddering breaths as they slowly, tenderly explored the soft flesh they'd both ached for for so long.

But it wasn't enough. It could never be enough, and when a tiny, frantic little whimper escaped her, it was too much for him. With a ragged groan he threaded his fingers through her hair and took her mouth in a kiss so wild, so needy, so desperate that when he lifted his head long moments later it was like tearing away part of his soul.

'Sam?'

Her voice was trembling, her body quivering against him, and he forced himself to take a step back, to distance himself from the one person in the world who could still hurt him.

'No, Gemma. I'm not going there again. I can't.'

'I didn't ask you to.'

'But I want to,' he said, the words dragged from him. 'How can I want to? You walked away from me—you just walked away—why?'

She felt pain close like a fist around her heart, wishing she could tell him the truth but not really knowing how, not now, after all this time. 'We were kids, Sam. It was a long time ago. And maybe it was wrong. Maybe I shouldn't have gone, but at the time I felt I had no choice. My life was—it was going in a direction I hadn't planned, and I didn't know what to do. And I made a mistake.'

'So—what are you saying, Gemma? You want to try again?'

'No. Yes. I don't know,' she said tearfully, not wanting it to be like this, so very different from what she might have planned. 'I really don't know what I want, and I certainly don't know you, not now. Maybe I never did. Maybe you never knew me. Maybe we need to find out who we are now, what we're looking for—because we haven't moved on, either of us, have we? Not really.'

He stared at her, his eyes shielded again, although she could see the emotions on his face from the set of his lips and the slight flicker of a muscle in his jaw.

'I don't know,' he said at last, his voice taut. 'I'm not sure I can do this. I don't want to talk about it, and I haven't got time for it. I've got other priorities now. I've got to go and do a surgery, and then I have to take Jamie to see my mother. He still hasn't been.'

'Maybe he's frightened she'll die? Or that she'll lean on him, and he's afraid he can't cope? Sound familiar, Sam?'

His laugh was bitter. 'Yeah, but she won't lean on him. She'll lean on me, like she's always done, because that's my job, isn't it? I'm the man of the house, the head of the family. And I don't need it any more than I need this all raking up again. So forgive me if I don't feel like exploring my emotions with you to see if you made a mistake or if you really did mean it when you walked out on us. I've got enough on my plate. You made your bed, Gemma. Go and lie in it.'

And turning on his heel, he walked away and left her there, her slender hope for their future happiness in tatters.

'Mummy! Mummy, can we have Matt to stay tonight? Please please *please*!'

Kate smiled ruefully down at her son, hanging on her arm and begging, while those dark brown eyes so very like his father's implored her to say yes. 'Darling, we can't tonight, I'm sorry, because I've got the barbeque to set up in the morning with Uncle Nick, but maybe tomorrow night?'

'Could I offer to have Jem instead?'

She looked up into the man's kind, straightforward

face and wondered about him. He was a teacher at the senior school, a widower, apparently, and his son Matthew Werrick was one of Jem's friends, but so far she'd never really had anything to do with him.

He held out his hand. 'We haven't been properly introduced. I'm Rob.'

She smiled and took his hand, warm, firm and uncomplicated. She had a feeling it matched its owner. 'I'm Kate. It's nice to meet you—and I'm sorry about Jem. He's been asking for ages about Matthew coming to stay, but tonight's really not good. Maybe another time.'

'I can have them tonight. I'm more than happy to.'

'Oh, we wouldn't dream of imposing, Rob.'

'It's not an imposition at all. Actually it would be fun. The weekends can get a bit long, can't they?'

Oh, yes. And the children were begging. Yet still she hesitated, and his mouth curved into an understanding smile.

'Don't worry about it, Kate. You don't know me. That's reasonable, but perhaps instead of the night, why don't you drop him off in the morning on your way to the barbeque, and I can bring them both down later and meet you there? We were planning on coming, anyway. Would that be better?'

'Oh, Mummy, I want to go to Matthew's for the night! Please, please!'

'Jeremiah, don't, that's rude,' she chided, but Matthew was pleading with his father, and Rob gave her a 'suit yourself' shrug and a smile, and she gave in.

'If you really don't mind, I'm quite happy for him to stay with you. And it's nothing to do with not knowing you, it's more that I have problems returning favours because of work.'

'Well, I don't think we need to worry about that, do we?' he said with an understanding and good-humoured smile. 'I'm more than happy to have Matthew's friends over. So—do you want to collect his things and drop him round to me? Or come with him at six and I'll feed you both. Rumour has it I can manage to hurl together a half decent Bolognese sauce—so if you'd like…?'

Actually, yes, she realised suddenly, she *would* like. She'd spent the last thirty years waiting for Nick to notice her, and the only time he had, it had been devastating. She hadn't been on a date since she'd started going out with James, and it was nearly eleven years since he'd died. And apart from James, there had only been that one time with Nick, on the night of the storm, the night James had died…

So, yes, she would like. And although it was only a simple supper invitation, for Kate it was a quantum leap. So drawing in a breath, she smiled at Rob and threw herself into the void.

CHAPTER FOUR

'I'M NOT coming.'

Sam propped himself up against the worktop and folded his arms. 'Why are you scared, Jamie? Is it because you don't know what to expect?'

'I'm not scared.'

Sam sighed. 'Of course you are. Your mother's had a stroke, and people die of them. Every day. So, sure you're scared. It's only reasonable. Dammit, I'm scared.' Scared he'd end up trapped here, scared he'd never get away again and he'd be stuck with Gemma in the same town, bumping into each other and driving him insane with wanting.

'Is she going to die?'

'Well, of course she is, we all are, but not now. At least, I don't believe so, anyway. They think she's got an underlying heart condition—nothing serious, just an irregular beat that could cause her blood to clot, and if that's the case, she'll have anticoagulant drugs to slow her clotting and antiarrhythmics to make her heart beat evenly.'

'What, to go with the blood-pressure drugs and the anti-depressants?' he said lightly, but Sam could tell there was real fear there lurking underneath his flip remark, and he wished he knew him well enough, wished he was close enough to his brother to pull him into his arms and hug him.

Wished there'd been anyone there to do it to him, when his father had walked out and left him—literally—holding the baby.

But there hadn't, and Jamie wouldn't let him anyway, so instead he opened the fridge, poured two glasses of juice and pushed one towards Jamie across the kitchen table. 'She'll be all right, Jamie. She's already so much better.'

'It's my fault.'

'No, of course it's not your fault. It's her fault. She's never looked after herself properly.'

'No. It's my fault. We had a row. I got really angry with her, and we were yelling, and I went out. And I didn't come back until after midnight. And if Gemma hadn't found her…'

'She would have died?' he said softly. 'Maybe. But that's not your fault. Lots of people have rows. It doesn't kill them.'

'It nearly killed Mum.'

'No. The stroke nearly killed her. You didn't. And she misses you. I think she wants to make up.'

'Did she say so?'

He shook his head. 'No. But she's very keen to see you.'

Jamie sat there for a moment, then drained the glass and stood up. 'So what are we waiting for?' he asked, and headed for the door.

'Hi, Mum.'

'Jamie! You came!' his mother said, and, holding out her arms, she wrapped her youngest son against her heart, and Sam swallowed the lump in his throat and turned away.

And there, catching him with his emotional trousers down, was Gemma, carrying a vase of flowers. 'Hi. You got him here, then,' she said softly, and he nodded.

'Yeah. Thanks.'

'Thanks?'

'It was what you said, about him being scared. They'd had a row and he thought it was all his fault. Look, are you done here? I was thinking—maybe we could go and get a coffee?'

'So you can salve your conscience about being nasty to me at lunchtime?' she said, her eyes reproachful. 'I don't think so, Sam. And, yes, I am done,' she added pointedly. 'I'm going home—to lie in my bed.'

She put the flowers down on the locker and dropped a kiss on Linda's cheek. 'You take care, and I'll see you when you get home. Bye, Jamie. Nice to see you again.'

And she walked out of the ward, her back straight and her head held high.

His words echoed back at him, and he felt a wash of guilt. Damn. He gave his mother what had to be an awkward smile. 'I'm just going to go and get a coffee. I'll leave you two alone for a minute, you've got a lot of catching up to do and I missed lunch. I won't be long.'

She smiled knowingly, and Jamie just grinned, and he ground his teeth and followed Gemma out.

'Gemma? Please, wait.'

She stopped and waited, but her face was expressionless. 'What?'

'Just—I'm sorry. I didn't— Look, this isn't easy.'

'Tell me about it,' she muttered.

'Please. Come and have a coffee with me. Give me a chance to apologise.'

She looked up into his eyes, saw the signs of strain around them, and because she loved him—had always loved him, ever since the first time she'd seen him walking on the beach twelve years ago, a boy on the brink of manhood—she nodded. 'OK. But you're buying.'

They found a canteen that was open, and he ordered two lattes, picked a couple of sandwiches out of the fridge at random and paid for them, then followed Gemma to a table.

'Tuna and cucumber or roast beef and horseradish?'

'Chicken salad,' she said, taking the tuna, and smiled, and saw the tension drain out of him.

'They're going to give me hell for this. Mum gave me such a knowing look, and Jamie was grinning. I should have let you get further ahead before I came out after you,' he grumbled, struggling to open the other packet of sandwiches.

She watched discreetly, noting that he was obviously finding his finger and thumb uncooperative and the lack of feedback was hampering him. She concentrated on unwrapping her own sandwich and munching into it, and after a moment he succeeded, and she was able to relax.

'Your mother seems quite keen to get us back together again,' she said conversationally, and he stopped, his sandwich halfway to his open mouth.

'What's she said now?'

She shrugged. 'Just asked how things were going at work. I didn't tell her.'

He felt his neck heat. 'That was—I was just—'

'Defensive? I'm a nurse, Sam. I've seen worse.'

But not on him, and it had shocked her much more than she would have believed possible. She took another bite of her sandwich to give her mouth something to do, but even so the silence stretched out until Sam broke it, his voice taut and strangely impassive.

'She kept telling me that you asked after me. In her letters. Why did you do that?'

Because I love you? Because I needed to know—anything, any scrap of information, anything to keep my love alive...

'Well, I have to talk about something during a consultation,' she said lightly, 'and you're as good a topic as any.'

And the only one of any interest to her, but he didn't have to know that.

'So it wasn't that you wanted to know?'

Oh, lord, she couldn't do this. She put her sandwich down and met his eyes. 'Sam, of course I wanted to know how you were doing,' she said, giving up the pretence. 'It's not as if I hate you.'

'But you don't love me. You didn't—not enough to stay.'

Or too much...

'Sam, we were so young.'

'I *loved* you,' he said roughly, throwing down his sandwich and leaning forwards, his eyes glittering. 'I really, really loved you, Gemma—and you just walked away. And you didn't even tell me to my face. That was the thing that hurt most—that you couldn't even talk to me. After all we'd shared—'

He broke off, sat back and shook his head.

'This was a lousy idea. I can't do it, Gemma. I'm sorry. It would be too easy to let myself get sucked back in, but I've been hurt too damned much by you, and I'm not letting it happen again.'

And without another glance at her, he got to his feet and walked away from her, leaving her in a litter of unwanted sandwiches and half-finished coffee and broken promises.

The barbeque was in full swing when he walked down there the following afternoon, and the first person to greet him was Lucy.

'Sam? Oh, Sam, it's so *good* to see you!' she cried. Handing a tiny baby over to the man at her side, she threw herself into his arms and hugged him. Then she let him go, stood back and stared at him, laughing and shaking her head in disbelief.

'Goodness, you have got *so* damned good-looking! I can just hear the clatter of the locks with everyone shutting their daughters up! Come, I want you to meet Ben and the children.'

And she dragged him over to the man he assumed was Ben, and took the baby back out of his arms. 'This is Ben Carter, my husband, and the little tyke round his neck is Annabel, and this is Josh. Guys, this is Sam Cavendish. He taught me how to light fires and climb trees and—'

'I'm not sure I want to know what he taught you,' Ben said with a dry chuckle, but his handshake was friendly enough and Sam could see the bone-deep confidence in their relationship that shone from both of them.

And he envied it. God, how he envied it. To have a love that profound and know it was returned...

'Gemma's here,' Lucy said softly, her eyes concerned.

'I know.' Of course he knew. His radar had clocked her the moment he walked into the surgery car park which turned annually into the site for the Penhally Bay Independent Lifeboat Association fundraiser. She would be here, he'd known that. Maybe in a perverse way it was even why he'd come, unable to stay away. Even after yesterday, after all that had been said, after two failed attempts at building bridges, he couldn't stay away.

But Lucy was one of the few people in Penhally who knew the whole story, and he knew he could rely on her to keep her thoughts to herself.

'Dad tells me you're working at the practice. That must make things a bit interesting,' she murmured.

'It's fine,' he said, trying not to think about just how fine it wasn't.

'That's what Dad said, but I didn't believe him, any more than I believe you. So—how's your mother? That was a bit of a shocker.'

'She's OK. She's coming home on Tuesday.'

'Oh. Right. Will you be OK to work?'

'Yes. I have to be, I can't sit and look at her all day, and anyway she's made fantastic progress. The new specialist stroke unit's brilliant. And if she needs it, she'll have physio and occupational therapy and maybe even someone from the community psychiatric team to make sure she's coping with the changes in her life. And she'll need to rest and get her confidence back slowly, and I'm only going to be working part time.'

Ben laughed at that. 'That's what Lucy said—but somehow, if you aren't careful, the part time grows. There's the odd clinic here and the occasional surgery there, and before you know where you are the only thing missing is the on-call.'

'Well, it's all a change from working all day and being on call all night seven days a week in a shanty town or some isolated clinic in the bush. And having drugs on tap is a revelation, as is being able to drive down the road without wondering if you're about to be ambushed or blown up.'

A frown crossed Lucy's face. 'Yes, Dad mentioned that. How are you now?'

He smiled. 'I'm fine,' he said, his stock reply, and really, he supposed, he was, if you didn't count the scars and the horrified look on Gemma's face. And he was enjoying being back at work, just as he was enjoying seeing Lucy again, and meeting her husband and her babies, and being there at the barbeque. Tame and bucolic and very, very English, he thought drily, but somehow safe.

And if it wasn't for Gemma threatening his peace of mind, he might almost be tempted…

Nick turned the sausages on the barbeque while he smiled mechanically at the busy throng and wondered if Kate was right about Sam and Gemma. They'd been avoiding each other—not hard, in the crowd, but it seemed odd that Gemma hadn't gone up to Lucy and said hello, and he wondered if that was because Sam was there talking to Ben and cuddling the baby. And ignoring Gemma, in turn?

Possibly. Frankly, he had no idea, and he wondered if that should worry him. Was he really so blind to people's emotions as Kate implied?

Or was it just that his own life was so filled with pain that he'd shut himself down?

Take the business of Jeremiah—

'Mummy, we're here! Hi, Uncle Nick. We're starving. Can Matt and me have a burger please, Mum?'

'I should think so, love,' Kate said, smiling indulgently at him across the barbeque while Nick stood poised with the tongs and stared at the boy who was his son, and then she lifted her eyes and smiled at the man with the children. Robert Werrick, Nick realised, and felt a prickle of something that felt uncomfortably like—jealousy?

Ridiculous! Of course it wasn't! But her greeting to Werrick then made it obvious that the boys had spent the night at his house and been with him for the day, and he suddenly wondered if—

No. Of course she wasn't seeing him! And, anyway, it was none of his business if she was. But it didn't stop it feeling just a little bit odd, and not altogether pleasant...

Gemma spent the rest of the bank holiday weekend blitzing her house.

Her parents had bought Seagull Cottage with the express intention of having somewhere convenient, easy to maintain and with a lovely setting, and all of those things made it ideal for Gemma, so when she'd moved back, she'd persuaded her parents to let her rent it from them.

And it had been perfect.

The garden was just a paved area with pots standing around on it and enough room for a little table and chairs, and because of the mild climate many of the things in the pots over-wintered, so it was just a case of tidying up from time to time. No grass, no hedges, no weeding—but that weekend, frankly, she could have done with all of them, just to keep her a little bit busier and take her mind off Sam.

She would have gone to St Piran's and visited Linda, but she knew Sam's sisters would be there over the weekend and, besides, so would he. There would be plenty of time to visit her once she was home, and she could choose a time when Sam was out. So with nothing better to do and the garden tidied within an inch of its life, she spring-cleaned the house.

Completely.

She turned out her bedroom, changed the sheets, wiped down the woodwork, polished the furniture—she even wiped the bulbs in the light fittings—and then she did the same to the other two rooms and the bathroom before moving downstairs and blitzing the living area.

She even cleaned out the fridge, her least favourite job in the world, and by the end of Monday the washing was done, there was a pile of ironing she could scarcely see over and she was exhausted.

So exhausted that when she went into work on Tuesday morning, having girded her loins for bumping into Sam, she'd completely forgotten that Linda was being discharged and he wouldn't be in.

And the disappointment was extraordinary.

Oh, well. She threw herself into her work—mostly baby inoculations with some travel vaccinations for people planning their summer breaks, and then she went upstairs to the staffroom to make herself a drink and found Lauren there.

Damn.

'Hi, there. Can I make you another drink?' she asked cheerfully, but Lauren wasn't fooled. Not that she said anything, just shook her head and asked how Linda was, but the jump from Gemma's 'Do you want a drink' to Lauren's 'How's Linda' was pretty darned remote—

unless your mind was already there, Gemma thought with resignation.

'She's fine, I think. Doing really well, but you can tell me more once you've treated her. I take it you're going to be doing her physio?'

'I expect so. Are you going to hand her over to Rebecca for her continuing care, or are you going to pop in on your way home so you can give her more continuity?'

And see Sam. 'I'll see how she is, I think,' Gemma said, trying hard to sound casual. 'If she's relatively stable, there won't be much to do apart from regular INR checks for her anticoagulants, so Sam could take the bloods and bring them in. In fact, he could do all of it. He's only here part time.'

'So you don't have to go there?' Lauren said softly, and Gemma looked up swiftly and met her concerned eyes, teabag poised on the spoon, and then she turned back and threw the teabag in the bin, put milk in her tea and sat down.

'Why wouldn't I want to go there?' she asked, and Lauren sighed gently.

'OK, you don't have to tell me, but if you need someone to talk to—I know Sam had a thing for you all those years ago.'

'A thing?' she said, trying to sound puzzled, but Lauren wasn't stupid and she gave her friend a patient look.

'The girls in his year were gutted, so it was hardly a secret, Gemma. And I saw your face on Friday. You were devastated when you saw his injuries, and if you ask me he was pretty devastated that you'd seen them. He wasn't going to come after you, but then he asked my advice.'

'And you told him to follow me?'

'No. I told him to follow his heart. And then I was

upstairs getting something from the treatment room and I saw him kiss you.'

'That would have been right before he told me I'd made my bed and I should lie on it,' she said with a trace of bitterness, and Lauren sucked in her breath and reached out a hand.

'Gemma, I'm so sorry. It must be so difficult for you, working with him. Why on earth did he agree?'

She shrugged. 'I have no idea. Because Nick's very persuasive? Because he genuinely thought it would be all right?'

'Or because he thought it would give you a chance to get to know each other again in a way that gives you both an opportunity to retreat without loss of face?'

She thought about that for a moment, but it didn't seem to feel right. 'I don't think so. I don't think it was that premeditated. And he didn't look any more pleased than I felt, to be honest, so, no, I don't think it was that, but I can't for the life of me work out why—especially as Linda's making such amazing progress. By Friday night, you'd hardly know she'd had a stroke on Tuesday. It's incredible.'

'I know. I've seen other people who've been treated there, and it's fantastic what that rapid intervention with clot-busters does,' Lauren agreed, and to Gemma's relief the subject moved away from Linda—and, more specifically, from her elder son.

But only for now. She knew perfectly well that Lauren would be watching, and because she'd be treating Sam, too, and because patients having physical therapy often talked quite revealingly to their therapist, Lauren would probably hear more than Gemma wanted her to.

But it would be safe with her. Her friend wasn't a gossip and, apart from her professionalism, she was the soul of kindness. She'd look after Sam, support and encourage him, and give him the help he needed to get his life back on track.

And if that meant that in the end he left Penhally again to return to Africa, Gemma would just have to accept it…

CHAPTER FIVE

'JAMIE! Get up! You've got to be at school in twenty minutes, and I need to get Mum up and dressed before I go to work in half an hour, so I haven't got time to drive you!'

'For God's sake, bro, chill! I'll be fine.'

'No, you'll be late,' Sam said, stripping off the quilt and hoisting Jamie out of bed one-handed. 'Now get washed and dressed and get to school before you get suspended.'

'I should be so lucky,' he mumbled, but Sam wasn't going to pick that one up in this lifetime, so he went downstairs and found his mother tangled in her bra.

'Oh, Mum, let me help you with that,' he said gently, and sorted her out, getting the straps in the right place and then hugging her as the tears of frustration filled her eyes. 'Come on, you're doing so well.'

'It's just all so unnecessary! If only it hadn't happened…'

'I know. But it did, and luckily Gemma was here.'

She put a hand on his arm. 'Sam, don't hurt her.'

He stared at his mother in astonishment. 'Me, hurt Gemma? Mum, she walked out on me!'

'But she loves you, Sam. It's so obvious.'

'Not to me, it isn't.'

'Well, then, you're blind, and you probably don't deserve her. Come on, help me into that top and then you'd better go or you'll be late for work.'

He waited until she was settled in her favourite chair opposite the window with a view over the harbour, and then he paused.

'Are you sure you'll be all right?' he asked, still torn about leaving her, but she just smiled sadly.

'I'll have to be, Sam—and you're not exactly far away. And I've got the phone and all I have to do is press 1 and I'll get the surgery, so I'll be fine, and I've got Digger for company. Go on—and take Jamie to school or he'll be bunking off again.'

'For heaven's sake, he should just—'

'Please, Sam. He's in enough trouble.'

'OK, I'll take him. There are drinks in the fridge, and I'll leave the back door unlocked so Lauren can get in. And don't boil the kettle!'

'No, darling,' she said with a long-suffering smile, and he kissed her cheek, grabbed his keys, yelled for Jamie and started the car.

'Linda?'

'Gemma? Hello, sweetheart. How kind of you to drop in.'

'Not at all, it's always a pleasure to see you. I'm parched. Do you fancy a cup of tea?'

'Oh, I'd love one! Sam won't let me near the kettle at the moment, and I know fruit juice and water are good for you, but, oh, I do miss my tea!'

'You'll be telling me in a minute that he's hidden

all your chocolate,' Gemma teased, and Linda rolled her eyes.

'Don't. Don't even go there. He rations it. I don't know where he keeps it, but I'm allowed one square a day, apparently. Too much saturated fat. And it has to be the dark stuff, like you said, or he won't let me have it at all. He's a tyrant.'

'But you love him.'

'And I'm not alone, am I?' she said softly, and Gemma nearly dropped the teapot.

'Linda, really—I don't think—'

'Don't panic. He doesn't see it, but if he'd only give you both a chance…'

'Linda, he doesn't like me.'

'Sam? Of course he likes you. He's just wary. Now, I don't know what went on between you two, and it's not my business, but he hasn't been the same since you left. He's like he was after his father went—defiant and defensive, but I thought he'd get over it—get over you, but he doesn't seem to have done. So—don't give up, Gemma. Please, don't give up. Not without trying.'

'Don't give up what?'

'Sam!'

This time she did drop the pot. It slipped through her fingers and hit the worktop, and only Sam's hand flying out to steady it prevented an accident.

'Guilty conscience?' he murmured, and she turned and glared at him.

'Not at all! You frightened the life out of me, sneaking up behind me like that!'

'Sneaking? It's my house! I'm allowed to walk in— and I didn't sneak. I'm just not noisy.'

'I didn't hear your car.'

'That's because I could see yours here, so I left it at work and walked home in case there wasn't room on the drive. I'll go and pick it up later—take the dog out for a run. So is there tea in that pot, or are you just posing for effect?'

She nearly threw it at him.

'Ron Reynolds is home.'

Sam was lounging in the doorway to her room the following afternoon, and Gemma looked up from her notes.

'Is he? Good. How's he doing?'

'OK. It was an MI, so he's another one on anticoagulants for your INR checks. They've done a balloon angioplasty apparently and he's much improved. He'll need checking on, but he should be all right to come here to your clinic.'

'Well, if not I'll ask Rebecca to do it. So how come he knew you? Because it sounds as though he did, quite well.'

Sam's face was wry. 'Oh, he did. He lived quite near us, and I guess he had quite a lot to put up with. I took their washing off the line one night and hung it in the top of the fir tree in the front garden. It wouldn't have been so bad if it hadn't been for his daughter's underwear. She was a bit of a goer, Amy Reynolds, and her underwear was a legend.'

Gemma laughed. 'And were you familiar with the underwear before this occasion?'

He chuckled. 'Sadly not—well, only from the washing line. We could see it from the top of the tree in the Tremaynes' back garden next door. Jack, Ed and I used to go up there and try and spy on her through her bedroom window.'

'Sam!'

'What? We were about fourteen! We were just kids, Gemma. We didn't know anything about sex then, really. It was just a bit of harmless fun.'

'You weren't so harmless when you were nineteen,' she said rashly, and then could have bitten her tongue as he went still.

'No. But that was different, Gemz. You were my wife.'

Gemz. He'd only ever called her that when they were alone. She looked away, her mind flooded with memories. Intimate memories, of the time they'd spent together. His touch, his soft, coaxing voice, his gentleness—his passion, finally unleashed and exquisitely shocking in its awesome power to thrill her. She swallowed hard. 'Sam, I—'

'It's all right,' he said softly. 'It's in the past, Gemma. Let's just leave it there. I have to get on. I'll see you.'

And shrugging away from the doorpost, he crossed the landing and went down the stairs, and she listened to his limp and wanted to cry for everything they'd lost and the fact that there just didn't seem to be any way back.

Damn.

He couldn't concentrate. He couldn't think about anything other than Gemma, about how she'd felt in his arms, how much fun they'd had, the laughter they'd shared, and how it had felt to hold her long into the night, just talking about anything and everything.

He couldn't remember anything they'd not been able to talk about, and yet now—now every conversation seemed to lead back to them, and the fact that they'd split up, and it was like a minefield. And he knew, from bitter personal experience, just how dangerous *they* could be.

But he couldn't stay away from her, couldn't ignore her. Couldn't, despite his best efforts, manage to keep away. And at the bottom of his heart, hidden low down behind all the disillusion and pain, was a gut feeling that there was something going on, something he hadn't known about—something she was keeping from him. So maybe she was right. Maybe what they needed to do was try again, see if they could make a go of it this time—and maybe now she'd trust him enough to share whatever it was that had taken her away from him.

No. He felt himself recoiling from the idea, curiously unwilling to disturb the status quo, the unstable truce they seemed to have established. Perhaps to try and pick up their relationship where they'd left off was too much, too soon—but what if they wound the clock back further, maybe, to when they'd met? Pretended they'd just met now, that they were strangers and they were attracted to each other and they were just starting out?

Would it work? Give them a chance to get to know the people they were now, and see if there was any way forward from there?

He didn't know, but he was going to give it a damn good try, because his time back in Penhally had proved to him, above all else, that he couldn't live without her. Not live. He could exist, as he'd been existing for the last eleven years. But live? No. Not without his beloved Gemz.

So he'd suggest they start from scratch, as if they'd just met. Strangers. It could be interesting. Fun. And maybe…

All he had to do was talk her into it. Whistling softly, he left his consulting room and ran upstairs and tapped on her door, but it was opened by Lara Mercer, the other practice nurse.

'Ah. Is Gemma here, Lara?'

'No, sorry Sam, she's gone home. She said something about dropping in on your mother on the way, but that was half an hour ago.'

'Right. OK, thanks.'

'Is there a message?'

'No. No message.' At least, not one he'd leave with anyone.

He drove home, wondering if she'd still be there, and she was, so he pulled in behind her—to stop her getting away? Maybe. Then he went inside, calling as he did to avoid the possibility of her accusing him of sneaking up on her.

She was just leaving, picking up her bag and keys, and he wondered if she'd seen his car pull up and decided to get out of his way. He couldn't blame her if she did, because every encounter seemed to peel another layer off their defences.

'Could you move your car for me, Sam?' she asked, not quite looking at him, but he wasn't ready to let her go.

'Can we have a chat first?'

She looked at him, searching his face for clues. 'What about?'

He gave a crooked, slightly uncertain smile that tipped her heart off kilter. 'Oh, this and that. Can we take the dog and go up to the headland? He could do with a little run.'

She hesitated, but then Linda came out into the kitchen and kissed Sam on the cheek. 'Hello, darling. I'm just going to have a lie-down for a few minutes. It's been a long day. Call me when you get back from your walk.'

So there was no excuse she could give him, no way she could suggest that his mother needed him, not while she was sleeping.

She nodded. 'All right,' she agreed, but her heart was pounding and she didn't know what he was going to say. Probably nothing. She was being silly, it was probably about Linda or work or telling her he was going back to Africa.

He picked up the lead and Digger was there, coiled ready for action, and he clipped it on, opened the door and ushered her out.

'Well?' she asked, unable to bear the suspense any longer. They were up on the headland; they'd walked up Harbour Road to the church at the top of the rise with its pretty lychgate, and now they were heading down to the lighthouse on the end of the promontory, above the cliff. And she couldn't bear it any more.

'Can we sit down?' he suggested, and she looked at the grass. It had been sunny all day, it might be dry enough. And they'd often sat on the headland and talked.

'Sure,' she said, and watched as he lowered himself carefully to the ground and stretched his left leg out in front of him, bending the other one up and wrapping his arms around his knee.

'Sam?' she prompted when he still showed no signs of speaking, but even then he didn't say anything or look at her, just stared out over the sea while Digger sniffed around his feet and finally lay down. And, like the dog, she resigned herself to waiting patiently until he was ready.

'I was wondering,' he began at last. 'We can't turn the clock back, it just doesn't work. We can't pick up where we left off, not really, and as you said, we were just kids then. We're adults now, different people. Different things have happened to us, to shape us, strengthen us—change us. And you're right, we don't know each other. So why don't we start again? Right from the very beginning, back before we ever met, as if we don't know each other, have no history, nothing to beat each other to death with. Just two people, with common career interests, getting to know each other.'

She stared at him, because of all the things she'd expected him to come out with, that wasn't one of them. And odd though it sounded, maybe it could work.

She felt a glimmer of excitement, a flicker of hope. She moistened her lips, took a deep breath and started.

'OK. So—I'm Gemma. I'm a nurse, as you know, and I work in the surgery here, as you know, and I'm twenty-nine, and I'm sort of single—well—am I?' she asked, and he turned his head and smiled a little wryly.

'Yes,' he murmured, his voice low and slightly gruff. 'Yes, you are.'

'OK,' she said, suddenly feeling a little less confident because she hadn't ever thought of herself as single in all this time, more as—a wife on ice? 'So, I'm single, and I like children and animals, and daytime TV when I get a chance, and I read crime fiction and biographies, and I like swimming in the sea but I can't surf to save my life, and I love walking on the moors. How about you?'

He gave her a funny little smile that made her heart turn over again, and said, 'I'm Sam, I'm thirty, I'm a doctor, and I'm covering for an old childhood friend until her replacement can be found, and I've been working in Africa for an aid agency but I did something stupid and got myself blown up, which is why I walk with a limp and can't feel much in my left hand and why—why I've got some pretty horrible scars.

'And my mother's not very well, but because you did your job and checked on her even though you were off duty she's going to be fine, and I'm really grateful, and I'd like to get to know you better. And I'm single, I suppose, but there was a girl a long time ago who broke my heart, so I'm a little wary.'

That made her eyes fill and her heart twist with anguish, and she bit her lip as he went on, 'I love swimming in the sea, and I used to be able to surf but I'd probably fall over now because of my leg, and I read thrillers and crime fiction and car magazines, and I used to ride a motorbike but I can't any longer, but I still love walking on the moors, even though my ankle's not too keen on it. And I have two younger sisters, both married with children, both living fairly near but not apparently near enough to be of much help to my mother, and I have a younger brother who's off the rails a bit but basically a good kid.'

He smiled again. 'And that's me, really. Any questions?'

She shook her head. 'Not really.' Not that she could ask, anyway. Not under the terms and conditions of this new relationship. 'How about you?'

'Are you an only child?'

'No, I've got an older brother, he's thirty-three and he's married with two children, and he lives in Bristol. He's an architect.'

'Interesting. So—did you always want to be a nurse?'

She gave a strangled little laugh, then shook her head. 'No. I was going to be a doctor, like you, but then…' She faltered. Should she tell him? Explain what had happened, why she'd gone? But, no, they were playing let's pretend, and she wouldn't have told a stranger about it, so she carried on, choosing her words carefully, 'Then something happened, and I met some nurses, and I realised I'd rather do that. I'd met lots of doctors, because my father's a doctor so I've grown up round them, but I'd never really had anything to do with nurses before, and the more I talked to them, the more I thought it was a better direction for me.'

Sam was silent, assimilating her words. There was something missing, some gap in her story—something vital. But he didn't know… 'What was it that happened? Was it while you were travelling?'

Oh, rats. Tell him? Or not tell him? She wanted to, but at the same time she didn't, because she was so afraid he'd feel obliged to stand by her, just as she had all those years ago, and she didn't want that. She wanted him for himself, and she wanted him to want her for herself, not feel saddled with her out of duty or a mis-placed sense of responsibility.

So she lied—well, no, because it wasn't really a lie, but she was flexible with the truth, and it hurt. 'No, I wasn't travelling at the time, but my circumstances changed and I ended up living amongst nurses.' Well, it was true, in a way. She had, and she'd been there for ages. 'And it changed my conception of them and what they do.'

No. She was still holding something back, still not telling him all of it. But he let it go—for now. He'd get it out of her later, make her tell him everything. For now, he'd let her tell him what she wanted, and he'd try and fill in the blanks.

'So—why practice nurse rather than hospital nurse?'

'For the continuity, really,' she said, relieved to be off the sticky subject of the past and onto something she could talk about with genuine enthusiasm. 'I love the fact that I can watch an entire family grow, from inoculating the babies and giving them advice all through childhood to routine health checks on their parents, and continuing care clinics for the grandparents—like your mother, for example, who comes in regularly for her blood pressure and cholesterol, and Ron Reynolds with his angina, and then there are the children with asthma and the mums who want to give up smoking because they've just found out they're pregnant, and the drop-in contraceptive clinics to keep the youngsters out of trouble and the weight-loss clinics, and the diabetic clinics, and the travel clinics—it's just so varied. Everyone thinks it's just inoculations and smear tests and dressings, but it's not. It's fascinating, and it's all about the people. And it's the people who make the job.'

She looked at him again. 'Does that answer your question?' she asked, and he gave a slight smile.

'Yes, I think it probably does.' For now…

'Can I ask you something now?'

'Sure.'

'Why Africa?'

He looked away, his smile vanishing. 'Why not? God knows, there's a need.'

'But not everybody goes. Why you?'

'Because I was—single? Because nobody was going to be hurt if I was?'

'Except your mother. She was terribly upset.' And me…

He shrugged. 'Accidents can happen to anyone.'

'But that wasn't an accident, Sam. It was a booby trap laid by insurgents.'

'Whatever. I gave the people much more back than was taken from me during the time I was there, and that's what matters. I remember one occasion when I had to contact a colleague in London and ask for advice on a procedure I'd never done before, and the only way to contact him was by mobile phone. We had satellite phones, and he was able to text me instructions. And I saved this kid's life because of that. Without me, without the team, without people going out there and having a go in often impossible conditions, these children and their mothers and fathers would die. And it's the simple things—like appendicitis and not having clean water and not having basic antibiotics and anti-malarials that kills them so often. And I was able to make a difference.'

'And you don't think you can make a difference here? What about Ron Reynolds? If you hadn't been there in the surgery when he'd come in, he might have died.'

'No, because Hazel would have got you, and you would have taken one look at him and called an ambulance, and got Nick back from fiddling with the barbeque arrangements and he would have been fine. But there are kids out in Africa now who are dying because I'm not there.'

'Sam, that's nonsense, because if you're there, then there are children dying in India or Indonesia or South America or Birmingham or even Cornwall because you aren't there. You can't save the world. You can only do your bit.'

He turned and searched her face, then his eyes softened in a smile that made her breath catch. 'You know, you're beautiful when you get worked up about something. You come alive inside, and your skin glows and your eyes are bright and—you're just gorgeous.'

She felt her skin warm, and she couldn't stop the slightly embarrassed little laugh that escaped from her chest. 'Sam...'

'I want to kiss you,' he said softly. 'Will you let me?'

She nodded, speechless with need and emotion, and, leaning over, he angled his head and touched his lips to hers.

Just gently, just the lightest touch, but it struck a spark to the tinder of her withered, lonely heart and brought it to life. But all too soon he was lifting his head and moving away, his eyes still locked with hers.

'Can I see you again?'

She nodded. 'Of course.'

'Tonight?' He closed his eyes. 'Damn, no, I can't tonight, I promised I'd go up to the Carters' for a drink later. You could come?'

She shook her head. 'No. I don't think so. I think this should just be between us.'

A shadow crossed his face. 'Yes, of course. I was forgetting. Saturday, then? Saturday night. We could—I don't know, we could go out of town somewhere.'

'Or I could cook for you,' she suggested, and then wondered if that was too much, too soon. 'Or we could just go for a walk.'

'We could go for a walk and then you could cook for me another time.'

She smiled. 'That's two dates.'

'Mmm.' He smiled back. 'It is. Well?'

She nodded, still smiling. 'Yes. Let's go for a walk on Saturday, if it's not raining.'

'And if it is?'

She shrugged. 'We could go to the cinema?'

'And sit in the back row?'

The little bubble of laughter wouldn't stay down. They'd done that so often when they'd first started going out together. And he'd taken full advantage of the darkness…

'Maybe. If you promise to be good.'

'Oh, I'll be good,' he vowed, and she felt her heart stutter in her chest.

She sucked in a deep breath. 'OK. We'll do that, then. Walk or cinema, and then on Sunday I'll cook for you.'

He pulled a face. 'I should probably be at home on Sunday, cooking a roast for my mother. Sunday is always a roast, or it always used to be. And if I cook it, there's a fair chance it won't be drowned in saturated fat and there'll be lots of fresh vegetables.'

She cocked her head on one side. 'That sounds very civilised.'

'Oh, I can be—when the occasion demands it, I can be very civilised. But most of the time it's something fast, cheap and easy.'

She laughed. 'That sounds a little suspect,' she teased, and he chuckled.

'Well, if the cap fits…' He turned back to the dog and scratched his ears. 'Shall we go back to Mum, little man?'

Digger jumped up, tail wagging, and Sam got stiffly to his feet, flexing his left leg which was obviously giving him trouble still.

'Are you sure you're OK for a walk on Saturday?' she asked, and he shot her a curious look.

'Yes—why?'

'I just wondered. Your leg?'

'My leg's OK. I have to keep using it. It's getting better all the time, and a walk will be just what it needs. And Digger will have a great time, won't you, mate?'

They walked back to the house side by side, not quite touching but close enough for little electric currents to zing between them, and when he slipped his hand behind her back to usher her across the road she felt the warmth of it curl through her, right down to her toes.

'Have you got everything?' he asked as she stopped by her car, and she nodded.

'Yes, I picked it all up on the way out.'

'I'll just put the dog in and move my car, then.'

She unlocked her car and got in, wondering if he'd kiss her again, but instead he opened his car door once the dog was safely inside, fired up the engine and moved out into the road so she could get out, and then he gave her a lazy, sexy wink and a wave as she moved off up the hill.

It was going to be a long time till Saturday...

CHAPTER SIX

FRIDAY was busy, and Gemma hardly saw Sam.

Probably just as well, she told herself, as she wasn't sure she could control her reaction to him well enough in front of patients, but it was curious to know that he was in the room just below her. Curious and comforting, in an oddly exciting way. But then she saw him go out on his visits just before lunch, and wondered how the surgery could suddenly feel so empty.

Ridiculous.

But in her heart was a little bubble of hope, and she kept seeing that little sexy wink and the waggle of his fingers as he'd waved her off last night, and she couldn't wait till tomorrow.

'Right, that should be OK for a few days, but if you have any trouble, come back to me on Monday,' she said to Mrs Jacobs as she smoothed the dressing firmly into place over her leg ulcer. It was healing well, and hopefully the dressings could come off altogether soon.

She glanced at her watch as she showed Mrs Jacobs out of the door. Ten to twelve. Time for a bit of paperwork—mostly reminders for smear tests and well-person checks, baby inoculations and so on. Necessary, but dull, and not the part of her job she liked best, by any means.

Still, she had a good clinic this afternoon, a nice mix of young and old, well and not so well. And with any luck, it would make the day whiz by and take her mind off Sam for long enough that she could do her job!

'Sam?'

He stopped on the path of his patient's bungalow and looked in at the intimidatingly familiar face of his old headmistress in the window next door.

She was tapping on the glass, and she beckoned him in with an imperious finger. He felt a smile curve his lips, and without ceremony he crossed the grass, tapped on the door and went in. 'Well, hello, you,' he said, crossing over to her and crouching down beside her chair. 'How are you? You look well.'

'I'm very well. Back in my home at last—have you got time for a cup of tea?'

He glanced at his watch. He did, but only if he didn't stop for lunch at the practice—which meant not seeing Gemma. But he could live with that. It would heighten the suspense—as if that was necessary! But Gertrude Stanbury had been one of the very few people who'd believed in him, Nick being the other most significant one, and he owed old Gertie a damn sight more than the time for a cup of tea. Not that he'd get that if she heard him refer to her as Gertie!

'That would be lovely,' he said with genuine warmth, and he stood back and watched as she struggled to her feet and limped painfully into the kitchen.

'You're in pain,' he said, and she turned and raised that autocratic brow at him as of old.

'And just who are you to tell me that?'

He grinned. 'Ah, well, it was a medical comment.'

'Was it, indeed? I've had a knee replacement, and I need the other one done. Going to fast-track me?'

He chuckled. 'You know I would if I could, but it wouldn't be fair and, anyway, I'm only locuming. I have as much clout as you do, probably a damn sight less. So—how are you really?'

'Oh, not so good, but I manage. Sam, could you put the kettle on for me? I find it hard to lift if there's more than just a cupful in.'

'Sure.'

He wondered how on earth she did manage, and asked.

'Oh, I have a home help who's marvellous, and I get by. But I'm all the better for seeing you back home. I'm sorry about your mother. I gather she's made excellent progress.'

'She has. Who's your spy?'

She chuckled. 'Lauren. She came to put me through my paces this morning. Sam, could you pass me down those cups, please?'

'Sure. I gather you had to move out after the flood.'

'I did, but it's done me a huge favour. I've got new furniture and carpets and everywhere's redecorated—it's like a new house, and yet all my precious things were safe, because they were in the top of a wardrobe. And the rest...' She shrugged and smiled. 'Well, I won't have to worry about replacing anything again in my lifetime. The insurance company were wonderful. So—tell me about Africa. What's this I hear about you having an accident?'

'Nothing passes you by, does it?' he said gently,

taking the carefully laid tray from the worktop and following her into her sitting room.

'Not much, but I can see that you survived it, more or less. I gather young Jamie's in trouble, though, talking of things that don't pass me by,' she went on. 'You want to keep him away from Gary Lovelace. I don't often give up on a child, as you know, but—well, some people are just plain bad, and I'm afraid he might be one of them. Keep him away from him, Sam, before something awful happens.'

He sighed. 'I don't know if I can. I can threaten, cajole, bribe—but it has to come from him. And I can't find the motivator.'

'I think it all stems from your father leaving—just as yours did. That sense of abandonment—and then you left, when he was six, and now his mother's ill and could so easily have died—he's just scared to love, Sam, scared to care.'

Hell, he knew that feeling so well. He was aching to be back with Gemma, but he was so afraid to trust her, and there was something she wasn't telling him.

'How's it going with Gemma?'

He narrowed his eyes. What the hell did Gertie Stanbury know about Gemma? Could she read his mind? Apparently, because she went on, 'Oh, come on, Sam! I know you loved her—and I know she loved you. And ever since she came back to Penhally, I've been waiting for you to come home. I knew you would. You all do, in the end.'

'Maybe,' he said, and then changed the subject—or at least, the subject of the subject. 'What do you remember about Polly Searle?'

'Oh, dear, that poor child. Little mouse. She had the

most dreadful home life—awful man, her father. I was so worried what would become of her after her mother died. I thought she'd waste away at one point but she always had brains, just like you. Thank goodness she got away and she's all right. She'll be a marvellous doctor—a really good listener. Not enough people are, you know. Kate Althorp was wonderful to her, and I think they're still in touch. She's her godmother, I believe. Why do you ask?'

'Kate was talking about her. We need a woman doctor and Kate was suggesting she might be available.'

'Oh. Well, I don't know if she'll come back. It'll take a lot of courage, but she was never short of that.'

Sam tried to remember, but his image of Polly was blurred by time and had never been a strong one. 'Oh, well, time will tell, I suppose,' he said, and got to his feet. 'I need to get on. It's lovely to see you again.'

'You haven't told me about your accident.'

He grinned. 'No, that's right, I haven't. I'll have to come back again.'

'You do that, young man. You're always welcome in my house. And good luck with Gemma.'

He opened his mouth to correct her, but then shut it again and smiled. 'Thank you. And you take care of yourself. I'll see you soon.'

'Bring me good news!' she called as she watched him down the path, and he laughed and waved her goodbye, then got back into his car and drove down to the surgery, listening to the weather forecast as he went.

Tomorrow was going to be warm and sunny, with light winds and the odd bit of high cloud. Pity, he thought with a wry smile. He'd been looking forward to the cinema…

* * *

'Kate? It's Rob.'

'Oh, hi, Rob.' Kate cradled the phone against her ear and watched Jem through the open door to the sitting room. 'What can I do for you?'

'I was just wondering what you and Jem are doing today. I was hoping to see you to ask you last night at school, but you weren't there.'

'No, I'm sorry, I was working late—but we haven't any plans today,' she told him, wondering what he was going to suggest and discovering that she was actually looking forward to it, whatever it might turn out to be. 'What did you have in mind?'

'A bike ride. It's so lovely, I thought I'd take Matthew up onto Bodmin, and I wondered if you'd like to join us?'

'Oh. That would be really nice—although I can't remember when I last rode my bike. Jem's is getting a bit small for him. I'm going to have to get another one soon, I think, because he's growing like a weed. Maybe for his birthday—actually, that's a good idea. It's this month. Perhaps you can give me some guidance, because I really don't know what's good for kids or not.'

Rob chuckled. 'No problem. So I'll pick up the school minibus with the bike rack on the back and come and get you—what time?'

'How about ten? Does that give you long enough? Either then or later, so it's not too hot—and I could bring a picnic.'

'That would be really nice. I'll see you at ten, then.'

She hung up, a little smile playing around her mouth, and went through to the sitting room. Jem looked up as she walked in. 'Who was that, Mum?'

'Mr Werrick. He wondered if we'd like to go for a bike ride up on Bodmin.'

'Cool! Can we go?'

'I said yes—and we're going to take a picnic, so you need to check the tyres on both our bikes while I have a look and see what I can find in the fridge.'

'Tuna sandwiches,' Jem yelled, running out of the back door, 'and chocolate biscuits!'

'OK!' And humming, Kate took out the bread and set to work.

It was glorious up on Bodmin.

Glorious because, with the wind in her hair and Sam at her side, she could have been eighteen again, back in the days when nothing had troubled them and everything had seemed wonderful.

They'd ridden out across the moors on his big, powerful bike the summer he'd met her, when she'd only been seventeen and he eighteen, dark and dangerously exciting in his black leathers with the shadow of stubble on his jaw and that wickedly enticing twinkle in his eyes, and they'd lain in the heather and kissed for hours on end, till her lips were full and swollen and her skin was raw from stubble rash, but she wouldn't go any further. Not until she was married. She was saving herself—it was a promise she'd made to herself ages ago, and she'd meant it, but hadn't stopped Sam trying everything else that he could think of, and he'd had an amazing imagination.

But it hadn't been enough, and so the second summer, after a frustrating year of letters and phone calls during term time and seeing her only when she was down in Penhally with her parents at their holiday cottage, he'd asked her to marry him, in a crazy moment, and she'd been so stunned and so in love with him she'd said yes.

They'd been up here on the moor when he'd asked her. Lying on a picnic rug, hearts racing, their bodies screaming for that last step that she wouldn't take, and she'd often wondered if he would have asked her if she hadn't held out, or if their affair would just have fizzled out.

But he had asked her, and it seemed incredible now that they'd gone through with it. She'd gone home to Bath on the pretext of needing some more clothes and had tracked down her birth certificate, and they'd gone straight to the registrar and arranged it, booked a time for the first legal opportunity just sixteen days later, and then, without telling anyone, they'd made their vows, with Jack and Lucy Tremayne, sworn to secrecy, as their witnesses.

They'd spent forty-eight hours of hedonistic bliss in the ramshackle beach house he was renting just a mile along from the centre of the village, and with incredible patience and restraint, Sam had gently, tenderly, shown her just what her body was capable of. They'd had so much fun, shed tears of laughter and of joy, eating, sleeping, talking and above all making love again and again and again, and then reality had intruded with a thunderous knock at the door in the middle of the night, and her parents had stood there, incandescent with rage. And telling them they were married didn't help. At all.

'Hey, what's up?'

She dragged herself out of the past and looked up at him, still miles away. 'Nothing,' she said, blinking away the bitter-sweet memories of that long-ago summer. 'Just remembering.'

'Remembering?' he said, a teasing light in his eyes. 'Have you been here before, then?'

And she reminded herself that they were starting

again, without the past, without the hang-ups and heart-aches, and she smiled a little mischievously. 'Oh, once or twice, but I was much younger then. I always loved it up here. How about you?'

'Likewise—but I have to say the present's every bit as good,' he murmured.

She gazed up into his eyes, her breath lodged in her throat, and then he seemed to free himself from his trance and reached back into the car. 'Here, I brought us some lunch. We can take it with us and find some-where to sit and eat it.'

'Oh! How lovely! Thanks, Sam. Let me take it, you've got the dog.' And he couldn't manage both, not with his torn shoulder.

'Thanks. Wretched dog. He needs to learn not to go down holes so I can let him off for a run. It took five days to dig him out last time, and he was lucky to survive, apparently. Personally, I would have left him there, wouldn't I, Digger?'

Digger wriggled his tail and grinned, tongue lolling, lead taut as he stood poised for his walk, and Sam grinned back and locked the car and headed off along the path with Gemma at his side.

They walked over the rise, not too far because of his ankle, listening to the sound of the curlews and the bleating of the sheep, and then they settled down with their faces to the sun and their backs to an outcrop of granite, and ate their lunch.

'This is gorgeous,' she said round a mouthful of smoked-salmon sandwich, and he grinned.

'Ah, well, a little bird told me you like smoked salmon,' he teased. Stealing her sandwich from her hand, he opened it, peeled out the salmon and dangled it over her mouth. 'Open wide,' he instructed, and then slowly lowered it to her lips.

She took it from him, their eyes locked, and he threw the bread to the dog who was poised waiting.

'Mmm,' she said, licking her lips, and his eyes darkened, his breath hissing out and touching her face. Another inch, she thought. Just another inch, and his lips…

The contact brought a shuddering sigh from his chest, and she could feel his hand trembling against her cheek.

'God, Gemz, I want you,' he breathed, and she heard a whimper of longing—hers? Oh, yes, hers, a longing for the touch of his body, for the feel of his skin against hers, for the weight of him poised over her, his solid, muscled body trembling with restraint.

His hand slid up under her T-shirt and cupped her breast, and she arched up into his palm, aching for him just as she had all those years ago. But it was worse now, harder to hold back, because she knew what she was missing, knew just what his touch had to offer, what his body could do to hers and the heights it could take her to, but she couldn't let him, couldn't go there again, not without telling him…

Sam hauled himself back under control. He couldn't do this. Not up here, on the moor, where anybody could walk past and see them. They weren't kids any longer, they were adults—married to each other, for heaven's sake, although now that was little more than a technicality, he thought with regret—but he needed her. God, how he needed her, the healing touch of her hands on his body, the tender kisses, the sweet sighs, the fractured little screams as she neared her peak, and it was driving him mad.

'Gemz? Let's get out of here,' he groaned softly. 'I want to make love to you, and I'm not doing it with an audience of sheep and ponies and dog-walkers.'

'We can't, Sam.'

'Why not? Give me one good reason why not.'

She swallowed and forced herself to meet his eyes with an unsteady smile. 'Because we've only just met.'

She saw confusion in his eyes, then frustration and then, finally, irony. He laughed softly and dropped onto his back beside her, his wry chuckle making her smile. 'Oh, you witch. Really?'

Her smile faded. 'Really, Sam,' she said quietly. 'There's still a lot we don't know about each other. So many things have happened, so much water under the bridge—'

She broke off and he searched her face for clues. *So many things have happened.*

But what things? And why—?

'Digger, no! Come back! Oh, hell.'

He leapt up, letting out a sharp groan and clutching his thigh, and headed off after the dog. 'Digger, damn it, come back here!'

But Digger had seen something, and he was off. Gemma scrambled to her feet and ran after them both, and then watched in horror as the terrier leapt into the path of a group of cyclists and tried to bite the front wheel of the leading bike.

The bike wobbled, all the others swerved and crashed, and the first bike arced through the air and landed on top of the child in the heather.

Oh, lord, she thought, and, racing past Sam, she arrived to a scene of chaos and sobbing, with Kate Althorp in the middle of it.

'Kate! I'm so sorry, he's a naughty dog. Digger, come here, baby. Good boy.' She caught the limping dog and held him while Sam went to the child who'd fallen off. Jem, she thought. It's Jem. She didn't recognise the other boy, or the man who was hovering over him, but she knew Kate's son, and she heaved a sigh of relief as he got to his feet, flexing his wrist and trying not to cry.

'Are you all right, Jem?' Kate was asking, and he nodded.

'How's Matthew?'

'He's fine,' the man said. 'He's banged his shin but I think he's all right.'

'Here, Jem, let me have a look. I'm a doctor,' Sam was saying gently, feeling the boy's forearm and wrist carefully with his fingers. 'I think it's OK, but it's hard to tell. It could be a sprain. If you can come down to the surgery, I'll X-ray it for you and check, and we can plaster it if necessary, but I don't think it will be. I'm just so sorry—I was distracted, and the dog just got away from me.'

Distracted by kissing Gemma, who was standing a few feet away from him looking shaken. Idiot. He should have tied the dog's lead to his foot, not just assumed that the promise of food would be enough to keep him there.

'It's all right, accidents happen,' Kate said, but Gemma could see she was shaking as she bent over her son. 'All right, my love?'

Jem nodded, sniffing a little and struggling to be brave, and Kate said, 'I'm sorry, I should introduce everyone. This is Rob Werrick and his son Matthew, and this is my son Jeremiah. Rob, this is Sam Cavendish, our locum doctor, and Gemma, our practice nurse.'

'Sam—of course,' Rob said, nodding at him. 'I should have recognised you, you're the spitting image of your brother.'

Sam grunted. Was he? Of course he was—and they were both the spitting image of their father, although he'd left his mother because he didn't believe Jamie was his, of all the ironies. And now was not the time to get into that.

'Where's your car?' he asked, and Rob jerked his head towards the top of the hill.

'Up there—it's next to a silver hire car. Is that yours?'

'Yes. So we're going in the same direction. How are we going to get us all back there?'

'I'll go and get the van—it's the school minibus, it'll go over these tracks. I won't be long. Matt, stay here with Jem and Kate, and I'll be as quick as I can, all right?'

He nodded, and his father set off for the car park at a run, and they settled down to wait. Sam glanced at the injured boy, and felt a vague flicker of recognition. Jem looked familiar, but he couldn't work out why. He was nothing like James Althorp, that was for sure, but he reminded him so clearly of someone…

'Why don't we sit down and wait for him?' he suggested, and they all sank down on the heather, the bikes still lying where they'd fallen, and Gemma brought the dog over to him, a worried look in her eyes.

'Sam, I'm not sure, but I think Digger might be hurt.'

'Oh, no! I didn't mean to hurt him!' Jem said, sounding worried, but Sam just gave him a rueful smile.

'It's hardly your fault, Jem. He's a rascal. Digger, come here, boy, let me see.'

But he was holding his paw up, and Sam could see without getting closer that it was swelling.

'I think it might have got run over,' he said quietly. 'Silly, silly dog. That'll teach you to chase bikes. We'll have to take you to the vet later.'

'You can go now. Uncle Nick can X-ray my arm,' Jem said. 'He won't mind.'

Uncle Nick? Or…?

The recognition was sudden and startling, and Sam let out his breath on a quiet, surprised sigh and turned back to the dog while he assimilated the information. Nick and Kate? Really? When?

'Mum, I think my bike's broken.'

'Oh, no,' Sam groaned. 'Look, I'll pay for a new one, OK?'

'No, you won't,' Kate said with a smile. 'It was too small for him anyway. I was going to buy him a new one for his birthday—it's this month.'

May. Nine months after August. So that summer, the summer he and Gemma had got married, the summer of the storm, Nick and Kate had been having an affair?

God. Had Annabel known? Had Jack, or Lucy, or Ed?

No. Surely not? There'd been no sign—not that he would have noticed, he admitted, because he'd been so wrapped up in Gemma the world could have fallen apart and they wouldn't have noticed.

The sound of an engine interrupted his thoughts, and the minibus appeared over the rise and bumped its way down to them. Minutes later they were packed up and away, and although the dog was injured, Sam insisted that they drive down to the surgery to make sure Jem was all right before they took Digger to the vet.

They were met by Nick, who examined the boy's arm and X-rayed it with a curious detachment that Sam found puzzling. Almost as if he was keeping his distance…

'Well, it's just a sprain, I think,' Nick said, and Sam, looking at the X-ray over his shoulder, nodded in relief and turned back to the others, to see Rob's gaze flicking curiously from Nick to Jem and back again. So he can see it, too, Sam thought. It's not just me. And who else has worked it out? Did Nick know? Surely to God he must?

But it was none of his business, and he forced himself to concentrate. 'Thank heavens for that,' he said, and smiled at the boy apologetically. 'I'm really sorry, Jem, but I'll make sure you get a new bike out of it, OK? It's the least I can do. Right, if it's OK with you all, I need to take the wretched dog to the vet now,' he said. 'Who do I call?'

'Oh, that'll be Melinda Lovac. Dragan was complaining that she was on call and so he'd be left with a grizzly baby,' Gemma said with a smile. 'He's teething, and he's had a cold. Give her a ring—here, we've got her number,' she said, and, going behind Reception, she looked it up, dialled the number and handed him the receiver, then went to put a support bandage on Jeremiah's arm.

'Oh, Digger! What a smart paw!' Gemma said, popping in later to see how he was and admiring his bandage. 'And what a lovely hat!'

'Idiot dog,' Sam grumbled as Digger turned round and smashed the clear plastic Elizabethan collar into his leg. 'How's Jem?'

'Fine. He's a bit sore, but I've put a support on it and he's OK, and everyone else is all right. Matthew's got a little bruise on his shin but, apart from that, the only other damage is to Jem's bike.'

'I still think I should replace it.'

'No. Kate's insistent she's buying him one for his birthday.'

'Well, she can, but I'm paying for it,' he said stubbornly, and Gemma chuckled.

'I'll let you two sort it out between you,' she said, knowing just how stubborn Kate could be, too. 'So what happened to his paw?'

'Fractured metacarpal. Melinda said he'll be fine, but he needs to keep the bandage on as long as possible—which will be as long as we can stand him crashing into things in that lampshade. Hopefully it'll teach him a lesson, but I'm not holding my breath. He's a terrier, and terriers are born to chase and to dig. He does both, with knobs on!' He tipped his head over to one side. 'So—we never got to finish lunch,' he said softly, 'and there's the remains of the picnic sitting in the cool box in my car. How's about going down to the beach to finish it? Without the dog?'

'Oh, Digger, he's so mean to you!' she murmured, scratching his head inside the collar, and then she straightened up with a smile and met his eyes. His sexy, smouldering, midnight-blue eyes. And then she remembered what they were doing, what he was saying, when the dog had run off, and her heart pounded.

'That sounds lovely,' she said, and she pulled herself together with effort. They were supposed to be getting to know each other all over again—but not that fast! And there was so much she needed to tell him before she let him get that close, but they should be safe on the beach. 'But I can't stop for long,' she added. 'I've got lots to do.'

Which was a total lie, because she'd cleaned her house until it squeaked the previous weekend, apart from the ironing—well, OK, the ironing was still there, and would take her the rest of this weekend, so it wasn't really a lie, except that now she'd have to do it!

'Come on, then, we'll take the car. All that running over rough ground hasn't done my ankle any good. I reckon Lauren will kill me.'

'No, she won't. She'll just sigh and fix it,' she said, and followed him out of the door, leaving the disappointed dog behind.

They drove up over the rise past the church and the Smugglers' Inn, and then past the surfing beach and on to the next cove, to the beach where Sam had been camping out in the tumbledown little wooden shack all those summers ago.

The place where they'd spent their honeymoon, she thought, with the single bed against the wall and a Primus stove to cook on and not much else, but it had been home, for one glorious and utterly romantic weekend. It wasn't there any more, of course. It had been in a terrible state even then, and she imagined it had fallen to pieces long ago.

'There used to be a little cabin here on stilts, just on the edge of the beach, by the sand dunes,' she said softly, carrying on their game of let's pretend as they settled down on the sand with their backs to a rock. 'Along there, at the end.'

He met her eyes, his expression sombre. 'Yes. It got smashed to bits in a storm, just after my…' He hesitated, then went on, 'Just after the girl I loved left me.'

She felt tears fill her eyes. She hadn't known that. Hadn't known that the house had been destroyed by the storm, that Sam could have been in it, that everything inside must have been washed into the sea. And all those memories…

'I'm sorry,' she said, her heart aching for him, because it had been his retreat, the place he came to escape the pressures of home. And for those few days, it had been like living in paradise. 'Were you—were you here? When it happened?'

'No. I was up in the village, trying to help get the kids off the rocks,' he said bleakly, remembering how he'd helped them, how he'd watched James Althorp being washed away, and Nick's brother Phil being smashed against the cliff by a huge wave, but none of it had reached him because he'd been numb inside, so overwhelmed with pain because she'd left him that he'd shut down. 'I didn't think about the house at all. But then I went back later, and it was gone, everything washed away, just broken matchwood flung up on the foreshore and a few bits of clothing lying around in the seaweed like so much flotsam. I didn't come here again for years.'

'Oh, Sam. I'm so sorry.'

He smiled, a fleeting, sad smile, and shook his head. 'Don't be. It was a long time ago, and nothing to do with us.'

Really? He was still persisting with that? OK. She took a deep, steadying breath and prodded the cool box with her foot. 'So are you going to feed me, then, or is this going to be yet another occasion when you tease me with food and then leave me hungry?' she said lightly, and he gave a soft huff of laughter and pulled the lid off.

'Oh, I don't want to leave you hungry, Gemma.

That's not my style. Not my style at all. So—what do you fancy?'

You, she thought, her heart thumping. I want you, Sam. Nothing else. Nothing more. Just you. But I don't know if I can have you, and I don't know if it's fair to ask…

CHAPTER SEVEN

SUNDAY was dull.

Gemma spent the whole day ironing and daydreaming about Sam, and the night doing the other sort of dreaming—the sort of dreaming that had been more and more frequent since he'd come back, and which, since Saturday's kiss, had started to spiral out of control.

And on Monday morning she went back to work, and he was the first person she saw, coming upstairs to the staffroom to grab a cup of tea before his surgery.

'You don't have to do that, my duck, I'll bring it down to you in a moment. You go on,' Doris said, fussing around him, and Sam thanked her and shot Gemma a wry smile over her head—a smile that said had they been alone, there might have been another kiss.

She went into her room and was buzzed almost immediately.

'Morning, gorgeous,' he murmured in a wonderfully growly purr that sent a shiver down her spine. 'How's the ironing?'

'Done,' she said with a smile. 'How was the roast?'

'Good—except that Jamie went out straight afterwards and didn't get home till three. I had to drag him out of bed again this morning—but you don't need to hear that. I just wanted to tell you—oh, thank you, Doris, put it there, that's great.' He paused, and she heard his door click shut before he went on in that deep, persuasive rumble, 'My mother's got an appointment at the hospital today, so I'll be going in after lunch with her and then after that I'm free, and you did mention the other day that you'd cook for me at some point, so I thought tonight might be a good opportunity…'

She squashed a smile. 'Are you inviting yourself to dinner, Dr Cavendish?'

She could hear his answering smile down the phone. 'Do you know, Nurse Johnson, I believe I might be?'

And then there was a funny silence, while they both thought about that. Because of course she wasn't Johnson any more, but she wasn't Cavendish either, not really, and she wasn't sure if she ever would be again. It took her a second to get her mind back in order, to remind herself that they were playing a game and she needed to stick to the rules, for now at least, and then she took a deep breath and said, 'Well, then, I suppose it would be churlish not to extend a formal invitation, wouldn't it?'

'It might very well be. Seven-thirty or eight?'

'Or earlier. I have to be at work tomorrow morning at eight, so if you don't want to be kicked out the moment you've scraped up the last morsel, you could make it seven.'

'Seven will do nicely. Can I bring anything?'

'Just yourself. You know the way to Seagull Cottage, don't you?'

'I'm sure I'll find it,' he said with a chuckle in his voice. 'I'll see you later.'

'I'll look forward to it.'

She cradled the phone with a smile, and tried to concentrate on her patients, but then a man hobbled into her room and asked if she could put something on his leg to support it, because it was swelling a bit since he'd trapped it between the boats on Friday. Alarm bells rang instantly.

'Friday?' she said. 'But it's Monday.'

'Well, I've been busy, and I didn't think it was anything to worry about really, but it's giving me a bit of stick now.'

'Well, let me have a look,' she said, and when he rolled up his trouser leg she had to stifle a gasp. It was black. Literally black, from the knee down, and she couldn't imagine how much pain he must be in. 'I really think you need to see a doctor with this,' she said, comparing it to his other, undamaged, leg. It was nearly twice the size, and she was worried for the circulation to his foot.

If it wasn't too late to worry. She hoped not. The foot was cool—colder than the other one, but not too much so, and she buzzed Sam and asked him if he could pop up for a moment when he was free.

'I'll come now, you've caught me between patients,' he said, and she heard his uneven tread on the landing and then a sharp tap as he entered.

'This is Mr Polgrean, he trapped his leg between two boats on Friday,' she explained, and Sam took one look at it and nodded briskly.

'Hello there, Mr Polgrean, I'm Dr Cavendish.'

'I know who you are, and your brother's no better. Don't know what your mother's thinking about the way she's let you both run around, causing havoc and making people's lives a misery. I want another doctor. I don't want you anywhere near my leg.'

Sam folded his arms and nodded from the other side of the room, but Gemma could see the withdrawal in his eyes and knew he must be hurt. 'OK. Fair enough. But I'm the only doctor on the premises at the moment, and I don't know if you have any idea of the seriousness of this injury, but even from here I can tell you that there's a possibility you'll lose the leg if you don't get to hospital immediately. I think you have a thing called compartment syndrome—'

'This is no time for one of your jokes, young man,' Mr Polgrean said. 'I know what you're doing, and it won't work.'

Sam ignored him and carried on. 'When you caught your leg between the boats, you bruised it, but there's a problem with that. Each of the muscles in your leg is enclosed in a sheath, and you've sustained such severe injuries to the muscles that they've all swollen and because of the tight sheath around each one, the pressure on the muscles is going to cause them to die. And then you'll lose your leg. And if you ignore it for too long, you could die. Now, clever money would go to hospital and have an operation to cut a little slit in each of the sheaths to reduce the compression on the muscles and save your leg, but if you like, I'll go back downstairs and we can let nature take its course.'

Mr Polgrean stared at Sam for an age and swallowed hard. 'You're just trying to frighten me. You're blinding me with science and trying to scare the living daylights out of me, but I know you and your practical jokes, Sam Cavendish, and I'm not falling for this one.'

'No. I'm not joking,' he said quietly. 'I'm sorry you

don't like me or my family, but that's nothing to do with this. I did a lot of things when I was young that I regret, but I'm not going to let that lead me into doing something else as an adult that I'll regret even more, and if I walk away from you now and you lose your leg, I won't be able to live with myself. And I have to say, dumping several stone of spoilt herring on our drive was pretty good revenge,' he added softly. 'I was clearing it up for days.'

Mr Polgrean grunted, but his leg was obviously extremely painful, and Gemma was getting worried. Sam was standing there waiting, Mr Polgrean was lying with arms folded over his bulky chest and the faint aroma of rotting fish drifting from him, and she wondered what it would take to break the deadlock.

But then he started to chuckle. 'Days?' he said. 'Did it take you that long, boy?'

Sam's mouth twitched. 'It did, and I never forgot it. I thought I'd never get the smell off my hands.'

'I've still got that mermaid painted on my boat,' Mr Polgrean said slowly. 'You did a good job. Best endowed mermaid I ever did see,' he mused, a smile flickering on his face. 'But your brother—'

'My brother is nothing to do with this, and I'm dealing with him.'

'Not fast enough. He was outside last night with that Gary Lovelace, causing all sorts of mayhem. Wonder they weren't all arrested.'

Gemma saw Sam close his eyes and sigh quietly.

'So—what's it to be? Hospital, or sit there and argue until your leg drops off?' It was said quietly, very matter-of-factly, and after a moment the man nodded.

'All right, then. Do your worst, young Dr Cavendish, but I tell you, if I die, I'm coming back to haunt you.'

Sam grinned wryly. 'I don't doubt it, Mr Polgrean. I don't doubt it for a moment.'

The tap on her door was a minute early, but it wouldn't have mattered if he'd been ten minutes early, or ten minutes late, come to that, because she was still in her bedroom vacillating between the blue jeans with a long-sleeved T-shirt, the black trousers with a lacy vest top and a shrug over the top, and a little sundress that was probably too thin for the cool May evening but was so pretty she really, really wanted to wear it.

And now here he was, and she still hadn't made a decision.

'Eeny, meeny, miny, mo,' she said, and grabbed the little dress at random, hauling it over her head and fluffing her hair into place before running downstairs in bare feet.

'Hi,' she said, opening the door, and he came in, took one look at her and dumped the flowers he was carrying and kissed her.

'Hi, yourself,' he murmured when he came up for air. 'You look gorgeous. I brought you some flowers and some of Mum's chocolate stash, in the interests of preventative medicine.'

She chuckled and went up on tiptoe and kissed his cheek. 'Thank you. That's very public spirited of you, and I'll do my best to justify your faith in my ability to protect the community from harm.'

He laughed and pulled her back up against him and kissed her once more, then he freed her slowly and sniffed. 'Something smells good. What are we having?'

'Moules marinière, and fresh home-made bread—
well, it will be, when it comes out of the breadmaker—
and steak from the Trevellyans' with a green salad and
some new potatoes, and I've got a nice bottle of Chablis
in the fridge and some Merlot if you'd rather. Except
of course you're driving.'

He grinned. 'That's fine. I can still get you tipsy and
have my evil way with you,' he murmured, and she felt
a quiver of need race through her.

'Ever the gentleman,' she murmured, and turned
away to the stove, only to find his arms sneaking round
her and easing her up against his hard, muscular body.

'You wouldn't really want that,' he murmured into
the angle of her neck, his lips nibbling at her skin.

'Maybe not, but I want to eat first,' she said, and then
there was a breathless silence before he reached out and
switched off the hob, then turned her slowly into his arms.

'First?' he said, his face taut, his body rigid with
tension.

She gave in. 'Oh, Sam,' she whispered, and going up
on tiptoe, she cradled his face in her hands and drew him
down for her kiss. 'I've missed you so much.'

'Hell, Gemz,' he muttered, and then his mouth was
plundering hers, searching it hungrily, his lips moving
over her face, her throat, over her collar bones while his
right hand slid up inside her dress, dragging it up so he
could curl his fingers over her hipbone and haul her closer.

'I need you, Gemma. It's been so damn long and I
just want to hold you.'

She eased away from him, took his shaking hand in
hers and led him up the steep, narrow staircase to her
bedroom. The bed was made, the linen freshly washed
and ironed, courtesy of yesterday, and she threw the

jeans and trousers off it and then gasped as he seized the hem of her dress and peeled it over her head.

'Oh, God, you look the same,' he said, his eyes, as black as midnight, trailing over her and leaving fire in their wake. 'So lovely—so damned lovely.'

'And you're overdressed,' she said, and heard her voice shake a little.

She reached for his belt and unbuckled it, her hands trembling so much she could hardly shift the zip, and he took over, heeling off his shoes and shucking his jeans and boxers and socks in one smooth movement.

His shirt was next, dragged over his head with a muffled groan as he raised his left arm too high for his torn shoulder to tolerate, but it slowed him down, gave him time to draw breath and get himself back under control before he reached for her again.

Because he wanted to do this right. He had no idea what had been wrong before, but something had, he was sure of it, and he wasn't making any mistakes this time; not if it killed him, but after eleven years his control was hanging by a very frayed and tattered thread.

He held out his arms to her, and she walked straight into them, wrapping her arms around him so that he felt her warm, soft body against his for the first time in so long, and he gave a shuddering sigh.

'God, I've missed you. That feels so good,' he mumbled into her hair. 'So soft, so warm. Gemma—'

'Shh. Come on,' she said. Taking him by the hand again, she led him to the bed and turned back the covers, then lay down beside him and drew him into her arms and lifted her face to his.

Oh, dear heaven, it felt so good to hold him, to kiss him, to hold his big, strong body against hers after so long.

She was shaking all over, and she could feel the tremors running through him every time she touched him.

And she did touch him. She had to, her hands greedy for the feel of him, starved of his touch for too long. Their mouths sought each other, their breath mingling on gasps and sighs as they each rediscovered yet another place, another area of skin that seemed suddenly unreasonably sensitive.

And then he was moving over her, his body shaking as he held himself poised above her, his eyes burning like black coals as they held hers and he entered her with one long, slow, steady thrust that took her clean over the edge.

'Sam!' she screamed, and he drove into her, again and again and again, until with a savage, agonised cry he followed her into oblivion.

'I'm starving. All I can smell is that fresh bread, and I am so damn hungry my stomach's attacking me.'

She chuckled and lifted herself up on one elbow, staring down into his eyes. They were smoky now, the pupils back to normal, the expression slaked—for now, at least, as other needs took over.

'I'd better go down to the kitchen and get stuck in, then, hadn't I?' she said. Throwing off the covers, she pulled her sundress on over her head and padded down the stairs, turning on the stove again and throwing the mussels into the pan on top of the softened onions and garlic and humming softly.

She was stirring them when he appeared, dressed only in his jeans, with the top button undone and that delicious arrow of hair tempting her to follow it down...

'Don't look at me like that or we won't eat tonight and I swear I really will fade away.'

'Yeah, right,' she said, but she turned back to the stove, smiling to herself, and he came up behind her and inspected the food over her shoulder.

'If you want a job, you could take the bread out of the breadmaker, but mind you don't burn yourself.'

'I'm not six,' he reprimanded gently, tipping the golden, steaming loaf out onto the breadboard. 'Wow. I could just rip it in half and eat it.'

'And die. Back off. You can open the wine, I need some for the sauce.'

'Nag, nag, nag,' he grumbled, but he did as she'd asked and handed her the bottle.

'Here, pick out the ones that haven't opened and chuck them,' she said, tipping out the mussels and throwing the wine and cream into the pan.

He leant over her shoulder and sniffed. 'Oh, that smells so good. Funny, I've never thought of you as domesticated, but it works, you know? I think I could go for that, the whole barefoot and pregnant in the kitchen thing—'

He broke off, then swore softly. 'Oh, hell, Gemz. I didn't think about that before.'

She felt a shiver of something that could have been fear but could just as easily have been hope, and her eyes filled. If only it was so simple. If only she could just assume, like everybody else...

'Don't worry, it's a safe time,' she said, without going into details, and kept her eyes firmly fixed on the bubbling sauce.

He grunted, then handed her back the sorted mussels and held out the bowls as she dished up. 'Shall I cut the bread?'

'Mmm—big hunks, but not too big because we've still got the steak to come, and then there's the chocolate.'

'We'll see. We may have to have an inter-course break.'

She spluttered with laughter. 'Did you mean that quite like that?' she asked, and he grinned wickedly.

'I believe I meant it exactly like that. Eat up, I want to take you back to bed, my lovely girl. We've got a lot of catching up to do.'

It was nearly ten before they ate the steak, meltingly tender and bursting with flavour, and Sam thought he'd never tasted anything so good in his life. He pushed the plate away and met her eyes.

'That was fan-tastic,' he said slowly, and smiled. 'Utterly gorgeous. Beautiful. Sexy as hell.'

'Are we still talking about the steak here?' she asked, and he chuckled.

'Probably not. But that was pretty special, too.' He glanced at his watch. 'I wonder if Jamie's home?'

'Was he meant to be?'

'After last night? Damn right. I gave him hell, courtesy of Mr Polgrean.'

'What was all that about a mermaid, by the way?' she asked, fascinated. 'What *did* you do to his boat?'

'Ah,' he said, and grinned. 'Yeah, well, there were some marks on the paintwork, and they just suggested this shape to me, so I got some paint—proper marine paint, not any old stuff—and I painted a mermaid over the marks. And she—ah—she was a bit generous in the—ah…'

'Top-heavy?'

He frowned thoughtfully. 'Not really. Just very, very lush.'

'Not like me, then,' she said, wondering if it was utterly unreasonable to be jealous of a mermaid, but Sam just laughed.

'Nothing like you. For a start, you don't have scaly legs.'

'Thank God for that!'

He laughed again, and then getting up he cleared the table, put the plates into the dishwasher and pulled her to her feet. 'I think it's time for chocolate.'

'In the sitting room?'

'No—upstairs,' he said, smiling. 'Go up and wait for me.'

So she went up and sat in the middle of the bed, still in her sundress, and he came up a few minutes later with a tray.

'What on earth have you got there?'

'Grapes, apple, banana and chocolate. Melted chocolate.'

'Oh, wow. DIY chocolate fondue.'

'Exactly. And I'll feed you, but first you have to take off your dress.'

'Done,' she said, flinging it aside. 'I'll have apple first.'

'Uh-uh. We haven't started yet. Lie down.'

She lay, and he picked up a slice of apple, dipped it in the chocolate and dangled it over her mouth. 'Open—now suck.'

She sucked, and his eyes widened.

'Oh, hell, this is not going to work.'

'Works for me,' she mumbled round the apple.

He sighed and dipped a slice of banana into the bowl and trailed the warm chocolate over her chest, then licked it away, and she shivered. He did it again, but then his tongue encountered a little bump in the skin, and he licked it clean and looked at it. A tiny scar. He didn't remember it, but there was plenty of time in eleven years for her to have picked up a scar. He pressed his lips to it and lifted his head, meeting her eyes with a smile.

'Get the idea?'

'Oh, yes,' she said, and, taking her finger and dipping it into the chocolate, she tipped him onto his back and dribbled it down his chest and across the flat, taut plane of his abdomen before putting her finger into her mouth so she could suck it clean while he watched her through narrowed eyes, his breath hissing through his teeth. Then slowly, inch by inch, she followed the dark, glossy trail down his ribs, scooping it up with her tongue while he lay and groaned.

'This was a lousy idea,' he muttered.

She lifted her head and grinned at him mischievously. 'You think? I've never had so much fun with chocolate.'

She straddled him and reached for another fingerful of warm temptation, and as she stroked it over his dark, flat nipples they pebbled under her fingertip and she felt his body harden even more.

'I want you.'

'I know. I can feel.'

'I love you, Gemz,' he said then, and she stopped, her finger halfway to the sauce, and tears filled her eyes.

'Oh, Sam, I love you, too. I've never stopped loving you.'

'Then why—? Oh, hell, what now?'

She stared at him, and then gradually the sound of his mobile phone got through to her. She moved off him, and he sat up and reached for his jeans, pulling the phone out of his pocket with a short sigh.

'Jamie. What the hell does he want?' He flipped the phone open. 'Yeah, hi. What is it?'

'Sam? Sam, where are you?'

'With Gemma,' he said, picking up a note of panic in his brother's voice. 'Why? What's going on? What's the matter?'

'Sam, you have to come. It's Gary—there's been an accident!'

'What! Where? What kind of accident?'

'A car accident. He stole a car, and he's rolled it, and he's trapped underneath, and— Sam, I can smell petrol! You have to come.'

He stabbed a button and put the phone on hands-free. 'Where are you?' he asked, dragging on his jeans while Gemma pulled clothes out of the cupboard and got dressed, handing him his shirt so he could put it on, sorting out his socks and shoes.

'Up at the top of Dunheved Road, near the old mine workings. The car's upside down in a field, and I can hear him screaming!'

'Screaming's good,' Sam said. 'Don't worry, I'm coming. Dial 999 and get police, ambulance and fire brigade there now. I'll be with you in two minutes.' He hung up and turned to Gemma. 'I have to go.'

'I'm coming. You might need help.'

'No, it could be dangerous.'

'Sam, shut up and move,' she said, and ran downstairs after him, her heart in her mouth. No way was she letting Sam put himself in danger without adequate back-up, and, besides, he might need help.

And she'd just have to put her feelings for the boy aside and try and remain professional.

They found the car easily, from the wreckage strewn across the road and Jamie standing by the verge, his face striken.

'Sam, he's here, come on, you've got to get him out!'

'Have you called the emergency services?'

'What? No, Gary said no, he didn't want the police.'

'Don't be ridiculous,' Sam growled. Pulling out his phone, he dialled 999 and ran towards the car, handing the phone to Gemma. 'Keep out of range of the fumes and tell them where we are. I'll give you an update on Gary.' He ducked down beside the car with a sharp grunt, and stuck his head under the edge of the wing. 'Gary? It's Sam. Tell me what hurts.'

'Everything,' the youth sobbed. 'Everything hurts.'

'Can you move?'

'No—I'm stuck, and I can't move at all. It really hurts if I try, but I'm scared and I can't breathe properly.'

'Don't worry, we'll get you out. Are you bleeding anywhere?'

'I don't know. It's wet, but I don't know. And my back's lying on a rock or something, because it really hurts.'

'Sam? Gemma said to give you this,' Jamie said, handing him a torch with shaking hands.

'Great.' But it wasn't, because in the torchlight he could see pink froth around Gary's lips, evidence of lung trauma. And that meant he was running out of time. 'Gemma?'

'Yes?'

He turned his head towards her but toned down the words for Gary's benefit. 'Tell them he's trapped under the car. He's bleeding from a head wound, but his pupils are equal and reactive, and his GCS is 14 at the moment. He's having trouble breathing and he says his back hurts. He could be stuck on a rock. Tell them to get a wriggle on, I think he'd like to get out quite soon.'

'OK,' she called, but he could hear the tremor in her

voice, and he cursed his brother and this stupid, stupid idiot he'd got himself mixed up with. Joy-riding, of all the dangerous and lunatic things, and their timing…

'Right, I'm going to try and get closer and see what's going on,' he said, but he just couldn't. The gap was too small, and every time he tried to shift himself, he got a shaft of pain through his shoulder.

And then Gemma was at his side, handing the phone to Jamie and telling him to give directions and stand by to flag down the emergency services, then tugging at his clothes.

'Sam? Get out of the way, you're too big to fit in there.'

'No way! You aren't going in! Gemz, no!'

'Shut up and move,' she said under her breath. 'Someone needs to assess him, and you can't get in there, and if one of us doesn't he might die.'

'He's not going to die.'

'Do you know that?'

And of course he didn't, but there was a chance they all would, with the petrol leak, and just the thought of Gemma trapped under the car if it went up brought bile to his throat.

'You can't—'

'I can. Please.'

And because she was right, because she was smaller than him, and fitter, and more agile, he had to let her, even though it tore him apart.

He couldn't lose her now—not now, after eleven damn years of wanting her back. Not when they were so close to sorting it out. He felt hot tears sting his eyes, but there was no time for sentiment, and he ran back to his car and pulled his medical bag out of the boot.

'Here, I've got a cannula. See if you can establish

IV access, and I've got some oxygen and a mask. And, Gemz?'

'Yes?'

'I love you.'

CHAPTER EIGHT

I LOVE you.

The words stayed in her head, echoing round and round for the next dreadful minutes as she struggled to get IV access and keep him oxygenated.

'Gary, lie still, you mustn't move your head, you might have a neck injury. Just lie as still as you can for me, that's great, and we'll get you out of here as soon as we can.'

She could hear the sirens approaching, the blue flashing lights flickering on their surroundings and casting weird shadows under the cramped space she was squeezed in with the injured boy. And what she could see in those pulses of light didn't reassure her at all.

She reached her hand under his shoulder and felt something warm and tacky, and her heart sank. Blood. Lots of it, seeping out of him at an unsustainable rate, and he was starting to fit.

'OK, we have to get him out of here *now*!' she yelled, and Sam ducked down behind her and laid his hand on her thigh.

'What's going on?'

'He's fitting, Sam, and there's so much blood— Oh,

hell, he's gone off. He's not breathing. Sam, we have to get the car off him or we don't stand a chance!'

Behind her, she heard Sam relaying her message, then the voices of the other men arguing, and then she felt someone grab hold of her feet and pull her out.

'What are you doing?'

'We're going to roll the car off him. Come on, out of the way, Gemz.'

He hauled her to her feet and they stumbled backwards as the fire crew and policemen heaved in a concerted effort, and the car hovered and then rolled away, bouncing back on its wheels with a series of creaks and groans.

Light flooded the scene, and Sam dived in almost before the car had settled and put his ear to Gary's chest. 'Quiet!' he yelled, and everyone fell silent. 'Right, he's still with us, we need to stabilise his spine and then scoop and run! Move!'

They moved, and in a matter of moments he was log-rolled onto the spinal board, supported and strapped in place and loaded into the waiting ambulance. And Adam Donnelly was there, too, getting into the ambulance and telling Sam to go back to Jamie.

'He needs you, he's in a hell of a state. I've got this one. Maggie's coming, she'll see to him. Right, let's go, everybody!'

Sam turned and looked at Jamie, who was hovering on the fringe, his face ashen and his body shaking. And for the first time he realised there was blood running down his cheek.

He must have scratched himself climbing through the hedge, he thought dumbly, and then Jamie held his stomach and turned away. 'I feel sick,' he said, and retched violently onto the ripped-up grass at the side of the road.

'Jamie?' Gemma crossed to him and put her arm round his shoulders, and Sam stared at him in consternation. Was it just shock? Or…?

'So can anybody tell me how it happened?'

Sam turned to see Lachlan D'Ancey standing in the road with a cluster of police around him, and his heart sank. Of all the things for Jamie to get himself involved in, he thought, and then he heard Jamie talking and his breath jammed in his throat.

'He said he'd borrowed it—I didn't even realise he had a licence, but then I realised it wasn't borrowed at all, and I begged him to stop, but he just went faster, and he was laughing and saying old man Polgrean deserved it if he trashed his car after last night, and then we started to skid and there was a thump and we were just flying through the air.'

Dear God. He'd been in the car?

Sam felt his legs give, and jammed his knees back to stop them collapsing. No! He hadn't been in the car! Surely not? He'd have been injured, and Sam hadn't even so much as glanced at him.

'Jamie, let me see you,' he said, crossing to him and taking the torch from Gemma. He flashed it in his eyes, but to his relief his pupils were equal and reactive and although he was obviously distressed, he was alert.

So he might be concussed, but he wasn't showing signs of brain injury yet. He was lucid, shocked but basically functioning, and Sam lowered the torch and handed it back to Gemma.

'What hurts?' he asked, scanning him quickly and noting he was holding his left arm. 'Were you wearing a seat belt?'

Jamie nodded. 'I was—Gary wasn't.'

Of course not. He'd thought he was immortal, beyond the laws of man or God, but he'd found out the hard way that that simply wasn't true. And he'd taken Jamie with him on that fateful journey with potentially disastrous consequences, and they could have both been dead.

He swallowed hard. 'I need to check you over properly,' he said, wrestling back his control and prioritising.

'Is he dead?' Jamie's voice was hollow, and Sam ached for him. He felt Gemma beside him squeeze his arm, giving him support. 'No, but he's in a very bad way,' he said softly.

'I want to go with him.'

'No, I need to look at you, Jamie. We can go to the surgery.'

'Can we talk to James now? We need to take a formal statement.'

He shook his head. 'Not yet, Lachlan. I want to check him out first. I need to have a proper look at him and X-ray his arm, amongst other things. But you could talk to Mrs Lovelace. She needs to know. Gemma? Keep an eye on him for a minute, I'm just going to pick up my things. I won't be long, bro.'

So while he retrieved his medical equipment from the midst of the wreckage, she put her arm round Jamie's waist and led him to Sam's car and put him into the passenger seat, then perched on the edge and held him tight as he started to shake violently.

'Are you OK, Jamie?' she asked softly.

'I'm fine,' he said, but his voice was flat and his body was shaking like a leaf.

'How's your arm?'

He looked down at it in confusion. 'Um—I don't know. Sore? I can't really feel anything.'

Oh, Sam, come on, she thought. Come and talk to him. Come and check him over.

But then Maggie Donnelly, Adam's wife, appeared and crouched down and asked him a few questions, then went back to Sam, who shook his head. Oh, no, Sam, she thought, because she'd heard Jamie's answers, and she didn't like them.

She went to Sam, taking his hand and gripping it tight. 'They have to take him to hospital, Sam,' she said, backing the paramedic up. 'Maggie's right, they have to get him checked over properly, make sure you haven't missed anything.'

'I can do it.'

'No, Sam, you can't,' she said firmly. 'He's your brother. You're too close. Just go with him and be with him, and I'll go and tell your mother what's happening and wait with her, OK?'

He hesitated for an age, then nodded. 'OK. How will you get back down to town?'

She smiled. 'I'm sure I can convince the patrol car to drop me off.'

He nodded, then, ignoring the onlookers, he bent his head and kissed her. 'Thank you. And thanks for going to Mum. Don't tell her too much.'

She smiled ruefully. 'I won't. Go on, go and look after him. He needs you. He's pretty shaken up. Are you all right to drive?'

He nodded again. It seemed to be all he could do. Words were deserting him and all he could see was the car flying through the air with his brother inside it. He could have been killed, and Gary might already be dead.

'Right, come on, let's go, we'll follow you, but pull over if he deteriorates,' Maggie said, and Sam got into his car beside Jamie, fastened his seat belt for him and then followed the ambulance back to St Piran's.

It was after three before they got home, and Gemma was sitting up with Linda in the kitchen drinking what felt like their hundredth cup of tea as the car pulled up.

'Oh, that's Sam. Gemma, make sure—see if he's brought Jamie.'

Her face crumpled, and Gemma hugged her swiftly and went out of the front door in time to see Jamie unfolding himself stiffly from the front seat, his left arm in a sling and with a back-slab on it, and steristrips on his cheekbone.

'Jamie's here,' she called back, and she heard Linda's sob of relief. She smiled at the young man as he stepped inside, trying not to wince at the rapidly emerging bruises on his face. Linda was going to have a fit. 'Hi, sport, how are you?' she asked gently.

'Sore,' he said, still sounding shaken, 'and I just want to go to sleep but Sam won't let me.'

'You can go to sleep, but I'm going to keep waking you,' Sam warned, 'just to be on the safe side.'

'But I don't want to wake up.'

'I know. Neither do I. But I need to make sure you're all right. You've had a head injury, Jamie, you need to be checked regularly.'

Then Linda was gathering her errant son gently into her arms and sobbing, and Jamie was patting her awkwardly and trying not to cry, and Gemma could see that Sam was struggling, too.

And it had all been so horribly, stupidly unnecessary.

'How's Gary?' she asked Sam in a low voice, and he shrugged.

'Touch and go. Ben Carter filled me in. He's got a shattered pelvis, a flail chest with penetrating rib injuries and a head injury—and that's just the obvious stuff. They're stabilising him, but he's got weak reflexes in his legs and he may have permanent damage to his spinal cord. They're going to scan him when he's stable, but he's on steroids now and they're fighting to keep him alive. The rest will sort itself out if he makes it.'

'Does Jamie know?'

'Yes. He saw him briefly in Resus, but Gary was out of it. He just needed to know he was alive.'

She rubbed his arm comfortingly. 'Sam, I'm so sorry. I'll go now. Call me if there's anything I can do.'

'Sure. Thanks, you're a star.'

He kissed her briefly on the cheek, his hand resting a moment longer on her shoulder, then he turned back to his family to pick up the pieces of yet another crisis.

How much more? How much more could he be asked to take? And how could she even conceivably put any more on him?

She left them to it and went home to bed, only to find the chocolate sauce bowl had been upended in the middle of her bed in all the confusion, and she thought of Sam making love to her, and the conversation they'd been having which had been so violently interrupted— a conversation they had yet to finish.

And she desperately needed to get to bed, but it was trashed, and the spare bed wasn't made up.

Pulling the bedding off, she carried it back downstairs, stuffed the sheet into the washing machine and took the quilt into the sitting room and curled up on the sofa with it snuggled round her. She was cold, she realised, and shaking with reaction now it was all over and there was nothing more to do. She could feel the sobs rising in her chest and she tried to hold them back, but she could still see Gary fitting, the terrible moments as he fought for his young life, and suddenly it was all too much.

'Oh, Sam, I need you,' she sobbed. Cuddling the bedding closer, she buried her face in it, in the scent of Sam's body, and wept for Gary and his family, and the close call Jamie had had, and Sam, struggling to hold it all together—and above all, the senselessness of the illness that had taken her away from him and wasted the last eleven years...

'How are things?'

Sam gave her a weary smile, pushed her backwards into her treatment room and closed the door, then pulled her into his arms and held her without speaking for several minutes.

'Are you OK?' she asked softly, and he nodded, his head moving against her shoulder.

'I'll be fine.'

'And Jamie? I didn't like to ask too much last night, but I've been wondering.'

'He's OK. He's very sore, and he's got some spectacular bruises, but they did an ultrasound aorta scan and X-rayed him all over and—well, he's fine. He's got several fractures in his lower arm and wrist and hand, and his sternum's really bruised from the seat belt, but on the whole he's been incredibly lucky. Unlike Gary.'

She sighed and rubbed his back comfortingly. 'Poor Amanda. Nick's been to see her at the hospital and she's devastated. She said everyone's going to think he's got his just deserts, but she's heartbroken. She's such a sweet woman, but hopelessly ineffectual. According to Nick her husband's a total waste of space, and she keeps letting him back every time he's out of prison. But at least she's got proper contraceptive cover now, so she's not still getting pregnant every time he's out, and maybe the other children will learn by Gary's mistakes and there might be a better chance for them.'

Sam let out his breath on a harsh sigh. 'Maybe. At least he can't hurt anyone else for a while now.'

'No. Amanda said that herself, apparently. Poor woman. Oh, well, if he survives maybe it'll be the making of him.' She straightened up and looked into Sam's red-rimmed, exhausted eyes. 'You don't look as if you had much sleep. What are you doing here? You should be at home in bed. They aren't expecting you.'

'I've brought Jamie in,' he explained. 'He needs another X-ray and a proper cast. Gabriel's just checking him over for me. Could you put the cast on? My left hand's not very useful, I might squeeze it too tight. No feedback.'

'Of course.'

She went down to the X-ray room with him and she and Sam looked at the plates with Gabriel while Jamie sat on the chair and stared blankly at the wall opposite, his battered face expressionless.

'Well, it looks good,' Gabriel said, studying the films on the light box. 'Nothing displaced. See here, a clean break of the radius and ulna, and two of the carpals, here and here, and the scaphoid and first metatarsal both have very fine cracks, but he's been lucky and I think he can have a proper cast now. There's only a little swelling. He'll need the thumb held out to keep the scaphoid aligned, but he should be OK. It'll need another X-ray in two weeks to check the alignment.'

'Great. Thank you, Gabriel. So, Gemma, can you plaster it for him?'

'Sure. Come on, Jamie, let's see what we can do. What colour do you want?'

'I don't care,' he said tonelessly, so she went for dark blue, and swiftly and carefully wrapped his arm in the fibreglass cast, checking it was comfortable and making him wiggle his fingers slightly, then glanced up at Sam. 'Happy with the position?'

'Very. You've done a lovely job, thank you.'

'Thank the time I spent in A and E doing nothing else,' she said, then smiled at Jamie. 'Right, you'll do,' she said, squeezing his shoulder in support. 'Keep it up, rest it and wiggle your fingers every few minutes. And don't get the cast wet, don't stick anything down it if it gets itchy and tell someone if it gets too tight or too loose or if your fingers swell or discolour. OK?'

'I'm fine,' he said, not looking at her, and she could see he was at the end of his rope.

'Take him home, Sam, put him to bed—and get some sleep yourself,' she said softly. 'You both look done in.'

'I can't sleep,' Jamie said. 'I just keep seeing it.'

Sam put an arm gently round his shoulders. 'You'll be all right. Come on, mate, let's go home and see if we can find a DVD.'

She watched them go, and Kate came out of the office and shook her head. 'Poor boy. He must be so upset.'

'He is—I think he feels guilty because he's got away with it so lightly in comparison. I've just been putting a cast on for him to replace the back-slab. Which reminds me, how's Jem's wrist?'

'Oh, he's fine. Back at school and proudly showing

it off to everyone. I think he wishes it had been broken! He's feeling terribly guilty about Digger's paw.'

'He shouldn't. Digger's fine, he's spending all his time on Linda's knee at the moment, and now Jamie's hurt he'll be snuggled up to him as well, so he's got plenty of company while he heals. He'll be spoilt rotten.'

She watched Sam through the glass doors as he put Jamie in the car and then drove away, and she wondered how long it would be before they could spend any time alone together, and when, if ever, they'd finish that long-overdue conversation...

'It's been really odd at school today—quiet. Nobody likes Gary, but they all remember him, and of course the middle brother's still there. It's as if everyone's holding their breath, waiting for the news.'

'Mmm.' Kate nodded at Rob and stirred the teapot thoughtfully. 'Jem said how strange it was without Tel and Tassie. They're above him and Matthew, of course, but he knows Tel.' She didn't let herself dwell on how he'd been so badly bullied by him, but somehow Rob knew that and gave her a gentle one-armed hug.

'He's OK now, Kate.'

'I know. I'm just so glad he's got Matthew for a friend.'

She looked up at him and smiled, and he stared down at her and for a moment she thought—no. Silly. Of course he wasn't going to kiss her. Although if he did...

But he moved away, and she took a deep breath and poured the tea, and the moment was gone. Rob took the tea from her and looked out of the window to where the two boys were playing in the garden.

'Can I ask something?' he asked quietly.

She followed the direction of his eyes and thought, Oh, no. Please, no. 'What?'

'You and Nick...'

He let it hang there in the air, and she looked down into her tea while Rob waited.

Then, when it was obvious she wasn't going to reply, he sighed softly. 'I'm sorry, I shouldn't have brought it up. Forget I said anything.'

She hesitated, then blurted out, 'Nobody knows.'

'Nobody?'

She gave a strangled laugh. 'Oh, Nick knows,' she said, and wondered if her voice sounded as bitter as it felt. 'But hardly anybody else, although that won't last. It's getting more and more obvious as he gets older, and it's only a matter of time.'

She bit her lip, staring at Jem through the window and feeling her heart swell with love. 'It was just once,' she went on. 'A stupid, stupid thing, and I know I ought to regret it, but—I love my son, Rob, and I wouldn't turn the clock back and undo it for anything, because then I wouldn't have him. He would never have existed, and I can't imagine life without him.'

'No. I know what you mean. Losing Annette broke my heart, but I don't think I could ever have dealt with losing Matthew.'

She felt her eyes fill with tears. 'I'm so sorry, Rob. It must have been dreadful.'

'It was—but it's a long time ago now, nearly five years, and I'm ready to move on.'

She looked up at him then, and realised he was talking about her, about them, and she thought, Yes, I'm ready, too. Not for a grand passion, maybe, because there'll always only be Nick, but a gentle love, a caring friend, someone to share things with? I'm ready for that.

'What are you doing on Friday night?' she asked.

'Why?'

'Because the children are both at Alex Pentreath's birthday party, and I wondered if you'd like to come for supper?'

He hesitated for a moment, then smiled. 'That sounds very nice. Thank you. I'd love to.'

'Good,' she said with a smile. 'More tea?'

Gary Lovelace made slight progress in the next few days, and by the end of the week he was downgraded from critical to stable. Not that many of the people in the village cared one way or the other, and not least Mr Polgrean, who was furious about his car and not at all surprised to hear that Jamie had been involved.

And because Jamie was getting better, Sam took him to see the man, to explain that he hadn't been anything to do with its theft and to apologise for all the trouble he'd caused in the past, and after he grudgingly accepted his brother's apology, he turned to Sam and said he owed him one, too.

'This leg business. They said I could have died. You were right, and I had no business bringing up the past like that. If you'd walked away…'

'I could have been struck off for neglect. Let's just forget it and let bygones be bygones, shall we?' he offered, and held out his hand to the crusty old fisherman.

And after an age, he took it, and Sam watched the anger and bitterness drain out of him. He took Jamie home, and the following day he returned to school, to Sam's relief, as he had significant public exams coming up in the next few weeks, and then everything quietened down.

On the home front, at least. Sam was able to go back to work, and it was mayhem, because the tourists were starting to come in larger numbers, especially the surfers, and then Adam Donnelly dropped a bombshell into the mix.

'Maggie and I have decided that the world's a fascinating place and we want to go and see it before we settle down and have a family, so we're going to be leaving Penhally at the end of August,' he announced at their weekly staff meeting.

Amid the exclamations and ripple of comment, Sam wondered what the staffing implications would be—and if Nick would try and talk him into staying on full time.

He wasn't sure, and he certainly didn't know what his answer would be, but that would rather depend on Gemma, he thought, which brought up the subject of the conversation they'd been having when Jamie had phoned him on Monday night.

And it was Friday now, four days later, and he was still no nearer finding out why she'd left him.

But he'd promised to take Jamie over to the hospital this evening to see Gary, and his mother needed his attention, and he would just have to wait. It wasn't the sort of conversation he wanted to rush. There was something she wasn't telling him, something so hugely significant that it had led to the end of their marriage, and he wanted time to talk it through, to get right to the bottom of it and thrash it out, once and for all.

He'd waited nearly eleven years, after all. What difference could a few more days make?

Nick drummed his fingers on the kitchen table and stared blindly out of the window at the dark sea.

He was lonely. Lonely and bored, and he knew Jem was at a party tonight. He glanced at his watch. Ten to ten. Kate might still be up. He could drive past, see if there were any lights on. He wanted to talk to her about Polly Searle—or Polly Carrick, as she now was.

He couldn't remember her at all, but he could remember her father, and he'd been a thoroughly nasty piece of work. No wonder she'd changed her name to her mother's maiden name. He couldn't remember much about her, because he'd not been her GP, of course, Phil had, but Kate would know.

And she was right, they could do with a woman doctor. He hated all the menopause stuff, it was utterly foreign to him and women got so emotional. Yes, a woman doctor would be good.

Tossing his keys in the air and catching them with a sweep of his arm, Nick headed out of the door, locking it behind him out of habit—not that he needed to, probably, with Gary Lovelace out of the frame for now, but old habits died hard.

He drove along Harbour Road past the fishing boats that were all getting ready to go out on the tide, and up Treligga Road to Kate's house. He could see lights on, but as he approached he noticed a strange car on the drive.

Odd. She must have visitors.

And then he saw her cross in front of the kitchen window, and a man—Rob Werrick?—walked into view.

Damn. So he'd been right, they were seeing each other. Unless Rob was picking up something Matthew had left behind? That could be it.

Except, if that was the case, why was Rob looking down at Kate like that? And why...?

Oh, God. He watched in horror as Kate lifted her face to his kiss, then sat, transfixed, as the kiss grew more passionate.

No! But then they moved apart, and he felt a wave of relief, but it was short-lived. The landing light came on, then the bedroom light. And Kate reached up and closed the curtains.

He felt a wave of nausea wash over him and, spinning the wheel, he gunned the car back down the hill and out along the Harbour Road, up past the Smugglers'.

He didn't stop, although he often dropped in for a quiet pint with Tony.

But not tonight. Tonight...

Tonight he just wanted to scream with frustration and bitterness and all the pent-up emotion that was normally locked down tight inside him, and until he had it under control, he was going nowhere.

But he couldn't get the image of Kate and Rob out of his mind, and he was eaten up with a nameless emotion that felt suspiciously like jealousy.

Ridiculous. He didn't even *want* Kate!

But he was damned if he wanted someone else having her, he thought bitterly. He contemplated going home and getting drunk, but dismissed the thought. There was a better way to deal with his frustration, and it was about time he dusted off his social life. Hauling his phone out of his pocket, he scrolled through his numbers, then paused and pressed the call button.

Moments later, it was answered, and he took a breath and leant back, calming himself.

'Louise? It's Nick. How are you? We haven't spoken for a while—I'm sorry, I've been rather tied up. Look, are you busy? I was wondering if I could drop by…'

CHAPTER NINE

'How's Gary?'

'Still in a coma.' Sam sighed and dropped into his chair, and Gemma pushed the door shut and went over and put her arms round him.

'I'm sorry. How's Jamie taking it?'

'He's racked with guilt. Thinks he should have done more to stop him, though God knows what he could have said to make him pay attention, when nobody else has ever succeeded. Even Gertrude Stanbury, our old headmistress, thinks he's probably just a bad person, and she doesn't write people off lightly. She never wrote me off.'

'Because you weren't a bad person, Sam. And neither is Jamie. Even if Mr Polgrean thinks you both are.'

'Oh, not any more,' he said with a chuckle. 'He actually apologised for being rude last Monday, because they'd told him how close he'd got to losing his leg, and he realised that if I'd listened to him and walked off, he might have lost it. Or worse. And he even accepted Jamie's apology for getting mixed up with Gary, so it was pretty cosy all round, really.'

'Good grief, wonders will never cease,' she said with a chuckle. 'And your mum?'

'Oh, she's all right, I suppose, but still a bit shocked and she's struggling to get over her own problems, but Lauren's been great with her and she's doing all right. Her hand's still a bit weak and her legs are a little unsteady, but fundamentally she's fantastic, considering.'

'And the dog?'

'He's getting along.'

'Good.'

Gemma perched on the edge of the desk facing him, and ran her finger over his knee thoughtfully.

'So—does that mean you're able to get out a bit more now?'

He raised a brow, the smile he couldn't quite prevent playing around his mouth.

'Well, that very much depends, of course, on what's on offer.'

'On offer? I was rather thinking it might be your turn to do the offering.'

He sat up slowly, leaning forwards and reaching up to pull her down onto his lap. 'Well, now, let me think. How about dinner somewhere? Not the Smugglers'. Somewhere a bit more private, where we aren't going to run into whoever's acting as Town Crier this week. Somewhere like Padstow, or Rock?'

She cocked her head on one side. 'That sounds rather posh.'

A little frown crossed his brow, and he gave her a quizzical smile. 'Maybe it's time I took you out and spoiled you a little.' And then afterwards, when he'd wined and dined her, he could take her back to her house and talk to her, get her to open up to him, tell him whatever it was that had torn them apart. 'Perhaps Friday?'

'Maybe,' she said, but she hesitated. There was so much he didn't know, so much she still had to tell him, and until it was out in the open, she really didn't want to get into the whole formal dinner thing. It just seemed wrong, and she didn't know how she could sit there and pretend that everything was all right.

'How about coming round to mine for supper in the meantime?' she suggested. 'And maybe this time we'll get to finish our meal.'

And that all-important conversation.

'That would be good. My sister Beth's coming over this evening with her brood to see Jamie and Mum, but I could do tomorrow or Wednesday.'

'Make it Wednesday,' she said, suddenly wanting to stall this whole thing and wishing she'd never brought it up. 'Seven-thirty? I've got a clinic before, so I can't get away too early.'

'Seven-thirty's fine,' he said, and then patted her on the bottom. 'Come on, off my lap, gorgeous, before I get too distracted to work. I've got a rammed surgery this morning, and a load of visits, and that's before the phone line's been open for more than five minutes!'

He was right, it was a hectic day, and Tuesday was no better.

By Wednesday she'd managed to work herself up into a frenzy about their meal—well, more specifically the conversation after it—and the last thing she wanted at a busy well-woman clinic was children running around. Not with what she was going to have to tell Sam later, anyway. And there were three of them, the

O'Grady children—although one wasn't running anywhere, and she frowned at him.

Liam. She knew him—and he was normally as lively as a cricket. He must be going down with something, she thought, and then dismissed it as she worked her way through her list of patients.

Until she got to the last, Siobhan O'Grady and her little brood, and then as she ushered the children in, Gemma glanced down at Liam and frowned again. He had bruises on his arm, big bruises, like finger marks, and she thought, No, not Siobhan. She was a wonderful mother. And the father was a nice man, a policeman. So what…?

'Hello, Liam,' she said, crouching down beside him. 'You're very quiet today, you're normally tearing around. Aren't you feeling well?'

He shook his head, and Siobhan said worriedly, 'No, I don't think he can be, he's been so quiet, you know, and he's not the quietest child. And he's so pale. I thought, if it went on much longer, I ought to bring him to the doctor and have him checked out, but perhaps you could have a look at him since he's here with me now, just in case he's picked something up at school.'

'Of course, you're at school now! What a big boy. Can I have a look at you, Liam? Want to pop up here?'

And she lifted him carefully to the couch and sat him on the edge and studied him. And her heart began to pound slowly. 'How long has he had the bruises?'

'Oh, I hadn't even seen them! Good grief, there're dreadful! Niall, what have you been doing to your brother?'

'Nothing! I didn't do nothing, I swear!'

But alarm bells were ringing, and Gemma lifted

trembling fingers and felt the sides of Liam's neck. Peas. Chains of peas, running down each side, and under his chin, and in his armpits.

'I think we need to get a doctor to have a look at you, my little fellow,' she said, lifting him down and putting him carefully onto a chair. 'Siobhan, stay here with them, I'll be back in a moment.'

And she went out of the door, closed it behind her and took a long, steadying breath. Thank heavens there was nobody in the waiting room, because she was shaking like a leaf, her heart was racing and she thought at any moment she might be sick.

Her legs wobbling, she walked down the stairs and over to Reception. 'Is there a doctor free?'

'No—oh, yes, someone's just come out of Sam's consulting room. Nip in now, quickly,' Hazel said, and she thought, of all the doctors, but maybe he was the right one, and maybe this would open the gates to that conversation.

She tapped on the door and went in, and he glanced up and his eyes softened and he smiled at her. 'Hello, my gorgeous girl. What can I do for you—? Gemma? Are you all right? What is it?' He got up and crossed over to her, a frown pleating his brow, and she forced herself to smile.

'It's not me.' Not this time. 'It's a little boy upstairs— Liam O'Grady. He's tired, pale, listless, his glands are up.' She swallowed. 'And he's bruising.'

Sam frowned and tilted his head to one side. 'Leukaemia?'

'I think so.'

'Oh, hell. Right. Who's with him?'

'His mother, and his brother and baby sister.'

'Is there a father?'

'Yes. He's a policeman. He'll be at work—he's in the CID.'

'OK. I'll come up. They'll have to take him straight over to St Piran for blood tests, if you're right, and then they'll let them know in the next day or so, I guess.'

Or sooner…

'Has she got a car?'

'Yes. She lives up near me, I see her quite often.'

'Right, let's go and have a look at him—Liam, did you say?'

'Yes.'

And she led the way back up, hoping she was wrong, hoping that Sam would tell her she was imagining it, that this dear, delightful little boy wouldn't have to go through the hell of—

'Siobhan, this is Dr Cavendish.'

'Sam! Oh, I'm so pleased it's you!' Siobhan said, her eyes filling.

He smiled warmly. 'Hello, Siobhan. Long time no see. We were in the same year at school,' he explained to Gemma. 'So, which of these little men is Liam?'

'He is,' Niall said, and Sam, having already zeroed in on Liam, nodded and crouched down beside his chair.

'Hello, Liam. I'm Dr Sam. I'm an old friend of your mummy's. Can I have a look at you, do you think?' And at Liam's nod, he lifted him onto the couch, laid him down and gave him a gentle but thorough examination. And then he pulled the T-shirt down over his skinny little chest, straightened up and met Siobhan's worried eyes.

'It's serious, isn't it?' she whispered. 'Holy Mother of God, Sam, tell me it's not serious.'

'Gemma, have we got any toys?'

'Of course. I'll just…' She stuck her head round the other treatment-room door, where Lara had just finished her clinic. 'Lara? I wonder, would you mind playing with the children for a moment? They're a bit bored in here.'

'I'm sure I've got lots of toys. Shall we go and have a look?' And Lara smiled at the children, scooped Liam up gently and held her hand out to little Caitlin.

And as the door shut behind them, Siobhan started to shake uncontrollably. 'So—come on, Sam, for the love of God tell me!'

'He's going to have to have some blood tests, and then the haematologist will talk to you, but, yes, I'm afraid it may well be serious, Siobhan. I'm very sorry.'

'But…' Her eyes swivelled to Gemma's, desperately seeking reassurance. 'No. Tell me—tell me it's not leukaemia.'

So she had known, or suspected. Oh, dear help her, poor woman, Gemma thought with a detached part of her brain, because the rest of her was screaming in denial and just wanted to run away, as far and as fast as she could.

'I'm sorry, but it's the most probable cause of his symptoms. They'll take blood, and as soon as they have the results, which is usually within hours, they'll do a bone-marrow biopsy if it's indicated, and then if that confirms it they'll start chemotherapy straight away, possibly tomorrow.'

'Tomorrow!' she gasped, sagging into a chair and staring at Gemma open-mouthed. 'No! They can't! My baby!'

'Siobhan, it may not be. They have to test for it, but—'

'But you know, don't you? You know. Oh, God, I want Sean. Can I call him now?'

'Of course you can,' Sam said, but she couldn't hold her phone, far less speak, so Sam took it from her and asked her husband to come down to the surgery, while Gemma sat beside her and held her hands and waited.

And then, because he'd only been at the other end of Harbour Road, Sean was dropped off by the patrol car he'd been in and was shown up to the room, and Siobhan threw herself sobbing into his arms and Sam filled him in on what they suspected.

'So—what's the prognosis?' Sean asked directly, meeting Sam's eyes head on, and Sam shrugged.

'I can't tell you. We don't even know if it is leukaemia. We do know that it's a classic presentation, but that's all. He will have to have the blood test to be sure, and the bone marrow biopsy to confirm it and to indicate the best treatment, and only then will you have any idea—but treatment is better than it's ever been, and children do survive this in great numbers. But you have to have it confirmed, and until then, there's no point in torturing yourselves.'

Out of the corner of his eye Sam saw Gemma shake her head slightly, as if to clear it, and then he looked more closely. She was chalky grey, her fists were clenched and her knuckles white, and she was shaking. All over.

'Gemma?'

She jerked to her feet. 'I'll go and see how the children are. You take as long as you need. We'll be next door.'

She went out, closing the door behind her with trembling fingers, and then took a moment to breathe in deeply before following the sound of giggling. She dredged up a smile. 'Hello, all. How are you doing?'

'What's wrong with Mummy?' Liam asked, and she crouched down beside him and swallowed hard.

'Nothing, sweetheart. She just needed to talk to the doctor, and we thought it would be boring for you all.'

'Is it because I'm sick?'

Oh, hell. But experience had taught her that honesty was the best policy, and age was no barrier to understanding. It was just a case of pitching it right, and she had no idea if she would. But she had to answer him, because he was waiting, and so she nodded slowly. 'Yes. She's worried, but she would be. You're her big boy, and you aren't feeling well, and she wants you to be better.'

'So will I have to have medicine?'

She nodded. 'I think so. The first thing is you'll need to go to the hospital and they'll need to take a little bit of blood from you.'

'With a needle?' he asked, his eyes wide, and she remembered that Liam hated needles. Passionately. His pre-school booster had been a work of art to get into him, and had taken her weeks of patient persuasion.

'Yes,' she said, because there was no point in lying. 'Yes, there will be a needle, but they'll be very gentle.'

'No! I don't want to go to the hospital! I want you to do it here!'

And then Sam was sticking his head round the door and frowning. 'Everything all right?'

'Liam wants me to take his blood.'

The frown grew deeper. 'How?'

How what? How would she do it? Or how did Liam know? How had she been so stupid as to tell him?

'He asked if he would have to have medicine, and so I told him the truth,' she said simply, and after a moment, Sam nodded.

'OK. I'll ring the hospital. It might be possible for you to do that. I'll ask.'

'No, let me. I'll know what bottles we have and if we can do it. Liam, stay here with Lara and Caitlin and Niall, and I'll be back in a moment, OK?'

He shook his head. 'I want to come.'

She looked at Sam, and he shrugged, as much as to say, Well, it's his illness, and you know him. Your call.

'Come on, then,' she said, holding out her hand, and when they were back in the other room, he went straight to his mother and climbed on her knee and sat there, watching Gemma as she explained what she'd told him.

'But, Liam, you have to realise that if I take your blood today and they say you need to go to hospital for your medicine, you'll have to go. I can't do it here. So although I may be able do this first bit, I can't do any more. You do understand that, don't you? It's not that I don't want to, it's just that they have special people to do it, and they're very good. They have lots of children there, and they know how to do it so it doesn't hurt and they can look after you.'

His chin wobbled a bit, but then he nodded.

'OK, let's ring them,' she said, and dialled the hospital number and asked for Jo in Haematology, while Sam watched her thoughtfully.

'Hi, it's Gemma Johnson at Penhally Bay Surgery— hi, Jo. No, I know. It's about a patient this time,' she said, and he thought, What an odd remark, as if she knew the person on the other end and talked to them about other things. What other things? Maybe she'd had some training there or knew them socially. Whatever, she was still talking, and the part of him that wasn't trying to work out the sub-text was listening.

'We have a child with suspected ALL—can I do the bloods here? He's needle phobic and we've been working together on this, so he wants me to do it. No, they can bring them up straight away. OK, tell me what I'll need, and I can do that.'

She scribbled down the tests that would be required, and the tubes she'd need, then thanked Jo and hung up, then smiled at Liam. And if you didn't know her well, she looked fine now, he thought, except for something in her eyes, some shadow that haunted them. But what? What was going on here?

'OK, Liam, I can do it here, so do you want to lie down or stay on Mummy's lap?'

'Mummy,' he mumbled round his thumb, snuggling closer, and Sam could see his eyes beginning to fill.

Oh, hell, so were his. He blinked hard and concentrated on Gemma, ready to step in if she needed help, but she seemed to be managing fine. More than fine. Except for the look in her eyes.

'Right. I'm going to put a little strap round your arm to stop all the blood in it from disappearing back into your body and running away from me, and then I can find a tiny little vein and get some out. Here, pull this end and stick it on there—no, bit tighter—that's lovely. Oh, yes, look, here's a lovely little vein. I'll put some special magic jelly on it like we did before, and then it won't hurt a bit. Now, do you know what colour your blood's going to be when it comes out?' she asked, and he nodded.

'Red,' he said. 'Timmy had a nosebleed in the playground last week and it was bright red.'

'Well, that's a funny thing, because when it comes out and hits the air, it changes to bright red, but when it's in your arm, it's actually quite dark, almost purple.'

'Purple?' he said, giggling. 'No, it's not purple!'

'Shall we see? I tell you what, shall we ask Mummy to hold your hand out here for me, so I can see better? That's lovely, Siobhan, just hold it straight on your arm like that. Fantastic. Right—red or purple?'

'Red!'

And with a chuckle, she slid the needle in, clipped the first bottle on and they watched it fill.

'It *is* purple!' Liam said. 'I thought it would be red!'

'I wonder what colour the next one will be?' she asked, swapping bottles, and in the end she had several, and to Liam's disappointment not one of them was red.

'But,' she said, pressing a swab over his vein as she drew the needle out, 'when we take this swab off in a minute, I bet you the blood on it's red.'

'Wow. That's really odd,' Liam said, resting back against his mother and watching as Gemma wrote his name on all the labels.

'OK, you need to take these in straight away, and go to the haematology lab and ask for Jo. She's expecting you. And they'll process them immediately.' She ruffled Liam's hair. 'Well done, sport. You're a good boy. And don't worry, they'll look after you.'

'What about Niall and Caitlin?' Sean asked, and she could see he was pale and hanging on to his control by a thread.

'Is there someone you can leave them with for now?'

'My mother—we'll drop them round there on our way. I'll ring her from the car. Gemma, thank you so much.'

Siobhan broke off, and Gemma bent and hugged them both, mother and son, then said, 'Right—what colour is the swab?'

And lifting it away to replace it with a little plaster, she showed it to Liam.

'It's red!' he said. 'So I *was* right!'

'Yes, we both were. Clever, eh? Now, you need to keep your finger on that for a while to make sure the bleeding's stopped, OK? Good boy. Right, here are the bottles,' she said, handing the plastic bags to Sean. 'Let us know.'

'We will,' Sean promised, and he ushered his family out, with Sam following, while she sank down into her chair and closed her eyes.

She felt drained, exhausted, and her mind was whirling, dragging her back down into the vortex, and she had to get out of here. Had to escape, to run away, to forget the awfulness, the fear, the terrible loneliness of that dreadful journey that Liam and his family were about to make.

A journey she knew all too well…

What the hell was going on with Gemma?

Sam wanted to go back up, to see her, to get to the bottom of it, but his patients were backed up wall to wall, and when he rang her room, there was no reply. Damn. And he couldn't see the car park from his surgery, so he had no idea if she'd left the building, but—she'd said she had a late surgery tonight, and he was going round for a meal at seven-thirty, so she should be here.

Maybe she'd taken Lara's room? Or gone to the loo, or made herself a cup of tea. The waiting room upstairs had been empty, he remembered, and told himself not to worry. There were other things demanding his attention, and he could think about her later.

Except he couldn't get her out of his mind, and he kept replaying the scene with Liam over and over in his head. She'd been so good with him, and she'd known so much about it. Almost too much. As if…

Cold dread washed over him as the thought crystallised. No. It couldn't have been her, but maybe a member of her family had suffered from it—perhaps a sibling who'd died? But he knew she only had one brother, and she hadn't mentioned it, and he was sure—absolutely sure—that she would have done.

Unless…

Oh, God. His heart began to pound, and his palms felt damp. Not Gemma. Surely she would have told him? Surely…

But there was a scar on her chest. Just a tiny scar, to the side of her sternum, high up below her collar bone. He'd noticed it last week, when he'd been making love to her, licking chocolate off her soft, pale skin. And he'd seen it, felt it, a tiny hard bump in the skin. The sort of scar that would be left by a central line during treatment for leukaemia.

He stood up and went over to the window, staring out across the headland at the side, past the building work which was still in progress, but he didn't see anything except the scar, and the look in her eyes as she'd taken Liam's blood and comforted his parents and calmly told them what to expect.

Because she knew, he realised, every inch of the road they'd have to travel. She'd taken every step, walked every mile of it—and she'd done it alone, without him.

But when? Surely not then? Surely that wasn't why? She hadn't been ill—had she?

He cast his mind back, trying to pick up clues from their time together that summer, but he could only remember the good times. The laughter, the loving, long into the night, so that the next day he could hardly wake her.

Because she'd been so tired.

And he'd chased her up the beach and back to the house, laughing and giggling, and she'd turned just as she'd been going in and she'd missed the step and hit her shin, and she'd come up with a hell of a bruise.

She'd hit it hard, but—that hard? Hard enough to turn her shin black? It only took one little vessel to rupture, but what if it had been more than that? And she'd had a niggling cough, too—a cold that seemed to linger. She'd been working hard for her A levels, and she'd said she was run down, but it just didn't clear.

He went back to his desk, logged into his computer and found her patient file. He could look it up—scroll through it and get the answers, but he wanted to hear it from her and, anyway, he knew.

He logged off again and squeezed his eyes shut, the certainty devastating him.

She'd had leukaemia—his dear, darling, precious Gemz had had leukaemia, and instead of telling him, she'd shut him out, let her parents whisk her away, and all she'd left him was a note.

How could she?

How could she have done that, excluded him, when he loved her so much he would have died for her.

He sprang up again, shoving his chair back so hard it hit the wall, and picking up his jacket he headed for the door.

'Where's Gemma?'

Kate was behind the desk looking for something in the filing cabinet, and she hesitated at his sharp tone.

'She's gone.'

'Gone where?'

'I don't know. Home, I suppose. She said she wasn't feeling well. Lara's covering her clinic. Did you want a nurse for something?'

'No. It doesn't matter. Can you ask Hazel to reschedule the rest of my patients, please? I have to go.'

'Of course—Sam? It's not Jamie, is it? Is everything all right?'

No, it bloody well wasn't all right, it was about as wrong as it could get, but he wasn't talking about it with her, or with anybody but his wife.

'It's fine,' he said, and shoving the door out of the way, he limped out into the car park, got in his car and drove to her house.

CHAPTER TEN

SAM pulled up outside Gemma's house and sat there, unable to move.

He felt sick, his heart racing, grief and anger and bitterness churning through him violently so that he wasn't sure if he could even talk to her. Not now. Not like this.

But she was there, standing at her door watching him, and he could see it in her face.

So he got out of the car and walked up to her door, and without a word she stood back and let him in. He could see tearstains on her cheeks, and her eyes were red-rimmed, but sympathy was a long way down his list of boiling emotions at that moment and so he ignored it and walked through the house and out onto the deck at the back.

He couldn't sit inside tidily on a chair while they had this conversation, because frankly he just didn't trust himself at the moment and he needed air, needed space. He heard her footsteps behind him, and turned to her, needing to see her face while she made this explanation.

And it had better be damned good.

'You had it, didn't you? That's why you left. Because you had leukaemia,' he said, making himself say the words although they threatened to choke him.

Her eyes wavered, but held his, and he could see the tears welling again. 'Yes.'

'Why? Why did you leave me? For God's sake, Gemma, we were *married*! I'd promised to stand by you, to be there for you, but you didn't give me the chance! You just walked away, without explaining, without talking to me about it, and you left me hanging there in free space, with no clues as to why you'd gone, what I'd done wrong. Do you have any idea—*any* idea at *all*—of what that felt like? I loved you so much. I'd promised to be with you through thick and thin, and you couldn't even tell me when something was wrong.'

'Because I didn't want to stop you doing all the things you were going to do, Sam!' she said, and he could see the tears streaming down her face. 'You were nineteen, for heaven's sake! Nineteen! You had your whole life ahead of you, and I couldn't hold you back. I didn't have the right to hold you back.'

'Oh, you did. I gave you that right, Gemz—I gave you that right when I married you, for better, for worse, in sickness and in health. And I meant it, every last damned word I said to you. And you didn't give me the chance—'

He broke off and turned away, and then he felt Gemma's hand on his arm.

'Sam? I did it for you.'

'Well, you had no right!' he roared, turning on her with all the anger and frustration and hurt of the last eleven years spewing out of him in a hideous tide that threatened to destroy him. 'You had no right to do that on my behalf! It wasn't your decision! It was mine, and you took it away from me and you took away the only thing that mattered to me, the only thing I cared about, the only decent thing that had ever happened to me in my whole life! And I can never, ever forgive you for that.'

And pushing her aside, he strode out, ignoring the pain in his ankle as he ran down the steps to his car and got in, slamming the door and driving off with a squeal of tyres.

He didn't know where he was going, but he found himself at the beach—not the little cove where they'd shared their love with such innocence and passion. He couldn't go there, it would hurt too much, but he needed to hear the sea, to have the crash of the waves drown out the screaming pain in his heart.

He stumbled out of the car and down the steps to the sand, walking unseeing past the few people still there on the beach, down to the far end. And he sat on a rock above the water and tried to breathe, tried to slow his heart and let his feelings settle, let the grief and anger and betrayal die down to a level he could deal with before it destroyed him...

'Gemma?'

She heard the knock on the door, heard the woman's voice and got numbly to her feet.

Siobhan O'Grady was standing on the step, her tear-stained face pleading, and Gemma held out her arms as the woman fell into them, sobbing.

'Oh, Siobhan, come in,' she said gently, and led her through to the sitting room. Not the deck. She couldn't sit out there where Sam had...

'Tell me. What did they say?'

'He's got to have a bone-marrow thing in the morning to confirm it, but they think it's ALL—is that right?'

She nodded. 'Acute lymphoblastic leukaemia. It's the most common in children and young people. And it can be treated, Siobhan.'

She nodded. 'So—why do they look at the bone marrow? If it's a blood thing?'

'Because the bone marrow makes the blood cells. And in ALL, the white blood cells or lymphoblasts which have gone wrong don't work properly to mop up infections, which is why children are often run down and unwell. And they often have fewer red blood cells and platelets, which means they have symptoms of anaemia and difficulty clotting, hence the bruising.'

'So—what happens now? Oh, God, Gemma, I can't stand it, my poor baby…'

Gemma hugged her close and let her cry while her own heart was breaking, and after a while Siobhan pulled herself together and straightened up. 'I'm sorry, but I can't cry on Sean, he's falling apart, and so's Mum, and I just needed to talk to someone who knew what I was talking about.'

Oh, she knew. She knew only too well, but that was fine. Talking to Siobhan didn't hurt her, but talking to Sam…

She needed to talk to Sam, but not now. He needed time to calm down, time to think. And Siobhan needed her.

'Now they do the bone-marrow aspiration, and then they go from there, working out a treatment schedule, but he won't be in hospital all that time. He'll come backwards and forwards, spending a lot of time at home between cycles, and you'll get a great deal of support from the hospital and from the surgery, but you just have to take it one day at a time, Siobhan. And you will get there.'

'Oh, dear lord, I hope so, but I don't know how to be strong for them,' she murmured, and Gemma held out a box of tissues to her.

'You'll be fine. At least it's all under way now, and you just have to be strong for Liam. It'll be hard for him, and you have to help him, but it'll be hard for you, too, and you have to look after each other, and the other two children. I know it's difficult, but don't forget about them, and don't suffocate them. And lean on Sean, and encourage him to talk, because men are bad at that. And if you ever need to talk, I'm always here, and I'll always have time for you.'

'You're so kind. Thank you.'

'It's no problem.'

'I have to get back,' she said, standing up and mopping her nose again. 'I've got to do some washing for Liam, and I haven't even thought about feeding us—I've fed the children and put them to bed, but somehow, food...'

'You have to eat. Go on, go home and look after yourself, because you have to stay well for them all. And good luck tomorrow. Keep me in touch, won't you?'

'Oh, I will, thank you Gemma,' she said, and, giving her one last hug, she went down the steps and hurried back to her house, leaving Gemma to her tumbling thoughts.

She went back out to the deck, and sat down on a chair and waited. Would Sam come back, or did she need to go and find him?

What if he didn't come back? she thought suddenly, on a wave of dread. What if he left again, went off back to Africa? He'd said he couldn't forgive her. What if he'd meant it—really meant it, meant he couldn't, wouldn't forgive her, and so it was all over, back to square one, only this time it was his idea and not hers? The pain swamped her, even the thought was agonising, and she felt a sob jam in her throat, trapped there by the rising tide of panic.

She had to find him. Had to go and look for him and change his mind, but where?

The beach, she thought. Their beach.

And she grabbed her keys, slammed the door shut behind her and ran down the steps to her car. She knew exactly where to find him—but he wasn't there. And he wasn't at his house, and she drove round for ages, looking blindly through her tears for his car, but it was nowhere to be seen, and finally she had to admit that he might have gone, that it could be too late.

That maybe at last their marriage was finally at an end.

With the last shreds of her control, she pulled over to the side of the road, cut the engine and began to sob.

'Sam?'

He lifted his head and stared blankly at the French doctor.

'Gabriel—hi. Sorry, I was miles away.'

'So I could see. No dog today?'

'No, I—uh—I haven't been home.'

'Mind if I join you?'

Why the hell would he want to join him? But it was a public place, and he could hardly tell him to leave.

'Sure.'

Gabriel sat down on another rock, the slender greyhound leaning against his leg, and he idly pulled the dog's ears and gazed out to sea.

'I often come here when things seem—confused,' he said quietly. 'I listen to the gulls, and the sound of the water, and things straighten out a little bit.'

Sam grunted. Nothing was straightening out for him, that was for sure. He was as confused and hurt and bitter as before, and it would take more than a few seagulls to sort him this time.

'I saw your patients this evening, by the way.'

Sam sighed. 'Thanks. I'm sorry, I just had to get away.'

'Want to talk about it?'

'Not really. There's nothing you can do, nothing anyone can do. She made her choices years ago.'

'Are we talking about Gemma here?'

He sighed quietly, then nodded. 'You know, we were married, Gabriel. I was nineteen, she was eighteen, and I loved her so much it hurt. And I thought she loved me, so I married her—and then she found out she had leukaemia, and without telling me she just walked away. She just walked away, and she left me a note, for God's sake! She didn't even have the guts to talk to me, and I only found out today by accident.'

Gabriel made a soft sound of sympathy. 'You know, *mon ami*, maybe she did have guts. Maybe she was misguided, but maybe she did what she did for you.'

Sam grunted. 'That's what she said, but she had no right to make that choice for me.'

'Of course not. Lauren did the same for me. When she found out she was going blind, she tried to cut me out of her life, and gradually I worked out what she was doing—but at least I knew she had something wrong, and I bullied it out of Oliver, and then I confronted her with it. I asked her, if it had been me, would she have left me to cope alone, and she was furious. Of course not! But she asked this of me, to leave her to cope alone because she didn't want to be a burden to me. As if the woman I love more than life itself could ever be a burden.'

Sam felt hot tears scald his eyes, and turned away. 'I'm just so angry with her.'

'Of course. I was angry with Lauren. But you love her, *non*?'

'Oh, yes. I've loved her for ever. I've never stopped loving her.' His voice broke, and he felt Gabriel's hard, warm hand on his knee.

'Then go and talk to her, Sam. Tell her how you feel, forgive her. And don't waste any more of your lives apart. It's so obvious you belong together. Don't let one mistake be responsible for any more.'

And getting to his feet, Gabriel walked away, Foxy trotting quietly beside him, leaving Sam alone with the seagulls.

She wasn't there.

Her car was gone, and she wasn't there. And he had no idea where to start looking, so he sat there on her step and waited, his thoughts in turmoil. And finally, as the sun set, she appeared, turning into her little parking place and cutting the lights on her car.

She got out slowly and walked up to him, and he stood up stiffly and held out his hand to her, his heart contracting at the sight of her ravaged face.

'I'm sorry. I shouldn't have yelled at you. Can we try again?'

'Oh, Sam—I thought you'd gone,' she said, and fell into his arms, sobbing, just as Siobhan had fallen into hers. She fumbled for her keys and he took them and let them in, then shut the door and pulled her back into his arms.

'I love you,' he said brokenly, desperate to sort this out, knowing that he had to be with her, that he had to hear her side of it and learn to forgive her, because nothing else would be right. 'I've always loved you, and I can't walk away from you now. But we have to talk.'

'I know. Sam, I'm so sorry.'

He held her close, rocking her, and gradually her tears slowed and she eased away. 'Come in to the sitting room,' she said, and he picked up the soggy tissues and raised a brow.

'Siobhan,' she explained, taking them from him and binning them. 'She came to say they're doing the bone-marrow aspiration tomorrow, and she just needed to lean on someone.'

'And she chose you, of all people.'

'But at least I *know*, Sam. I know what it's like.'

'Tell me,' he said softly, pulling her down beside him, and she went into his arms and snuggled closer, loving the smell of sea air and soap and Sam that drifted to her nostrils, needing the strength of his arms around her while she did this, because to talk about it brought it all back, and it had been the most traumatic and terrifying and desperate time of her life, and she'd needed him so badly.

'What do you want to know?' she asked, steeling herself.

'Everything. Everything that happened, from start to finish.'

She nodded, took a deep breath and began with the facts. 'OK. It was the Monday after we got married on the Thursday. My parents had come down on Saturday afternoon and found us, and I hadn't talked to them, but I thought on the Monday when you went back to work that I ought to try and make peace with them, tell them how much I loved you, why I'd married you—but when I got up, I felt terrible. My leg was covered in bruises from when I'd fallen up the steps, but I noticed others that morning, ones I hadn't got a clue about. I'd put it down to—well, to all the love-making,' she said, feeling herself colour.

His breath sucked in. 'Was I so rough you thought I'd given you bruises?' he asked, sounding so appalled that she laughed a little unsteadily and lifted her hand to his taut, stubbled jaw, cradling it.

'No, of course not,' she murmured as he turned his face into her hand and pressed his lips to her palm. 'You were always gentle with me. That was why I couldn't understand it. But then I thought about the cough that wouldn't go, and I'd had a headache all Sunday and I was so tired all the time. Again, I thought, because of being awake at night, but we'd dozed all day, too, so it was silly. I thought it might be because I was so upset about my parents, but when I went to see them my mother took one look at me and burst into tears and told me I looked dreadful, and it was the first time I'd looked in the mirror for days, and I was chalk white under my tan, and I had black circles, and I knew then that it was more than that, that something must be dreadfully wrong.'

'Was that when you went home to Bath?'

She shook her head. 'No. No, that was later, after…' She trailed off, and felt his arms tighten around her in silent support.

'Later?'

'My parents took me straight to see Phil Tremayne, Nick's brother, and insisted he see me immediately. He took one look at me and sent me straight to the hospital.'

'On the Monday morning.'

'Yes. We got there—oh, I suppose it was about ten-thirty? And they did the bloods and asked me to wait, and then the consultant haematologist called us into his room and told me he wanted to do a bone-marrow biopsy because he thought I had leukaemia.'

She felt the tension in him ratchet up a notch. 'And?'

She closed her eyes, but she could still see everything—her parents' faces, the kind, professional sympathy of the haematologist, the room where they took her for the bone-marrow aspiration.

'He did it straight away,' she said, oblivious to the tears that were trickling down her cheeks, 'and by three I had my diagnosis—acute lymphoblastic leukaemia. And the treatment was going to take months, so obviously we couldn't stay in Cornwall, because my father would have to go back to work and, anyway, Bath has a brilliant treatment unit, so they packed everything up into the car, and I wrote you the note,' she said, trying hard to hold it together because writing that letter had been the hardest thing she'd had to do at that, oh, so difficult time, 'and we dropped it into the beach house on the way home.'

'But—why?' he asked, his voice cracking. 'Why didn't you find me and tell me? I would have come with you. Why shut me out, Gemz? I needed to be with you, I would have stood by you, come with you to the hospital, held your hand, stayed at your bedside.'

'Of course you would,' she said sadly, hating the anguish in his voice and wondering even now if she'd do the same thing all over again, for him. 'But you wouldn't have gone to uni, and you would have sacrificed your chances of a medical career for me, and I couldn't let you do that. I loved you too much to take that away from you.'

He shook his head. 'We could have worked it out. I could have gone to uni in Bristol, just as I did, and visited you every day. I came to see you—did you know? Your parents told me you didn't want to see me, and they turned me away.'

She nodded miserably. 'I told them to.'

He stiffened and turned his head so she could see his eyes. 'What? You were there?'

She nodded again. 'In the sitting room. I saw you outside, and I wanted you so badly, Sam,' she said, unable to hold back the tears. 'I wanted you to hold me, to tell me it was all going to be all right, but it wouldn't have been fair, and I looked so awful—I'd lost my hair again, and I was so thin, and I was feeling really sick, and I knew if you saw me you'd be angry with me for not telling you, and I couldn't cope with it.'

'No,' he breathed raggedly, folding her against his heart. 'Oh, no, my love, no. I would have held you. I wouldn't have cared about your hair, or how thin you were or how awful you looked, and I wouldn't have been angry.'

'You were today.'

He sighed and closed his eyes. 'I know. But that was different. Today I was angry because you'd taken away that choice from me, the choice I'd already made to be with you, to support you when things went wrong. But back then—Gemz, I made those vows meaning them, and I would have stood by you. It was a real commitment, and it didn't matter that I was only young. I meant every word, and I meant it for ever.'

'Did you? Or was it only because you wanted to

sleep with me and I wouldn't let you if we weren't married?'

He exhaled sharply. 'Is that what you thought? That I married you for sex?' he asked, his voice horrified. 'Dear God, Gemma—sex doesn't matter that much.'

'It does if you're nineteen and impulsive. I thought it was just a spur-of-the-moment thing, a crazy idea. I thought you'd get over me. I really thought you would, that it had probably only been about sex—well at least, for you.'

He shook his head emphatically. 'No! If I'd wanted sex, I'd have found it somewhere. But I'd already waited a year for you. All that last year, from the moment I met you, there was no one else—and there hasn't been, in all this time. No one. Because you're the only woman I want…'

His voice cracked again, and he rested his head against hers and dragged in a breath. 'So what happened after the bone-marrow aspiration?'

'We went back to Bath, and I was admitted the following morning. I had four cycles of chemo, over the next five months. I was meant to have five, but they couldn't give me the last one because my immune system was so knocked off that it was taking too long to recover each time, and they were afraid they'd wipe it out completely, so they stopped, but I was ready to stop.'

He hung on tight, and she hung on back, remembering the time she would really, really rather forget.

'Was it horrendous?'

'Not horrendous,' she said honestly, 'but not good. I felt sick—not horrifically, but I had a sore mouth, and so I didn't really want to eat or drink, so not being hungry was probably a bonus. And I was tired—so, so tired. I slept most of the time. And of course I lost my hair, and every time it started to grow back again, I'd have to go back in and have another cycle and it would fall out again. I'd go in for the infusion, then home for forty-eight hours, then back in, in isolation, until my bone marrow had recovered, then I'd have a week or two at home before the next time. And they checked my bone marrow every time, and after the first cycle I was in remission, which is what they expect, but they have to go on to make sure they've got every last cell.'

'And have they?' he asked, and she could feel the tension building in him as he waited for her reply.

'Yes. I've been clear ever since, and they gave me the all-clear at five years, but they still test me every year—it's only a blood test, but they keep checking, and they'll do that for the rest of my life.'

'So it never goes away? The fear, the possibility of it returning?'

'Not really,' she said, thinking about it. 'I don't tend to dwell on it, but I suppose it's always there, and something like little Liam today brings it all right back.' She sighed. 'Poor Siobhan. I always thought my parents had a harder time of it than I did, especially my mother. It's really tough on a mother. I can't imagine what it must be like.' And she might never have the chance to find out…

'So what will happen to Liam? Will it be the same?'

'Pretty much, I expect. They'll do the bone-marrow aspiration tomorrow, and then if that confirms it's ALL, they'd do other tests to establish exactly which sort, because that determines which drugs they use to target it. And he'll have a series of treatments in a complex schedule over the next couple of years—it's a longer treatment for children, but the hospital staff will get them through it. They're fantastic. The nurses were brilliant to me.'

'Is that why you went into nursing? You said the other day you lived with nurses for a while—is that what you meant? In the hospital?' he asked, as if it had been puzzling him and he'd suddenly worked it out, and she nodded.

'Mmm. I hardly saw the doctors, really, but the nurses were there with me all the time, hands-on and much more involved with my daily care, and it just seemed—I don't know, more me, really. And it's nothing to do with being clever. Everybody thinks if you're clever enough you should be a doctor and not a nurse, but it's so different, and you have to be clever to be a decent nurse especially these days, it's got so complicated.'

'You're a brilliant nurse,' he said softly. 'Watching you today with Liam, knowing something was wrong but not knowing what, but just watching you with him, the way you got that blood from him when he was clearly terrified, but you just distracted him with the colour thing and he was too busy trying to prove you wrong to notice. And the way you dealt with the parents—you were fantastic. I'm not surprised she came to see you. I just wonder that they all don't.'

'Well, today was a little different. I'm not that nice to all of them.' She laughed, but he just smiled.

'I bet you are. It's not in your nature to be nasty to anyone. You were even nice to Gary Lovelace.'

'So were you.'

He gave a soft laugh. 'Let's face it, life was doing a pretty good job of having a go at him at that point, I didn't need to do it, too.'

'No.'

He held her quietly for a while, while she lay in his arms and let all the hurt seep away, and then he lowered his head and kissed her. 'Come to bed,' he murmured. 'I want to make love to you.'

It was dark in the bedroom, the only light the pale shimmer of the moon across the sea in the distance, and they lay snuggled together, her head on his shoulder—the right shoulder, the one that didn't hurt—and his left hand was trailing softly over her, his little finger stroking her skin, because he could still feel with that side of his hand and he wanted to feel her, needed to feel her, to make up for all the time they'd lost.

She was so soft, her skin like silk, and he turned his head and kissed her tenderly. 'I love you,' he said quietly. 'I'm so sorry I wasn't there for you. You do believe me when I say I would have been, don't you?'

Gemma nodded. 'I know, and I'm so sorry I shut you out, but I did it for you, Sam, you have to believe that. You had your whole life, your career ahead of you. You'd worked so hard for it, your life had already been hard enough. You'd had your mother depending on you, your sisters and your little brother—for the first time since your early teens you were going to be free to do what you wanted to do, so how could I ask you to take me on as well? I couldn't burden you, Sam. It wouldn't have been fair.'

He'd never thought of it like that, and never would. He would never have walked away, because it—she—would never have been a burden. 'It was my choice. It should have been my choice, Gemma.'

'I know. I can see that now, and I let you down,

because I didn't understand about love then. And if I'd told you, we could have been together, then you wouldn't have ended up in Africa, and you wouldn't have been blown up and so badly hurt.'

'I'm all right,' he said, but she shook her head, her eyes filling with tears.

'No, you're not. And you won't be, unlike me. Your leg's always sore, your shoulder hurts if you move it too far out of its comfortable range, your hand can't feel properly, so it makes your job and everything else difficult.'

'And does that worry you?'

'What?'

'Does it worry you? That I'm—disabled?'

'You're not disabled! Don't be ridiculous!'

'I am. You said it yourself. My ankle will never be right, my leg will never be right, I'll always have problems with my shoulder and permanent sensory deficit in my hand which affects what I can do career-wise—but would that stop you wanting to be with me? Would it make you walk away?'

She stared at him, horrified that he should even think it. 'Sam, of course not!'

'Then why did you think that I wouldn't want to be with you? You were *ill*, Gemz. You could have died, and you denied me the chance to support you, to be with you.'

'For you! And because of that, you went to Africa and got blown up.'

'Because of my own stupid fault! The accident was all my fault, I should have taken more care. I had a duty to look after myself, and I failed. It's not your fault that I was blown up, I should have paid attention. And I'm fine, I can live with it, but I can't live without you, and

I'm never letting you go again, whatever the future holds for us, because I can't live without you. I need you so much.'

He turned her into his arms and held her tight. 'Promise me you'll stay with me. I can't lose you again. I just can't…'

His voice broke, and he felt the tears he'd held back for so long forcing their way out past his defences, but it didn't matter because Gemma was holding him, and telling him it was all right, and she was crying, too, her tears hot on his shoulder, like healing rivers taking away the pain in his heart and filling it with love.

But she couldn't promise this. Not yet. Not before he knew it all. 'Sam, it may come back,' she warned tearfully, easing away so she could look at him.

His gaze didn't waver. 'I know.'

'I may die. I don't think so, and I'm clear, but there's no guarantee. And we may never have children—because of the chemo. And if that's important to you, you need to know that there's a real possibility I'm sterile. You need time to think about it, to work out what you want from a marriage, because I couldn't bear it if we got back together again now and then a few years down the line you changed your mind because we couldn't have children and you realised you wanted them more than me after all.'

'No. No way. Of course I want children with you— but that's the key. *With you.* And if you're clear, you're no more likely to get it back than I am. That's not going to change my mind, my darling. None of that is going to change how I feel about you. Children are optional. You're not. I need you—for as long as we've got together, I need you.'

'Oh, Sam.' She reached up and cradled his rough, stubbled face in her hand, feeling the rasp of it against her palm, real and solid. Her Sam. 'I need you, too,' she said unsteadily, tears falling again, 'and I've missed you so much.'

'No more,' he said, drawing her back against his chest so she could hear the steady, even beat of his heart beneath her ear. 'That's all finished now. We're starting again.'

For a moment they lay in silence, simply holding each other and treasuring the contact, then she said softly, 'Sam—can we do it properly this time? Have a church wedding?'

He gave a low chuckle. 'But we're still married, sweetheart. We don't need to get married again.'

She tipped her head back. 'I know, but—I'd just like to do it properly, with our families, and our friends.'

He smiled. 'In the church, I suppose?'

'Can we? Have a church blessing?'

'If that's what you'd like.'

'It is—on our wedding anniversary,' she said, getting into it, because not having a proper wedding with their loved ones there to hear their vows in public was one of the things she'd always regretted. 'Can we do that?'

'Sure. And maybe this time, when I say my vows, you'll trust me enough to believe me.'

'Oh, Sam, I'm so sorry,' she said, filled with endless regret.

'I know. So am I. But we're getting another chance, so let's use it wisely, and talk to each other. Promise?'

She smiled at him, her eyes shining. 'I promise.'

Their wedding anniversary dawned bright and clear, a glorious sunny day in early August.

They had breakfast together on the deck, watching the sun rise, and then she went to have a shower—and ended up with company, Sam smiling that sexy, lazy smile and lathering his hands and washing her, oh, so thoroughly all over, until she could hardly stand, and then carrying her back to bed and loving her until she came apart all over again, taking him with her.

And then she smiled at him and said, 'I've got something to give you.'

'A wedding anniversary present?' he said, puzzled when she went into the bathroom, but then she came out with a little white stick in her hand and gave it to him.

A pregnancy test stick. And it was positive.

He felt his eyes fill with tears, and he drew her into his arms and held her close, wondering why the hell being so happy should make him want to cry. But these last few months they'd shed a lot of tears together, for all the time they'd lost, and these—these were good tears.

'I can't wait to see you with our baby,' she said. 'You'll be such a good father, Sam. We're going to have a very lucky child.'

'With a mother like you, it can't fail,' he said, hugging her hard and hanging on.

And then they were late, and she had so much to do she began to panic, and she sent him away.

'Go! Go on, I want to do this properly, you'll have to wait for me in the church, and Lauren's going to come and help me dress, so scoot!'

He scooted, and went home to his mother's house and found her dithering in a panic because he wasn't dressed.

'You'll be late!' she scolded, back to herself now, and he hugged her and grinned at Jamie and ran an eye over his suit.

'Very smart. Never thought I'd see you in tails.'

'It's that woman you married, wanting to do everything properly,' he said with a grin. 'Go on, go and change or you'll be late.'

'You're beginning to sound like Mum,' he said drily, but he went and changed, because he couldn't get there quick enough.

They walked up, leaving a reluctant Digger behind, and went through the little lychgate to where Jeff Saunders, the new vicar who'd replaced Daniel Kenner, was waiting for them.

And the church was packed, to his surprise. Gemma's parents were waiting in the porch for him, and Gemma's mother came up to him and hugged him.

'I'm so sorry I sent you away. Please forgive me,' she said, and he felt his eyes fill and hugged her back hard.

'I know you were only doing what she asked,' he said. 'And it's behind us now.'

'She's coming!'

'Oh! Sam, in the church, you can't see her, it's unlucky!'

He hid a smile. Unlucky? He didn't think so. Not after the wedding anniversary present she'd given him that morning. He shook hands with Jeff Saunders, greeted their friends as he and Jamie walked down the aisle and took their places, and then the organist was playing and he turned his head and...

His breath caught in his throat.

She looked beautiful. More beautiful than he'd ever seen her, her face radiant, her eyes shining with love as she walked towards him on her father's arm, and as she drew level with him, he chucked convention out of the window and bent his head and kissed her.

'I love you, Mrs Cavendish,' he said softly, and she smiled.

'I love you, too. But we have an audience.'

He glanced over her shoulder and grinned. 'So we do. Perhaps we'd better get on with it.'

And he turned back to Jeff Saunders who was smiling indulgently, and nodded.

'Dearly beloved, we're gathered her today to bless the marriage of Gemma and Sam, and to give them an opportunity to make their vows again, in front of you, their family and friends, to cement their marriage and help them make a fresh start on this their journey together.'

And then Sam turned to her, took her hands and stared into her eyes.

'I, Samuel, take you, Gemma, to be my wife. To have and to hold, from this day forward, for better, for worse, for richer, for poorer, in sickness and in health, till death do us part. I promise to love and honour you, to trust you, to listen to you, to talk to you, to share my worries and my joys, and to be here for you, no matter what, as long we're both alive. Everything I have, everything I am, is yours. I love you.'

They'd written the words themselves, but as Gemma repeated them back to him, her voice caught.

'…in sickness…'

She faltered, and he held her hands as she lifted her eyes to his again, and went on, 'In sickness and in health, till death do us part. I promise to love and honour you, to trust you, to listen to you, to talk to you, to share my worries and my joys, and to be here for you, no matter what, as long we're both alive. Everything I have, everything I am, is yours. I love you.'

And with tears in their eyes, they went into each other's arms and held on tight, through all the readings, through the hymns, and through the final prayer, then, letting go, they joined their hands and turned back towards their family and friends, and took the first step of their onward journey.

Together...

LET'S TALK

Romance

For exclusive extracts, competitions
and special offers, find us online:

- facebook.com/millsandboon
- @MillsandBoon
- @MillsandBoonUK

Get in touch on 01413 063232

For all the latest titles coming soon, visit
millsandboon.co.uk/nextmonth

MILLS & BOON

THE HEART OF ROMANCE

A ROMANCE FOR EVERY READER

MODERN

Prepare to be swept off your feet by sophisticated, sexy and seductive heroes, in some of the world's most glamourous and romant locations, where power and passion collide.

HISTORICAL

Escape with historical heroes from time gone by. Whether your passion for wicked Regency Rakes, muscled Vikings or rugged Highlanders, aw the romance of the past.

MEDICAL

Set your pulse racing with dedicated, delectable doctors in the high-pre sure world of medicine, where emotions run high and passion, comfort love are the best medicine.

True Love

Celebrate true love with tender stories of heartfelt romance, from the rush of falling in love to the joy a new baby can bring, and a focus on t emotional heart of a relationship.

Desire

Indulge in secrets and scandal, intense drama and plenty of sizzling hot action with powerful and passionate heroes who have it all: wealth, statu good looks…everything but the right woman.

HEROES

Experience all the excitement of a gripping thriller, with an intense ro mance at its heart. Resourceful, true-to-life women and strong, fearless face danger and desire - a killer combination!

To see which titles are coming soon, please visit

millsandboon.co.uk/nextmonth

JOIN US ON SOCIAL MEDIA!

Stay up to date with our latest releases, author news and gossip, special offers and discounts, and all the behind-the-scenes action from Mills & Boon...

 millsandboon

 millsandboonuk

 millsandboon

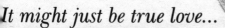 *It might just be true love...*

MILLS & BOON
MEDICAL
Pulse-Racing Passion

Set your pulse racing with dedicated, delectable doctors in the high-pressure world of medicine, where emotions run high and passion, comfort and love are the best medicine.

MILLS & BOON
True Love
Romance from the Heart

Celebrate true love with tender stories of heartfelt romance, from the rush of falling in love to the joy a new baby can bring, and a focus on the emotional heart of a relationship.